Main Character hides his Strength
Book 1: Enemy of the World

D1241835

Roadwarrior

Main Character hides his Strength
Book 1: Enemy of the World

Translated from the Korean by
Edward Ro and Minsoo Kang.

Oppatranslations

Oppatranslations, LLC.
5110 ravenna PL NE #201
Seattle WA 98105, USA

oppatranslations.com

Edited by - Josiah Davis, Sahil Bansal, Euijin Kang, Kitkat, Nas Versix, Curry, CheeseTakery, Luke Thompson

First published by Oppatranslations, LLC 2017

Paperback
ISBN: 978-0-9992957-1-7

Contents

Prologue

For the first time in his life, Devil Commander Veritas trembled in fear. It was ironic that he who had been called the "Commander of Terror" by all was terrified of a lesser lifeform. The source of his newfound fear was but a mere human. Humans were insignificant existences that could be killed with a single glance. But the one before him, wielding a massive hammer, was different. Just a bit TOO different.

Over a hundred Balroq Devils were strewn across the Demon Realm floor with their skulls split open. There hadn't been any flashy skills or spells. That stupid bastard hammered at and ripped apart all of the Demons' skulls with ease. This human, who effortlessly swept aside the guards, approached ever closer.

"W-what do you want, Human? I'll listen to all of your..."

The massive hammer flew over like lightning and dealt a critical blow to the Devil's goat-like skull. The High Devil of the Demon World's Third Circle, Veritas' eyes spun in separate directions.

WHAM! BLAM! SLAM!

The torrent of blows continued, not stopping until every inch of the High Devil's skull was completely flattened. The Devil perished, and his army was laid to waste. All that was left was the King of all Demons, Hesthnius Max.

Sungchul Kim opened the gate inscribed with an insidious hexagram, then turned towards the Demon King's Citadel. However...

"Hm?"

On top of the blood-tinted throne was a long, cold corpse. A hazy form appeared in front of the flabbergasted Sungchul.

"Kehahahaha! You can't kill me now, wielder of Fal Garaz!"

The Demon King had voluntarily shed his body. The reason for this was simple; Sungchul was just too strong. However, physical strength was not all-powerful.

"You can't kill me now."

Sungchul already knew this.

"..."

Physical attacks did not have any effect on ethereal targets. A strong blow would be able to disperse a weak enemy. But this was the Demon King; only a limited number of high-level spells had the potential to deliver a mortal blow. Furthermore, Sungchul couldn't use Magic. Rather, he had never bothered to invest in Magic. Not only did he dislike Magic, he even hated Mages as much as he did the Devils; this was the weakness the Demon King had taken advantage of.

"I may have lost my army, but as long as I, one of the Five Great Calamities, survive, the Prophesy of the End will still come to pass. As it stands, we may not be able to kill one another, but I can still crush the very world you stand upon. You may hate your own kind, but what could you ever obtain from a dead world, filled with nothing but monsters and Demons?"

Listening to the taunting words of the Demon King, Sungchul came to realize something important.

I need Magic.

Chapter 1 – Summoning Palace

A bright light poured from a colossal summoning formation and the night sky started to glow eerily. As he gazed up at the faintly lit sky, Sungchul reminisced about the time he was first Summoned. That had been more than two decades ago.

Back then, he had been naive and unprepared. Dangers were common, and it was nothing short of a miracle that he had managed to survive. Now, it would only take an hour for him to kill everyone in the Summoning Palace, but the terror and helplessness he had felt when he was first Summoned resurfaced from a corner of his memories. Sungchul approached the sewers of the Summoning Palace while shaking himself free of these memories.

In front of the sewers, a Werewolf was standing guard.

"Grrr…When will it end? My turn better come soon."

Creatures that were once human, Werewolves were people that had forsaken their humanity to embrace the feral side. Those who had a cruel and vicious nature would typically be seduced into walking this corrupted path which granted them high strength up front at the cost of having a low potential for growth.

The Werewolves, whose limits were clear, had but one joy and one purpose in their life, and that was to rip apart the newbie humans with their powerful teeth and claws. Werewolves had been one of the most feared enemies when Sungchul was first Summoned into the Summoning Palace, but they now couldn't even survive a single punch of his.

Sungchul comfortably walked towards the creature from the shadows.

"Grr…Who are you?" said the Werewolf guarding the waterways as he sniffed the air and looked around angrily.

WOOSH

A firm grip suddenly wrapped around the Werewolf's neck and his yellow eyes widened in fear.

W-what is this strength?!

Unable to even cry for help, the Werewolf could only watch helplessly as the mysterious human began looping a rope around his neck with one hand while holding him with the other.

THUMP!

The Werewolf struggled against the noose for a while before becoming limp. Sungchul took out a pen and paper and scribbled: "I can't go on living like a dog."

He silently shoved the piece of paper into the Werewolf's pocket and walked deeper into the darkness of the sewers, heading towards the Palace.

After passing through the dark waterways, a brightly lit hallway appeared. Sungchul reached into his memories and directed himself towards the Summoning Plaza. There were a few guards along the way, but at their level, they wouldn't be able to feel his presence. Sungchul freely strode through until he reached the Summoning Plaza.

The plaza was filled with massive inscriptions and numerous Mages who were chanting summoning incantations. They were conducting a Summon of a grand scale.

This was an accursed practice in which humans from a world called Earth were forcefully summoned here. The massive Summon teleported ten thousand people each time, but not even five hundred would walk out of the Summoning Palace in one piece. The rest would meet their end in pitiful tragedies, be used in Magical experiments, or be sold as slaves.

There were four plazas in which the summoning took place. These were: Azure, Scarlet, Blanche, and Crimson. Each plaza was able to convoke 2500 humans per Summon. Sungchul chose to quietly hide himself at the Blanche Plaza. The Blanche Plaza was defended by a total of 200 Summoners, Guardian Golems, and soldiers. A small abominable fairy was hopping around between them.

"Kekeke! What kind of trashy humans will be coming today? I can't wait anymore! Trash Mages! Hurry up, spit out the trashy humans!"

The small, ugly creature with red eyes wasn't actually a fairy. It was a Homunculus, an artificial lifeform created within a Mage's flask. They were in charge of the "introductory" course for the newly Summoned, and their greatest joy was looking upon the fear and dread etched into the faces of dying people. This Homunculus, which wore a green hat, was one of these sadistic bastards. Unfortunately for him, luck was not on his side.

"Kekekeke! How should I kill these newbies to receive praise? Happy worries...Eeehh?!"

The Homunculus, preoccupied with the summoning process, was suddenly pulled backwards.

"..."

The kidnapper of the Homunculus was none other than Sungchul. The Homunculus's crimson eyes were filled with horror.

"How can a mere normal human do this to the noble me?!"

Though Homunculi were only as large as infants, their Strength and Dexterity were about five times stronger than the average adult. It wasn't uncommon to see two Homunculi tearing a human apart. This Homunculus, however, was now powerless after being captured by a seemingly average looking man.

"Hand over the quest log."

Sungchul bluntly spat out his demand.

"Q-quest log? Do you even know where this is...?! Keeeee!"

Act first. Ask questions later. Sungchul tore away a single leg from the Homunculus, and its red blood splattered all over.

"Hand it over."

As he spoke, he tore off another leg. It didn't matter if it died since there were countless other Homunculi left to replace it. In fact, a dead comrade would serve as a strong incentive for the next one to obediently comply with his demands.

It hastily answered before Sungchul could grab its arm.

"I-I'll hand it over! Human, sir!"

The Homunculus spat out a bright orb from his flapping gullet, and a message popped up as Sungchul grabbed the item.

[Obtained Summoning Plaza's Quest Log!]

[Would you like to see the Quest Log?]

With a simple nod, words began to fill Sungchul's vision.

[Summoning Plaza's Quest Log]

Charismatic Person – After being Summoned, introduce yourself to more than 10 people within 10 minutes. / Reward: Fire Seed

Sports Man – Within 3 days of being Summoned, perform 300 sit ups and 3 hours of running. / Reward: Strengthening Dumbbells

Cook – Using more than 3 types of ingredients provided by the Summoning Palace's Quests, prepare a meal. / Reward: White Bread (Ration) x 3

...

All the quests and their requirements provided by the Summoning Palace were written concisely within the orb taken from the Homunculus. Sungchul carefully sifted through all the quests to find those that were useful to him.

Observant – Read aloud the inscription posted at the main entrance. / Reward: Intuition +1

I have to raise Intuition. Especially because of those curses.

As he resumed searching for more quests, he could hear a pained voice beside him.

"H-human, sir. Y-you're letting me go now, right? It h-hurts."

It was the legless Homunculus. The reply was…CRUNCH! A merciful, painless death. Sungchul tossed the limp corpse into the air. Blood had splatted all over the place, but that didn't matter; this entire place was about to overflow with human blood soon.

Are these all just the common ones? There are no Hidden Quests listed here.

This was a decent find considering the fact that he had obtained it from a low-level Homunculus. Sungchul retreated back into the darkness to wait for his next opportunity.

Soon, modern humans suddenly appeared from the bright lights of the Magic Formation. The Summoned had arrived.

"Where am I?"

"What…What happened?"

Having been pulled out of their comfortable, civilized world, they inspected their new surroundings with innocent and confused faces. However, there was no time for them to be surprised.

All the Mages and the guards left the plaza, and only the rough looking Homunculi remained to face the humans.

"Kekekekek! Humans! Welcome to the Fields of Judgement!"

The people didn't know what to make of these infant-sized creatures that were hopping and shouting about. Some of them looked around blankly, some kept bashing at their phones, and others kept badgering another with questions. Each person's reaction might have been different, but the crises facing them were all the same.

Sungchul, who had slipped in amongst the crowd, was quietly waiting for a message to appear.

Will…it succeed?

He, who had been banned and made enemy of every Circle of Mages, had never had the opportunity to learn Magic. If there was a way to learn Magic by beating the knowledge out of a Mage, he would have tried it by now. But Magic could not be learned without obtaining a Mage Class first, which wasn't as easy as it sounded.

Along with precise planning and some luck, he would need to find an altar and a skilled Mage who could breathe life into that altar. It wasn't difficult for him to crush a kingdom, but if someone was to find out that he was trying to learn Magic, all the Mage circles would put their lives on the line to stop him. Those people were the craziest of fanatics. They put their reputation even above their lives.

The only solution Sungchul could come up with was to sneak into places that bestowed Classes for free, like the Summoning Palace. If one could receive the Summoning Palace quest, there would be an opportunity for them to learn Magic. He wasn't sure if it would work, but this was the safest bet he could have made. Suddenly, a message appeared before Sungchul's anticipating eyes.

[Welcome to the Summoning Palace.]

[Summoning Palace's Quest will now begin.]

[Battle will soon commence, please be prepared.]

It happened. The Summoning Palace's quest had been triggered. In his mind, Sungchul was celebrating when another message appeared.

[Warning! You could die.]

"Me? Die?"

His lips curved into a cynical smile.

***

The iron gates on the walls surrounding the plaza opened, and an alienesque creature squirmed through. A man with particularly good sight spoke uneasily.

"Is that a Mantis?"

The man's guess was correct. However, there was no way that something as simple as that would appear in the Blanche Plaza. What had really appeared was a Man-Eating Mantis, standing at the height of an adult male. There was a swarm of them numbering in the hundreds.

"Now! Trashy humans! Weapons are going to start appearing. Pick one! Fight...or run! If you don't do either...kekeke! You can just let yourself be eaten!"

The Homunculi began dancing as they taunted the Summoned. The crowd remained still, unsure of what to do. But Sungchul was different. Without showing any particular emotion, he patiently waited for the arrival of the weapons. A worn blade suddenly appeared in the air.

[Blade of Beginnings]
Grade: Common – Lowest Grade
Type: Blade
Effect: None
Note: Wield and fight. Die. Or Kill.

It has been a while since I've used a blade.

He had been solely using his hammer for quite a while now. This didn't mean he couldn't use a blade. Sungchul's mastery level with a blade was at the Master rank. It fell short of the "greatest" ranking of Grand Master, but it wouldn't be wrong to say he was humanity's most powerful swordsman.

Sungchul hid amidst the rumbling crowd and observed the transparent beings that were meandering above their heads. It was a summoned creature with the appearance of a transparent blood shot eye. Most people wouldn't be able to notice it due to its invisibility spell, but such illusion spells were ineffective against Sungchul.

That must be the Observer's Eye. Have they already started filtering people out?

Sungchul could see a large Observation Tower above the walls surrounding the plaza. The bastards who held power in this part of the world were sitting in that tower. They were watching through the Observer's Eye for any seeds or "special talents" they could nurture. But at this point it was still too early for them to tell, so they were mostly just watching the people who were of interest to the higher ups.

As if on cue, the Observer's Eye focused their attentions onto those special individuals at the same time. This was a type of a mark.

All of The Observer's Eyes are enchanted with a low-level repellent spell. I suppose it could keep away trash mobs like those Man-Eating Mantises.

Some of the Observer's Eyes hovered over the men and women who looked promising. These eyes were the property of the slave traders. Most likely they would reveal themselves at a moment of peril, offering a contract with horrific terms in exchange for saving the Summoned's life, just so that the innocent life can be plunged into the depth of despair and suffering.

"Now now, trashy humans! The game will begin!"

The Homunculi with the red hats were hopping over to the humans. A man walked over to one of them.

"Hey! What the fuck are you? Huh?"

It was a relatively muscular man in his mid-twenties who looked agile. He must have used his fist quite a bit in the old world, but this was Other World; old ways of thinking did not apply here.

One of the Homunculi with the red hat tottered along and asked,

"Trashy human, you have something you want to say to me?"

The man, seemingly full of energy, suddenly kicked the Homunculus. However, the kick carrying all of his weight was easily stopped by the Homunculus' child-like hands.

"Uh...? Huh?!"

The man's eyes only briefly reflected the horror welling up inside him before the surrounding Homunculi gathered like vultures and each happily held onto a limb. The man desperately tried to swing his blade, but it was all to no avail.

"H-hey! Let go of me! Shit!"

The red hatted Homunculus smiled viciously as it said, "Trashy human, struggling without knowing your place! Time for a lesson!"

"This place is OUR playground! Break our rules, and this is what happens!" snickered another Homunculus while pulling the man's limbs apart.

"KYAAAAAA!"

The man's limbs were torn apart, accompanied by a sickening cry of agony. After a brief and shrill scream of a woman onlooker, the entire plaza plunged into a horrified silence. The Homunculi, basking in the tangible fear of the humans watching, arrogantly proclaimed, "From now on, you must all listen to what we tell you to do. Run over to that door as fast as you can! Or else Mister Mantis is going to make a tasty meal out of you!"

The seal surrounding the plaza fell away, and the starving Mantis swarm suddenly perked up. The humans finally understood the fate that awaited them. There was a desperate cry, followed by pandemonium. A huge group of 2500 people all bolted towards the door. Everyone pushed and shoved until the weakest of them were trampled to death. Sungchul calmly made his way through the chaos towards the front of the crowd. This was all a familiar sight to him.

The Homunculi's repertoire hadn't changed a bit. There would still be an unwelcome surprise waiting for them at the exit.

"Kwuuuuuh!"

A hand shot out from the exit, followed by a creature shaped like a human. It was a Ghoul, a zombie-like creature that sought human flesh. Although the creature still retained a bit of its human consciousness, their insatiable hunger prevailed over their sense of reason.

The starved Ghouls became frenzied at the sight of fresh, living humans. They caught the more athletic among the Summoned who were at the front of the crowd and started eating them alive. Witnessing the traumatizing scene unfolding before them, those at the front came grinding to a halt. However, the remaining herd of two thousand didn't stop with them. The people at the back continued to press forward, while those at the front began to scream, "Stop pushing! Stop pushing!"

Those facing the Ghouls held the crowd back with all their strength, but in the end, they were slowly being pushed forward inch by inch until they, too, were grabbed by the Ghouls.

"KYAAAA!"

"So…hungry…! HUNGRY!"

Accompanied by the screams of their victims, the Ghouls began to feast. However, there was a stronger, even more terrifying predator hunting those who had fallen behind.

"D-dear!"

A middle-aged man feebly tried to defend his wife with his blade, but a beginner was no match for the Man-Eating Mantis.

CLANG!

The mantis' foreleg shattered the blade and snatched up the despairing survivor.

CRUNCH! CRUNCH!

The Homunculi made satisfied smiles while listening to the music of flesh and bone being devoured.

"That's why you have to run faster, you slowpokes! Being lazy led to this! Kehehe!"

It was a hellish scene, but all of this failed to affect Sungchul. To him, there was something more important that demanded his attention, which was to read the inscription that was at the front gate.

"…Death will set you free."

[You are a possessor of sharp observation. You have astutely observed the inscription written at the front gate, and completed Observant (Common)]

Reward: Intuition +1

The first quest had been completed. However, it was still far from over.

[Oh Ho! What a nice guy! You have completed Samaritan (Common) by helping 3 people who have fallen over.]

Reward: Apple x2

[You are a true romantic, gazing up upon the two moons longingly even in the most dangerous of times! Romanticist (Common) has been completed.]

Reward: Palace Token x1

Even during the process of escaping, he was able to finish a few trivial quests. Things like apples could be earned at Sungchul's leisure, but the Palace Token was the most important item to collect from Palace Quests. Palace Tokens were required to pick a class. One would have to feverishly collect them if one wanted to take one of the Hidden Classes, but Sungchul only wanted the common Mage Class. He could easily collect 9 of the 10 tokens with little trouble. Trying any harder would only garner the attention of the large guilds and sects.

I can probably get away with earning 15 tokens without raising an alarm. Now that I've managed to get some intuition, maybe I should check my status window for once.

In this brief moment, a Ghoul rushed towards Sungchul. Sungchul reflexively swiped across the Ghoul's skull with the back of his blade. However, he forgot to control his strength. The Ghoul's head broke through the reinforced floor.

"Shit."

He tried to hold back, but he was still too strong. It couldn't be helped. His physical strength far exceeded the level of a human and approached the realms of divinity.

There is definitely a need for me to conceal my strength. By a lot.

Thankfully, his action went completely unnoticed; no one was in a position to notice anything out of the ordinary. That was only natural. Preserving one's life here was difficult enough without watching what someone else was doing.

The end slowly came into sight. The Homunculi were waving blood-soaked cloths while shouting at people. Those who arrived first felt as if they were suffocating both physically and mentally. Sungchul softly muttered "Status Screen" under his breath. Overall, the Status Screen of newcomers would be pathetic beyond compare. It wouldn't be rare for it to be filled with just some meager stats and nothing else. This wasn't the case for Sungchul. His Status Screen unfolded like a legendary epic.

[Current Status of Sungchul Kim, "The Destroyer"]

[Blessings]

1. Covenant
   (Unknown)
2. Unshakeable
   (Immune to Mental Attacks)
3. Blessing from God of Chaos
   (10% Bonus to Strength, Dexterity, Vitality)
4. Heir of Heracles
   (+100 Strength)
5. Bloodline of Zealot
   (Major Bonus to Regeneration when Below 10% Vitality)
6. Champion of Humanity
   (+ 50 Resilience)
7. Rapid-Bow of the High Elven Kingdom
   (+ 30 Dexterity)
8. Heart of an Ancient Warrior
   (+5 Strength, Resilience, Vitality / Resilience)

[Curses]

1. Covenant
   (Unknown)
2. Final Declaration of Grand Mage Balzark
   (-10 Intuition)
3. Blessing of Blademaster Karakardra
   (+ 1 Dexterity, -1 Strength)
4. Ancient God's Champion, Arrak – Garr's Criticism
   (-3 Strength)
5. Dark Dragon Groteus's Karmic Curse
   (- 20 Strength, -20 Vitality)
6. Adelwight of the Haunted Forest's Common Curse
   (- 5 Strength, Erectile Dysfunction)
7. Enemy of the Kingdom
   (Faction: Nemesis of Human Kingdom, Blank Check
Reward)
8. Destroyer of Hora Mountain Sect
   (Faction: Nemesis of Hora Mountain Sect, Destroyed)
9. Destroyer of Mewra Sect
   (Faction: Nemesis of Mewra Sect, Destroyed)
10. Enemy of the Allied Mage's Guild
    (Faction: Nemesis of Allied Mage's Guild and Sub guilds)
11. Steel Fist Curse of Crimson Orc Chief, Drakuul
    (Race: -30 Orc Favor)
12. Recorded on Dwarven Book of Grudges
    (Race: -200 Dwarf Favor)
13. Recorded on Allied Merchant's Guild's Blacklist
    (Faction: Trade impossible with Allied Merchant's Guild and
their affiliated factions)

...

Too long. It would take ages to read completely down to the class screen. This was why he had avoided opening his Status Screen before. There also hadn't been any need to.

Sungchul sifted through the tightly packed lines of words to find what he was really looking for.

Ability power, Class, and Soul Contracts.

[Class]
Main Class – Primordial Warrior (Mythic)
Sub Class – High -Class Chef (Rare)

[Stats]
Strength 999+ Dexterity   853
Vitality   801   Magic Power   3
Intuition -9   Magic Resist 611
Resilience 501   Charisma   18
Luck   18

[Soul Contract – 6 Slots]
1. Soul Harvester
([Legend] Vitality Leech 15%, Vitality restored from fallen enemies)
2. Thunder Shield
([Legend] All Magic Damage reduced by 50% / Negate all mental attacks below legend rank)
3. Eye of Truth
([Legend] Negate all blessings below Epic rank / Identify all items, consumables, and skill details)
4. Soul Storage
([Epic] Can store 1500 different items)
5. Deceiver's Veil
([Rare – High Tier] Conceals status window)
– Blank –

With the comparably lighter data, Sungchul first looked over the Classes.

I suppose Mage should be slotted to the sub Class. I haven't really messed around with it like some other people have.

Sungchul then looked over his 5th Soul Contract, Deceiver's Veil. Soul Contracts were, as the name suggested, an agreement where a deity or a similar being inscribes some of their power into the user's soul. Each of these contracts were exceedingly difficult to obtain, but they also granted significant power.

Deceiver's Veil effectively deceived other users. It not only hid the user's stats but also their name. It was something essential for an unreasonably powerful loner with more enemies than friends like Sungchul.

I should play around a bit when I get the chance.

He finally looked over his stats, or more importantly, his Intuition.

Intuition is -9. That curse from the geezer, Balzark, is holding me back now.

The image of an old man, covered in countless inscriptions, spouting curses while being turned into tenderized meat, flashed through his mind. Intuition was a core stat for a Mage, going along with their Magic power. Higher Magic Power represented the Mage's destructive power and the size of his or her Mana reserve, while higher Intuition unlocked higher tiers of Magic spells. But, no matter how large your Magic Power was, spells simply could not be learned without their required Intuition. As far as he could recall, the Mage class required minimum of 10 Intuition.

It is critical that I raise my Intuition, but upper limit for increase in Intuition through common quests is set to 10. Limit for Strength gain is 23, so why is the limit for raising Intuition set so low?

He did not plan for it, but a need for Hidden Quests arose. However, Sungchul didn't know the requirements for triggering any of the Hidden Quests within the Summoning Palace. And he had only managed to get his hands on the common quest log. It wasn't like there weren't any other ways...

Sungchul searched for the most unnaturally calm individuals among the survivors. He found one. One with the Observer's Eye floating above. In other words, a "Preselected." A way would appear if he trailed him. A way to uncover a Hidden Quest.

Chapter 2 – Forsaken Cathedral

The Homunculi gathered around the survivors and began counting their numbers.

"How many of the trash survived? At a quick glance…Keke! Around 1500?"

Among the Homunculi, there was one that was abnormally large. It wore a white hat and, as the leader of the Homunculi, it called itself the Drill Sergeant. All of the Homunculi gathered around it.

"There are exactly 1534 heads!"

"Oh, my! Not even reduced by half? Such a disappointment. However, I am a benevolent Homunculus."

The Drill Sergeant's tone was not only shrill and cracked, but also loud, so it had no problem reaching its audience. The voice sounded unpleasant, but it still bored through into their ears. Sungchul also had to listen to its voice.

Is it the same one from twenty-five years ago? It's still alive.

The Homunculi usually lived short lives. Not only were they treated harshly by their masters, but they were also often cannibalized by their fellows. It seems that this Homunculus managed to survive so long by increasing its size to gain power and by taking in followers after helping them grow stronger.

"Now now, trashy humans! This gracious Drill Sergeant shall show mercy upon you all. I declare a week of rest! Please use this week well to adjust to this new world!"

The Homunculi followed the Drill Sergeant out.

This announcement snapped the people into conversation.

"W-where is this? Just where is this?"

"My phone…There is no signal, not even wifi."

"This is a dream…it has to be a dream…"

Most of the Summoned were unable to accept the reality they were facing and were still in denial. But being in denial was counterproductive. The smart thing to do was to accept their circumstance and act quickly to tackle the problems they were facing one at a time.

This week isn't a gift, but a death sentence.

There were no rations or water in this place. Only people. Other than the wall protecting them from the demonic creatures, there were no merits to staying in this place. People would have to venture beyond the walls to survive. Or they would have to eat other people.

Sungchul stayed with the crowd and observed the situation. A short while later, a few people started to move. They walked in a way that could be considered erratic in the eyes of a normal person. Some circled the plaza, and others pretended to swing a sword in the air. Normally, people would assume that they had lost it, but Sungchul saw things differently. There was an Observer's Eye on top of each one of these "lunatics" without exception. They were getting their instructions through a Summoner who was teaching them how to survive in this place. Completing small quests while others remained idle out of indecision and ignorance would quickly add up and make a critical difference in the end.

Among the "normal people," some were showing a bit of initiative.

"Excuse me. Are you by yourself?"

A middle-aged man in a ragged suit made his way through the crowd to form a group. Although some ignored him, insulted him, or outright refused to join him, he still managed to form a small group of ten people. As he watched that man, Sungchul began recalling an old memory.

Thinking back, there are those kinds too. Spouting annoying nonsense like, "a bundle of sticks is harder to break" to gather people.

He was then reminded of someone, a memory which darkened his expression rapidly. But there was no more time for him to soak in the past. Sungchul quickly tailed a group of twenty people exiting the plaza. However, someone in the background thoughtlessly called out to him.

"H-hey."

Sungchul turned his cold, emotionless gaze over to the speaker.

"Got any cigs?"

"…"

Sungchul didn't even bother acknowledging him any further.

Past the walls, a forest overflowing with demonic energy awaited them. It was home to demonic creatures. Those marked by the Observer's Eye were the first who dared to cross the barrier and step into the forest.

Sungchul noticed that even among the "Preselected," their large number indicated that these people were not ordinary.

They must have the backing of a big organization.

The Summoning Palace was a neutral zone under the protection of the God of Neutrality.

No powers were allowed to freely abuse their authority here. It required great sums of money to bribe enough people to influence things in the Summoning Palace; only major factions had enough wealth to bring several dozen officials under their sway. This meant that these people were most likely the ones who Sungchul had been searching for. He nonchalantly slipped into their group. The younger men and women gave him a glance before turning their attention away.

In this awkward silence, two more joined the group.

"Twenty-five people…I think that's everyone."

A stylish man in a suit was the first to speak out; everyone focused their attention on him. It must have been nerve-wracking, but he still continued calmly.

"I apologize if I seem forward, but that's just how it is. My name is Yuhoon Lee."

He received a reasonable response from the group. Everyone other than a squinty-eyed man with bleached hair seemed to welcome his attempt at breaking the ice. Yuhoon continued to address the crowd after gaining their approval.

"Can everyone hear their Guide's voice?"

Everyone's head nodded in response.

"…"

Sungchul also calmly nodded his head and turned his attention to their Observer's Eyes. There were slight differences in their shapes; each was summoned by a different Summoner. At this moment, Sungchul noticed something.

The quality of the assigned Mages is low. Their vision and telepathy must be spotty at best.

The Mages that Sungchul usually dealt with were of "High Rank." Even the Necromancers that Sungchul had frequently and casually beaten to death were capable of raising an army of undead numbering in the thousands. Compared to Mages of the caliber Sungchul was used to, these Summoners were apprentices at best.

Not bad. I should stick with this group.

By Sungchul's expectation, there would be Hidden Quests attached to the training course prepared for these twenty-four people.

"First off, my Guide has notified me that time is very precious. There is no time for us to dawdle. After a brief introduction, I believe we should quickly move on with whatever our Guides have directed us to do."

Yuhoon approached the people around him first, casually introduced himself, and enticed a friendly atmosphere. No one approached Sungchul, and that was because of his messy appearance. It was extremely difficult to obtain decent clothes in Other World, much less stylish ones. Sungchul did make some effort to try and look presentable, but he could only manage to get his hands on some worn-out military fatigues; he looked like some sort of homeless veteran. He also hadn't had any hygiene products with which to wash for a while now so he didn't smell too great, either.

Next to Sungchul, there was a teenager in hip-hop clothing and a woman in her twenties wearing only branded products, but they spoke to each other with their backs towards him. It was a clear sign of rejection.

"…"

Sungchul didn't particularly mind. There were no benefits in him caring what they thought of him; all he wanted were the Hidden Quests. However, someone noticed him from afar and approached him.

"Hey, mister, why are you standing here alone?"

Sungchul looked up, wondering who it might have been. It was Yuhoon Lee. The man spoke with a wide smile maintaining eye contact, and a hand outreached for a shake.

What a well-trained etiquette.

Sungchul had dealt with a lot of people before. His instinct told him that Yuhoon might not be as friendly as he appeared, but he accepted the handshake anyways.

"Just Kim. Please call me Kim."

"Then, we'll have to compromise with calling you Mister Kim."

About the time when introductions finished, an eerie glow emanated from deep within the forest. The group slowly gathered together and turned towards the light.

"Kekekeke…"

It was a familiar laugh. As expected, a Homunculus revealed itself from the darkness. The glow was coming from the lantern it held in its hand.

"You have already gathered here, humans!"

Sungchul recognized this Homunculus by its voice.

Drill Sergeant.

The Drill Sergeant was significantly larger than the average Homunculus, and also revealed a significantly more sinister set of razor-like teeth as it greeted the group. It stood at the height of everyone's stomachs, but they all understood just how savage and powerful these midget creatures were; how could they dare look down on the much larger Drill Sergeant?

The Drill Sergeant reveled in the humans' fears and smiled gleefully as it looked over them.

"Please do not fear, humans! This Drill Sergeant is but a smart Homunculus! I senselessly kill trashy humans, but to the selected few, I provide assistance."

The Drill Sergeant tottered back through the forest with a lantern in hand.

"Follow closely! Preselected humans! You might just die to some monsters if you fall behind! Kekeke!"

Everyone became flabbergasted at this situation.

"I think we can follow him. That's what the voice is telling me."

Yuhoon led the way in, following after the Homunculus. The others also followed after their impromptu leader helplessly. Only two people stayed in their place.

"Ah, shit. I really don't like that bitch."

A man resembling a catfish spat out a quick bit of profanity before following. Sungchul quietly moved after him.

—

The Homunculus led the group to an abandoned Cathedral. On top of the Cathedral's steeple there stood a rectangular ornament; this was the symbol for the God of Neutrality. The God of Neutrality was one of the five gods that ruled over the pantheon.

"You are to go in! Humans!"

The Drill Sergeant stepped in first. The rectangular ornament filled with a strange light as it stepped into the Cathedral.

"Woah...What? This..." Disparate words of admiration spilled out from the group.

There were sarcophagi with open lids within the Cathedral. There were twenty-five in total.

"Now now, humans! Don't dawdle, step into whichever one suits your fancy!" the Homunculus spoke with a smirk.

One by one, everyone eventually began lying within the sarcophagi. Sungchul Kim also found one somewhere in the middle and laid down. The sarcophagi began levitating with power, and the lids closed shut on their own. Bright letters began to appear within the suffocating darkness that surrounded them.

[You have found the martyr's sarcophagi and laid down with resolute hearts.]

[Determination of the martyr uplifts your body.]

Effect: +10 Strength, Dexterity, Vitality (Region Restriction: Summoning Palace)

***

In essence, this was a buff for beginners. But the amount granted was outrageous. An average, healthy adult male would have a Strength stat of 6. What would happen if you added 10 to this number? Even the feeblest of women would suddenly exceed the normal physical limit of human anatomy.

Sungchul's eyes revealed his surprise.

I've heard stories, but I never imagined that the Preselected would get this significant of an advantage.

He was one of the original Summoned. Delicate dandies like the "Preselected" hadn't existed back then; everyone had to claw their way through depths of hell each day. He knew that everyone who made it out alive had done so by the merit of their own strength and their luck. In that way, it had been truly equal; those who lacked ability, died. What Sungchul had witnessed just now in this Cathedral threw the concept of a fair game out the window.

"Now now, wake up! Great humans!"

They saw a pile of weapons and rations that had been prepared in front of the sarcophagi. There was a week's worth of food, and weapons that were visually similar to the basic ones. Everyone looked confused, but Sungchul had already spotted the difference.

These are enchanted weapons.

Physically identical weapons could have a drastically different performance with enchants. The impact of enchants was more drastic for lower-grade weapons like the ones they had been provided with at the start. These weapons were worlds apart from the ones the group was currently equipped with.

"Now now, humans! Throw away those trash weapons you are carrying, and take hold of these new weapons, please! These are ten times better!"

They hesitantly exchanged their old weapons for the new ones.

"Woah! They look the same, but I think the new ones seem better somehow."

"Yeah, don't they feel lighter...and stronger?"

The Drill Sergeant saw the delighted eyes of the group and spoke even louder with its usual grating voice.

"You selected few! You are protected! I, Drill Sergeant, shall dedicate myself to guiding every one of you in safely passing through the tribulations of this Summoning Palace!"

The members began relaxing and smiling after hearing these words. They had completely accepted the Homunculus's words that they were the chosen ones.

"Everyone. We will soon return to the plaza! There is no need to fear! You have obtained a few powers beyond those of the trashy humans! Kekeke!"

The Drill Sergeant's words bolstered the group's pride. Laughter could be heard from the people, but Sungchul saw a faint light approaching the group. It was another lantern. This lantern was held by a single Homunculus who was leading a single person in this direction.

"Huuuuh? What's that?" The Drill Sergeant revealed its razor-like teeth as it questioned the other Homunculus.

"Manager! There is another chosen human!"

"What? Chosen human...?!"

The Drill Sergeant's eyes lit up with a crimson light.

"There are already twenty-five people here. What's going on here, assistant?"

The Drill Sergeant began huffing and threateningly approached the smaller Homunculus before it replied fearfully.

"T-that is…The human said he needed to take a shit first, so he was late."

"Shit…? Does that even make sense?"

The Drill Sergeant drew close to the newly arrived human and glared at him. He was a twenty-year-old male with a decent appearance and a balanced physique. He seemed to have an extremely friendly personality because he continued to smile despite the Drill Sergeant fuming before him. A few of the women took note of him.

"Anyways, it's impossible! All the Buffs of the Martyrs and the overpowered weapons have already been distributed to the twenty-five people gathered here. Those who are tardy have no right to get anything!"

The Drill Sergeant crushed a candy while shaking its head in anger. However, the small Homunculus' face now started to pale.

"B-but, Manager… this human…is not ordinary."

"What do you mean? Assistant?"

"This human is someone directly chosen by the Order of the Iron Blood Knights' Head Captain!"

"O-Order of the Iron Blood Knights?!"

The Drill Sergeant jumped up in surprise. It was so surprised that even the candy flew out of its mouth.

Order of the Iron Blood Knights, huh.

Sungchul recognized the name. They were once the preeminent steward defenders of humanity against the demonic forces. But they fell to corruption and instead became the shield of the elites. An image of the Knight Captain's stubborn face with graying beard flashed across Sungchul's mind.

"Hey, you call yourself the Drill Sergeant, right? Don't be so stiff; I haven't really adjusted to this world yet."

The tardy guy finally opened his mouth. There wasn't a speck of him trying to confront the Drill Sergeant. He passed by the flabbergasted Drill Sergeant and began smiling while warmly shaking hands with the rest of the group.

"Hello, everyone! Sorry I'm late, my name is Ahram Park. As you can see, I am a 'Preselected' just like you all."

It was an astounding display of self-confidence and adaptability. He had already understood his status within this new society and was now making full use of it. The man clearly knew that no matter what he said, the Drill Sergeant could not harm him.

The Drill Sergeant was shaking in rage, but it could only savagely chew an ever-increasing number of hard candies. The Drill Sergeant eventually addressed everyone other than Ahram.

"Among you, there is a bad boy that has deceived this Drill Sergeant. Please come forward now. Before this Drill Sergeant becomes very angry."

The people in the group continued looking at each other and exchanged gazes filled with suspicion. Sungchul met two distinct gazes himself. They were the hip-hop boy and the brand-name girl he noticed from earlier.

"Isn't it that person?"

"I think so too."

The two eventually stood before Sungchul.

"Hey, hobo."

The Hip-hop boy took on an aggressive tone with Sungchul.

"It's you, isn't it? Everyone can see that."

Sungchul laughed to himself as the kid glared at him with arrogant eyes.

I guess I must look like I'm a pushover.

The Drill Sergeant's grating voice once again punched at their ears.

"Hey, you. Why did you raise your hand?"

Drill Sergeant was looking at Yuhoon Lee.

"Are you confessing that you're the rat?"

Yuhoon's shoulders fell away at the Drill Sergeant's murderous tone.

"No."

"Then why did you raise your hand?"

"I'm not sure of the exact circumstance, but if I understand correctly, someone among us isn't a Preselected, is that right?"

The Drill Sergeant nodded. Yuhoon, with a voice markedly more pleasant than the Drill Sergeant's, continued speaking softly towards the crowd.

"The one guiding me has provided a wonderful suggestion. We could reveal the name of our Guides."

A very simple, but effective method. There was an Observer's Eye above all of the Preselected. The Observer's Eyes were limited to transmitting the Mage's telepathy to only their assigned candidates and were invisible to one another. But this wouldn't matter if their candidate were to verbally relay the information. Only the Preselected would be able to answer this question. There was no possibility that someone could reason themselves out of this.

"For reference, the name of the person guiding me is Leonis!"

Yuhoon was the first to announce his Guide, which was the conservative and smart choice.

The Drill Sergeant, who had been shaking in rage, quickly started smiling grotesquely.

"There, human! Truly brilliant! You have earned points in this Drill Sergeant's books! That is a great honor!"

Yuhoon simply scratched his head and smiled sheepishly.

That guy…

Sungchul questioned the claim that the idea Yuhoon proposed came from the Guide; thick-headed interns wouldn't be able to think up such an idea on the fly like that.

"My Guide's name is Dolores Winterer. She says she is on a different level than average Mages!"

Ahram followed up with a raucous laughter. The Drill Sergeant ignored him and continued asking down the line.

"Human, your Guide's name?"

"Choi Hweyun."

One by one, the group revealed their Guides' names, and the smaller Homunculus followed behind the Drill Sergeant and recorded them on a sheepskin. When half the group was done, the young pair standing beside Sungchul started glaring at him once more.

"Hey, hobo. Trying to bounce now? That monster is going to split you in half when it finds out you clowned him, ya know."

"Is that right?"

Sungchul replied calmly. However, he wasn't looking at the kid, he was actually focusing on the Observer's Eye above him.

Should I try taking that...?

It was just a simple construct; its telepathy was probably automatically directed to the closest individual.

"Then I'll go before you," said Sungchul and as he spoke, his right hand moved; it moved at a speed faster than anyone could see and grabbed the Observer's Eye above the man's head.

Don't fight with other Preselected...Don't fight...

Telepathy flowed in. It was a pathetic quality of telepathy that sounded weak and distant.

"Why are you standing in front of me?"

The man, who hadn't even realized that his Observer's Eye had been stolen, continued to glare at Sungchul. Sungchul feigned weakness and lowered his gaze, to which the man smirked victoriously.

"Can't wait to die, can you? I won't stop you."

The brand-name girl and the kid continued chattering behind him. It was as though they were celebrating Sungchul's imminent death. However, they could never imagine that his hand was currently wrapped around something.

Why does everything look so strange...What...is there a problem...?

Primitive telepathy from the Observer's Eye continued buzzing in. Sungchul quietly reflected on this new revelation about the Preselected.

Now that I think about it, none of these people actually ever talked to the Observer's Eye.

His gaze fell on the distant Drill Sergeant and the woman in front of it.

"Elipas…is the name."

The woman, and even Yuhoon, never muttered to themselves but were still able to respond quickly to the question. That could only mean there was another method of communicating to the Mage; a very strong mental thought.

What is your name?

Sungchul leaked a concise and strong thought through the Observer's Eye. A reply soon followed.

Didn't I tell you before…? My name is Krill…Krill Regall…

Krill Regall. As soon as he heard the name, Sungchul threw the Observer's Eye into the air. It didn't go far before a small explosion happened followed by a splattering of blood, but no one was able to see this. Now it was Sungchul's turn.

"Umm…the human with colorful clothing! State the name of your guiding Mage!"

The Drill Sergeant revealed its razor teeth and demanded an answer.

"Krill. Krill Regall."

The hip-hop man's face crumbled at the mention of that name.

"What…What did you say?"

It was only natural to be surprised. It was the name he was going to give. However, the Drill Sergeant wasn't interested in fair trials or figuring out who was truly guilty. It stood indifferently before the man whose Guide's name was stolen and demanded an answer.

"Hey you! Human with earrings! State your guiding Mage's name!"

"U-um…"

The hip-hop boy was soaked in cold sweat. He finally pointed at Sungchul and began shouting.

"That fucker! He said my Mage's name!"

"What? Human?"

The Drill Sergeant and the small Homunculus with the paper and pen both tilted their heads.

"No...shit. That fucker! He said my Mage's name before I could! Krill Regall was mine!"

There was no one here, no Homunculi, who was willing to listen to him. The Drill Sergeant lifted the hip-hop boy by the collar with its pudgy hands.

"Got him! The rat! I finally found the criminal!"

"No...! It's not me!"

Sungchul looked indifferently at the boy being dragged off, and quietly raised his middle finger. Finally, the boy understood what had just transpired, but by now it was much too late.

"H-hey!!!"

The boy was soon torn apart by the hands of two Homunculi. His pitiful screaming rang eerily throughout the Forsaken Cathedral.

Chapter 3 – Nightmare of Vestiare

It had been four days since the mass summoning, and an unpleasant energy was circling the Blanche plaza. 1500 people were busy stewing in the stench of rotting flesh without any food or water. There were no conversations, just constant glares from across the plaza.

RIIIP!

The sound of plastic rustled from one corner of the plaza. Several hundred pairs of eyes shot towards the man that was pulling something from his clothes. It was just an empty cigarette carton.

"Anyone…Anyone have some cigs…?"

The man kept asking with hollow eyes even as his voice grew taut. A few of the men standing nearby spat out profanities as they started beating him up. Nobody tried to stop them, and not even his pitiful screams could stir up any sort of reaction.

After the beating was finished, the man kept on muttering as he lay on the ground.

"C-cigarettes, please…"

Sungchul unconsciously recognized the face. It was the face of the idiotic guy who had asked for some cigs on the first day. Looking at the man's crooked nose and his bruised eyes, he estimated that the man had two more days left at most, or perhaps he wouldn't even last the night. His spirit looked to be even more dead than his body was.

Sungchul only cared about how to best spend his time here; he refocused his mind on his objectives.

In the end, I didn't manage to find any Hidden Quests.

There weren't any more gatherings of the Preselected after they left the Forsaken Cathedral. It was completely against his expectations; he had hoped that some of the Preselected would be called away one at a time, but none of them had moved discreetly.

The most he could do was keep track of what they did throughout the day.

They had taken over the northern corner of the plaza and the training center located there. The Preselected were inside, training with the practice and spinning dummies. There were also ordinary people who were pointing at and mocking them as if they were lunatics.

"Tsk tsk. There's nothing to eat, and they're just wasting their energy. They're just asking to die faster."

"They gone crazy, is all. Those idiots."

These people were just ignorant. The Preselected would quickly grow strong inside the training center.

"Haha, the sound of your punch on the dummy is becoming crisp! How much strength do you have now?"

"22 now. The sound changed after I hit 20."

"I haven't hit 20 yet. I gotta try harder myself!"

A small, yet distinct disparity was beginning to grow. This would become a critical factor to them during the future crisis.

PUNCH. PUNCH.

Sungchul thoughtlessly punched a dummy in the corner of the training center and continued with his eavesdropping. There were two people worth taking notice of in this group.

Yuhoon Lee: A natural-born leader whose wit could charm any person coupled with a calm voice that even an announcer would envy.

And then Ahram Park: He had arrived conspicuously even on his first day, and revealed himself to be backed by one of the most powerful factions. He had already proven his authority over the Drill Sergeant and was more noteworthy than the former due to his powerful background. The chances of him being granted a Hidden Quest was quite large. The problem was, Ahram seemed to be more interested in his sexual conquests than any training.

"Do you have a boyfriend? It looks like you might have one...but maybe not anymore? Keke."

He didn't even pretend to be training. He avoided any form of labor, including hitting the dummies, and had become even more of a bother with his endless supply of pick-up lines. The women who were interested at first due to his powerful supporter and fashionably late entrance quickly lost interest due to his lecherous and flighty attitude.

"Ah...why does everyone hate me? It's a short life anyway. I might as well enjoy it while I can."

He was eventually turned away by all of the Preselected women and now turned to women outside of the group. Their faces all looked tired and despondent, but some still retained some of their former beauty. He drooled lecherously as he held his rations under his arms.

"Ah...what should I do? What am I to do?"

Sungchul thought that Ahram looked like an animal in heat, locked in a cage; he predicted that Ahram would cause a major incident in not too distant future. Sungchul didn't have to wait for long. Ahram left with a pretty young thing beyond the wall, but he returned alone. Only Sungchul knew what had really transpired.

"..."

Within an isolated area covered in foliage, there was the corpse of a naked woman. Sungchul acknowledged it without showing emotion. There was a distinct handprint around her neck; she had died from asphyxiation. The most incriminating piece of evidence was the slight bit of blood and skin embedded underneath her nails. Few rations were left next to the body as if to mock the victim.

What a broken person.

He had felt that Ahram was twisted from the start, but being granted so much authority so quickly could only make things worse. Who knew how many more would be sacrificed. It was up to Sungchul to find an opportunity to put an end to this.

I need to set up some sort of special experience for him and his Guide.

Sungchul closed the woman's eyes that were left open frozen in fear, and quietly whispered under his breath.

"May you find happiness in the afterlife."

He turned away from the woman and put the dangers of the dark forest behind him.

—

After sundown, the Preselected would gather beyond the walls to eat their food while sitting on the forest floor. The rations they'd been provided by the Drill Sergeant only contained stale bread and small beads that would turn into a mouthful of water when placed into their mouth. It wasn't tasty, but it was still something precious. They were the only ones among the 1500 that would be able to eat something in this week. Sungchul sat a distance away from the group, but he was still listening to their conversations.

"What did you do before?"

"College. I was still attending when I was suddenly dragged here."

"Same here. I'm a college student as well."

"Oh, is that right? What major?"

"I was a Music major."

That was the brand-name girl. People tended to talk more during their meals. Conversation acted to close the gaps in people's hearts and could bolster a person's spirits even in situations like these. However, all conversations stopped when a group of three drew near.

The Preselected exchanged glances with each other. The cold calculating glances gave proof of an unspoken consensus that they would commit murder together.

"Wow, there really is food here!"

The man briefly exclaimed before he suddenly fell silent as if his mouth was sealed. Obnoxious chewing sounds could be heard.

CRUNCH. SMACK. CHEW.

The sound dissipated, and the uninvited guests licked their lips longingly before leaving.

"What was that?"

"I don't know."

The Preselected who were riled up then dropped their murderous intent and resumed their meal, continuing with their conversations. No one had noticed Sungchul's disappearance.

"…"

Sungchul stared down at the crimson slime wedged under a heavy rock. Its name was "Blood Pudding," it was usually a green herbivore that was about the size of an adult woman. But during its mating season, it would turn red and become extremely aggressive and start devouring everything in sight. The problem, though, was that this species' mating ritual was very unusual.

Sungchul lightly pushed away the rock holding the slime in place. Freed from its binding, the slime leaped aggressively towards Sungchul.

WHAM!

The Blood Pudding exploded with a single punch.

"Any other fuckers want to try?"

Sungchul spoke coldly towards the slimy, crimson silhouettes deeper in the forest. Several hundred Blood Puddings resided within the forest, and the naked woman's carcass had lured some of them into this pit. Sungchul was keeping them away from the pit. Two more tried jumping out at him.

WHAM! WHAM!

The results were no different. Next, dozens of slimes attacked simultaneously but their crimson ooze splattered everywhere following sounds of heavy impact. This was a genocide; the Blood Puddings of the forest were at risk of extinction.

The Blood Puddings which surrounded him broke the encirclement and ran away from Sungchul. It was for a simple reason; Sungchul had managed to teach a creature lacking sentience to fear him, that he was the bane of their existence. He covered the corpse in the pit with dirt by using his feet and noted the direction the Blood Puddings were heading in.

"Hm? What is this?"

The Preselected only discovered the Blood Puddings after the unwelcome guests had left. A few men who had grown bored after having their meals began approaching the Blood Puddings.

D...danger...run...

As they approached the Blood Pudding, the Observer's Eye began transmitting the Mage's warnings. However, it was too late. The stationary Blood Puddings suddenly jumped into the air and swallowed one of the men.

"Uwek! H-help!"

The man's clothing slowly started being digested by the Blood Pudding's digestive fluid.

"Hey! Let me go!"

The man next to him tried attacking the Blood Pudding with his blade, but it was to no avail. A slime's constitution made them impervious to physical attacks, which made them very difficult for newcomers to handle. While the men continued to make their futile resistance with the swords, the slime finally enveloped the victim's face.

"Ummph!"

The man's face being dissolved as he drowned in the digestive fluid was clearly visible from outside the slime's transparent body.

"UWAAAA!"

The other one abandoned his sword and fled the scene.

"What happened?"

The rest of the group finally realized that something had occurred, and quickly rose from their meal. However, by now, the forest was crawling with crimson slimes. The Preselected finally experienced fear in their hearts. Only Ahram still didn't fully understand the situation.

"What? What happened?"

They abandoned Ahram with his ignorant question and scattered into the forest exit. Ahram figured something was up and started to stand up. His eyes caught sight of a man sitting with his back turned towards him. The man was wearing ragged jeans with military fatigues.

Ah, that smelly loner bitch.

"Hey, Mister. What happ-?"

His vision suddenly turned yellow. When he awoke, he was surrounded by overgrown grass and could feel the dirt on the ground.

W-what?

He couldn't remember what had happened. However, he did feel a sharp pain coming from his ankles.

"AAAAUGH! Shit! What the fuck!"

Something had broken his ankle. He had barely managed to lift himself when countless Blood Puddings came rushing in his direction.

"Ah...AH!!!"

The Blood Pudding's slick body crawled up on Ahram's sneakers.

PSSSHH

Ahram began foaming at the mouth and lost his consciousness at the sight of his sneakers being dissolved from the acid.

At that moment, a Magic formation appeared.

"Ice Bolt."

From the seal, a lightly dressed woman appeared and swung her staff. Her hair was red, but her eyes were dead cold.

"Damn it. Stuck with such an annoying bastard..."

The young woman spat on to Ahram's face and continued swinging her staff. The destructive blizzard of frost annihilated the nearby Blood Puddings.

"Haaa...What do I do with this son of a bitch? It's not like I can kill him."

The woman in question looked at Ahram with an annoyed expression and disappeared after shoving a healing potion down his throat. It was the epitome of a hit-and-run. But despite her best efforts, there was one person who had still witnessed everything from start to finish.

"..."

His name was none other than Sungchul Kim.

Dolorence Winterer. She must be at least a mid-grade Mage.

The number of well-trained Mages was low. In turn, they also received better treatment. Mid-grade Mages would even be able to manage a whole division of a small Guild. For this type of person to be stuck with this man meant Ahram must be of utmost importance to the backers. Sungchul digested the information, and then nonchalantly picked up Ahram before heading back to the group.

—

Two days later, Ahram disappeared into the forest without anyone's knowledge. The Drill Sergeant was there waiting for him.

"I have been waiting, Great Human!"

The Drill Sergeant led Ahram through the forest to a cliff using its usual tottering sort of steps. Below the cliff, there was a cave entrance. Ahram silently entered the forest, then popped out after an hour.

"Haa, haa…Shit…it's still too hard."

"Kekeke! Great human! There is no need to rush! There will definitely be progress if you challenge it again tomorrow!"

Sungchul carefully stepped out towards the cave after the pair had left.

"..."

He stepped in without a second thought. A series of brightly lit letters appeared before him.

[Vestiare of the Seven Heroes' Memorial]

[You have entered Vestiare's Dream World]

[Which dream of the Seven Heroes do you wish to view?]

[The difficulty varies with each dream.]

There were six different dreams listed ascending in difficulty.

[A Summer Day's Dream]

[False Dream of Spring]

[Dream of Troubled Sleep]
[Lucid Dreams]
[Memories of the Divine War]
[Eternal Nightmare]
"One of the Seven Heroes, Vestiare."

Seven Heroes, they were the legendary figures once known for having saved the Other World. However, their names had been listed second among the five Calamities. Sungchul's lips curled into a frosty smile. He chose one of the six dreams.

[You have dared to select Vestiare of the Seven Heroes' Eternal Nightmare]

[Be prepared to face death within the eternal darkness!]

*****

In an unfathomably distant past, there was a time when an unbelievable number of humans were summoned en masse into Other World. The irresponsible gods left the fate of Other World in the hands of the insignificant humans. The humans were unaccustomed to the world and were quite primitive, but they had been able to overcome Other World's tribulations after many sacrifices. The Seven Heroes were at the center of this.

The Seven Heroes, as they had been called by the people, suddenly disappeared one day, leaving behind a legend stating that they would return when they were once again needed. This legend was fulfilled in the most ironic form possible.

[…The seven forgotten beings, who disappeared after trampling over the Devil's demonic forces, will one day return to fulfill their promise. And with them, blood, death, war, and pestilence will come.]

The forgotten saviors of the past were now rewritten as a Calamity, becoming one of the symbols of extinction within the minds of the people. However, no one could answer as to what kind of individuals these Seven Heroes actually were. It was one of the

41

most heavily guarded secrets in this world, known only by the highest levels of authority. Sungchul was also counted amongst them.

Vestiare. She was definitely one of the Mage heroes. A High Elf. She created a class of Magic called Echo.

His blood had started boiling as soon he had heard the name Vestiare. Vestiare had reached the peak of all Mages. She must have created this cave in order to pass on her techniques and skills to a worthy student.

It must have been from before they fell. Back when they still cared about humanity...

Faith in humanity. The thought brought a bitter taste to his mouth, but it was almost over. He had already witnessed so much betrayal, change of heart, and corruption. He had seen enough evil to fill even the Devils with disgust. If it hadn't been for his promise, he would have given up a long time ago. It was the first and only promise he had made, back when he had still been an ordinary person. He might have even decided to give up all his strength and return to his world otherwise.

"Whew..."

A sigh welling up from deep inside his chest spilled out. Sungchul's eyes sharpened like the stars of the clear midnight sky, and he shook off the foggy memories of the past.

Another set of bright letters appeared before him.

[Be ready. The Eternal Nightmare is about to begin.]

His surroundings turned a bloody crimson, and the metallic stench of blood tickled his nose. Sungchul slowly moved forward. Within the blood mist, creatures that looked like a compressed brain came into view. They were cloaked in invisibility Magic, but couldn't trick Sungchul's eyes. They were Dream Demons, commonly known as succubi or incubi. These demonic creatures would use the suction cups beneath their brain-like bodies to drain their victim's life force while injecting sweet dreams into their minds. It was similar to how mosquitoes also used anesthetics to drain blood.

A suction cup attached itself to Sungchul, but he continued, moving forward without giving it another thought. The incubus began to induce sweet dreams through the suction cups directly into Sungchul's mind. Sungchul, however, did not react to it at all.

One by one, other Dream Demons began attaching themselves to him. The massive swarm of Dream Demons soon formed something similar to a grotesque helmet sitting on his head. These Dream Demons continued to inject the most euphoric dreams imaginable into his mind. The average person would never have wished to wake up from such sweet dreams, but Sungchul suddenly stopped moving.

"Let's see…is that all of them?"

He lightly brushed his hand across his head. Five Dream Demons were caught by their suction cups.

"…"

Sungchul swung them wildly over his head using their suction cups.

SLAM!

"Kyaaaak!"

"Kiiiiii!"

They struck the walls of the cave and disappeared in a bloody mess. Sungchul brushed across his head again and grabbed some more.

"Kiiii!"

The Dream Demons began emitting threatening noises, but these were meaningless acts of defiance. Sungchul gave them a full swing and a few more disappeared in a similar mess. The Dream Demons began detaching themselves from his head, finally feeling a sense of terror. Some of the Dream Demons doubled down with even more euphoric visions while others even tried injecting paralyzing nightmares. However, all forms of resistance were meaningless.

SQUEAK!

Another batch of Dream Demons was pitifully killed after being mercilessly smashed into the wall. After several more repetitions, almost all of the Dream Demons had been eradicated. Sungchul grabbed the last remaining Dream Demon and brought it to his eyes. His emotionless eyes stared at the glowing eyes of the incubus.

"Watch carefully, you bastards. I am your worst nightmare."

Sungchul crushed the last Dream Demon in his hands.

"Kiiiii!!!!"

The Dream Demon screamed in agony as it became deformed while leaking brain fluid, before finally exploding.

DRIP. DRIP.

A mixture of blood and brain fluid was dripping from his hands. The reason he was able to overcome the Dream Demons was simple. Unshakable: a blessing that nullified all forms of mental attack. The creatures who had died by his hands did not realize this truth until the very end.

A ghostly doll lingered before Sungchul, who had handily cleaned up all of the Dream Demons. It emitted an unusual aura. He recognized it as a Mana Automaton.

A Mage.

The ghostly doll slowly approached Sungchul and revealed its form. Blond hair flowing like moonlight, sparkling eyes like fallen stars, long pointy ears. It was a High Elf woman.

"You have killed all of my demonic servants."

The familiar woman spoke as though in a dream. Sungchul could surmise her identity from her appearance and her manner of speaking.

"Are you Vestiare?"

The woman only faintly smiled. Sungchul then realized that he couldn't feel a presence from this woman.

This isn't Vestiare's physical body. It must just be some vestige of her memory.

He might have called it a "vestige," but it still contained a significant amount of Magic Power. Enough to make him feel admiration towards Vestiare.

"I don't think we can continue the trial anymore. Only those that can overcome thirty-three euphoric dreams and twenty-seven painful nightmares would be eligible for obtaining the rewards. And you just destroyed all of the tools."

"Didn't I win, then? I've 'overcome' all those things that would inject the dreams."

Vestiare's remnant laughed at Sungchul's words.

"You are interesting."

"I suppose you have some level of consciousness, despite being just a remnant. Seeing as you have some ability to form judgement."

"Ah, have you already noticed my identity?"

Sungchul feigned ignorance at Vestiare's question by raising his shoulders. In one of his open hands, an oversized hammer appeared. Fal Garaz, the divine armament forged by the shards of the sky itself by the Dwarven God. The weapon that filled the arrogant Devils of the Demon World with terror had revealed its form inside this cave.

"Would I get a reward for destroying you?"

Vestiare's remnant looked shocked at first but then smiled approvingly at Sungchul's blunt question.

"If you can."

As soon as the words left her lips, Sungchul instantly tore across the floor towards Vestiare's remnant. The remnant once again looked shocked, but still managed to cast a Magical trap and blink away.

BLAAAAM!

Sungchul's body, snared by the Magical trap, was enveloped in blue flames and had his movement dulled. Vestiare's remnant concentrated on continuously blinking away to maintain some distance away from him. A massive blue flame began to roar above her head as it took the shape of a spear. When Sungchul tried to leap forward once again, several traps all triggered at once.

BOOOM!

The blue flame exploded. Sungchul had tripped the triggers. The effect was the same, but the cause was different. He was intentionally triggering the traps with the tip of his toe as he ran by them.

BOOOM!

Dozens of traps began chaotically triggering at the same time. Vestiare's remnant flew into the air with the explosions concealing her target. A large shadow loomed across her face due to the geysers of blue flames and the flaming spear that she had conjured.

WHAM!

One-hit K.O.

Vestiare's remnant was splayed upon the floor, and the flaming spear she had conjured above her head unraveled.

"...Stop exaggerating. I didn't hurt you that badly."

Sungchul stood before her without a scratch. The remnant's lashes trembled slightly.

"You are strong. Very strong."

Sungchul simply glared at the remnant coldly and asked,

"Where are the Seven Heroes?"

An update on the Seven Heroes. This was the sole reason he had kept the remnant alive. Vestiare's remnant briefly closed its eyes and spoke with a soft voice that was filled with respect.

"We will appear before you when the time is right, when the Prophecy of the End draws closer, even without anyone seeking us out."

"I see."

Fal Garaz rose into the sky. Its shadow drew onto the remnant's face, but the remnant laughed instead.

"You are the same as us."

"I am?"

Sungchul's hammer shook slightly.

"I could feel it through the Dream Demons. You have the same...no, maybe a lot more disappointment and rage against humanity contained inside of you."

"I won't become like you, Seven Heroes."

"Will that be so? If the misplaced promise that sustains you ever goes awry..."

"Shut up."

The hammer abruptly fell. Vestiare's remnant shattered like glass and scattered across the floor. The blood fog weakened and the blood drained from the surroundings, which eventually returned to its original colors. Sungchul quietly waited in silence for his well-deserved reward.

[You have destroyed Vestiare's Dream.]

[You have completed the Objective "Destroyer of Dreams (Hidden – Epic)"]

Reward:

30x Palace Token

+10 Magic Power / Intuition / Magic Resistance

The Magical Staff "Moonlight" (Rare)

"..."

Disappointment passed across his eyes. The rewards were pitifully lacking. An "Objective" was rated higher than quests. They were interchangeable with quests, but they were one-offs, and unique to each Objective. They were also much more difficult compared to quests, but usually, the rewards were also comparably great. This time, however, proved to be the exception.

Did they compensate for the fact that this was inside the Summoning Palace? I suppose Vestiare's remnant could only be compared to a mid-grade Mage. This staff also would be invaluable to a newbie.

The rewards also held a unique value to Sungchul. He was able to obtain 10 Intuition, which was beyond precious to him. Sungchul quickly opened his status window.

```
[Stats]
Strength  999+   Dexterity     853
Vitality   801   Magic Power    13
Intuition    1   Magic Resist  621
Resilience 501   Charisma       18
            Luck   18
```

Intuition had finally escaped the negative values. This meant that he would be able to accomplish his Mage Class by simply completing the common quests obtained from the Homunculus. He also had more than enough Palace Tokens needed for the class change.

Should I slowly put an end to this act...?

He had accomplished his goal. He just had to take it easy for the rest of the trials in the Palace. He had started to turn back with these carefree thoughts when more words appeared.

[The Seven Heroes acknowledge your existence.]

[The Seven Heroes has placed you in their sights.]

"I didn't really need this..."

Sungchul felt annoyed, but words kept appearing.

[Vestiare of the Seven Heroes is overjoyed by your completion of her Objective.]

[Vestiare of the Seven Heroes grants you an additional reward for overcoming the mission.]

Reward: Tome of the Echo Mage

"Echo Mage...?!"

Sungchul recognized the class. Echo Mage. This was Vestiare's unique class. Regular mages could only cast Magic once with each cast, but an Echo Mage could fire the same spell multiple times with just one cast. This ability had allowed Vestiare to raise the firepower of a simple fireball to that of Hellfire Flames. This legendary ability was now within his grasp.

"…"

Sungchul silently touched the Tome of the Echo Mage, and its information revealed itself.

[Tome of the Echo Mage]

Grade: Legendary

Type: Class Transfer (Compact Form)

Effect: Legendary Class Echo Mage Acquisition

Note: On the final day of the Summoning Palace, open the tome. Vestiare's vision will reveal itself to you.

Restriction: 20 Magic Power / 20 Intuition / 20 Magic Resist

Required: x50 Palace Token

"Shit."

It was still too early for him to take it easy.

Chapter 4 – Krill Regall

"Shit! Shit...!"

Krill Regall was being faced with the greatest disaster of his life. He had skirted life and death several times after he was first summoned into Other World, but that was nothing compared to his current predicament.

"The week is ending soon; all the Mages will be made to report on the physical conditions of their Charges before the next sunrise."

The muscular Grand Knight from the Order of the Iron Blood Knights made this announcement in a gravelly voice. The Order of the Iron Blood Knights were one of the three greatest factions from the northern region of the main continent. They were known for their immovable strength, as well as holding their own against the mightiest of the Demon tribes' main forces.

It had just been a year since he had been summoned. Krill couldn't afford to offend such a powerful faction. He had lost contact with the newly summoned Preselected whom the Iron Blood Knights had put him in charge of. Death was a common occurrence within the Summoning Palace, and a failure of this magnitude would almost guarantee his execution. Just how had this happened?

Krill anxiously began to recall the day he had lost contact with his Preselected. Hyunsuk Jang had asked for his name; it wasn't an unusual event when the Preselected asked for their Guide's name. Krill didn't think much of it and had replied properly; there hadn't been any risk in doing so.

Being Preselected within the Summoning Palace meant they would have a faster growth and also have access to valuable secrets of the large factions. Investment of goodwill with an upcoming big shot was well worth it. The problem was that his charge had asked for his name twice.

Because the communication via telepathy through the Observer's Eye was unstable he could not be certain, but he suspected that something big must have happened between the first and second time his name was asked.

The image through the Observer's Eye got cut off. Did it get hit?

The Observer's Eye was an extremely convenient tool, but its combat capabilities were pitifully lacking. It wouldn't survive an assault against even the average stray cat. This was why they were veiled by an invisibility spell, though it wasn't uncommon for a stray rock or bird to bump into them and put them out of commission. Krill placed all of his hopes on this being the case. He had to hope that the Eye was just down and that Hyunsuk was still alive within the group. The simplest way to confirm this was with another Mage. They could ask their own Preselected Charges and easily verify his suspicions.

However, these grounds weren't so amiable. There were forty-eight Mages residing within the Northern Observatory of the Blanche Plaza, and only twenty-five of among them were in charge of the Preselected; Not a single one of them was on good terms with Krill.

It was because taking care of the Preselected was among the best possible jobs to hold as a low ranking Mage. Competition for the position was why no one was willing to help one another. Instead of helping, they would more likely search for any mistakes to report to the supervisors to eliminate a competitor.

It might have been a bleak hope, but there was one person that might be willing to help him.

"What? You want to borrow my Observer's Eye?"

Dolorence Winterer. She was the Observatory's only mid-grade Mage. She was a senior from the same Magic School and a member of the same faction. Normally, he would never dare talk to her, but now she was his only hope.

"Yes…I'm begging you!"

Krill poured out all of his sincerity and bowed at the waist. Both his eyes were clenched shut in desperation as he waited for her reply. But all he could hear was a snicker. Not good. It was enough to completely shatter all hopes he had of salvaging the situation.

"You expect me to treat someone that can't even keep track of his own Observer's Eye like my underclassmen? No, I refuse. Get out of my sight, you disgust me."

"I-I'm sorry!"

"I won't report you to the higher ups. You won't last another day before they find out anyway."

After looking at him with disgust clear in her eyes, Dolorence left the Observatory with proud strides. He could hear chilling words from down the hall.

"Fucking idiot."

"..."

His body trembled, and cold sweat trickled down in beads. Humiliation and anger suppressed all the air in his lungs.

"...Shit! Damn bitch!"

He wanted to tear her apart, but he lacked the strength; he didn't even have the power to fix his own pitiful fate. He couldn't do anything but fall to the floor and cry silently. He cried there until a middle-aged Mage found him.

"Hm?"

Their eyes met. Krill didn't know his name, but he knew of the man's identity. A Slave Hunter. They were tasked with poaching any talented recruits among the newly Summoned batches. Krill couldn't be proud of his own position, but it was still several times better than a Slave Hunter's. It was a heartless job, meant for heartless people. Now, a Slave Hunter was looking at Krill with great interest.

"Why is such a young man crying so pitifully? Did you miss out on some meals?"

Krill would never associate with such a character. The man might be older, but these fallen Mages had already had their names removed from the Mage Guild's ledger. There was no reason to treat them as fellow Mages.

However, things were different at the moment.

"Did you lose your pet rabbit?"

The middle-aged Mage smiled widely and took a step towards Krill.

"I do not wish to talk to you, sir."

The middle-aged Mage feigned surprise but kept smiling mockingly.

"Looking at you, you've definitely lost your pet rabbit."

"..."

Krill didn't bother hiding his irritation and stood up to walk away. The man's final words clung onto Krill's back.

"Such a shame. I might not be completely out of ideas on how to help…"

It was enough bait to successfully hook Krill. He reluctantly turned around and approached the man. His eyes were still bloodshot from his crying.

"You remind me a lot of myself."

The man stretched out his left arm as he spoke. His arm began revealing itself from the long sleeve of the robe. Amputee. His left arm had been completely removed down from the elbow.

"Thankfully, Typhoon is a generous guild; they were satisfied with taking just one arm. If it was anyone else, they might have decided to take my tongue or neck instead."

He spoke lightly, but his tone was vindictive. Krill shook slightly.

"So…you too…?"

"Yep. I was also a candidate sitter. No luck though. Who knew he'd get stabbed by an ally before the Rank Match?"

The Slave Hunter's confession adequately softened Krill's guarded heart. As his natural guard fell, Krill voluntarily clung to the Slave Hunter, as he really didn't have anywhere else to turn to.

"Before...I apologize, but...please help me. I-I'm running out of time!"

The Slave Hunter closed his eyes, as if sympathizing with Krill, then handed him a single key.

"You know about the tunnel for the slaves on the lower floor, right? There will be things that are unsettling, just shut your eyes and keep on going. It'll lead you to the Summoning Plaza."

"...You mean go out personally?"

"That'll be the most reliable way. No one's letting you borrow one anyways, right? An Observer's Eye."

The middle-aged mage's words were simply this: there were no other options. Krill held onto the key while deep in thought but eventually hurried away after a quick nod.

It can't be helped. Since it has come to this point, I might as well check on Hyunsuk's condition personally.

Everything would return to normal if Hyunsuk was alive. It would take a considerable sum to summon another Observer's Eye that was enchanted with invisibility, but what did money matter at this point?

Krill made his way to the slave entrance at an impatient pace.

"Ugh..."

It was an awful stench. The combined odor of human feces, rotting flesh, and sewage was enough to make one dizzy. He could see the slaves chained to the sides of the tunnel, and the brutal Slave Hunters who were breaking the slaves' wills through the use of a special incense. All of this was accompanied by pitiful screams echoing throughout the length of the tunnel. He could hear the sizzling sound of burning flesh.

"Kukuku! Look at the bastard's strugglin'. He'll be a good product."

The sharp eyes glowing from the burning embers turned to focus on the uninvited guest.

"Kukuku...A little chick Mage came here for some playtime? You can already see the slaves here, so take a pick."

"..."

Krill gritted his teeth and picked up his pace. It chilled his heart upon hearing another pitiful scream intermingled with the sound of burning flesh.

Fucking trash.

He saw a pile of corpses further down and a pair of red eyes that flashed within the pile.

"Kekek...Human! Do you have any candy?"

"If you have any candy, hand it over immediately!"

It was a group of Homunculi. However, these Homunculi were much more disfigured than the average ones. They all wore ripped clothes and a broken expression; some were even lacking a limb or two. These were the outcasts.

"Human! Why are you ignoring us?!"

A Homunculus missing an eye and a leg grabbed onto Krill's pants after crawling over to him with its arms.

"Give us your candy!"

Krill's face crumpled. He simply crushed the Homunculus' head with his heel.

"Tchyaaaaa!"

He was classified as a Mage trainee, but he was still someone that had survived all of the Summoning Palace's trials. Someone like a Homunculus was no match for him anymore.

"Shoo! Filthy things!"

The Homunculi scattered like roaches into the corpses.

Krill finally managed to find the rusty gate after crossing through the tunnel of corpses. He stared at the key in his hand and gritted his teeth as he looked at the gate.

I'll definitely find you. For sure.

—

The cave no longer emitted any Magic after the trials ended. Sungchul stored Fal Garaz and the Tome of the Echo Mage into his Soul Storage and looked over his other rewards. 30 Palace Tokens and the Magic staff "Moonlight." Palace Tokens could be hidden inside his pocket, but the staff was much more conspicuous. He continued to stare at "Moonlight" until its stats displayed themselves.

[Moonlight]
Grade: Rare – Low Grade
Type: Magic Staff (Rechargeable)
Effect: Fires an energy bolt after activation
Charge: 100%
Note: A staff crafted from the bark of a cypress tree bathed in moonlight. It is packed with Magic Power, but the staff itself is quite fragile! Use with caution!

Its capabilities weren't anything worthwhile, and physically it was just a wooden stick. He would normally have tossed it without a second thought, but it was significant to earn items before the first Rank Match.

What should I do? Should I keep it or just store it?

He contemplated for quite a while but decided to just hold onto it for now. Moonlight was a rather high caliber weapon for this stage of the trials, and it would also allow an alternate method for him to progress without having to rely solely on his actual strength. It was not like anyone would question him, but it also wouldn't be too hard to make up a lie about how he had gotten this weapon.

Sungchul grabbed Moonlight and walked away from the cave.

Anyhow, I need nineteen more Intuition. I should just barely be able to obtain enough Palace Tokens as well. Palace Tokens have to be earned by standing out...but that's not something I want to do.

He had wanted to leave the group of the Preselected when he had earned the ten Intuition. Now, if he wanted to become an Echo Mage, he would need to meet the additional requirements by tracking down some more Hidden Quests.

Can't be helped. I'll just have to fit in for a little bit longer.

Ahram's life was extended without his knowing.

As Sungchul stepped back inside, a loud noise, followed by shrieks, reverberated within the plaza.

*　*　*

The Homunculi were at the center of the chaos.

"Now now! This is a special ration provided for the Rank Match tomorrow! Humans! Eat plenty and bring out your strength!"

The Homunculi were distributing hard bread with mystery meat inside, from a large cart pulled by eight goats. The starving people flew into a frenzy at the first sight of food after several days. 1500 people swarmed the cart like bees and began fighting for any reason whatsoever. In the worst cases, they fought with their weapons and even killed each other for the food.

Sungchul ignored the chaos and focused on what the Homunculus had said.

Rank Matches are tomorrow? Did it get pulled forward?

Rank Matches were the most important events in the Summoning Palace. There were four plazas: Blanche, Azure, Crimson, and Scarlet. Within the Summoning Palace, they would hold a death match with special conditions between the plazas. These matches were the Rank Matches.

In Sungchul's time, these Rank Matches would kill off at least a hundred people each time. Sometimes, it would cut down a group by half its number. These Rank Matches also provided plentiful rewards for the survivors. The Summoning Palace's original objective was to prepare the Summoned to integrate with Other World by subjecting them to hellish conditions.

It felt like that objective had changed now. The privileged few, the "Preselected," were an indisputable proof of this.

"Now, watch that. Isn't it fucking funny? They are crawling like dogs just to eat some rotten bread."

"What else are they going to do? They haven't eaten anything else."

While the average Summoned were fighting for food with their lives, the Preselected were busy mocking them while sitting underneath the shade of the training center. Some silently continued training, but others were embracing their first form of entertainment in a while. Sungchul quietly claimed a corner of the center and fell deep into meditation. One of the common quests required him to meditate at a set time for two Intuition.

When the meditation ended, he circled the plaza looking for inscriptions that were hidden along the walls to read aloud. It wasn't well known, but the Summoning Palace's inscriptions changed daily. Even the former "Death shall set you free," was now, "Life might be painful, but there might also be value."

He had continuously worked on common quests so he could gain Intuition, but now, he also needed Magic power. The targeted Hidden Class, Echo Mage, required Intuition and Magic power of 20 to unlock it.

Sungchul scoured through the list obtained from the Homunculus and memorized each relevant quest. Especially the long-term quests, or the repetitive quests which needed to be completed first. Sungchul efficiently utilized each moment of his day so he could continuously progress through these quests.

He didn't slack off on observing the others in his group, especially Ahram. It was thanks to him that Sungchul was able to come across Vestiare's cave, and a similar opportunity might arise again.

Since Vestiare's Memorial had been completed, Ahram's guiding Mage ought to be busy preparing a new growth opportunity for him. They couldn't guarantee his survival in the trials otherwise. No matter how superior the people in this group were, this place was like the jungle; there would be plenty of geniuses among the crowd who were lying in wait. Careless people were constantly losing their lives around these parts. Sungchul got up as he noticed the sunset.

"Let's slowly begin our meals."

Yuhoon, who had been sweating by the spinning blade dummy, finally called the group together. The few who had grown tired of the endless fights followed along without a fuss. Sungchul woke from his meditation and followed after them.

As he was brushing off the dirt, a man approached him.

"Um...Mister."

It was the man who resembled a catfish, the one who had shown animosity towards Yuhoon on the first day. He was ostracized by the group along with Sungchul. He didn't outright refuse socializing with them as Sungchul did, but his outward appearance and brash attitude had caused the others to avoid him. He felt a strong sense of rivalry with Yuhoon but had low ability and talent. So Sungchul saw him as a man with an inferiority complex.

"If you wouldn't mind, would you like to eat together?"

He forced the words out with much difficulty. He had a tough exterior, but he was still human and must have started feeling lonely after a while. Sungchul returned a smile.

"Let's do that, then."

After the Blood Pudding incident, Yuhoon had moved his usual eating spot from the forest to underneath the walls. It was more likely to be discovered by the others, but it was less dangerous. As usual, Sungchul sat slightly apart from the group and chewed on his hard bread. The only difference now was that another person was sitting beside him.

Yungjong had been preparing for a government position in the old world. He'd lived a short life of twenty-five years, but with an empty smile, he spoke bitterly about how nothing had worked out as he'd planned.

"The competition was so fierce. It wasn't so easy to overcome half of the youth population in Korea, you know?"

"Is that so?"

It had been a while since he heard any recent stories from the old world. He only managed to obtain his current appearance through several facial reconstructions and surgeries, but the time that had passed in this world hadn't been short.

"That's so strange. I didn't think people would be so eager to become a Government worker."

"What crazy planet are you from?"

It had been more than twenty years since he had been summoned to Other World. That was enough time to carve a river into a mountain. He recalled the times he used his bus tokens to get a ride to the roller disco so he could skate along with the disco music.

I wonder if those who have returned are doing well.

Some of the Summoned had managed to amass great achievements which gave them the right to return to the home world. They were called the Returnees. A few among Sungchul's old companions had chosen to return back to the old world at the cost of the majority of their strength. Sungchul had also wished to return, but he had cleanly given up on the idea. It was enough for him to listen to stories through others.

Snapping away from his thoughts, he saw Ahram chewing on bread away from the group; it didn't seem to have any special meaning. As he was about to turn back his gaze, he noticed a being he had never seen before. A man was standing at a distance. He was dressed in a conspicuous outfit and was looking over in Sungchul's direction. Unlike the modern clothes of the other Summoned, he wore a Mage's robe of this world.

A Mage? It's interesting to see a human other than the Summoned in the Summoning Palace.

Sungchul's eyes sparkled with curiosity.

—

"Not here...Not here. Hyunsuk, that piece of shit..."

The Mage in the distance was none other than Krill Regall. He had taken the slave tunnel leading to the plaza and took quite some time to find the group of Preselected. He knew only one face from the group, but he couldn't find him. Hyunsuk, the Asian man with a detestable face.

Did he really die?

He felt terror crawl up his spine as he counted the people in the group. There were twenty-three of them sitting in the circle eating, two less than the amount chosen originally. It was possible that his Charge was still alive and well within the plaza, but it seemed more likely that he was already dead.

Shit. What happened? How did this happen?

He suddenly noticed one detail. Among the twenty-three Preselected, there was one person without an Observer's Eye. He had a slim build with average height. A man wearing military fatigues and old jeans. He confirmed again with his Glasses of Truth, but the man truly didn't have the Observer's Eye around him.

Could it be...? Did this guy do something?

Krill's eyes emitted a cold, murderous intent. He carefully walked towards the group. It was then that the man in military fatigues began heading towards the forest on his own.

A chance.

Krill felt a twinge of excitement at the tip of his tongue as he followed the man into the forest.

I don't know what your plans are, but I'm planning on making you sing.

He had a squeamish personality and didn't enjoy doing anything violent, but there was no time for him to be picky. He had to get through this disaster at any cost. He kept reassuring himself with these words as he pulled out a Magic staff and followed after the man.

"Looking for me?"

An unexpected voice came from an unexpected direction.

What is this guy?

He was grabbed from behind. However, this was only a newly Summoned. He should be able to handle him even without using any of his Magic, solely through the physical strength he obtained from completing quests during his time in the Summoning Palace. He tried to counter the assault while keeping this in mind.

WHAM!

His vision turned yellow in one blow.

"Ugh!"

When he came to, the man was pressing on Krill's chest firmly with his foot. Krill tried to move, but it felt like he was nailed to the ground. He finally realized the man in the military fatigues was no normal person.

"Hey, Mage. Why are you looking for me?"

The man, Sungchul, asked coldly.

"T-that is…"

"Are you looking for your Charge?"

Krill was ambushed verbally, and his weak spot was immediately exposed.

"How is that kid?"

Krill asked desperately. It was all but an impossible dream, but he still hoped against hope. Sungchul's reply, however, couldn't be blunter.

"He died."

"Uuu…"

Krill's shoulders finally lost all strength. The word "despair" flooded his mind. All hope crumbled away, and the image of the Slave Hunter who had helped him appeared in his head. What he had thought was crude and disgusting at first was now a vision of his future. It was at this moment that another glimmer of hope appeared.

"Looking for a hole to hide?"

It was Sungchul. He removed his foot from Krill's chest and spoke quietly.

"Help me, and I'll give you a way out of this."

CLACK…

Something shiny fell near Krill's face. It was a blue emerald.

***

Money makes anything possible.

This was true for both the old world and this one. Two of the Preselected belonging to the Order of the Iron Blood Knights were dead, but only one death had been reported. The other Mage who had lost his Preselected was dragged off by the Iron Blood Knights and never seen again. In Krill's short lifetime, there had never been a moment that had caused him to shudder more. He was now standing at attention in the office and in front of a high-ranked and armored Iron Blood Knight.

"You are wise, my friend. You said you were Krill Regall?"

The high-ranking Iron Blood Knight brought up the thick emerald to his eyes and carefully examined it through one eye. He had had many accomplishments, as the scars on his face gave witness. This man was the Captain of the 3rd Assault Regiment, Sanggil Ma. In this Mass Summoning, he was the one in charge of nurturing the Preselected.

"I wouldn't have let you off easily if you tried to bribe me with pocket change. You might have even suffered a worse fate than the other idiot who got dragged away earlier. In a place called Korea, insolence is a grave crime," said Sanggil with a bone-chilling smile.

"I…I wouldn't dare…!"

"I know that. That's why I've called you over."

The Captain placed the emerald deep into his pocket and said in a low tone.

"For now, return to the Observation Tower."

"What? You said…return?"

His Preselected was dead. What was there to be done even if Krill returned to the Tower?

Sanggil trimmed his fingernails with a nail clipper as he spoke in an annoyed voice.

"I thought you had a good head on your shoulders, but maybe I was wrong."

"..."

"Hyunsuk is alive."

When he heard this, Krill sensed a chill running all over his body.

It's exactly like that guy had said!

The man, who hadn't revealed his name, had told Krill with a cold voice,

"At the very least, they will leave you alive for the moment. But remember, they will never let you go, nor will they forgive you."

The current situation was flowing exactly as the unknown man had predicted. Sanggil sent Krill back to the Observation Tower to wait on standby. In the bird cage, there was a small Sky Squirrel with white, striped fur moving about busily. Krill tied a letter the size of a sesame seed to the leg of the Sky Squirrel then whispered as he opened the back window,

"Please deliver this to that person."

"Kyu kyu!"

The unusually intelligent Sky Squirrel nodded and then let its small body fly out through the open window.

-

"Kyu kyu!"

Sungchul Kim untied the paper on the squirrel's leg and confirmed the contents within.

[Tomorrow's Rank Matches will go by Alamo Rule. You will go up against zombies.]

[The reward cutoffs are at 1/3/10/30 zombies]

[The bonus monsters will be wearing red hats.]

"..."

Sungchul memorized the contents in his head and rubbed the paper between his fingers. The paper became dust and scattered in the wind.

"You did well."

He took out a piece of bread from his pocket and offered it to the Sky Squirrel.

"Kyuing?"

The Sky Squirrel nibbled on the bread, then stared at Sungchul with some interest before disappearing into the darkness.

He's intelligent, thought Sungchul as he recounted the information Krill Regall had provided him.

"Zombies will be coming out with Alamo Rule. That's not a bad start."

Rank Matches had many methods. There could be Death Matches amongst the Summoned of each plaza or fights arranged between elites representing each plaza or even a Pac-Man game where you had to avoid the monsters, and many other odd rules with names of unclear origins.

The Alamo Rule, which would begin soon, was one in which the Summoned would work together to defend against numerous demonic creatures. Although the demonic creatures were easy enough for newbies to overcome individually, there would be a great number of them. As the defenders, it would feel like they were fighting against endless waves of monsters.

However, this was also an opportunity. Even though these were weak monsters, as long as you could take care of them you would be rewarded. Krill Regall had mentioned cutoffs for the rewards, which changed at thresholds of 1, 3, 10, and 30 kills.

In other words, it meant the finest rewards could be had from hunting over 30 of them. Of course, top 3 were granted additional bonus reward, but Sungchul had no intention of being in the top 3. He would do just enough work to get maximum standard rewards. That was Sungchul's goal. And most importantly, he was interested in the bonus monster that would appear.

The zombies with the red hats, these bonus monsters, were slightly stronger than the normal ones, but defeating them yielded great rewards.

Sungchul wasn't certain about exactly what the rewards would be, but based on his past experience, it definitely included Palace

Tokens. This information was valuable to Sungchul, who was in dire need of 19 additional Palace Tokens.

On the dawn of the second day, Sungchul opened his eyes to a familiar demonic energy.

The Necromancers had arrived at the Summoning Palace and were chanting an incantation to raise the dead.

"Guuuuuuh"

In the morgue below the Summoning Palace, the dead were coming to life. These were the victims from the first day of the mass summoning. Thousands of these corpses followed the Necromancer's orders to move through the underground tunnels and stand just outside Blanche Plaza's entrance, which was connected to the palace. Most of the Summoned couldn't imagine such a scene, but the Preselected were told ahead of time of what was happening

"Kim Hyung[1]! Did you hear that voice?"

Yungjong acted rather friendly.

"You mean the part where Rank Matches will start today?"

"Yup. According to their Guides, they were told to fight at the front instead of heading towards the backlines."

"Is that so?"

"They said to get at least 30. God damn it…I'm a bit nervous."

Getting 30 kills was the minimum requirement to get the best rewards. Krill Regall's information seemed reliable. A little after sunrise, the Homunculi, including the Drill Sergeant, appeared at the Blanche Plaza.

"Now now, humans! Rise and shine! The most important event, the Rank Matches, starts now!"

The people who were hungry and thirsty all stared at the Homunculi with vacant eyes. The Drill Sergeant showed off its razor teeth as it smiled and started speaking in its particularly annoying voice.

"All of your friends who had come with you will be here soon! It's simple! Just play with your old friends for one hour! And remember! If you kill your friends, you can get water and rations. The rewards will grow the more you kill!"

After the Homunculi disappeared, a low trumpet sound was heard over the palace walls. The gargantuan walls that were always closed were now slowly being opened wide. Each member of the crowd had a blade in hand and was watching nervously to see what lay beyond. Outside the palace doors were humans; humans who were staggering and walking strangely. While the crowd was bustling, Sungchul read the message that appeared in front of his eyes.

[First round of the Rank Matches begins now.]

[Rule: Alamo]

[Featured Monster: Zombies]

[Raise your sword and fight. Cut down your enemies. Here, your value will be measured only in what you prove through your own actions.]

"A sword."

Sungchul smirked as he grasped the staff in his hand. Moonlight, one of Vestiare's gifts. Today, Sungchul had thought of using Moonlight instead of a sword for the audience at the Observation Tower.

The ruling class of Other World often gathered in the Observation Towers on Rank Match days and gambled great sums of money on which Plaza would win. Among those gathered in the Plazas, there were some who were able to wield a sword well in their own right, as well as those who are natural born fighters.

Using Moonlight would help him stand out, but the bastards up in the tower would lose interest quickly; what they wanted to see was not some wimp who relied on items, but diamonds in the rough who showed a genuine talent for fighting. The strong, hidden among the crowd, would awaken to their true nature on the battlefield today and would henceforth push themselves during the remaining trials to grow even stronger.

"Kim Hyung, let's try our best."

The Preselected were all on the frontlines, as if by a previous arrangement. Sungchul found Ahram among them. He was also on the frontlines, but he was not holding onto a sword; he held a staff instead. It looked a little different from Sungchul's, but it appeared to be a Mage staff charged with Magic power.

Did they have to babysit him with that staff because he refused to train properly?

Sungchul had destroyed Vestiare's fragment, so the Mage in charge of Ahram didn't really have much of a choice. Even though it was conspicuous, in order to raise Ahram's capability immediately, he had to be given an item that could be used instantly to boost his power. To Sungchul, this was good news. It meant that he did not need to be careful about holding back with Moonlight.

[Rank Match begins now.]

[Restrictions have been removed.]

[Warning! You could die!]

As the message disappeared, the zombies outside the palace door pushed forward into the Plaza with a singular purpose.

"Uwoooooh!"

Most of the Summoned stepped back in fear at the sight of the zombies pouring in.

"Uuuh…! Please let me live!"

"What the fuck is this bullshit…"

There were some who edged back from the fight.

"All right, everyone! Let's go!"

Some of the Summoned who had the will to fight got into a formation and faced off against the zombies. Sungchul noticed that the man who was leading them was the middle-aged office worker from the first day, who had recruited a party despite being told off numerous times. The man lacked strength, but fought on desperately and engaged in a hit-and-run battle tactic.

On the other hand, there were those who firmly held their ground and fought head on. It was uncertain if they were also one of the Preselected, but they had courage on par with a Preselected and good instincts for battle. They were the type that got the feel of it with each zombie kill and quickly grew stronger. These were probably the types that the ones at the Observation Tower watched with the most interest. Of course, the Preselected behind them were not just idling either.

"Now! Everyone, let's go!"

The Preselected, including Yuhoon, entered the fray as well.

SLASH!

Zombies were cut down easily. This was inevitable; the zombies' power was on par with the average Summoned's power on their first day in the world. In the past week, the Preselected had been bestowed blessings, given enchanted weapons, and undergone training; to them, the zombies were nothing more than smelly lumps of meat.

"Wo…Woah! I got one of these!"

Among the Preselected, Yungjong was rather cowardly, but even he was able to cut down a zombie easily. Some of the women stubbornly refused to go out and fight, but the Preselected were already doing their part. Meanwhile, Ahram Park was standing with the women in the rear until he decided it was time. From his staff, two spirit wolves emerged and leaped at the zombies, whipping up a bloody storm.

"Excellent! You're doing great!" said Ahram as his raucous laughter reverberated over the battlefield.

"…"

Sungchul waited until there was a lull in the battle before he began using his staff. He aimed his staff at the zombies and poured his strength into it. Energy bolts shot out of the end of the staff and pierced through the bodies of the zombies.

"Woah! Kim Hyung! What was that?"

Youngjong asked in surprise.

Sungchul Kim replied nonchalantly.

"This? I picked it up in the forest."

As he said this, Sungchul made a quick work of the zombies. Ten, Twenty, Twenty-nine. With one more left, Sungchul scanned the masses of zombies rushing in. Finally, he found the bastard he was searching for; the zombie wearing a red hat. Sungchul headed towards the bonus monster. However, two spirit wolves passed by him and rushed at the red hat zombie first.

He could hear a giddy laughter coming from behind him.

"Ahahahaha! That one's mine! Nobody shall touch it!"

It was Ahram. Anger erupted from Sungchul's eyes.

That son of a bitch is asking for a beating.

Sungchul held himself back in the hopes that the kid would still have some uses in the future. He grabbed the head of a zombie off the floor and threw it backwards. The zombie head flew like an arrow straight towards Ahram.

"Ack!"

Ahram cried out and crumpled to the floor. He had dropped his precious staff before he fell unconscious.

As soon as he let go of the staff, his connection to the spirit wolves was severed. Sungchul now had the opportunity to take the red hat zombie for himself. As he was aiming his staff, he noticed a woman who ran like a cheetah towards the red hat zombie.

On the outside, she looked like an ordinary Summoned. However, the vigor and skill with which she ran…the energy in her focused gaze was unusual; if he wasn't careful, he could lose the red hat to her.

"…"

Sungchul poured his herculean strength through his body, and in a flash, he was standing between the mysterious woman and the red hat zombie

STAB!

Sungchul's sword pierced through the heart of the zombie, and their gazes met. Her eyes were filled with astonishment, but her unwavering gaze was abnormal even by his battle-hardened standards. However, the message which popped up concealed her from his eyes.

[You have eliminated the bonus monster!]

Rewards:
1. Palace Token x 3
2. Light Shield of Vitality (Common)

Chapter 5– Alchemist

The first Rank Match drew to a close. There were countless zombies and human corpses strewn about on the floor. This had been relatively easy compared to some other trials, but there were still more than a few casualties. Their numbers had been cut down to below a thousand. Most of the injuries had come from the latter half of the fight when the zombies had managed to push past the forward group with their sheer numbers and lay waste to those hiding in the rear.

However, the overall strength of the Summoned had also grown. Those that had contributed in killing the zombies were granted bonus stats and rewards.

[The first Rank Match has ended.]

[Blanche Plaza has slaughtered 852 creatures.]

[4th Place of the 4 Colored Plazas.]

[Overall rewards will be based on Plaza ranking.]

[The Administration of the Summoning Palace will judge the rewards.]

An unexpected turn of events had occurred. No, it would be more accurate to say that he had a brief lapse of memory. Even twenty-five years ago, the rewards had been handed out based on a Plaza's overall merit. He reflected on the reason he could have forgotten such a crucial detail and came up with an answer.

Blanche Plaza was always number one. We didn't let go of that position even once. It was unimaginable to think that the other Plazas could beat ours. That must be why I had chosen this Plaza without a second thought.

Twenty-five years ago, many famous figures appeared from the Blanche Plaza: the ones with great charisma who had held the people together, the smart ones who had cleverly formulated how to

72

overcome each trial, and then the silent ones who resolutely held the front; Sungchul was of the third category.

He had always stood at the frontlines to protect the others and grew stronger unintentionally. Faded faces flashed through his mind. Some were still alive, while the others were dead. The survivors had become major players; each of whom by now had a great deal of influence in their own area.

"…"

His reverie was interrupted by a new message.

[The division of Rewards for each Plaza is complete.]
[Congratulations! You have completed the first Rank Match!]
[You have qualified for grade A reward.]

Basic Rewards:

2x Palace Token
1x Fresh Meat
5x Apple
1x Week Supply of Rations

Selection Rewards:

1. Divine Elixir of Escape
2. Explosion Scroll
3. Wind Master's Blade
[Please Choose]

The basic rewards were as bare as he'd expected. However, the selection rewards drew Sungchul's attention. They were quite balanced in value: Divine Elixirs of Escape and Explosion Scrolls were consumed upon use, but in turn were very powerful. The Elixir guaranteed someone's survival during Pac-Man rules, and Explosion Scrolls were powerful during Alamo rules or Death Match rules. The blade was also useful for people who had confidence in their own abilities. It raised their dexterity and added a critical strike effect. It would be a relevant weapon for a beginner until they graduated the Palace.

Twenty-five years ago, Sungchul had chosen the Windmaster's Blade. However, this time, Sungchul decided on the Explosion Scroll. The sword was useless to Sungchul, and the Explosion Scroll had more utility to it than the Divine Elixir of Escape. The Elixir was only effective against demonic creatures, but the Explosion Scroll could also be used on humans. It would be difficult, but the Explosion Scroll could be used to seriously wound the predators during Pac-Man rules.

Sungchul looked through the small package of rewards. Palace Tokens, food, and Explosion Scroll. He packed up his rewards and returned to the training center. As expected, the Preselected were fine, and some had even managed to get into the rankings.

"Taeksoo, that's awesome! You're third place. You got the highest score among us!"

The ranking results could be seen from numerous Stone of Records scattered around the palace. Sungchul looked at the record out of curiosity.

[1. Ahmuge – 142]
[2. Jungshik Chun – 100]
[3. Taeksoo Kim – 85]
...
[6. Yuhoon Lee – 64]
...
[21. Yungjong Ha – 44]
[22. Sungchul Kim – 35]
[23. Ahram Park – 29]
...

Sungchul allowed himself a grin. *Ahmuge and Jungshik Chun. I've never heard of them.*

Sungchul recalled the face of the woman he had seen during the battle. They had competed over the bonus monster, and she had been quite skilled. It might be that her name was amongst the two listed there.

Sungchul continued down the list until another name caught his eyes.

Ahram Park. Only 29.

The zombie he had thrown during combat had hit Ahram on the head, and although it was unintentional, Ahram had fallen unconscious and had his Spirit Wolf summoning staff stolen.

Sungchul could see Ahram's despondent face in the corner of the training center. He continued to skillfully operate the record stone.

[Would you like to see previous records?]

Sungchul visualized "Yes" in his mind, and the messages in front of him changed.

[Historical Ranking]

[1. William Quinton Marlboro – 301]

[2. Shamal Rajput – 275]

[3. Sungchul Kim – 256]

...

Looking at the records, he couldn't help but scratch his head.

William...Shamal...Such nostalgic names. Even my name is in the records. I wonder what happened? Isn't it much easier now to set higher records than before?

There weren't any privileged people in the past; everybody had to face the oncoming demonic creatures. He had expected much better scores to arise compared to the past, but reality didn't reflect his expectations. Either the Preselected had little motivation to try very hard when they were this spoiled by their backers, or perhaps the current generations of Summoned might just have fallen in quality.

Sungchul felt satisfied with what he saw as he returned to the training center. Several Preselected were admiring their rewards. However, there were dark faces among them. The Preselected who received no reward, despite having been given privileges and advantages, could do nothing but hang their head as their comrades celebrated.

"Kim Hyung! Come here!"

Yungjong shouted tactlessly from across the group and walked up to Sungchul. He held a transparent glass bottle containing a liquid in his right hand. It was the Divine Elixir of Escape.

"Kim Hyung has one too, right?"

Sungchul shook his head.

"No."

"What? Why?"

"What do you mean why?"

"I saw that Kim Hyung also killed over 30 of 'em. What did you pick? Did you ignore your Guide and pick something else?"

Sungchul simply nodded, and Yungjong jumped up in shock.

"Dang...you've got guts. Mine said you could die on the next Rank Match without one. That Pac-Man or something game."

"Don't worry about me."

After listening to Yungjong, Sungchul glanced at the others in the group and saw that they were likely told the same thing. Their Guides had probably urged them to get the item that guaranteed their survival in the Pac-Man round. This must be why those without the rewards looked so grim.

"Uuu...Shit..."

Even Ahram, who was usually full of energy, also sat in a corner and picked at his nails. He had even lost his staff which was his fail-safe.

There were others who were also marked for death among his group. Sungchul recognized one of them; it was the girl wearing all brand-name clothes who had been friendly with the man who was executed by the Homonculi on the first day.

Sunghae Bae.

She didn't manage to kill a single zombie. It wasn't because her strength was lacking; her weapon was better than the average Preselected. Her score was zero because she couldn't muster the courage to strike down her foes. It could have been out of disgust, or might have been out of fear. No matter the reason, the result was that she now had to worry about her immediate future.

Sungchul had felt her gaze on him for a while now. She kept peeking over at him every now and then. She couldn't approach him because Yungjong was making such a large ruckus next to him.

Previously, she had looked down on both of them. The reason was that ugly, unsociable, shy men were the perfect target for mockery. Things were different now; although her glamorous persona and her status as the daughter of a wealthy family in the old world had given her a golden ticket, none of it held any value due to the failing score she had earned in this match. Even the "friends" that had socialized with her during meals now completely ostracized her.

Shortly after, Sunghae finally approached Sungchul.

"Now now, humans! You might catch some nasty disease from the zombies and corpses lying around! Let's work to move them quick-quick!"

The Homunculi brought over a goat-driven cart in order to load the corpses. Sungchul joined in the clean-up and began tossing the bodies into the cart one at a time.

"Excuse me."

He could hear a hesitant, yet familiar voice from behind him. Sungchul turned around and faced Sunghae. He wasn't confrontational, but neither did he show any warmth. Sunghae felt tense receiving this sort of indifference.

I…why do I have to…beg to him…

However, this was a matter of life and death. Sunghae channeled all of her strength into forming something similar to a smile on her face as she said,

"Hello."

"What do you want?"

There wasn't even a second to waste on such a woman. Sungchul replied very curtly.

Sunghae already felt quite frustrated, and now she could only crawl even lower. She avoided Sungchul's chilling stare and spat out her rehearsed speech.

"Um…I am really sorry for the first day. It was all because I was so shocked and scared…I must not have been myself."

"And you are here because?"

Sungchul quickly cut her off. Sunghae had always felt that, in all her years of popularity, she knew better than most how animals called "males" worked. That is why she understood that this man did not care to entertain her for even one bit; this conversation had been impossible from the start. Sunghae could feel a cold sweat trickling down her back.

"If that's all, then."

Sungchul turned around and began walking towards another pile of corpses. She quickly blocked his path and spoke in a mocking tone.

"You're also a man, right? A young one at that. How about having someone like me?"

She had abandoned her pride and thrown herself at his feet. Sungchul continued looking at her with cold eyes and spoke plainly.

"What about you?"

"Stop pretending. I'll just say it straight, then: help me."

"What do you want?"

Sunghae looked over at the staff tied down to Sungchul's back. The energy-bolt-firing Magical staff, Moonlight. With this, she might be able to overcome her weak resolve and raise her score. This was why she had approached Sungchul.

"That staff. Let me use it, and I'll do anything you ask."

As she finished, she unbuttoned the top of her shirt. Her cleavage peeked out tantalizingly from beneath her black brassiere.

"You must be pent up after so long, right? I can do it right now if you want."

The people passing by looked at her with shock and disgust, but she had nowhere else to turn.

If I can just take his staff…It doesn't matter what anyone says.

However, Sungchul didn't show any response. He looked at Sunghae's cleavage with the same indifference as Warren Buffet would look at gold. Sunghae suddenly started feeling nervous.

This bastard…did he hang around that catfish guy because he's actually…?!

"Miss."

Sungchul finally spoke, and Sunghae buttoned her top back up.

"Yes?"

He spoke indifferently while pointing at his lower half.

"I commend your courage, but mine doesn't stand anymore."

He quickly turned and left. Sunghae's mind was spinning in chaos.

Rejected by a bastard like that…that smelly country hick bastard!

She was unaware that she hadn't washed in a while either and now smelled just as bad, if not worse. However, Sunghae was a resilient woman. She caught up to him again and blocked his path once more.

"Move."

Sungchul didn't have any compassion this time. Sunghae's confidence couldn't help but collapse under his cold eyes, coupled with their murderous intent that made her break out in goosebumps. Tears started pouring out of her eyes, and her voice tumbled out pitifully.

"Please…please, that staff…let me use it…please…"

Sunghae clung to him desperately.

"What are you going to give me?"

Sungchul turned around. It wasn't out of some half-baked sympathy, but to check if there was anything worthwhile he could get out of this woman.

"W-what do you want?"

When she asked, he spoke in a different tone pointing above his own head.

"Ask him. Ask what he can offer me."

Mages didn't want their Charges to die. It could be said that her guiding Mage might be just as desperate as Sunghae. Sungchul recalled Krill's desperate face and laughed to himself.

***

"Now, this is the place. Keep your promise."

All things considered, Sunghae was very quick to act. Within an hour since they had spoken she had already come up with something new to offer to trade and reattempted the negotiation. And what she offered was what Sungchul sought; a Hidden Quest. But once he learned more about it, he found it not all that attractive. Sunghae had brought a Class Change Quest, but the problem was that the class itself was not all that great. No, in fact it was considered the worst class.

The Alchemist Class.

A class that was universally looked down upon.

There was a good reason why the Alchemist class was avoided like the plague. Mages only needed to raise their stats high enough to meet the prerequisite to learn "Fireball" from the "Pyromancy" School of Magic, then spend some of their Mana to cast it. Alchemists also had access to something similar to "Fireball" called "Magic Grenade" from the Alchemy School of Magic.

Like the Mages, an Alchemist had to raise their stats to meet the prerequisites and learn the skill for crafting the item. But it didn't end there. They then had to spend time gathering materials, prepare ingredients with specialized tools, and then mix the components to synthesize the item, and even then, there was a chance of failure. Most people preferred the simpler power-to-investment ratio of Mage Classes and simply ignored the Alchemist Class. People even mocked Alchemists as masochists.

"By following deep into this dried-out well, I was told that you could get the 'Hidden Class': Alchemist."

She emphasized the word "Hidden Class," but Sungchul knew better. As someone that had been through hell and back, he knew that Alchemist was a trash class.

"I refuse your offer."

Sungchul didn't speak to Sunghae, but rather to the Mage backing her.

"For what reason?"

Sunghae asked impatiently.

"I don't like it. Something like Alchemy…I'm confident in my ability to break things, but I hate putting things together. Bring me some other Hidden Quest, especially something that raises Intuition, or I won't hand over the staff."

"…Wait. Just wait a bit."

Sunghae took a step back and turned around. She didn't speak for a while, so she must have been exchanging a blood curling conversation with the Mage in the Observation Tower. After a long while, Sunghae finally turned around, an awkward smile forming on her lips.

"You said you wanted a Quest that raises Intuition, right?"

Sungchul nodded in response.

"That's great, then. The Hidden Quest that I proposed could raise your Intuition by 15 when completed."

"15?"

It was an outrageous amount. The average stat gained from Hidden Quests, even from an Objective, was below 10. This wasn't even an Objective, and yet it raised a stat by 15? It was far outside of his expectations.

"That is hard to believe."

"It's the truth! Well…it is only when all the requirements are completely met, but…"

"Full completion?"

"Yes. My Guide says it normally grants only around 3-4, or 5 in rare cases. But if you fulfill all conditions and trials, it is possible to get up to 15."

"Is that true?"

Sungchul's eyes lit up brightly. Sunghae's eyes trembled in response, though it didn't seem like it was from the fear of getting caught, but rather from fear of him.

"Yes, you can trust me."

She bit her lips while nodding.

Sungchul handed her the Magic staff, Moonlight.

"If you're lying, there will be consequences."

"D-do whatever you want!"

Sunghae's voice shook as she escaped from the scene as quickly as she could.

Now, left on his own, Sungchul expressionlessly stared at the bottom of the dry well.

—

BOOM!

There was a ladder leading to the floor of the well, but Sungchul ignored it and simply leaped in. All the dust gathered on the floor made it difficult to see, but he was more interested in observing the faint Magical energy that was surrounding the area.

[Wonder of the Generation. Memorial of the Eighth Hero, Eckheart]

Eighth Hero...? Eckheart?

One of Sungchul's brows shot up. He had heard of the Seven Heroes, but this was his first time hearing of an eighth one. He had never heard of the name Eckheart.

[You have observed the Wonder of the Generation.]

[The Amazing Test of the True Hero, Eckheart.]

Sungchul rarely expressed his emotions; however, the series of messages mentioning this person left him baffled.

"...Who are you?"

Suddenly, the entire well shook slightly. It felt like someone was striking a distant wall. The well's wall opened after a while. This hadn't been done by Magic, but rather by some primitive device.

To make matters worse, the door struggled to open, as though the machinery had rusted.

Looking at this scene, Sungchul couldn't help but feel regret. This felt extremely cheap compared to Vestiare's Dream.

It might be better not to go through with this.

The Alchemist class was a problem in of itself. He couldn't waste a precious subclass slot on a trash class which would only hamper his future growth. He could erase a useless class later on at the Temple of Knowledge, but it was still a troublesome thing to have to do.

Sungchul sighed in regret and turned around. However, a sudden message stopped him in his tracks.

[Would you pass by the Wonder of a Lifetime like this?]

Sungchul didn't miss a beat as he continued to walk out, after which another message appeared before him.

An amazing test of the Eighth Hero (Seven Heroes is incorrect), Eckheart, the Wonder of the Generation
   * 1 Free Intuition JUST BY TRYING (15 Max!!!)
   * Investigate Ancient Artifacts
   * Obtain a Familiar after fulfilling special conditions
   * Opportunity to fulfill an Objective
   /// Try it now, all of this is FREE!

"…What…is this?"

He had completed several thousand Quests and Objectives, but this was the first test of its kind. He could feel the Quest maker's desperation. How few challengers must there have been for it to have reached this point?

Did they refer to this message when they told me about the 15 Intuition?

The Mage guiding Sunghae seemed to have arrived here at this point. There was no way to tell whether that person chose to become an Alchemist or not.

"Mm..."

This was quite troubling. Sungchul was extremely weak to exaggerated advertisements. Not that he fell for its seduction, but he allowed himself to be tricked on purpose. It couldn't be helped if it turned to out to be a bust, but there was still a great deal of satisfaction to be had when it turned out that the advertisement was telling the truth and gave great rewards. For someone like Sungchul who led a very difficult life, it was one of the few hobbies he had.

Sungchul tightened his grip and turned around once more. Rather than the 1 free Intuition per attempt, the familiar and the opportunity to fulfill an Objective tugged at his heartstrings. Whether this Hidden Quest contained an Objective or was filled with ordinary common Quests depended completely on the grade of the Quest-Host who had created this Hidden Quest.

"..."

Sungchul used both of his hands to grab the wall that was stuck part way open and tore it apart. A series of candles lit themselves as he walked deeper into the well. He walked for about a minute until he reached a dead end with a block protruding from the wall. There were two glass bottles upon an altar made of a pile of rocks: one was a red vial and the other a blue vial.

[First test of the Eighth Hero, Eckheart.]

[Grab the vials]

He followed the instructions. The blue vial was labeled Elixir of Frost, and the red vial was named Elixir of Fire. Once he had grabbed both of the vials in his hand, a completion message appeared.

[You have grasped the Wonder of the Generation, Eckheart's inheritance.]

[You have experienced the oppressive knowledge within Eckheart's inheritance]

Reward: Intuition +1

I haven't felt anything like that.

It was an annoyingly talkative Quest, but at least it hadn't been lying about the rewards. Sungchul quickly confirmed the Intuition had changed from 1 to 2 with his stat window. Another door suddenly shook awake, but as if there was a problem with its mechanism, it struggled to open once again. Sungchul forced his way through once more.

Beyond the door was a spherical area with a human-sized stone doll in the center. It appeared to be a golem. Sungchul couldn't help but doubt himself. He had never seen a stone golem so small. Golems were typically large; miniaturization of the internal components was difficult. Although their combat capabilities would be lacking, wooden marionettes were better suited for this size than stone golems.

Is that an actual golem?

He had only entered this dungeon half-heartedly, but he now felt a bit more excited. A series of messages popped up once more.

[The Magic Golem created using the Eighth Hero's superior technology will be difficult for your current self to deal with.]

[However, it is the duty of Alchemists to make the impossible a reality!]

[Use the two colored vials to block the Magic Golem's attack! This is the Eighth Hero, the Wonder of the Generation, Eckheart's End of the Tutorial Test!]

RUMBLE

The Magic Golem's eyes flashed as it began to move. Its movements were slow and exaggerated, but it was definitely a golem.

The Magic Golem turned itself in Sungchul's direction, but then stopped. Sungchul waited to see what it was doing when it started glowing bright red, heating up to an incredible temperature.

Sungchul grabbed one of the two bottles which read: Elixir of Frost.

I guess he wants me to use this one.

A chill, cold enough to freeze the air, poured out as he opened the bottle. Sungchul lobbed the Elixir of Frost at the Magic Golem.

PSSH

The overwhelming cold of the Elixir created white steam over the overheating golem. The steam flooded out, covering the room before slowly subsiding. The Magic Golem reverted to its original color. It then began to change once more.

This time, it began to emit a chilly blue aura. Sungchul tossed the final Elixir in the same way, thereby neutralizing the chill. An overwhelming amount of steam flooded the room then dissipated.

The Magic Golem stopped its operation, and its eyes lost their luster. A message appeared in the silence.

[You have perfectly neutralized the Magic Golem!]

[You have felt the Alchemist's Potential awaken deep inside of you!]

Reward:

+1 Intuition

Tome of the Alchemist

"..."

Easy. It was laughably easy. Even a dolphin or a chimpanzee might have been able to complete this Quest with ease. It was almost as if they were giving away the Alchemist Class for free.

I always wondered why some people chose Alchemist as their main class, but I guess this is the answer.

Ultimately, they were being scammed. They must have thought a "Hidden Class" would separate them from everyone else and so they must have used their main class slot on it.

What an interesting fellow.

Sungchul continued past the door that was behind the Magic Golem while having these thoughts. It led down a tunnel which was illuminated by an eerie red light and had bone-chilling ambient noises.

[The true test starts from this point onwards.]

[For those that wish to know the true path, continue forth with resolution.]

Sungchul broke into a faint smile. He stored the Tome of the Alchemist in his soul storage and pulled out Fal Garaz.

WHAM!

Fal Garaz's impact shattered the Magic Golem, and he then picked up one of the Golem's pieces. Curiosity sparked inside Sungchul; the heart-shaped mechanism in his grip contained countless gears click-clacking together as they emitted some form of pure light.

As to be expected, this isn't some low-grade creation like a marionette. This is a perfect internal mechanism from a golem. Peculiar to a degree I have never seen before.

He dropped the mechanism and stood up.

Self-proclaimed Eighth Hero, Eckheart. Sungchul couldn't guess who this guy was, but if Eckheart was capable of making a golem of this level? It had been a long time since he'd last smelled the rich scent of a jackpot. Like a thirsty man drawn to water, he headed down the corridor.

***

As he continued forth, an altar came into view. The altar was wrapped in steel and copper and had a crude appearance. Two Magic Golems were standing on either side of the altar. A message popped up as he approached.

[Open the Tome of the Alchemist over the altar.]

Sungchul's eyes turned towards the altar. A considerable amount of Mana could be felt coming from it. However, it felt different from a Mage's Mana. If a Mage's Mana could be compared to the constant rhythm of breathing, this Mana had a consistent presence with no fluctuations. Sungchul recalled the mechanical noise of a flat-lined heart monitor coming from an emergency room. A similar steady flow of Mana could be felt from the Golems.

This is a proper altar. It could almost sell me on this class all on its own.

Eckheart the person, was interesting, but Sungchul was not so interested in the Alchemist Class itself. He simply passed by the altar into the passage beyond. As soon as he entered, a message in red brought him to a stop.

[Only those with Alchemic abilities can challenge the trials which lay beyond.]

Several blades and hidden traps made intimidating noises as they activated from all sides. Looking at the message, Sungchul felt despondent. Only allowed to advance after becoming an Alchemist. What a childish trick.

Sungchul could pass through the traps with his own strength, but he felt like playing along for at least a little while longer, and so he retrieved the Tome of the Alchemist and opened it.

[Class Change Tome of the Alchemist]
Grade: Rare – Hidden
Type: Class Change (Compact Form)
Effect: Acquire Hidden Class Alchemist
Restriction: None
Requirement: 20x Palace Token

Everything else was fine, but the Palace Tokens made him hesitate. Sungchul had 36 Palace Tokens. He needed 14 more to become an Echo Mage. It wasn't like these Tokens were very easy to get, and there was the chance that he could be hit by some misfortune and miss his mark for becoming an Echo Mage if he were to spend 20 Tokens here. Taking this was like stuffing oneself on ramen before going to a high-class restaurant and then missing out on the main course due to being too full.

Mm…what to do…

He didn't hesitate for too long. Sungchul reached into his pocket for 20 Palace Tokens and placed them, along with the tome, onto the altar.

The reason he was confident in doing this was simple. He was humanity's greatest warrior. There were at least two more Rank Matches left, and he could earn more than enough Palace Tokens just by maintaining a good ranking. There was the risk, however, of being noticed by the spectators, but missing out on this curiosity would linger too much in the back of his mind.

What's there to life? Might as well bet it all.

A lengthy message then appeared.

[You have felt the breath of truth.]

[Congratulations! You have acquired the Hidden Class, Alchemist!]

Reward: Class – Alchemist acquired

A wind, interwoven with Magic, blew out from the altar and wrapped around Sungchul's body. The wind grew brighter and brighter and flowed even faster before finally disappearing into his body. He immediately opened his class window to take a look.

[Class]
Main Class – Primordial Warrior (Legendary)
Sub Class – High-Class Chef (Rare)
Sub Class – Alchemist (Rare)
*2 Additional Sub Class slots available

He had acquired the Alchemist Class. There were two Sub Class slots left; more than enough room for the Echo Mage Class. Personally, it bothered him that he had wasted two of his precious Sub Class slots for personal hobbies. But hadn't he done fine without worrying about his Sub Class slots so far? He reassured himself with these thoughts and continued past the altar, into the corridor. Unlike before, none of the traps were activated.

Past the hostile corridor sat a table and a stone cauldron. The hole under the cauldron lit up with bright, orange flames and heated itself, while different kinds of minerals, plants, and shells from unknown organisms could be seen on the table as he stepped closer. A purple Magic Golem appeared on the other side of the room, but it appeared to be tightly wrapped in something similar to a spider's web.

[The Fundamentals of Alchemy: Synthesis]

[Combine the prepared ingredients on the table and synthesize an item capable of freeing the Magic Golem.]

[Being unable to free the Magic Golem will result in disqualification.]

[Time limit is 10 minutes. There will be no second chances.]

As expected of a trial for Alchemists. Sungchul glanced over the ingredients on the table. There was some grass, a rock, a vial of water, some pieces of a shell, and other tedious bits of junk. He was at a loss regarding what he should do with the ingredients in front of him.

Sungchul continued to stare thoughtfully at the ingredients before holding up the grass, then took a whiff.

It smelled just like grass.

After he'd finished smelling it, an unexpected message appeared in front of him.

[Blindman's Grass]

Level: 1

Grade: E

Attribute: Wood

Effect: None

Note: It is a commonly seen grass, but due to its agreeable nature, it is generally used as a buffer during Alchemic experiments.

Here in Other World, appraisals were usually limited to weapons or potions that had some practical use. Grass, stone, or other natural objects could not be appraised at all, but more than that, only a few books, meant for herbalists and the like, contained any information regarding these.

Is this a basic skill for Alchemists?

Sungchul checked the fine details of the Alchemist Class window.

[Class: Alchemist]

Class Skill: Synthesis

Class Skill: Inspection

After reading about Inspection, Sungchul understood what had just occurred.

I must have gotten the message screen because of the Inspection skill.

According to its description, an Alchemist could determine the attributes of an ingredient after having a sniff. Sungchul continued to investigate the other materials in the same manner: Vaporizing Liquid, Riverside Stone, Glacial Crab's Shell Fragment, etc. They all had their own description and effects.

Sungchul obtained all the information and paused to ponder briefly before tossing the Vaporizing Liquid into the cauldron. The Vaporizing Liquid was the base, the foundation for the ingredients. The Riverside Stone with its polar attribute was pulverized by his fist and then tossed in afterwards. The Vaporizing Liquid emitted a white light as the stone powder began to react with it.

Next, he pulverized, then added, the crimson wings of a butterfly. They were called the Wings of the Infernal Butterfly. It contained a fire attribute that could be used to amplify a weaker ingredient. The Riverside Rock essence flared up as the crimson powder entered the cauldron and the liquid turned a bloody red. However, the Riverside Rock, added before the wings, had an earth attribute and began to emit a black smoke once it started mixing.

To neutralize this, Sungchul added the Blindman's Grass which acted as a buffer. Once added, the black smoke stopped, and the cauldron turned purple.

Sungchul began to stir the cauldron with the large spoon next to it. This was when the Alchemist's next skill, Synthesize, would start to be useful. Every time the cauldron was stirred, he could feel a small amount of Mana leaking out of him.

This must be why the Alchemist Class remains unpopular.

After several minutes of stirring, a bright light came pouring out of the cauldron.

[Synthesis Complete]

For the first time in a long while, Sungchul felt his heart race in excitement as he checked his work. The product was a sticky, colorless liquid. He collected the liquid into a provided container then inspected it.

[Low-Grade Acid]

Level: 1

Grade: F

Attribute: Fire

Type: Common Clutter

Effect: It melts sticky substances

This was exactly the result he was looking for. He was slightly bothered by having used only some of the twelve ingredients on the table, but he'd still managed to make something as he had intended. Sungchul took the low-grade acid and poured the liquid over the Magic Golem.

SSSSS

The spider web emitted white smoke before slowly beginning to melt. Sungchul watched his success with smug eyes as he waited for the web to melt away completely, but it didn't dissolve any further. He had used all of the acid but had only managed to melt some of the spider web. It seems he actually needed to use all of the ingredients provided to him. He stood still for a moment to consider his options when a message popped up before him.

[30 seconds before time limit ends.]

[Acid of Rank D or higher required to melt the spider web.]

[Before the road of truth, a peerless mind is required. Those without talent shall be turned away.]

There was no more time or ingredients to spare, but it was also a waste for him to turn back now.

"…"

Another message appeared as if to mock him.

[10 seconds before time limit ends.]

[Turn back, you who lacks talent!]

It was once said, a man will be more willing to make promises when he needs to use the bathroom, than after he's already relieved. Sungchul couldn't help but feel this was an apt saying to describe his current feelings. He stood over the Magic Golem, and looked over the spider web, before roughly spitting out a single phrase.

"Aaaah, fuck it!"

He pulled apart the spider web covering the Magic Golem with his bare hands.

RIP!

It was something that could never be pulled apart by an ordinary human being, but it was no different than any other type of spider silk before Sungchul's god-like strength. The Magic Golem's eyes lit up as the spider web covering it was harshly pulled apart.

"Thank you for freeing me. You have great talent as an Alchemist. I will lead you to the next test."

[You have torn the Spider Queen's silk, which even a legendary blade could not sever, using your knowledge of Alchemy.]

Reward: +2 Intuition

The end justifies the means; freeing the Magic Golem was the only requirement for the test. Creating the acid was only one of the

93

methods to passing the test. Of course, this probably wasn't the intention of the Quest-Host who had created this Quest because no matter how sharp or powerful the weapon, it would still take no less than ten minutes to unravel this web. The host could not have possibly foreseen Sungchul's overwhelming strength.

After passing the first test with ease, Sungchul headed towards the next course. Another trial, similar to the previous one, awaited him. He'd failed the first time, but he wouldn't make the same mistake twice. Sungchul used his wealth of experience and adaptability and his occasionally surprising innovation to move forward. If all else failed, he temporarily unsealed his massive strength to brute-force through each one of Eckheart's tests. Now, as he approached the final trial, a massive three-headed golem stood to block his path.

[Eighth Hero, Eckheart's final exam]

[The ingredients prepared before you are seeds of possibilities.]

[No questions asked. Destroy the Three-Headed Golem!]

The requirements were simple, but by now, Sungchul had also become tired of needing to think and create items to pass the tests. He immediately pulled out Fal Garaz and smashed the Golem across the chest.

SLAM!

[You have completed all of Eckheart's exams and come to accept the glorious potential of Alchemy.]

[Eighth Hero Eckheart could not be more excited to bestow his inheritance on you who has completed all of his tests.]

Reward:
1. Tome of the Creationist
2. Familiar: Living Book Bertelgia
3. Eckheart's Portable Alchemic Cauldron
4. + 5 Intuition

The rewards fell in front of Sungchul. There were two books. One of which was significantly larger, but as he reached for it, it floated into the air as if to reject him.

"Ah…what a blatant scam artist…"

A depressed and cold voice of a little girl could be heard, but it wasn't coming from a human.

"…This is the worst. This kind of person is my owner…"

The voice was coming from the book.

Chapter 6 – Pac-Man Rule

"You're definitely not a normal person. I didn't have a chance to see how you managed to use your thick skull to figure out a way past the extremely complicated and difficult first test, but looking at how easily you took care of the Battle Golem personally created by Eckheart…"

The flying book spoke with its pages fluttering about as though it were alive.

"You might be good enough to be a mid-grade Guild Master or a general of a small nation, right?"

"…"

It wasn't the first time that he had seen a familiar. He had received several familiars from his friends in the past, but whether it be plant or animal, anything he tried to raise all died quickly in his hands without exception.

"What are you?"

Sungchul asked the book.

"Me?"

The large book stopped its movements, and Sungchul nodded impassively.

"I am Bertelgia. A living book, as you can see. I have ended up as your familiar. Not that I wanted to be."

She spoke like a tsundere[2], but her attitude wasn't what mattered to Sungchul.

"What are you capable of?"

This was the only question that mattered.

Bertelgia was struck dumb for a moment, before speaking again in a depressed voice.

"It's very rude how you are treating me like a tool, but seeing as I have no personal desire to get close to you either, I'll accept your behavior. As you can see, I am a living book."

Bertelgia began opening her pages on her own accord, revealing the contents written within to Sungchul. Her pages contained beautifully written formulas and descriptions, complete with illustrations, all for the purpose of aiding the process of Alchemic creation.

"Contained within me is all of the knowledge left behind by Eckheart, the self-proclaimed Eighth Hero. Eckheart wasn't a very smart guy, so the knowledge isn't all that great, but…Hey! Don't touch!"

At this point, Sungchul began to forcefully flip through the pages.

"If you want to see something, you can just tell me! I'll find it and show it to you!"

Bertelgia struggled desperately, trying with all her might to break free of his grasp.

"Yeah?"

Sungchul let go of her. Bertelgia, finally freed from his monstrous strength, shot up to the ceiling before floating back down to where she had been before.

"Yes. Just ask away. Eckheart was a mediocre Alchemist, but he also had some clever tricks."

"Mm…"

Sungchul gazed off into the distance, before staring sharply at the book.

"Can you undo the Curse of Extinction?"

At the mere mention of the curse, a memory he had been suppressing bubbled up in his mind. Bertelgia twirled from left to right.

"Oh? That? That guy also tried solving it, but he didn't succeed."

"I see."

He wasn't disappointed because he hadn't had any expectation in the first place. He bent down to pick up the other book from the floor.

[Tome of the Creationist]
Grade: Legendary
Type: Class Transfer (Compact)
Effect: Legendary Class Creationist Acquisition
Note: My beloved daughter shall lead you to the True Path of Wisdom.

"What is this?"

Creationist: a legendary grade class. It was a class that Sungchul, who was steeped deep in the lore and knowledge of Other World, had never heard of before. Not only that, but the note was also odd. It was unreasonable to request finding the daughter of someone who lived at least a few thousand years ago.

It wasn't long before Bertelgia began to speak again.

"Can't you read? That is the Tome of the Creationist."

"And where is Eckheart's daughter? Won't she be dead by now?"

"Who died? She's right here."

Bertelgia put herself on display like some kind of bird as she flapped her pages. Sungchul stopped breathing and focused his sharp senses to search through his surroundings, but he couldn't perceive any other presence around him.

"Where is 'here'?"

After Sungchul asked for clarification, Bertelgia shoved her paper-packed body towards him and said as she sighed.

"Really, you can't even see who is right in front of you...I'll reintroduce myself then. I am Bertelgia: the daughter of the self-proclaimed Eighth Hero, Eckheart. I am your familiar who will be guiding you on the path of becoming the Creationist."

He had gained 15 Intuition, a tome for a never-before-seen class, and a familiar who claimed to be the daughter of Eckheart. He would have to wait and see how useful the Tome of the Creationist or Bertelgia would be; nevertheless, he had gained a lot of unexpected things.

"Hello? Mr. Musclehead? Can you hear me?"

Sungchul smirked as Bertelgia let out her sharp words.

—

Night had already fallen by the time he reached the Plaza. Sungchul headed towards a clearing near the training center where the Preselected were staying. Everyone had followed after Yuhoon and gone to sleep. Sunghae appeared to be sleeping, her arms wrapped around the staff, but on closer inspection, she was actually cautiously looking over in his direction with her barely opened eyes.

Sungchul headed towards his own spot farther away from the main group. An appreciated guest was waiting at Sungchul's sleeping space which was made from the clothes of those who had died.

"Kyu kyu!"

It was the Sky Squirrel that had been following Krill Regall. Like before, there was a pouch with a message tied to the tiny paws of the Sky Squirrel. He fed the creature some bread crumbs before retrieving the message.

[1. More bribes needed. Urgent.]

[2. Rules of the next Rank Match decided. Pac-Man Rules / Tam Tam]

[3. Requested standard for distribution of rewards: 1st – 100% / 2nd – 80% / 3rd – 60% / 4th – 40%]

[P.S. Without additional bribes, I might not be able to send out this guy anymore.]

After grinding the note into powder with his fingers, he leaned against a training dummy and began to contemplate.

It's Pac-Man rules, with a Tam Tam included to boot.

It was the worst combination of the most difficult rule with the worst of the monsters. Pac-Man rules were one of the many different types of Rank Matches that distributed scores based on the number of people who managed to survive against a powerful creature within the time limit. It might be argued that other rulesets were designed to allow the survivors to fight back; Pac-Man rules, in theory, offered no such opportunity. They released a monster that even a mid-grade fighter, let alone newbies, would not stand a chance against alone. The only way to stay alive against such a monster was to keep away from it until it managed to eat its fill.

The creature, Tam Tam, was one of the weakest monsters that the Summoning Palace kept. It was also one of the more popular monsters to be hunted by the strong. However, there was a valid reason that this monster was called the bane of all newbies. While other monsters hunted humans solely to serve as food, the Tam Tam would play with its meal. The number of casualties it caused during the rounds had never once fallen below that of the other monsters.

Are the Preselected within the Blanche Plaza lacking? I thought the Order of the Iron Blood Knights was a big name around here, but maybe they still hadn't completely recovered from the Demon Army's second invasion?

Blanche Plaza was not the only Plaza to have the "Preselected."

All the other Plazas had Preselecteds backed by major factions as well.

Within the Plaza itself, the Preselected were given special treatment, but this problem extended to the overall Summoning Palace as a whole. In other words, there was a difference in treatment between different groups of Preselected.

The Preselected backed by the strongest faction would have relatively comfortable and safer trials in the Palace, whereas the Plazas not backed by the strongest were forced to face the more difficult and dangerous ones. The Blanche Plaza had received the trial that was rumored to be the most difficult of them all: The Tam Tam.

Sungchul vividly recalled how violently that demonic giant monkey toyed with people before it killed them. His companions, who had numbered over 500, were reduced to below 50 in just one match. The Plaza, soaked completely in blood, was a scene he could recall vividly even to this day. This might have been why Krill had emphasized his need for additional bribes. He knew that the Tam Tam would be in the next match and had no expectations that Sungchul would survive.

Sungchul pulled out a rose-tinted ruby and placed it into the Sky Squirrel's pouch, then petted the squirrel's head with a bent finger.

"Kyu Kyu!"

The Sky Squirrel disappeared into the night sky.

Sungchul closed his eyes and began planning, while the Preselected continued to sleep.

The difference in rewards between ranks is larger than I had expected.

According to Krill's information, the highest-ranking Plaza would earn more than twice the reward of the lowest-ranking Plaza. This means that, within the last ranking Plaza, there was a limit to how much an individual could earn as the pool of rewards were effectively 40% of what the first rank's total rewards were. This difference would prove to be critical. Being in a lower-ranked Plaza would inevitably lead to earning relatively fewer Palace Tokens.

There was also another problem, which was the Tam Tam's presence. Leaving it alone would not only guarantee Blanche Plaza's continual last place, but would also make the following Death Match rules all the more difficult for them. There was only one way to avoid this disaster; he would need to get rid of the Tam Tam.

He now needed to find a way to kill it without being discovered. The Pac-Man match would inevitably draw a crowd of skilled onlookers that would come to enjoy the senseless violence and chaos within the Summoning Palace. If he revealed his strength at that time, he would immediately draw their attention and cause all activities within the Summoning Palace to come to an end and lead to various nations and guilds sending in armies to try and kill him. There was no other way to solve it; Sungchul looked back at Sunghae, who was cautiously watching him through the slit of her eyes with an anxiously beating heart.

—

It wasn't like there was a strict standard or anything, but a large, demonic creature would usually be classified as a Monster. To be more exact, large, demonic creatures that had low intelligence would be classified as Monsters. Tam Tams were smarter than most Monsters, but their level of intelligence was still comparable to wild beasts, hence their classification.

The Tam Tam was a twelve-meter tall, massive primate. It could run quickly, use its extended arms cooperatively with its legs, and, like a human, was able to freely manipulate objects with its hands. Its strength was lacking in comparison to other monsters, but it could still split a man in half with just its spear-like teeth. This did mean, however, that it wasn't a completely impossible threat for the newbies to face.

It was certainly impossible for a newly arrived Summoned to defeat it, but there were those who became much stronger after surviving the first Rank Match, and many had begun to push themselves to train or explore the forest to strengthen themselves after coming to accept their grim realities.

Of course, the probability of winning was realistically stuck at a permanent zero, but Sungchul planned on raising the chances by a significant margin.

I don't need that many. But I need to gather help. If I can gather those who can cause real damage to Tam Tam and have them bring it down, I can use the Explosion Scroll to kill the Tam Tam without raising suspicion.

The Preselected were the ideal candidates for this purpose, but most of them had already acquired the Divine Elixir of Escape. They couldn't be counted on for his plan. They would secure their own survival by slathering on the contents of the Elixir and going to hide in a corner.

Fortunately, there were also a few among them who haven't received the Divine Elixir of Escape. Ahram and Sunghae were a prime example of this. There were four such people in total, including that pair, who hadn't gotten the Elixir. Sungchul approached the one he was already acquainted with: Sunghae.

"…What do you want from me? I believe I've kept my promise, haven't I?"

She quickly drew the staff behind her as she spoke out nervously. Her voice caught the attention of two nameless Preselected men who moved closer to her from the side. It appeared as though someone was worried that Sungchul would attack her to take back the Staff and had prepared a few bodyguards in advance. However, this kind of petty planning meant nothing to Sungchul.

"I didn't come here to take away the staff. I'm just here to give you a warning."

Sungchul pointed to above his head, and her tension dropped by a small bit.

"Didn't your Guide tell you what the upcoming Rank Match would be?"

"I've heard of it. Pac-Man? He said it would be Pac-Man Rules."

"You know which monster is going to be in this Pac-Man game, right?"

"Mmm, maybe I do…"

"Tam Tam"

"Tam Tam? That's a funny name."

"It's a funny name, but what it does is anything but funny. Do you have an item that can replace the Divine Elixir?"

Sunghae pulled out Moonlight and spoke in a trembling voice.

"Isn't this enough?"

Sungchul looked at the staff with emotionless eyes and shook his head.

"That kind of thing can't guarantee your life."

Sungchul turned around. With his broad back to the group, his deep voice could be heard,

"If you want to live, come find me in the forest. Come with anyone that doesn't have an Elixir."

On the first day they were Summoned, no one could have predicted that this would have happened; that the most destitute and unremarkable looking man among the twenty-five Preselected would one day speak down to the most beautiful woman and give her orders. But one week after arrival, everything had changed.

"Um...Hello?"

Sungchul expressionlessly watched as three Preselected cautiously entered the forest.

***

[Ten Thousand Sword Swings (Daily)]

[Ten Thousand Dummy Strikes (Daily)]

[Thousand Lifts with Every Dumbbell in the Training Center (Daily)]

[Eight Thousand Blade Dummy Dodges (Daily)]

[One Thousand Laps around the Plaza (Daily)]

[Low-Grade Monster Hunts]

[Low-Grade Monster x10 Hunts]

[Mid-Grade Monster Hunts]

[...]

This was only a part of the list Sungchul had scratched out on the dirt with twigs for the Preselected. The list of seemingly impossible tasks had a total of thirty entries in it, causing those who were reading to become slack-jawed.

"This is the list of common Quests that I've been suggested to do by my Guide, and they increase the three basic stats: Strength, Dexterity, and Vitality. If you don't believe me, then check with your own Guide."

There were a few false ones mixed in, but the majority of them were real. He borrowed the authority of the Guides to convince the Preselected before him, leaving the responsibility of proving his words to their Guides. The three Preselected showed hostility, but they also couldn't say anything to his face.

"I won't force you. You can spill sweat and train like your lives depend on it, or you can spill your blood at the Rank Match in front of the other Preselected. It's up to you."

There were a total of four Preselected gathered here: Ahram, Sunghae, and her two bodyguards. Ahram, despite being a latecomer, only listened to a bit of the explanation then left while yawning. He leaned against a tree off in the distance and began to hum to himself, attempting to nap. He was the epitome of carefree irresponsibility. Then again, what did someone who looked down on even the Drill Sergeant have to fear?

Only three people remained listening to Sungchul's advice.

"Excuse me."

A pale hand rose in the middle of the uncomfortable silence. It was Sunghae's.

"You are certain that there will be an effect if we do all of this, right?"

"Open your status windows. Ignoring the other stats, your Strength, Dexterity, and Vitality don't exceed 20, do they?"

The eyes of Sunghae and the other two became unfocused as they looked at their Status Screens. Sungchul looked over towards Sunghae and said.

"How do your Strength, Dexterity, and Vitality look?"

"Eh. They are 15, 16, and 16."

All three Preselected had similar stats. It wouldn't be surprising for the average Summoned to be limited at around 10, but it was disappointing for the quality of the Preselected to only be this high.

"My average numbers are higher than 20."

They heard a familiar voice; it was Ahram. He had been leaning on a tree trunk, pretending to sleep while actually listening to everything they'd said.

"I said I got more than 20. 20! So, I don't have to do that stupid list, right?"

Sungchul completely ignored him. Instead, he turned his head and called out loudly.

"Come out."

A man revealed himself from deeper in the forest. It was Loner #2: Yungjong Ha.

"Ah, this is a bit embarrassing. Do I have to do this?"

The other Preselected stiffened. It was quite unpleasant for them to be associating with just Sungchul, but now there was another unwelcome face in the mix.

Sungchul didn't mind the chilling gaze that the two of them were being shot with and spoke to Yungjong.

"Yungjong, how are your stats?"

"Ah, Kim Hyung. I really don't like this kind of thing."

"Come on, it's not hard. I'll even grill you some meat."

At the mention of meat, Yungjong opened his status window with a bitter smile and unhesitatingly recited the numbers within.

"Strength 28. Dexterity 27. Vitality 25. That's how it is."

The other Preselected were shocked by the numbers.

"How can that be? That bastard's stats are higher than mine?" said Ahram as he rose with a stretch from his tree trunk. An indecipherable smile appeared on his face.

"Some bitch like this is better than I am? Huh? Don't joke around with me! Fuck! This guy with a rotten expression is better than me?"

No one knew what had bothered him to such a degree, but Ahram was clearly angry.

"I'm already pissed for getting bitched at for losing the staff, and now some bitches are trying to fuck with me."

The rotten interior hidden underneath his handsome exterior revealed itself. He began looking over everyone with hatred in his eyes before eventually screaming out spitefully.

"Hey! Fuck it! Don't even bother! What do you fuckers know? Fucking worthless idiots. Do you know who my backer is? Do you?"

Everyone either turned their gazes or simply ignored him completely.

Ahram, who was throwing a tantrum like some drunkard, suddenly reached out and grabbed Sunghae's wrist.

"What are you doing?" exclaimed Sunghae looking aghast as she pulled her arm out of his grip. Ahram smiled lecherously and reached out for her once again.

"Do you know who my backer is, Sunghae? Hm?"

"What the fuck do I care about that?"

"Oh shit. Look who's talking back now. What a step up for a whore like you."

"What? What did you just say?"

Sunghae jumped back in surprise and pointed her Moonlight towards him, seeming ready to kill.

Ahram pointed at her staff and looked at her mockingly.

"Am I wrong? You got that fucking staff from that hobo, for a night."

"Are you crazy?"

"Give me a turn. Don't act so coy. I can get you something better than that shit if I ask my idiot Guide, Dolorence or some shit. Come on!"

Ahram struck Sunghae's staff out of her hand and once again held her wrists.

"Let me go! I'll kill you!"

Sunghae struggled with all her might, but her strength couldn't overcome Ahram's. Ahram dragged Sunghae by her arms to some taller bushes, in plain sight of everyone. He continued laughing the whole time. He was like a crazed dog that had broken free of its leash; a loose mad dog with a terrifying backer. Even the two men who'd assigned themselves as Sunghae's bodyguards could do nothing but watch with their heads lowered.

"…"

A man stepped up just as Sungchul was about to move. It was Yungjong.

"Little baby, shut up now, you hear? Or else your chin just might go flying."

Ahram would often throw a tantrum over every little thing, but this time, he went too far.

"What?"

Ahram glared, eyes blinded by anger. He raised his chin and walked rapidly over to Yungjong and got into his face.

"Flap those gums again, bitch. You stinkin' garb…"

The sound of an impact echoed in the forest. Yungjong had landed a refreshing punch in his face. Ahram's face was crumpled as he fell making an inexplicable cry of agony.

"AgeaaaAAa!"

The strangeness of the cry must have been caused by being interrupted in the middle of shouting insults by a punch. Ahram twitched like a cockroach hit by bug spray as he trembled in the ground, twitching and grabbing dirt.

"Ugh…Ugh…"

Everyone was reminded of the age old saying "A stick is the only medicine for an unruly dog" after the incident resolved anticlimactically. Ahram soon left the area, muttering profanities under his breath as he went.

"You'll all see. Fuckers. I'm going to get dad to fucking crush all of you. Bitches…Just you wait. Just you wait…"

The most cowardly of threats could be faintly heard coming from between the trees.

After Ahram left, Sungchul gathered the group again and spoke to them.

"I'll be in the Plaza. If there is anything you want to ask regarding the common Quests, don't hesitate to come to me."

Sungchul left the Preselected behind and exited the forest with Yungjong. Yungjong leaned over to him and whispered.

"Uh…shit. I ended up blowing it. That was the one bitch I shouldn't have hit."

He had acted instinctively, but there seemed to be a lot of regret remaining.

"Ah…what should I do? Shit…Should I apologize later?"

Yungjong turned out to actually be quite a decent guy. His mouth was foul, and his appearance was intimidating, but he always supported his friends. It was rare to find a person like this within the Summoning Palace where everyone's true face was soon revealed.

"Then why did you step up? I could have dealt with it myself," replied Sungchul.

"Ah…but that bitch was so uppity. Really, though…I did do it, but…whew…"

"It's fine. Don't worry about it. Didn't you see him call his Guide an idiot? The Guide probably felt her blood pressure shoot up. She might even be grateful to you."

"R…right? It'd be sweet if that was the case."

His face relaxed slightly after being reassured. He had punched out of anger, and his naturally anxious personality couldn't be changed so suddenly.

"Anyways, Kim Hyung. Do you think those kids will actually do as you said? They're as spoiled as they come."

"Well, it's their loss if they don't. Your example will only be of benefit to them."

"Okay. Also, let me taste that amazing meat that you were talking about. I've only been eating that trashy bread, and I want to chew something which has meat juices flowing."

"I'm not bragging, but I'm confident in my cooking skills. I'll be grilling it for dinner, so don't come crying to me if you've filled up on the Homunculus's bread."

"Of course. I'll be waiting!"

Yungjong returned to the training center with his thumb in the air.

Now that Sungchul was alone again, he looked around the Plaza center a bit. He was looking at the established factions between the average Summoned.

It's not enough with just the minority of the Preselected. Everyone's stats have to be raised across the board.

Sungchul looked at the outer ring of the people gathered in the Plaza with passive eyes. He quickly found what he was looking for. That middle-aged office worker who had wanted to gather people to form a group on the first day; he had become the leader of the largest faction in the Blanche Plaza.

***

The middle-aged office worker was called Hakchul Kim. In the real world, he had been the division leader of a mid-sized company. He had neither great physical strength nor superior intellect, but he was determined to preserve goodness and righteousness. He wished to gather people in order to the end chaos and violence which ruled the place and restore public order.

The group which had started out with only a few people who shared his ideals grew to the current size of five hundred after the first Rank Match. This was indisputably the largest faction within the Blanche Plaza.

However, this faction had a critical weakness. Due to their open-door policy, they were mostly composed of people who were weak in body and spirit. Hakchul also enforced an equal distribution policy emphasizing that all rewards had to be split evenly among all of their members. This resulted in too many leeches infesting his organization despite his ideals. The problem was exacerbated during the last Rank Match, as those who were starving because they hadn't been able to kill a single zombie all flocked to this group to get a free handout. This allowed the group to explode in membership, but the internal stability and happiness were at the brink of collapse.

It was an organization on its last legs, but Sungchul decided to approach this group first simply because of their numbers. Their large membership meant that even the smallest increase in overall combat strength would show a greater effect than any other faction. Raising the Strength of 500 people by 1 was easier than raising a single person's Strength to 500. Although, the increase of stats by 500 distributed across many individuals was less dramatic than a similar increase in an individual. However, it was important for them to get as close to it as possible.

"I have something to say."

Sungchul waited for an opportunity to approach Hakchul. Hakchul was surprised by Sungchul's sudden appearance but welcomed him amiably.

"You're one of the people hanging out at the training center. Okay, what did you want to talk about?"

Looking up close, Hakchul seemed weaker and more pitiful than Sungchul had expected. His eyes were still resolute thanks to his ideals, but his wrinkled face showed his doubt and his anxiety. He looked as though the uncertainties of his future were starting to affect him.

This man…He's bearing a burden beyond his capacity.

Sungchul had seen many different types of people in this world. Too many times he had seen pure ideals get corrupted or ruin lives. Lofty goals, hanging high in the sky, seem so clearly defined. But every path leading up to it is shrouded in fogs of doubt and uncertainty. Hakchul was just one of many that were lost in this fog.

"Look at this."

Sungchul showed the same list of common quests to Hakchul as he had shown the Preselected.

"There will be a Rank Match soon. This one will be incomparably more terrifying than the previous one. Please warn your companions and advise them to raise their Strength."

"Thank you. All this is…"

Hakchul appeared to be very grateful at first, but as soon as he looked over the contents himself, he suddenly drew back. Sungchul's observant gaze didn't miss the other's hesitation. Hakchul grew more and more hesitant the further he read.

"I have read it over, and I am grateful for your help."

"It's not enough to be grateful. You need to at least tell your people about the Strength-enhancing Quests, right now."

"For the Strength-enhancing Quest...That was ten thousand sword swings...but ten thousand..."

"Is there a problem?"

"I mean, it's one thing to say the number ten thousand. But, who would actually swing that many times? One might say that it would be crazy of them. I'll let the people know, but I doubt that anyone will follow through with it."

He spoke amiably but in a skeptical tone. Some of his subordinates who were next to him simply laughed.

"Exactly. Who would do that kind of exercise?"

"Can't do it. We're running low on food now, and you want us to move around?"

"It's impossible. Not even worth trying."

They were the expected responses. Hakchul's faction had the largest number, but its large size didn't allow for effective control. Hakchul could give advice to his subordinates, but he lacked the authority to force them into action. This was the limitation of Hakchul's faction.

This will be difficult. These people...

Sungchul pointed off to the Observation Tower on the other end of the Plaza and spoke coldly.

"You think your objections mean anything to people in that tower?"

"Mmm..."

"At least try to force your most-trusted men. If you can't, you should get ready to go through hell."

He had said everything there was to be said. Their reaction was still lukewarm. There was nothing more to expect from Hakchul's faction. The result was completely below his expectations, but Sungchul moved on to the next location unfazed.

He arrived at the western end of the Plaza where the food cart that the Homunculi used was stationed.

"Now now, humans! We'll give out some food! Don't spill it, make sure to eat everything!"

The Homunculi tossed around rotten bread in their usual mocking manner. However, a group of muscular men stood in everyone's way.

"Shove off! You wanna try me?"

"Anyone who comes near is dead! Hey! Red hood over there! You wanna die? Ey!"

They had surrounded the cart and monopolized the food by force. They swung their blades and shouted at the other starving people that were approaching the cart. There were just about a hundred or so of these men, but the others could only bitterly swallow their spit as they looked on from a distance. This was the second faction Sungchul had decided to approach.

Unlike Hakchul and his faction, this group had gathered only for profit, and they only had one rule: strength.

Is he the leader?

A man was sitting arrogantly in the middle of the group; he was holding the food and had a beauty at his side. He looked to be in his early-thirties. His stamina was average, and he didn't appear particularly strong, but his eyes had a peculiar luster. His lean muscles were covered in yakuza-like tattoos, putting his former life on full display. Sungchul headed towards this man.

"Who're you?"

There was a rough-looking subordinate blocking his way.

"I have something I want to say to your boss."

"Who gave you the right?"

Sungchul effortlessly threw the thug to the ground and continued forward. The arrogant man gestured to the girl beside him to leave before staring back at Sungchul coldly.

"You, who are you?"

Sungchul knew the man's name: Jungshik Chun. With his grit, even though he had no particular "abilities," he had still taken care of 100 zombies at the first Rank Match. He was someone who had a higher score than any of the specially privileged Preselected. He truly had the natural talent to be a warrior. Jungshik probably didn't know about the Observer's Eye that had been placed on top of his head. Someone had already called dibs on him. It was rare for someone to receive this level of attention after only the first Rank Match.

"I've got something to say."

Sungchul said the same thing he'd told Hakchul. Jungshik, however, listened to him with great interest. The list of common quests was written below Jungshik's feet.

"So, you're saying that if I do this list of things you told me, my stats will increase?"

"That's right. However, the highest you can train up to with daily Quests is 25."

"25, eh? My boys are around 10 to 12, so they'll get twice as strong if I get them to grind this out, right?"

It was an entirely different reaction from Hakchul. His reply revealed an underlying assumption that he had complete control over his gang.

This is a dangerous man.

This wasn't some simple talent, but a man who had a natural tendency for violence. Looking at Jungshik's eager eyes, he recalled a companion that had become his enemy over time.

"Good. I'm correct, right? How about we give it a try?"

Jungshik stood and shouted towards a subordinate.

"Hey, bring me my dagger."

Jungshik's subordinate respectfully brought the blade, offering it over with both hands.

It was the Dagger of Swiftness. Jungshik gripped the blade in his left hand and glared at Sungchul with feral eyes before warning him.

"Stay right there. If you're lying, I'm going to skin you."

Sungchul replied with a bright smile on his face.

"Don't forget what I said. The Quests won't raise your strength past 25."

"Yeah? That's convenient. My strength just hit 24."

One of Sungchul's brow shot up. If he wasn't lying, then it was an amazing growth.

This guy…he's quite impressive.

As soon as Jungshik finished speaking, he began to swing his Dagger of Swiftness at a fearsome speed, and his goons surrounded Sungchul, all with a threatening expression on their faces.

Before long, ten thousand swings were finished. Jungshik wiped off his brow with a towel that was presented by one of his subordinates and checked over his stats.

"Oh wow."

Jungshik smiled with great satisfaction. He immediately gathered his gang and shouted.

"Gather around. From now on, it's time for hellish training."

Sungchul was no longer on his mind. He was so soaked in excitement at the prospect of strengthening his faction that he had already forgotten about Sungchul's existence. Sungchul left the group of men who were swinging blades with fervor and began thinking to himself.

We need those kinds of people at times too.

Jungshik's faction would probably grow at a scary pace under Jungshik's authority as long as he obtained a way of raising their strength. However, Hakchul had been given the same cards, yet his group didn't show any particular attempt to follow through with it. They just stared blankly from a distance like cattle, while Jungshik's group trained diligently. Hakchul's group might be five times larger than Jungshik's, but at this rate, comparing the two factions would be like comparing heaven and earth.

"Hey! Don't screw around! Hurry! Hurry up and do this so we can sweep up those annoying bastards."

Jungshik's sharp commands drew a clear vision of the future for Sungchul.

Hakchul's faction is soon going to get eaten up by Jungshik's faction.

If Jungshik hadn't gotten his hands on the common quest list, his faction would never have had enough strength to overcome such a large difference in numbers. There might be a bloodbath before the actual Rank Match between the factions. This was one of the basic natures of humans. However, this was well aligned with Sungchul's objectives.

I have to use everything available to me in order to kill the Tam Tam and secure Blanche Plaza to number one during the Rank Match. This is the most surefire way to getting all the Palace Tokens I need into my grasp.

He made his way out of the Plaza as the sound of Jungshik group's martial cries faded away.

—

The date of the Rank Match drew closer, and the rigorous training continued. The Preselected were physically exhausted, but the danger of death looming over them and Sungchul's guidance helped turn each of them into warriors in five days. They were now fighters that had an average Strength, Dexterity, and Vitality of 25. This was the greatest force that Sungchul had for the upcoming Rank Match.

He let out a contented smile and brought out a gift he had prepared for the Preselected for growing stronger. It was a slab of meat wrapped in leaves; this was the reward he had received six days ago. Other Summoned had greedily eaten their shares on the day they received it, but Sungchul was different. He had flavored the meat with salt and pepper, then fermented the meat in a dry location after wrapping it in leaves.

"Wasn't this from a week ago? It must be rotten by now..."

Sunghae dried off her sweat and looked over the meat. Sungchul silently unwrapped the leaves.

It looked completely dry at first glance, and parts of it had turned black, but for those that knew their meat, it told a different story.

"Dry aging?"

One of Sunghae's brows shot up. He nodded and wrapped the meat up again.

"I don't mean to boast, but I am confident in my cooking."

In reality, Sungchul was a master chef who had High-Class Chef as a subclass; his skills would've embarrassed even the chefs of the royalty.

He placed the wrapped meat on top of a wide, flat stone then grilled it patiently at a slow rate. The Cathedral was soon filled with a delicious aroma.

"Wow. That smells awesome."

Yungjong wiped off some drool with his sleeves and begged to have a piece. The two bodyguards and even the wealthy princess, Sunghae, were not an exception. They all waited for it to be cooked, their eyes glued to the meat.

It had been two weeks since the mass summoning which had brought them here, and all this time, they had only managed to eat hard bread and apples. No one had eaten proper food in a long while. Now that the greatest chef had prepared a meal for them, how could they not start losing their composure?

Sungchul finally cut open the leaves wrapped around the meat with his beginner blade and revealed the meat within.

CHIIIK

The meat juices and the aroma stuffed within the leaves exploded out and melted the last few bits of awkwardness between them. Sungchul expressionlessly stared at the meat before nodding his head.

"It's good to eat now."

With a cheer, they began their feast. Delicious food always improved the mood; the four Preselected gathered here forgot their differences and fully soaked in Sungchul's world of delicious flavors. Conversation flowed freely, and the participants stopped judging one another.

"I'm really grateful, Mr. Yungjong. Thank you for saving me."

"No! It was nothing! Haha...I just did what I had to."

The two had gotten close before Sungchul knew it. He noticed the vial of Divine Elixir of Escape that Yungjong had been discreetly fidgeting in his grasp. Sungchul smiled, amused, before taking another bite out of the meat.

It is said that a man is helpless before a woman.

In that regard, Sungchul was superior, not that it was anything to boast about. He couldn't help but grin.

However, Sungchul suddenly noticed someone's gaze from behind him. It was Ahram. He had avoided everyone after being punched by Yungjong, but he suddenly appeared on the final day before the Rank Match. He stared at the happily feasting Yungjong and Sunghae before disappearing into the darkness again.

"Kim Hyung! Is something wrong?"

The excited Yungjong called out to Sungchul. Sungchul calmly memorized the direction in which Ahram had disappeared as Yungjong called him again.

"What's wrong? Kim Hyung."

"Ahram came by and looked over you and Sunghae before leaving."

"That bitch? Me? Why?"

"I don't know why, but you better be careful."

"Pfft. What can that kid do to me? Even Sunghae is strong enough to step all over him."

Yungjong felt Sunghae's gaze and exaggerated a bit. She laughed a bit and motioned for him to rejoin the feast.

He definitely wasn't wrong. Over the last five days, Yungjong had become much stronger, while Ahram had simply stared blankly from the corner of the training center doing nothing. However, there was something that bothered Sungchul. He recalled the red-headed female Mage with a freckled face in charge of Ahram. She had been rather skilled.

That woman couldn't possibly be called out by Ahram to take revenge? No...that can't...

That kind of event was unthinkable. The Summoning Palace explicitly forbade anyone from interfering with the Summoned directly without proper permission from the Palace. Strictly speaking, the existence of the Preselected was also illegal, but that was easier to justify because no Mage directly used their strength on any of the Summoned. To harm the Summoned meant to challenge the authority of the Summoning Palace. They say there is a fine line between bending the rules and breaking them, but the consequences of the two offenses were vastly different.

There was no way that a mid-rank Mage would give up their life for someone else, but there were always exceptions…Or so Sungchul thought as he cautioned Yungjong.

"There is no reason not to be careful."

"Pssh. You should also be careful, Hyung. That brat doesn't like either of us."

Yungjong smirked before returning to the feast. The joyous sounds of laughter rang out from the Forsaken Cathedral.

—

CLUNK!

The iron gates of the Plaza opened with a suffocating dread. Hundreds of Summoned watched quietly with hushed breaths as the monster slowly revealed its form through the gigantic gates.

"W…what is that?"

"Th-that's crazy…"

It was a massive primate covered in crimson fur. The humans trembled at the sight of the overwhelmingly large monster before running away without a second thought. The grotesque creature's tire-sized eyes gazed down at the humans on the ground. Their terrified faces filled its blue eyes.

"OOKIKIKI!"

The monster revealed its teeth with a wide smile and started to laugh.

Tam Tam.

The worst monster of Pac-Man rules had arrived at the Blanche Plaza.

***

The same message appeared before everyone's eyes.

[The Rank Match is about to begin.]

[The Tam Tam is an aggressive and savage monster.]

[Escape the Tam Tam's predation for an hour.]

[However, defeating it automatically fulfills the Victory Condition. If you can, that is.]

"I don't see Mister Yungjong."

Sunghae began looking around the arena nervously.

"What happened? We promised to help each other..."

Sunghae let her words hang as she desperately looked for Yungjong. However, it wouldn't be easy looking for a person in the large Plaza filled with a thousand people.

"Yungjong...Where are you?"

It most likely wasn't out of the goodness of her heart that she was now looking for him so desperately. Sungchul remembered the Elixir that Yungjong had been fidgeting with behind his back during his conversation with Sunghae. Like many other men, he might have overpromised when he was with her but then chose to disappear when the time came to keep his word; it was a common story.

Sungchul chose to look away towards the rest of the crowd positioning themselves in the arena, rather than reply to her muttering. On the right was the disorganized mob composed of Hakchul's faction and unaffiliated Summoned, and on the left side stood Jungshik's gang in a slanted single file line. Jungshik's faction stood closer to the Tam Tam, but he didn't immediately order his men back.

The Preselected were also split into two forces. The ones with the Divine Elixir stood harmoniously in the corner to the right, but the ones without the Elixir stood opposite Jungshik's faction, together with Sungchul. However, there was one thing that stood out. Ahram was within the right corner conversing loudly with people, wearing a very satisfied expression on his face.

Why is that bastard over there?

As he put the question aside, screams broke out towards the front of the crowd. The Tam Tam began its hunt.

"Ookikiki!"

The Tam Tam used his two arms to propel himself forward, like a quadruped, towards the right side.

"Everyone run! Hurry!"

With Hakchul's shout, hundreds of people began to scatter like leaves in the wind. The Tam Tam's massive hand swept across the floor and grabbed three people at once.

"UWAAK! S-Save me!"

"KWAAAAK!"

The struggling captives quickly entered the open maw of the massive creature.

SQUISH! CRUNCH!

His massive teeth tenderized their flesh and blood into boluses of meat which then slithered down his throat and into his stomach.

"..."

Sunghae's whole body trembled in fear.

"W-what is that? Just what is that?"

It wasn't just her. The other Preselected lost all will to fight in the face of the Tam Tam's oppressive show of force.

"Just run for now. There's no time to discuss this."

Sungchul ran forward with all his strength as if to lead the charge, and hundreds of people behind him began to follow his lead because of their fear. Behind them, the massive monster busied itself with tossing people into its gullet.

The feast of an oppressive monster, this was the traditional scene of the Pac-Man Rule Rank Match. On the other side of the Plaza walls, various powers of the Other World were enjoying the grotesque slaughter, smiling from the packed seats.

"Blanche Plaza has no luck at all, to get Pac-Man rules on their second Rank Match and with the Tam Tam at that."

A middle-aged man holding a glass of blood-colored wine who was surrounded by beautiful women acknowledged the fully-armored man.

"..."

The fully-armored man was tense, unlike the middle-aged man with the wine.

Fucking Summoning Plaza dogs. They're trying to suck us, the Order of the Iron Blood Knights, completely dry. Have we lost the support of the Empire?

The man was the Iron Blood Knight's Grand Knight, Sanggil Ma. He stood wordlessly and walked towards the Observation Tower. Two knights closely followed behind him like they were his shadow.

"Dolorence Winterer!"

Sanggil let out a roar as soon as the Observation Tower's door opened. The collective gaze of all the Mages in the tower gathered on Sanggil. A Mage coyly walked over towards him within the silence. Unlike most Mages, she wore a tight dress which revealed her feminine charm. She was Dolorence Winterer. Her freckled face greeted the incensed Grand Knight of the Iron Blood Knights with a smile.

"Were you looking for me?"

Sanggil glared at Dolorence with contempt and sternly asked her.

"How is the Captain's son? I've read from your report that he didn't receive the Divine Elixir in the first Rank Match."

Dolorence looked to be surprisingly comfortable under Sanggil's seething gaze.

"It has been taken care of."

"Meaning what?"

Sanggil's hand gripped his blade. His raging eyes emitted an undeniable murderous intent, creating a suffocating atmosphere for the Mages sitting within the Observation Tower with them.

"The Captain's son managed to get ahold of a Divine Elixir."

"How can that be?"

Sanggil looked as though he didn't believe it.

The Divine Elixir of Escape can only be obtained by the blessings of the 'God of Neutrality' that presides over the Summoning Palace. It is only granted through the trials and can't be reproduced with Alchemy or Magic of any kind. And this red-headed bitch still managed to get one for her Charge?

It sounded impossible. Sanggil believed as much and continued trying to drive her into a corner.

"I'm supposed to just take your word for it?"

Dolorence donned a smug smile and spoke in a cheerful tone.

"You'll see. But try not to blame me later."

"What does that mean?"

"I simply followed the Iron Blood Knights' doctrine."

"Speak plainly, Mage."

Sanggil finally pulled out his blade; Dolorence placed a scrying orb onto a nearby desk.

"'Sacrifice the few for the sake of the many,' isn't that one of the Iron Blood Knights' famous doctrines?"

Ahram's appearance was shown within the scrying orb. It closed in on his hands on the Divine Elixir held tightly within his grip.

—

"UWAAK!"

Twenty more died. The Tam Tam continued to loudly chew on the people and look around for more victims. The summoned were screaming madly in fear.

Among the crowd, it searched through those with long hair; it was hunting for women. Men were muscular, making their meat tough, but women tasted better with their fatty flesh. The Tam Tam wiped off his bloody mouth with his massive hand and reached out to his next victim.

123

"Kyaaaa!"

The victim quickly flew into the Tam Tam's mouth. It continued looking for its next meal as it chewed.

"How long do we need to keep running for?"

Sunghae asked with ragged breath.

"Until the bastard is full."

"When will it be full?"

"Around thirty people."

It wouldn't be long until the hungry predator became stuffed.

In Sungchul's grip was the Explosion Scroll. Retaliation would have to wait until it lowered its guard.

"UWAAAK!"

That moment came unexpectedly soon as the beast shoved ten more people into its mouth. It leaned back in satisfaction and then burped.

"Buuuuurp!"

It was easy to ignore the sound, but now there was a disgusting stench which filled the arena. The Tam Tam scratched its head as it looked around with even more savagery in its eyes.

"Ooki?"

It was play time now. The Tam Tam was an unusual creature that would also kill for sport. It grabbed another pair of victims with its hands. It looked at the struggling humans with curiosity filling its eyes as it began smashing them together like a child playing with his toys.

"S-stop!"

"Uwek!"

The two people cried out desperately a few times before they became crushed into tenderized meat in the Tam Tam's hands.

"Oookikikikiki!"

The Tam Tam laughed and bared its teeth as it sought out some more toys.

"Ookiki?"

It looked at a group of people that weren't running away like the others. The Preselected.

"Shit. It's looking at us."

One of the Preselected spoke hurriedly.

"Everyone be prepared."

Yuhoon calmly took a step back and pulled out his Divine Elixir. The Tam Tam slowly moved towards the Preselected.

"NOW!"

Yuhoon was the first to pop open the Divine Elixir and pour it over his head, with the rest of the group following his lead. The approaching Tam Tam hesitated and tilted its head in confusion when the group of Preselected disappeared before it.

"Ooki?"

It quickly lost interest, but there was one person that hadn't used his Elixir yet; that person was Ahram. He broke past the group of Preselected and headed over towards Sungchul, having no fear of the monster.

"Over here! Here, you stupid monkey! Over here!"

"Ooki?"

The Tam Tam was quick to respond to the provocation, and Ahram became even louder and more animated.

"Rip this fucker apart! Do it now!"

The Tam Tam turned around and moved towards Ahram. At that moment, Ahram pulled out something which caught Sungchul's eyes.

That…is the Divine Elixir of Escape. How did that bastard…

The bottle's shape looked extremely familiar. He dug through his memory before finding it: the image of a man and a woman sitting around a bonfire last night. An outspoken male, an experienced woman; the male nervously fidgeting with a small vial behind his back.

That must be Yungjong's.

Ahram fully displayed himself before he poured Yungjong's Elixir over his body.

"Kyahahaha! Now, you stupid fucking monkey! Go and kill that fucker!"

The Tam Tam simply ran past Ahram, who was now blessed by the Elixir, and roared out in anger rather than the curiosity displayed before.

"Ookikiki!"

"Yungjong…Where did he go?"

Sunghae began looking for Yungjong again as another disaster approached. Sungchul said resolutely in her direction.

"Yungjong is not coming, so do what we had discussed."

Sungchul gripped his Explosion Scroll and headed to the front. He waited for the perfect moment while the frenzied creature continued stepping on people like they were ants. He opened the Scroll and shouted out clearly after all the fearful people had fled far enough away from the creature.

"Explosion!"

The scroll became dyed in light and created a massive explosion beneath the creature's feet.

BOOM!

The Tam Tam, who had been running about excitedly, suddenly lost its balance due to the force of the explosion and fell forwards.

"Kkeeeeek!"

It was a great enough force to shake the entire Plaza, but the Tam Tam was still not dead. It had only fallen over; all within Sungchul's expectations.

"Now!"

Sungchul lifted his blade high and ran over to the unconscious monster.

"Ah...Where the fuck is Yungjong!"

Sunghae swore in frustration and began using Moonlight to fire at the creature's eyes, signaling the countless other Summoned to also start attacking the fallen Tam Tam.

"Now! Bastards! It's time to get our payback from that fucking monkey!"

Jungshik and his subordinates stood at the front lines.

"Everyone! Now is the moment! Let's also go attack!"

Hakchul lifted his sword and tried to follow with the momentum, but only a handful of people from the front bothered to follow him.

STAB! STAB! STAB!

Dozens of blades continued to stab at the unconscious beast, but its tough hide and even tougher muscles didn't allow the average Summoned to cause more than a few superficial wounds to it. The majority of critical damage was done by the Preselected and

Jungshik's faction. Their blades, unlike the average blade, could cut through its flesh and sever its muscles, causing it to twitch, but that was the limit to it; they couldn't deal decisive damage by reaching the organs or breaking the bones. Sungchul also appeared to be doing a similar level of damage, but it was deceptively different.

"..."

STAB!

It looked as though he was simply plunging his blade halfway like the rest of crowd, but he also twisted the blade, causing the Tam Tam's tough muscles to wrap around it, inflicting much greater damage to the beast. Sungchul seemed to move more slowly, yet he alone was the one who destroyed the creature's left leg.

"Ookki!"

Every time Sungchul drove his blade into the creature, the Tam Tam would scream in agony. Every one of the attackers believed it was their own doing and attacked with even more vigor.

The fallen Tam Tam eventually regained its senses and opened its eyes. When Sunghae aimed for the eyes once again, it brought up its arms to protect its face as it stood up.

"Fuck! The monster! It's still alive!"

"Everyone fall back!"

Everyone that had been excitedly stabbing the creature quickly fell in behind Jungshik's faction.

The Tam Tam glared at everybody with an enraged expression and began beating its chest. That was the worst signal the Tam Tam made; it meant that it was about to go berserk. The infuriated and blood-soaked monster inspired tremendous fear, enough to make them feel as if their souls was being sucked right out of their bodies, except for Sungchul, who was looking over the monster peacefully.

"Ooki?"

Without warning, the Tam Tam who was angrily beating its chest swayed. It soon lost balance and fell. The onlookers didn't know what to think of it, and looked at one another, but only Sungchul knew the reason.

I have ripped all of your leg muscles to shreds. You will never stand again.

His attacks seemed quite ordinary, but he had worked towards disabling the creature's movement.

"Now! Stick to it! Stick it to that fucking monkey until it dies!"

Jungshik and his subordinates rushed with the crowd at the monkey once more. The Tam Tam flailed its arms desperately in defense, but the tens of thousands of cuts slowly accumulated damage to its body, making the Tam Tam's movement weaker and weaker until the monster finally gave out.

[What a surprise!]

[You have felled the monster!]

[Beyond expectation, the trial was completed. Regardless of results, top rewards are granted to the Blanche Plaza.]

[Congratulations! You have survived the second Rank Match!]

This was how the worst of the trials was completed with the greatest of results, but Sungchul's objectives hadn't been accomplished yet. He quietly kept his sight on a certain man who was celebrating happily; it was Ahram. Sungchul finally decided that it was time to act.

Chapter 7 – Pure Discipline

[As the Tam Tam has been slain, a secondary reward based on contributions will be distributed.]

[The Summoning Palace's Department of Operations is currently judging the contributions.]

The Summoned lingered around the Plaza for a considerable amount of time after the monster had fallen. They could hear bizarre shrieks and feel a terrible quake shaking the earth from beyond the tall Plaza walls. It felt like an eternity had passed before another message appeared before their eyes.

"What...0.2%? Only that much?"

"I only got 0.1%?"

The majority of contributions among them hovered below the 1% threshold. The number that appeared before Sungchul, however, was an outlier.

[Your Contribution: 18.4%]

A preeminent percentage

And preeminent rewards to match.

[You have been judged for S-tier rewards.]

Bonus Reward:

1x Scorpion-tail Whip

Standard Reward:

14x Palace Token
3x Fresh Meat
15x Apple
1x Week of Rations

> Selection Rewards:
> 5x Holy Water of Escape
> 1x Potion of Berserk
> 1x Soldier's Crossbow
> Select One

Among the choices, Sungchul chose the crossbow. The pile of items, including the crossbow and the whip, fell in front of Sungchul. He pocketed the most important reward: The Palace Tokens.

There are only two more Rank Matches left, but I still require twenty Palace Tokens that I need to earn from them. This is going be close. I might just barely make it.

The number he needed was dangerously close; this round demonstrated that, even when Blanche Plaza reached 1st place with Sungchul taking the lion's share of the contribution, the maximum Palace Tokens he could be awarded per round was 14. In other words, to earn a similar amount of coins he would need to have Blanche Plaza reach 1st place at least once more, and obtain a large percentage of the contribution again.

There is only the Death Match rule and the Last-Man-Standing rule left. Last-Man-Standing is going to be all or nothing, but I still have to keep Blanche Plaza in first place for the Death Match.

This was the reason he had picked the crossbow. Explosion Scrolls were ideal for taking down a large number of targets, but unfortunately, it wasn't included in the rewards this time. So now it was ideal to focus on improving the individual strength of many warriors instead. The soldier's crossbow and similar long range weapons would be highly effective when battling large mobs of the Summoned in the Death Match, so if given to patient individuals, it could prove to be quite effective.

After he'd packed up his items, Sungchul looked through the Stone of Records. As expected, all of the results had been recorded within.

[1. Sungchul Kim – 18.4%]

[2. Ahmuge – 5.2%]

[3. Chun Jungshik – 4.3%]

…

[12. Bae Sunghae – 3.3%]

…

[782. Lee Yuhoon – 0%]

[783. Kim Taeksoo – 0%]

…

Sungchul was in first place. He knew that he deserved more than 80% of the contribution, but he guessed that the judges only attributed the use of the Explosion Scroll into his score; they couldn't account for how much damage Sungchul had actually done to the creature, especially since he had avoided hitting its vital spots. On the other hand, all of the Preselected that had hidden themselves with the Holy Water of Escape now received 0% contribution.

He fell into contemplation as he looked at Ahram, who was now spouting profanities with no trace of the excitement he had displayed during the match.

It wasn't in my plans, but I did do something to get noticed. It's not very likely, as most people will just credit it to the item rather than to me…but I'm bound to get caught if I keep putting up a show like this.

A difficult restriction attached itself to his plans. He now had to keep Blanche Plaza in first place while also avoiding being noticed. Sungchul slowly returned to the Preselected camp as the excitement of their victory simmered down. He decided to approach Yuhoon first.

"Where is Yungjong?"

"Yungjong? Well…where could he have gone? I was looking for him too."

Yuhoon's eyes slid over to Ahram on the opposite side of the camp. They were hiding something. If the "leader" Yuhoon was acting like this, there was no point in asking the others. He would need some bait.

Sungchul asked the same question, this time with a piece of meat and two apples in his hands, to a different group of Preselected.

"Where did Yungjong go?"

They all clammed up, but their eyes were glued to the meat. They all had managed to get some Palace Tokens and rations due to Blanche Plaza being ranked in first, but the zero percenters couldn't get their hands on a luxury item such as fresh meat. And now, the opportunity to taste some had surprisingly arrived before them.

He didn't have to wait long.

"Excuse me…"

An unknown man approached Sungchul discreetly.

"Will you give that to me in exchange for information?"

Sungchul offered the meat and the apple first, and after grabbing the meat the man started to speak in a hushed tone.

"Before the match, the Drill Sergeant pulled him aside. They left the Palace gates together as I remember."

"Do you know where they went?"

"That is all I know. Don't ask me anything else, and don't act like you know me."

The Preselected hugged the meat and fled from Sungchul. He must have thought that it would be a shame to leave behind a perfectly good apple as he ran back to grab the apple while avoiding Sungchul's eyes before taking off once more.

The Drill Sergeant.

Sungchul rose from his seat, left through the Palace gates, and quickly found a clue. He could see the Homunculus' distinct tracks which stood apart from the countless footprints on the trail. Since the doors had been closed during the Rank Match, the chance of them fading away was slim. He followed the tracks through the forest, and they soon led him to a very familiar building, the Forsaken Cathedral. This had been the first gathering place of the Preselected.

Sungchul took note of the Cathedral's eerie atmosphere as he entered the building. He could see traces of a fire from last night, and there was the faint scent of flames and meat lingering in the air. He slowly took in his surroundings until he discovered something. There was a hand peeking out of a casket.

"..."

He quietly approached the casket and pulled it open. It contained an unrecognizable corpse which had been torn to shreds. He could only confirm the body's identity from its lower half.

Yungjong Ha.

On the face, which looked closer to tenderized meat, Sungchul found a small tuft of hair.

Wolf's fur.

It was the work of a Werewolf. Many possibilities flashed past his mind, but suddenly he heard some noises that were coming from nearby.

"Ah. It's so annoying cleaning up after humans!"

It was a familiar, grating voice. The Drill Sergeant. He was entering the Cathedral with a smaller Homunculus pushing a wheelbarrow.

"But we can get lots of candy, so it's all right! Even my child can eat some now!"

The Drill Sergeant held out a piece of candy for the smaller Homunculus who happily ate it.

"It's so delicious. Mama! One more please!"

A human's shadow stood in front of the happy pair of Homunculi.

"Eh? A familiar human is here. What are you doing here, human?"

The Drill Sergeant looked towards the open casket.

"What did you see, human?"

She revealed her razor-like teeth.

"Answer me, human! What did you see? You didn't happen to see what's inside there, did you?"

"Did you bring this cart so that you could carry away the corpse?"

Sungchul asked in a curt voice. The smaller Homunculus standing beside the Drill Sergeant hopped up towards him and postured threateningly.

"How dare some human speak like this? How dare you talk back? Just because you've become a little stronger, you think…"

Sungchul grabbed the Homunculus by the leg.

"Uh…Hey…?!"

The Homunculus that was lifted into the air looked around in confusion for a moment before it crashed to the floor and turned into a bloody paste.

The Drill Sergeant's eyes grew wide.

"Child! My child!"

The Drill Sergeant's head twisted towards Sungchul like the hands of a windup clock.

"H-how dare you kill my child…I may not have birthed him, but I still can't forgive you; I will never forgive you. Even if you are a Preselected, I can't allow you to walk away after seeing that corpse…This Drill Sergeant will now gladly kill you!"

The Drill Sergeant took up a martial arts stance and gestured towards him.

JAB JAB

After a while, she began spinning her fists like a windmill. It looked like residing in the Summoning Palace for twenty years had given her a chance to learn martial arts.

"I'll turn you into my slave and keep you stuck between the boundary of life and death!"

However, on this day, she had picked a fight with the wrong opponent. Her opponent was the strongest being known to all of humanity. Sungchul wasn't someone that a Homunculus could face even in a million years. There was a horrifying scream that soon filled the Cathedral.

"Who killed Yungjong?"

Sungchul pulled out one of her fingers and crushed the wound with his thumb.

"UWAAAAAAA! Drill Sergeant doesn't know this! Human! Please release me! I can forgive the killer of my…Eeeeng!"

He ripped off the rest of her fingers, and then began to tear away the flesh of her hand.

"I'll ask you again. Who killed Yungjong?"

The Drill Sergeant finally realized that the human standing before her lacked any form of sympathy.

"Ahram…It was Ahram Park! Human! Spare me…Please…"

"Ahram? Someone like Ahram couldn't possibly kill him."

"No! Ahram is now a Werewolf! Human! That red-headed Mage turned Ahram into a Werewolf!"

"So that's how it is."

The whole truth finally revealed itself. This explained how Ahram could kill Yungjong with his meager strength. Werewolves had an abysmally low growth limit, but becoming one was the easiest way to a large boost in physical stats.

They didn't involve a Mage directly and simply gave him the method. What a vile woman. Truly disgusting.

Finally, he extorted the quest list from the Drill Sergeant, and she spat out the bright orb while trembling. He couldn't help but feel disappointed.

It's just the common quests. I guess that means even this bastard only amounts to so much.

"Now…how about letting me go? Human? Sir? Please?"

Sungchul looked directly at the Drill Sergeant and pushed up his hair that covered his face, then spoke icily.

"Do you remember my face?"

"Of course I remember, human! You are the greatest and most merciful among all of the Preselected!"

He sighed and put his hands on his face.

CRACK CRUNCH

After the sickening sounds of muscles and bones being rearranged, a completely different face appeared before the Drill Sergeant.

"You must have seen me twenty-five years ago."

Her memories flashed before her eyes when she heard this until she recalled whose face it was. The Drill Sergeant paled.

"C-could it be…you're the Enemy of the World?! How could that be…you died five years ago…to the Human-Dwarf Coalition…"

"It must be a disappointment that I didn't die. Also, it wasn't they who couldn't kill me, but rather I who chose not to kill them. Remember that."

Sungchul grabbed the sack of candy that filled her pocket and shoved it down her throat. Her razor-like teeth shattered as her esophagus was fully blocked. He dragged her across the Cathedral floor as she struggled painfully then punched her a few times before tossing her deep into the forest.

"…"

He turned away from the burning Cathedral and pulled out a small whistle from his possessions. A small squirrel descended from the sky and sat on his shoulder.

"Kyu Kyu?"

It was Krill Regall's Sky Squirrel.

– I want to know more about Dolorence Winterer.

He tied a small gem as well as the note to the squirrel before patting its head. The Sky Squirrel deftly flew off into the night sky and disappeared from sight.

***

There was a murderous aura surrounding the Plaza, and it was coming from Jungshik's faction. Early in the morning, he performed a funeral service for the comrades who had fallen during the battle against Tam Tam. There were over thirty of his people who had been sacrificed during the Tam Tam match.

No one had expected Jungshik to create this kind of situation since Hakchul's faction had also received some damage, although significantly less when compared with Jungshik's faction; Jungshik himself had led the charge, so it was only reasonable. After holding a funeral service for his men, he confronted Hakchul's faction with his group.

"I have something to say!"

He stabbed his bloody sword in front of Hakchul and growled at the people that were surrounding him.

"Starting today, we will be ruling this Plaza."

It was an explosive announcement. Hakchul was more than a bit surprised, but he still used all of his effort to keep it from showing on his face.

"I don't understand what you're saying? Why are you doing this?"

"You don't know? It's because you guys aren't doing jack around here."

Jungshik had realized that there were too many blatantly useless people in this place. And the situation hadn't changed since the first Rank Match either. Those who fought risked their lives, while the others simply sat back and watched, fully satisfied with just being spectators.

They couldn't even muster up the minimum amount of courage needed to contribute, yet they always had something to say regarding the rewards that others got. And it wasn't uncommon for them to resort to theft either.

"Drag them out."

With Jungshik's gesture, one of his subordinates dragged out two people whose hands were tied.

"Your people had the balls to covet my men's stuff."

Jungshik's subordinate grabbed the back of their heads to reveal their faces. They had been beaten so badly that it was difficult to recognize their original appearance.

Hakchul's face froze in shock, then grew red in anger.

"E-even still, how could you beat someone to this state before hearing them out?"

Hakchul raised his hand. Several lieutenants around him nodded their heads and snuck off to bring back a few dozen people; they surrounded Jungshik's faction through sheer numbers, but Jungshik didn't appear to be scared of them at all.

As though expecting such a development, he smiled widely and pulled out the bloody sword from the ground and spun it around dexterously. It spun wildly before its point aimed straight at Hakchul.

"You wanna have a go?"

The fuse had been lit. The tension grew to the point that a fight could break out at any moment. At this time, a man strode over arrogantly between Hakchul and Jungshik while whistling to himself. Several hundred pairs of eyes were aimed at him.

They first noticed his handsome appearance, tall height, and well-proportioned body, but soon they felt an unusual aura coming from him. It was as if he was the physical manifestation of arrogance itself.

"Let's not fight. Love and peace, you know? Isn't that right, pretty lady[3]?"

Even under the gaze of the crowd, he didn't wilt but rather continued to jest as he approached both of the leaders.

"..."

Sungchul watched the man's movements from a distance. The other Preselected also took notice of the situation with great curiosity.

"Ahram? Why's he acting like that all of a sudden?"

"That's what I'm saying. He was all whiny about losing his staff…maybe he has finally lost his mind."

The man walking fearlessly between Hakchul and Jungshik was none other than Ahram Park.

There were dozens of subordinates standing behind both leaders, but they couldn't think of stopping him since he strode in so naturally and with such blatant arrogance. Ahram eventually arrived in front of both the leaders.

"Why so serious? Hm? Should humans be fighting with each other even after winning the Rank Match?"

Ahram looked at Hakchul and then at Jungshik as he spoke. Jungshik's cold glare pierced him like daggers. Ahram slightly opened his mouth in mock surprise, but that was all. He approached Jungshik, as though appeasing a child, and laid his hand on his shoulder.

"Woah woah, friend. Cool it, okay?"

Jungshik's shoulder moved slightly, and with great speed and accuracy, Ahram's shirt collar became ripped. If his blade had come any higher, it might have taken off Ahram's neck.

"I'm going to chop off your neck next time, so leave before I stop being nice."

Jungshik spoke frostily, and Ahram smiled in response.

"Che, this guy can't control his temper, can he?"

It was a dumbfounding situation. Everyone thought that Ahram was being overly brash. Jungshik was one of the strongest within the Blanche Plaza that everyone recognized. No one knew where this arrogance had come from, other than Sungchul.

He's aching to show off that ill-gotten power of his.

Ahram's body suddenly changed. It twisted, then grew fur along his face and arms. Everyone watched this transformation in shock and horror until a monster which was slightly larger than an adult man stood before them.

A Werewolf.

Like Vampires, Werewolves were one of the racial transformations that could be obtained voluntarily. It instantly granted 30 Strength, Dexterity, and Vitality. And, other than the critical weakness of the abysmal growth rate and inability to learn Magic, it was like being a wolf locked in a pen with the sheep being the recently Summoned.

"Now, let's cool our heads a bit. Mm?"

The transformed Ahram laughed loudly as he strode closer to Jungshik, one step at a time. Jungshik quickly realized that the monster would be difficult for him to deal with, but it was still a moment too late. Ahram had already targeted him and had no plans to show him mercy.

"What? Nothing more to say? Did your temper fizzle after seeing my true form? Huh? Did that rage fix itself suddenly? Huh?"

He took another step forward with an endless stream of taunts. Jungshik's subordinates stepped in between them with their blades drawn.

"Boss, we'll try to slow him down."

"Please escape!"

At that moment, Ahram took a step forward and his claws split the air, cleaving through the two humans' flesh as easily as through tofu. Blood and viscera splattered everywhere, and the two men hit the ground as corpses.

Jungshik's group had suddenly become smaller.

Ahram sneered as he licked his bloody claws.

"Now that I look at you, there's a lot of pretty pictures on your body. Is that a Dragon? Huh? Why won't you talk? Maybe you'll feel like talking after I've drawn a few more pictures on you, isn't that right?"

Ahram no longer held back his savagery, and as he revealed his strength, no one dared to step forward to stop him. Jungshik realized that he couldn't face this opponent and felt his impending death, but suddenly Ahram came to a stop.

"What? Why?"

He began speaking to himself. He looked off into the distance and swung his hairy arms.

"No, what more reason do I need than that of wanting to kill him? I don't know. Fuck, I said I don't know!"

Sungchul suspected the red-headed Mage had intervened behind the scenes.

Jungshik is a Preselected Summoned. I don't know who chose him, but if Dolorence had to step in, then it must be someone important.

However, Ahram wasn't so easily handled.

"It's fine. I'm sure my dad, whose face I've never even seen, will clean up the mess after me."

The beastly Ahram's yellow pupils glowed with frenzy, and he swung his arms towards Jungshik. Jungshik succeeded in stopping the claws but the force of the blow still carried through, throwing him back to roll on the ground.

"Che!"

He glared at the Werewolf rushing over towards him as he bit his lips nervously.

"?!"

His legs wouldn't move. He must've hurt his legs when he landed. The legs could recover quickly, but he would be defenseless until then. He watched helplessly as the Werewolf rushed towards him when a miracle occurred. Wolves appeared on both sides of Ahram. They ran like the wind through the crowd to bite and hold onto Ahram's leg, who was on his way to kill Jungshik.

"Fuck, what's this?"

They were Spirit Wolves. The same wolves that Ahram had shown during the first Rank Match. The two wolves now attacked their original master.

"These mutts!"

Ahram tore apart the wolves with his claws in a frenzy, and the wolves disappeared into the air with a pitiful cry.

"Who did it?!"

He sifted through the crowd of people with frenzied eyes.

"Who the fuck was it? The fucker who used my staff! Huh?!"

Ahram's attention had shifted away from Jungshik, so his subordinates efficiently took his immobilized body away. However, the situation hadn't quite resolved itself. Ahram's temper had simply transferred from Jungshik towards the rest of the Summoned.

"Which one of you fuckers was it?!"

Ahram blindly ran towards the crowd, and the horrified group scattered like leaves in their panic. Several dozen people were trampled and an unlucky few were tenderized into meat by his claws. The Plaza plunged into chaos.

In the middle of that chaos, Ahram began to breathe heavily as he slowly turned back to his original form. His transformation unraveled, only lasting for five minutes. But within those five minutes, he had changed the whole dynamic of power within the Plaza.

Jungshik, who had been rising, was now incapacitated and Hakchul had only been able to watch in horror as the Werewolf attacked his comrades. Ahram reveled in the tense atmosphere and looked around with a sneer. No one could stop him, nor could they criticize him. He had absolute power over this arena. He left with a knowing grin, aware of what he had just obtained.

At this moment, everyone fell silent as they gazed at Ahram, but unlike them, Sungchul was watching a certain woman instead. She was the one who had secretly conjured the two Spirit Wolves, and then nonchalantly hidden the staff within her cloak as she effortlessly blended in with the crowd to run away once the chaos began.

Sungchul recognized that woman's face.

It's her, without a doubt; the same one as before.

She was the one who had been aiming for the bonus monster during the first Rank Match. He'd managed to beat her to it, but she clearly was more capable than she had let on. The woman clearly had a level of intuition and ability that couldn't be learned in the field. Her painstaking effort and countless encounters with death were subtly hinted through her every move. He had come to suspect this only recently, but the critical timing of her discreet Summoning, along with her supernatural evasion, had confirmed his suspicion.

That woman...I've known this from the start, but she's definitely not an ordinary newbie.

He had never seen it directly, but he'd heard some interesting rumors regarding the Summoning Palace. There were those who were blessed by Gods or Lesser Gods with a chance to traverse back through time and start anew at the Summoning Palace. They were known as Regressors, people who returned back in time with their memories intact.

He recalled a forgotten memory because of that woman. There was a need to observe her further, yet there was something even more important that needed to be taken care of first.

A Sky Squirrel deftly landed on his shoulder.

"Kyu Kyu!"

Sungchul petted the squirrel's head then unraveled the pouch attached to its forearm to check its contents.

[Dolorence Winterer. Age 24. Frost Mage. An Airfruit Graduate. A hound for money and power with a rotten core, but her ability is also acknowledged as top-grade by her peers.]

"Ho...An Airfruit graduate. That's quite impressive."

Sungchul moved on to the next part of the letter with an amused expression.

[She ignored everything to observe her Preselected constantly, but there was a brief moment where she took her eyes off of him. That was when he was dragging an innocent woman into the forest.]

A rare smile formed as he finished reading the letter.

***

The opportunity arrived quickly. Ahram, who had already revealed his nature in front of everyone, had a much easier time hunting women now. He didn't even try to flatter them as he had done before; a single phrase filled with mockery was enough.

"Do you want to know the secret to become a Werewolf?"

Sungchul held himself back three times to be entirely sure. As the sun slowly began to set, a message from Krill Regall arrived on his shoulder.

[The time is now.]

It was a short message. At this moment, Krill Regall was watching Dolorence Winterer leave her post while spouting profanities.

"The fucker is at it again. Disgusting fuck. I can't look at this filthy shit anymore. I thought the son of the Captain of the Order of Iron Blood Knights would be more decent, but I couldn't have been more wrong."

When she stepped away, several rookie Summoners followed and tried to lift her mood.

"It is such a struggle. How did you get stuck with a guy like that…"

"There are only two more Rank Matches left! There will be rewards at the end, no matter how degrading it might be."

Honeyed words. No one would dare say that Dolorence was despised as a person who stepped on the weak and groveled to the strong. The reason why people still flattered her, however, was due to her large repertoire of spells. Without proper backers, it wasn't even possible to learn any spells. Buttering up to your superiors was a vital skill for a Mage, which was why it had become their second nature.

"If I were in that Plaza, I would have killed that bastard."

She sipped some alcohol while being surrounded by her lackeys. Not a lot of it, but enough to wet her lips. It was something she often did when stress overtook her. However, she then noticed Krill Regall, who was lingering nearby.

A cold smile formed on her lips as she asked, "Hey, you. What are you still doing here?"

"Oh…? Me?"

Krill froze in shock. Her sudden interest in him was surprising, but it was the uncertainty of what she might do which drove him to fear.

"Yes. You. Did you end up finding your lost Preselected?"

Despair. The only people who knew the truth were Krill and Sanggil; the news hadn't spread to the others yet.

"Yes. He's been found. He was fine."

Dolorence put on a mysterious smile and lightly shook her drink upon hearing the news. The blood red liquid in the wine glass swished around.

"Is that so?" she asked, her eyes sparkling.

"Hm?"

Her snake-like eyes snared Krill in place.

"T-that is…"

She stared at him for a while before taking another glass to her lips, then spat in contempt.

"You know, I am rather friendly towards fresh faces, but I detest the rookies that just categorically suck up to people."

"…"

"If you do not wish to repay a favor, by all means, you are free to do so. I won't stop you. But remember this: although it is possible that when you leave this place, you will never cross paths with high ranking members of the Iron Blood Knights again, but if you plan on living as a Mage you're bound to bump into me more than a few times."

She had taken the scenic route around the bush, but her demands were simple: I have something on you, now bribe me to keep it to myself. Krill could feel a cold sweat trailing down his spine. It was like a frog facing off against a snake.

As he slinked away, he couldn't help but sincerely wish for her demise. The mysterious Preselected's face popped up in his mind.

Krill only knew that the man had a lot of jewels and a strange amount of strength for a Summoned. He could think of many possibilities regarding the reason for it, but he decided not to pry into it any further. There was nothing good to be gained from this line of thinking. However, that man's actions still bothered him.

Why did that man ask for information about Dolorence…Could it be he's trying to screw with her? No way.

Krill found himself enraptured by unfathomable expectations as he stared at the scarlet moon hanging high up in the sky.

"…"

Another person was looking up at the same sky; a man with glistening eyes beneath his disheveled hair. Sungchul solemnly observed the atrocity happening below him. Ahram the Werewolf had finished eating the woman he had just fucked. Sungchul passively watched the woman's quivering eyes lose their focus and then let out a deep sigh. He jumped down towards this feral degenerate that had cut away his final link to his humanity.

"Ahram Park."

The small, but clear voice stirred the forest's melancholy. The Werewolf, with a piece of chewed flesh still in his mouth, turned around. A look of surprise flashed across his blood-smeared face.

"Who is it?"

Ahram threw away the corpse and stood up. The ravaged corpse fell between Sungchul and him. A muscular two-and-a-half meter tall creature stood before Sungchul.

"I was looking for you. Is this what they mean when they say, 'kill two birds with one stone'?"

Sungchul was unfazed by the aggressive questioning. Rather, it only caused him to raise his gaze slowly and look directly into the eyes of the Werewolf. Ahram, who had felt all-powerful until now, felt his breath catching and his legs buckling. His body couldn't move; it was as though he had been paralyzed.

W-what's wrong with my body?

At first, he thought that it might have been a side effect from his transformation into a Werewolf, but as time passed, he began to realize the actual cause; it was out of pure terror. The threat of danger coming from looking into Sungchul's eyes made his instincts scream out by impulse.

"Y-you bitch!"

Ahram tried to deny the terror reverberating within him and jumped towards Sungchul, but then he found himself suddenly spinning out of control. He stopped only after being embedded into the ground. The man that had turned his world upside down crushed something within his hand.

I-I lost? How did this happen…?! That red-head told me that being a Werewolf would make me the strongest in the Plaza…

Dolorence's promise would have been the truth, if not for a certain hidden master hiding his strength.

"…"

Sungchul briefly looked around before breaking off a thick branch that was within his reach. It would serve as a decent switch. Ahram realized what he was doing, but it was already too late.

WHAM! WHAM! WHAM! WHAM!

Continuous blows fell on the Werewolf's skin as if Sungchul were beating out dust from a rug. Ahram's hide began splitting as his blood and flesh splattered everywhere. He shrieked in pain, desperately wishing for someone to save him.

Red-head! Save me! Save me! Fuck it! Save me!

However, his guardian was outside her room, surrounded by her "yes-men," busy sipping alcohol.

As the senseless beating ended, Ahram finally returned to his human form. His body was covered with bloody bruises which triggered an emergency alarm, to which his guardian didn't respond. His eyes, covered with tears and snot, reflected the image of the man who was holding a large club. He finally came to understand the reality of the situation, and pitifully bowed his head to try and beg for his life.

"P-please…Mercy…"

[Drop]

Sungchul let the stick fall, and a small bit of hope blossomed inside of Ahram. However, his hopes were thoroughly crushed by Sungchul's boots.

STOMP! STOMP! STOMP!

Sungchul had simply switched from beating to trampling. He deliberately focused on stomping on the prone man's face, breaking all of Ahram's teeth.

"Uwuuugh!"

Ahram could no longer stand the pain and hugged the ground, raising his hips into the air. Sungchul stared at him in silence.

After he was given a brief respite, Ahram began to beg for his life once again.

"P-please…I'll do anything, please spare my life."

To which Sungchul pointed towards the forest. There lay the corpse of the woman whom Ahram had just killed. By unnerving coincidence, her unfocused eyes were pointing towards Ahram.

"What did you do when that woman begged for her life?"

"T-that's…!"

Sungchul slowly drew closer, and Ahram screamed as an unspeakable horror filled him.

"Get away from me! Y-you…if you touch me…you'll be killed!"

"Me? Killed?"

Sungchul grinned.

"D-do you know who my father is? He's the Captain of the Iron Blood Knights. The Iron Blood Knights' Captain!"

"The Captain of the Iron Blood Knights?"

"T-that's right! I don't really know him, but in this world, I've heard that he's very powerful…That's right, a strong backer! A backer! You won't be able to get away with killing me!"

"Is that so? How did you become his son if you had just been Summoned into this world?"

"I-I don't know. Fuck…Some Returnee or something like that came to me one day and told me! Told me that I was that guy's son! He said if I were to cross over into the Other World, I'd have money, fame, and power…That I'd get everything I couldn't on Earth!"

"A Returnee…"

It wasn't something that normally interested him, but his curiosity was satisfied. He finally knew how someone like Ahram had become a Preselected.

They used a Returnee. I suppose someone like Sungtek might know several individuals who have qualified to become a Returnee. But even if the world is facing the end, how could he think of bringing a fucker like this here?

The Captain of the Iron Blood Knights, Sungtek Jo, had three children in Other World, however like all of the other children, they had died before reaching the age of ten. It was probably desperation which drove him to seek out Ahram, a man he wasn't even sure was really his son, and bring him to the Other World. But his son turned out to be substandard to an extreme.

Sungchul lifted the stick once more.

"P-please…! Are you doing this because of Yungjong? That wasn't my fault. He was the first…"

Ahram crawled away pitifully.

" … "

Sungchul suddenly grabbed some vines from nearby and strung Ahram upside down from his feet.

"I'll tell you one thing. This is Other World. It isn't always true, but it is a world where strength is the law. In a place like this, it's problematic if you get cocky no matter how strong you get. Why? That's because there might always be at least one or two people who are stronger than you."

"I-I understand…I get what you're saying. I'm repenting, I'm serious!"

"And one more thing. There is no such thing as a second chance or mercy in this world. One mistake and you're done."

The stick rose into the air and struck Ahram's jaw before he could even utter a scream.

"Beasts will soon be attracted by the scent of your blood. Be thankful that the law of the jungle also accepts human garbage like you."

Sungchul dropped the stick and whispered quietly.

"Welcome to Other World."

As soon as the words left his lips, smaller monsters began to appear within the forest. They licked their lips at the sight of fresh blood pouring out of Ahram. He struggled desperately in his final throes, but his fate had already been sealed.

"…"

Sungchul quietly headed out of the forest, but before he could get far, a vague apparition appeared before him, leaving him slightly surprised.

It's rare that I fail to detect something.

A woman appeared amidst the darkness. It was a woman covering her face with a hood and holding a familiar staff in her hands. Once Sungchul stopped moving and silently acknowledged her presence, she removed her hood to reveal her face. A glint flashed across his eyes when he recognized the face.

This woman.

They had already met several times. They had competed for the bonus monster, and she had stopped Ahram as he was busy rampaging. This unknown woman spun around her Spirit Wolf Staff and opened her mouth.

"I was going to take care of him, but looks like someone beat me to it."

"…"

Sungchul stared at the silently approaching woman.

"You can't be just another ordinary newbie since you beat a Werewolf effortlessly."

Sungchul looked as though he was simply listening to her speak, but he was actually using his heightened abilities to uncover her identity. There wasn't anything that stood out for him. Even the Eye of Truth, one of his Soul Contracts, couldn't reveal anything special about her. She was a newbie Summoned that appeared to be normal, yet she wasn't so. His previous suspicions were only growing stronger.

She must be a Regressor.

The woman in question sighed.

"Such a solemn person. Or perhaps you have a bad impression of me."

"What is your business?"

Sungchul finally broke the silence and spoke. A brief look of surprise passed over the woman's face after he did, but lasted only briefly before she continued to speak, her eyes firmly fixed onto him.

"I'll be brief, so as to avoid any misunderstandings. I saw you kill that perverted bastard and thought that you weren't such a bad person, I'm also guessing that you might not be an average Summoned either."

Her voice was brief, but intelligent. Her gaze didn't falter during the conversation, and it sounded fluid, as though she was reading from a script.

"You also don't seem to be average"

"Correct. I won't tell you anything. But I also won't expect any information from you."

The mystery woman held out her hand towards him. It was a woman's hand that was just beginning to harden with calluses.

"I am Ahmuge. You must have seen my name on the Record Stone."

The figure that had dominated first place during the Rank Matches beyond the Preselected; The individual in question was unexpectedly a slim woman.

"I have reasons why I have to leave the Summoning Palace with a good score, but it will also be difficult for me to get the special rewards by myself. So, I also want another skilled person to work with me. Not some privileged trash, but someone with real ability."

"Is that why you saved Jungshik?"

Ahmuge smiled at his pointed question.

"He's a talented person. And he also has good leadership ability."

"Why did you want to kill Ahram then? He's a Werewolf; he would have been a strong addition to your combat strength."

She firmly shook her head.

"That man is incapable of benefiting a group. There might be something to be gained from him, but far more to lose. If you didn't act, I would have killed him."

Hearing these words, Sungchul smiled. They came to the same conclusion. Sungchul killed Ahram not only due to his despicable acts but also because he was proving to be nothing but an obstacle to achieving his goals. Not once had Sungchul strayed or forgotten his objective since arriving at the Summoning Palace.

"Okay. I'll cooperate, but I have a condition," Sungchul replied.

"Please don't pick anything too strange," said Ahmuge with a smile.

"Don't worry. Mine doesn't even stand. Instead, I wish to get information about hidden quests. Especially ones that raise Magic power."

"Magic power…Okay. I can teach you one."

Ahmuge held out her hand once again and grabbed his.

"What is your name?"

"It's Sungchul Kim."

"Sungchul Kim…?!"

Her voice and face took a sudden change.

"Is there a problem?"

She stared into his face directly before shaking her head.

"No, nothing in particular."

"Good, then let's get out of here. There will be some guests arriving here soon."

As the beasts that crawled out of the forest began their feast upon Ahram's upside down corpse which hung from a tree, Sungchul and Ahmuge quietly left the scene of the crime. Dolorence arrived at the scene only after a considerable amount of time had passed. After massacring the beasts with her Magic, she stood before Ahram's mangled corpse with a distorted expression.

"T-this...fucking...!"

She began to scream like a half-crazed banshee while pulling at her hair. The various creatures of the forest couldn't approach the frenzied aura of a berserk Mage. Some time passed before she once again stared at Ahram's cold corpse. There was one place that had remained somewhat intact; his face.

Dolores who noticed this fact felt her brain ticking away like clockwork as an evil plan began to form in her head.

"I can't let it end like this. Not after all I've done to get to this position. After all the groveling I've had to endure..."

An unsettling, crazed grin took form upon her lips.

It was an unremarkable morning. The Summoned greeted another day as they ate their meals or trained as the sun seen rising above the horizon quickly dissipated the fog.

Sungchul worked on common quests to raise his Magic power and intuition, and then returned to the Preselected's camp to have a meal. However, there was something unusual going on within the camp.

"Why is that guy like that?"

"Don't get close...his condition doesn't look so good."

Several Preselected were either fearful or annoyed while staring at a certain someone from a distance.

Sungchul walked through the crowd to see who the person was.

"..."

A slight wrinkle formed upon his forehead.

"Uuuhhhh…"

It was Ahram's corpse.

"Uuuuhhh…!!"

His corpse, with a hood covering everything except his face, sat while shaking from side-to-side like a crazed man.

They turned him into this brain-dead doll with necromancy. And an incredibly potent Preservation Magic was used to stop his decay.

He felt a bad premonition, and a bad feeling had an uncanny way of being right.

Krill Regall urgently sent a letter with the following message.

[Dolorence Winterer has finally lost it! She's planning to kill everyone in Blanche Plaza!]

Chapter 8 – Inextinguishable Fire

"You. Come help me."

Krill hadn't imagined that the embers would reach him. The fact that both of them had graduated from the same Magic Academy and committed the same crime drew Dolorence to approach him. He had welcomed it at first, but she had completely ignored his requests for help while still blatantly asking him for favors when she was in a difficult situation herself.

However, until she made a mistake and failed, Krill had no other choice. His only escape was if he reported Ahram's death to Sanggil. But Dolorence had dispatched several Mages in the area between the Observation Tower and where Sanggil resided to ensure her safety; acting too conspicuously would only result in his death. But…it wasn't like there were no other ways at all.

Once a week, Sanggil liked to check in on the Observation Tower to receive his report before each Rank Match. He then often "requested" bribes from Krill as he received his report, but this now proved to be the best opportunity for Krill. The only problem was that the next Rank Match was in four days. And, until then, he could not disobey Dolorence.

"You'll come to the Azure Plaza with me."

He really had no choice. No one knew what would happen if you annoyed her while she was cornered. Krill followed her through the Slave Hunter-only passage to the Azure Plaza. Dolorence put on a hood and shoved a dark crimson blood vial into his hand.

"Keep this. It's precious so you shouldn't spill any of it."

"W-what is this? Sunbae[4]."

"What do you think it is? It's awakened Lycan blood of course. It contains the ability to change an average person into a Werewolf when it's activated."

"Is that so…?"

156

"They don't teach you this stuff at school. Remember it well. I'll teach you the method to extract Lycan blood later when I have time."

Was this because she needed him? The previously cold and distant Dolorence felt like a completely different person as she replied happily. Krill felt nauseous enough to vomit on sight, but another thought also came to his mind as well. The thirst for knowledge, which was something that all Mages possessed, drove the desire in him to obtain the information possessed by a mid-rank Mage. But then he recalled all the grievances buried in his heart and managed to calm himself.

Dolorence discreetly approached a nameless Summoned within the Azure Plaza. She passed on the blood vial then put him under hypnosis.

"On the day of the Rank Match, you and your friends will kill everyone in Blanche Plaza. I'll show you the people you have to target first."

Krill caught on to her scheme while peeking at her from the side.

She wants to avoid personal responsibility by causing an artificial "Act of God," a situation where all the Preselected were wiped out. The responsibility would then naturally fall onto Sanggil or someone of a higher rank, and it would be considered a failure to coordinate within the Summoning Palace.

He had to admit; she was very brazen in her actions and abilities. He began to think that there might be much to learn from this woman if he were to shadow her.

Krill met a familiar face upon returning to the Observation Tower. It was the Slave Hunter with a missing arm. The Slave Hunter had seen Dolorence with Krill and walked up to him.

"Are you with that woman?"

Krill wanted to ignore him, but it was difficult as he had helped him in a time of need.

"It seems that way."

"There's nothin' more dangerous than a woman who puts average folks like us through ordeals."

He let out a lonely laugh as he disappeared into the darkness. And Krill's mood plummeted even further.

—

[Creation of six Werewolves in group D of Azure Plaza. Werewolves are expected to target the Preselected.]

The information brought by the Sky Squirrel threw Sungchul's thoughts into chaos. A single Werewolf had stirred up the Blanche Plaza so much that it was obvious what would happen if there were six of them. It would be a one-sided slaughter.

"Mmm…"

He had fought in countless battles, but he didn't have any clever plans for solving this situation. It would have been different if he had a month, but with only four days to prepare, it would be impossible to strengthen the Summoned in time.

It was possible to "incidentally" kill one Werewolf, but all his efforts would be wasted if he had to kill all six. He needed a conclusive solution to this problem. Thinking on this, his mind squeezed out a single person.

There was that.

Sungchul brought out a large book that had been shut away in his Soul Storage. It was the talking book, Bertelgia. She wasn't very reliable, but countless inspirations of the Alchemist Eckheart were recorded within her. There might be something inside of her that would be able to get him out of this situation.

"Why did you call me?"

She spoke with a yawn. It bothered him that a book would even bother yawning, but Sungchul didn't voice out his thoughts and made his request with a solemn voice instead.

"The next Rank Match turns out to have six Werewolves. I need Alchemic aid for dealing with the Werewolves with my current forces."

"Werewolves? Someone that can beat daddy's golems is asking me for help with something weak like Werewolves?"

Bertelgia acted indignantly and closed herself before falling to the floor.

"For the sake of a greater objective, I have to hide my strength. I need something that an average Summoned can use to kill the Werewolves."

"Mmm. So, you had circumstances like that, did you?"

"Can you do it?"

"Of course. I'm Bertelgia. I am the culmination of Alchemy. It might not be bad to show off a bit of my ability given this opportunity."

Bertelgia, with her pages fluttering, flew up into the air then circled around Sungchul. She let out a soft shout before revealing one of her pages to him.

[Inextinguishable Fire]

"What is this?"

Sungchul asked.

"As the name says, it's an inextinguishable fire. It'll only grow stronger with water, and it'll be effective against Werewolves who are weak against fire. Best of all, there are plenty of ingredients that can be found around this area, and it's also easy to make."

"Hoh."

Even though he thought the book talked a bit too much, she had still very efficiently taken care of his requests.

He scanned at the listed ingredients for Inextinguishable Fire: Golden Toadstool, Alchemic Charcoal, and three large Blood Pudding oozes. Other than the Alchemic Charcoal which had to be synthesized, the other ingredients could all be acquired through foraging or hunting. It also required an oven, and a mortar and pestle, but that wasn't an issue.

"You still have daddy's Portable Alchemic Cauldron, right? You didn't throw it away, right?"

"I didn't toss it."

"Good. Let's look for Golden Toadstools first. You can find them near the cliff edge."

159

Bertelgia fluttered excitedly as she flew ahead, but Sungchul grabbed her from behind and closed her.

"Hey, what are you doing? I was finally going to enjoy some scenery!"

As Bertelgia struggled with all her might, he began to run. He moved at such an unimaginable speed that even Bertelgia, who had been shouting, became speechless.

"W-who are you, really? What did you eat to get so fast?"

While she watched dumbstruck, he had already arrived at the bottom of a cliff.

"Where is the Golden Toadstool?"

"Mm...such a strange person. I got stuck with a really weird person. What am I supposed to..."

"I asked where the Golden Toadstool was."

"Such a boring and rude person. I really don't have any luck at all."

"Golden..."

"Okay! I'll find it for you! It's over here."

Bertelgia flew up to the edge and hovered over a small cluster of rocks sticking out from the cliff.

"This. This is a Golden Toadstool."

"Mmm? That is a Golden Toadstool? It looks like a bunch of stones to me."

"Try harvesting it."

Sungchul leaped up to the cliff and grabbed the Golden Toadstool.

Mm. This is not a rock.

Rather than a rock, it was much closer to a moss or a mushroom. Beneath the rock-like exterior, there were lots of golden spores and powder. It would be easy to mistake this for actual gold at first glance. He felt amazed as he put his nose close to smell it. An information window then appeared in front of Sungchul.

[Golden Toadstool]

Level: 2

Grade: D

Attribute: Wood

Effect: Ingredient

Note: It is named as an ore, but in reality, it is a mushroom. It catches fire easily and creates a strong blaze, so it is often used by dwarves as fuel. It forms a fungal colony, and its quality grows based on the size of the colony.

"Hoh."

Amazement appeared in Sungchul's eyes. It was fascinating. How long had it been since he felt the joy of learning something new?

"Next is Blood Pudding. Their ooze doesn't light on fire easily, but once it does, it won't extinguish easily either! This is the alpha and omega of the inextinguishable flame!"

Bertelgia hurried him to the next step. He put the Golden Toadstool into his pocket and carried her to the next location. It wasn't difficult to find Blood Puddings. Once blood was let out from an animal's corpse in an abandoned cave, they came like hyenas.

"Be careful. Blood Puddings are slime-type creatures, so they are highly resistant to physical damage. You might be strong, but it'll get dangerous if they surround..."

She couldn't quite finish her sentence because a Blood Pudding popped and splattered everywhere.

"W-what...you...who are you!"

Bertelgia froze in mid-air. Sungchul ignored her and pulled out a sack, gathering the Blood Pudding ooze inside.

"How do I make Alchemic Charcoal?"

"W-who are you...really..."

161

She must have been really shaken this time, and her shock wasn't so surprising either. It was known to be physically impossible to kill a slime-type creature with just a fist.

What kind of person is this? What is his identity?!

She finally realized that her master was truly not a normal person, and also without any form of patience.

"Alchemic..."

"Okay! I'll tell you!"

The ingredients were easily found in the area. All it took was a mixture of leaves and timber that could be synthesized into Alchemic Charcoal. It took quite some time, but when the Alchemic Charcoal was completed, he pulled out Eckheart's Portable Alchemic Cauldron from his Soul Storage.

The cauldron was small enough to fit in the palm of his hands, but when the seal was released, with a majestic bronze flash, a decent looking Alchemic cauldron appeared.

"Now, everything is ready. All we have to do now is to create it."

Sungchul nodded, and then stood in front of the cauldron. The fire, fueled by the Alchemic Charcoal and Golden Toadstool, was burning into quite a blaze.

***

BOOM!

A small explosion occurred inside the cauldron. Sungchul who breathed in the musky smoke then read the message which appeared before him with a blank look.

[Synthesis Failed!]

"Fuck!"

This was already his third attempt. His gaze naturally moved over to Bertelgia who was floating near the cauldron.

"Bertelgia."

"Hm?"

"How did this happen?"

"What do you mean, 'how did this happen?'"

She replied obtusely and opened up one of her pages before Sungchul.

"You're failing because you didn't read the book properly and only glanced over the ingredients before you started."

"..."

He didn't have anything to say because she was speaking the truth.

"Now, slowly read the page again. Starting from how much of each ingredient to add and followed by reading the instructions. Don't just eyeball it."

"I didn't eyeball it..."

Sungchul had pride in his status as a high-class chef. He calmed his heart, and then looked over the pages displayed by Bertelgia more seriously. His gaze gained a more solemn light.

Now that I've reread it, it does read like a cookbook.

Other than the final product, Cooking and Alchemy were mostly a similar process.

Prepare each of the ingredients properly and use exact amounts, work meticulously to focus on creating the finished product. Sungchul entirely focused all of his attention.

Bertelgia, seeing his changed attitude, muttered a few words.

"Well, maybe he has some talent."

After some time had passed, a blue light softly began to gather around the cauldron and the ingredients within turned into a single product. It had become a dark and congealed liquid.

[Synthesis Complete!]

Sungchul released a breath of relief as he was finally rewarded after having put in so much effort.

[Inextinguishable Fire]

Level: 2

Grade: D

Attribute: Fire

Type: Ingredient / Consumable

Effect: Flammable substance. Water excites the flames.

This time, it had been properly created. Sungchul gathered some dry branches and poured Inextinguishable Fire upon them.

"You're not trying to test it, are you?"

He nodded at Bertelgia's question.

"Hmm. It won't be easy to manage the flames. Dig a pit before setting it on fire. If you're unlucky, you might just burn down the whole forest."

Despite her warning, he took one of the Alchemic Charcoals that were burning underneath the cauldron with his hands and then tossed it on top of a pile of wood.

WHOOSH!

Fueled by the Inextinguishable Fire, the small ember burned fiercely.

It is a very controlled burn. I think this has some practical use.

He felt as if the fog blocking his path was beginning to lift. There were a lot of problems still left to solve, but discovering a possible solution let Sungchul feel much better about the whole situation.

"Hey? What are you going to do with that?"

The Inextinguishable Fire burned fiercely. At the rate it was going, it looked as though it would soon burn down the entire mountain.

"…"

Sungchul stood in front of the flickering flames and looked at it with passive eyes.

"What are you doing now?"

He suddenly punched towards the fire. An unbelievable amount of force was carried by the punch, which caused the flames to flicker weakly.

"Hiiii…"

Between Bertelgia's fearful gasps, he threw out a couple more punches and uneventfully extinguished the Inextinguishable Fire; then, after the fire went out, he grabbed Bertelgia.

"W-what are you doing?"

Bertelgia asked as she fluttered in panic.

"I'm finished, so I'm packing everything up."

"Finished? What do you mean finished? I still have as much knowledge as there is sand on the beach! Can't you just leave me be? The storage is dark and humid. I don't like it."

"You stand out too much."

"What if I just stay inconspicuous?"

"You're too big, and you fly."

"How dare you talk about a woman's size, so cruel."

"Well, Miss. Would you mind going into the storage now?"

"I-I can become smaller! I don't have to fly either."

She shone brightly and then became palm-sized as if to prove her words.

"Good?"

Her pitch grew higher relative to her reduced size.

Sungchul looked at the reduced Bertelgia for a bit before nodding.

"That size seems fine."

He put her inside the military jacket that he was wearing. She was a perfect fit for the pocket, as though she was made it. And as soon as Bertelgia was placed in the pocket she poked her head out. She spoke out quickly after seeing Sungchul glance over at her.

"I want to see some scenery."

He had no reason to reject her, so he redirected his attention elsewhere.

I made the weapon, but now I need to find a way to pour it onto the Werewolves.

Werewolves couldn't use Magic, but they did have a bestial instinct. It was so advanced that they could even dodge arrows coming from four different directions. They also had significantly higher dexterity than the average person, so it would be difficult to land even a drop of this liquid onto them with a half-baked plan.

"What are you thinking so deeply about?"

Bertelgia, who had been quiet in the pocket, popped a question.

"I'm trying to think of how to get the Inextinguishable Fire onto the Werewolves."

"Daddy often used a Dragon-headed tube and sprayed it like it was breathing fire, or he tossed out some pottery with a trigger."

"But that's too slow. They wouldn't fall for something like that unless they're stupid."

"It's just a matter of making them fall for it then."

After listening to her thoughts, an idea flickered in Sungchul's head. Krill's message and Ahram's living corpse. Both events seemed to be unrelated, but their timing was too opportune to call them a coincidence.

So that's it. Dolorence Winterer is actually trying to eliminate the Preselected. Among them, Ahram must be her number one target.

The Werewolves would have to target Ahram. They would also have to tear apart the corpse completely so that it was unrecognizable. That was the only way Dolorence would escape any fault. Sungchul decided to target these facts in his plan.

—

"Ey, Mr. Whatchurname. What do you have for me this time?"

Jungshik looked deflated from the incident with Ahram, but he was still a figure who had a large influence within the Blanche Plaza. The overflowing confidence and sharp aura, however, had withered. He moved his camp to the corner farthest away from the Preselected, and the number of guards also seemed to have increased.

"I have to talk to you about the next Rank Match."

Sungchul briefly summarized what was going to occur for the next Rank Match. It would be the Death Match rule with human vs. human combat, and the score would be based on the number of kills, etc. He omitted the part about Werewolves making their appearance in the match, though.

"Hoh. News sure travels fast. How did you get this information?"

"I can't tell you that, but if you cooperate with me, I'm more than willing to share it with you each time."

"Cooperate…"

A mischievous smile formed on Jungshik's lips.

"Well, let's leave it at that, then. What did you want from me?"

Sungchul requested to organize Jungshik's forces during the Rank Match. He wanted Jungshik's people to stay behind and stay in a safe place until the signal.

"Hoh. You're concerned about us? Or maybe you're more concerned about how many points we would earn?"

"If you only care about the points, you're welcome to ignore what I have to say."

Sungchul left Jungshik with these words. He knew it would be pointless to waste more words arguing after already having said everything that needed to be said. He was also confident that Jungshik would listen to him. Jungshik had already gained from his previous advice, and he was feeling cautious after his recent losses. Jungshik was also cleverer than he looked. Every loss from Jungshik's faction risked Hakchul regaining his control over the Plaza.

I think we can prevent major losses on our side from the Werewolves with this.

He had prepared a relatively sharp blade. All he had to do now was to prepare a shield to defend against the enemy's blade, which was several times sharper than his. Sungchul observed Ahram who was sitting outside of the training center and looking out with a blank stare.

"Uuu…Uuu…!!"

The hooded Ahram clacked his teeth while swinging his body from side to side like a roly-poly. Everyone continued to avoid him as he looked to be unwell and was continuously making unsettling noises. Sungchul made his way to the Preselected faction across from Ahram and sought out Yuhoon.

"You wanted to speak with me?"

He pretended to be polite, but his face and attitude clearly displayed that he didn't want to deal with Sungchul. Sungchul couldn't say when it had started, but Yuhoon had gotten a bad impression of him.

Sungchul realized this after the second Rank Match had finished. He had gathered up the ostracized Preselected and gotten high scores. Inversely, the other Preselected who had the Holy Water had now become undesirables. The leadership of the two had naturally been compared, which eventually got to Yuhoon.

"I'll be brief because I need to start training."

Sungchul acted naturally as if none of these insignificant squabbles bothered him. He spoke his prepared words calmly.

"I came to share some hot information, fresh from my Mage."

"What information is that?"

Yuhoon had been cautious around Sungchul, but hearing that it was from a Mage relaxed his guard. Sungchul looked around and spoke in a hushed voice.

"It is not confirmed, but I've heard that in the next match there will be people who're targeting us specifically among the opposition."

"Targeting us?"

"It looks like they are enemies of the people taking care of us. The Mage said that the people taking care of us would take a big hit if the opposition kills us. In the end, it's all rumors, but…"

"So what do you want?"

"I want us, the Preselected, to organize ourselves at the rear."

The enemies weren't just the Werewolves. There were as many Summoned enemies as there were people within the Blanche Plaza. It was also convenient to separate the average Summoned from the Werewolves to enact his plan. This was why he had approached Yuhoon to talk about how they would dispatch, but Yuhoon only looked at him coldly.

"I think that might be difficult."

Yuhoon was driven by his opportunistic nature and other petty emotions like envy. He stared without blinking at Sungchul. And with a mocking, chipper voice, he said,

"I have to achieve a good score during this Rank Match no matter what. You might be able to take it easy after getting the top score in the last match, but my friends standing behind me and I don't have that luxury. We have to make it up this match. My comrades and I will be standing on the front lines."

"Is that so? You might die."

"Is that a threat?"

Yuhoon frowned and bared his teeth. It was an intimidating face without a trace of the amiability he always carried. Sungchul had assessed him accurately during their first encounter.

Is this Yuhoon's real face? Truly pitiful. Staking so much pride on such a small amount of authority.

Sungchul decided there was no more cooperation to be gained from Yuhoon, then spoke again.

"Well…if you insist, then I won't press you anymore. I can only ask the others directly."

"I wonder how many people will listen to you."

"At the very least, I'll be taking Ahram with me."

Upon hearing his last words, Yuhoon finally let loose his guard and broke out in laughter.

"Take him. If you can, that is."

Sungchul smiled widely and headed over towards Ahram.

"Hey, Ahram! Let's go!"

Ahram, who had been swinging back and forth, turned and bared his teeth at Sungchul when he approached.

"KAAAAA!"

Between his clothing, the grotesque arm of a Werewolf began to appear. His self-defense mechanism kicked in. It was the only instinct Dolores installed into the corpse of Ahram. The arm could easily rip apart an average Summoned, but its opponent was Sungchul.

"Let's go, boy! It's time for your meds!"

Sungchul relaxedly supported Ahram and began walking forward. Strangers might have thought that it was just someone supporting a sick person. Yuhoon and the other Preselected whispered quietly, wondering since when have the two of them gotten so close with one another. No one knew the truth.

"..."

A living corpse had no need for organs; Sungchul examined Ahram, whose empty internal cavity had been filled with Inextinguishable Fire. Satisfied, he rewrapped Ahram's decaying body with a cloak and left.

"Uuuu..."

Ahram, finding himself alone again, once more began to swing his body from side to side.

The preparations had been completed.

***

[Third Rank Match will begin.]

[Rule: Death Match]

[Kill the Summoned from the other Plazas.]

[There is no good or evil here, only life and death. Do not hesitate to cut down your enemies; there is no place here for people who cannot take another's life.]

People from the other Plazas could be seen as the door in the center of the Palace opened. There were approximately seven hundred people. They were ordinary people no different from those from the Blanche Plaza. This might be one of the reasons people referred to Death Match as one of the worst rulesets. It was physically challenging to cut down a monster, but only by becoming a monster could one cut down another person. A message appeared in front of the hesitant Summoned.

[There will be a penalty game for anyone who hasn't scored a single kill until the end, this penalty game has a survival rate of 2.4%. You have been warned.]

[Furthermore, there will also be a reward honoring the one with the highest score, so give it your all.]

It was a cruel set of rewards and punishments. There was no better way to dominate a large group of people than the carrot-and-stick approach.

The Summoned already understood the way of the Palace. There would be rewards and progress waiting for those who overcame danger, but those who cowered would forever be left behind to continue their bare existence until eventually dying. There were many Summoned who were prepared to make up for their past mistakes and bet it all on this match. It was for this purpose that nearly half of the Summoned stood along the front of the Plaza. Most of them were Hakchul and his people.

"It is heartbreaking, but we must get a good score in this match to recover our strength."

Hakchul personally stood in the frontlines and made his speech with an awkward voice. Most of the people were listening halfheartedly.

Yuhoon's group of Preselected also stood at the frontlines and prepared for the battle.

"Don't be nervous. There aren't many out there that are stronger than us. And in case we come across one, we can always run or try to outnumber them. Above all else, remember this: whether you kill someone strong or weak, they are only worth one point."

Yuhoon put forth some common sense in a comforting voice. Most of the Preselected didn't really respond to his speech, but they all resolved to score well in this match in one way or another.

Kill those who are weaker than us.

The threshold for maximum rewards for the Death Match was set at five points. The sword-wielding Preselected gripped their weapons tighter.

On the other hand, Jungshik's faction stood far to the rear, away from the battle.

"There is no need to rush. Those trash at the front won't be able to get much anyways. They'll just be our meat shields. We'll go in when the meat shields have tired themselves out."

There was great unrest in his heart despite his confident words.

Will it really turn out the way he said it would?

With wary eyes, Jungshik observed Sungchul who was standing at the rear with him. Sungchul stood together with a few people; they were surrounding Ahram who clearly looked unwell. He couldn't figure out what Sungchul was up to, but they were both situated in the rear. This meant Sungchul was confident in his suggestion and was taking the same risk he was. Jungshik comforted himself with these words while waiting for the Rank Match to begin.

"…"

Sungchul stared off into the sky with an expressionless face. It was a clear day, and not a single cloud could be seen in the sky. The sun burned brightly, forming short but dark shadows. The soft breeze from the mountains felt cool and pleasant.

"Ah…I feel so nervous. Where could Yungjong have gone?"

Sunghae, caught in past traumas, began to mutter to herself. She had chosen to stand with Sungchul rather than with Yuhoon. It wasn't out of some "woman's intuition," but rather, out of a forced obligation. It was well known that her staff was once Sungchul's, and they had also acted together before. There were many within the Preselected who held the same assumptions Ahram once had:

that she was a pathetic woman who had slept with Sungchul to get his staff.

The two other men that were standing with Sungchul, Jungshik Park and Woojung Kim, had joined Sungchul out of their own free will. They had gotten acquainted because they both coincidentally were used car salesman and both disliked Yuhoon. They also benefited from Sungchul previously, and thus they had chosen to stick with him. However, they were put off by the sight of Ahram's cloaked body that was swinging in front of them.

"Pro Kim, you sure that guy will be alright like that?"

For reasons unknown, the used car salesman duo had decided to call him Pro Kim.

"Doesn't matter."

Sungchul spoke bluntly and looked over the entire Plaza with indifferent eyes. He couldn't find the person that he was looking for. Ahmuge the suspected Regressor; they had shaken hands with the idea of cooperating later, but she had concealed herself right before the Rank Match had started.

Intriguing. There is someone that can hide even from my eyes.

Some people were known to have "thin shadows." This meant that they had such a small presence that they were often overlooked. Ahmuge was also one of them, but in her case, it was more like her shadow didn't exist at all. She'd not only managed to evade his supernaturally honed senses, but also managed to slip beneath his guard and surprise him.

Could she have some hidden ability?

Although it was commonly known that Regressors normally return with the memories of their previous lives, there might also be some secrets which Sungchul was still unaware of. This was especially so in Other World, which was filled with both mystery and wonder.

The sound of a Homunculus blowing a horn sounded from a distance. Sungchul immediately returned to his group and shared some equipment with his comrades.

"Jungshik Park, I'll give you this shield. Protect Ahram with it."

Jungshik Park had a small stature, but he had spunk. His Strength and Vitality were among the highest in the group. But he had a trauma related to corpses, and so he hadn't been able to display his true strength in the first Rank Match. Other than his nasty habit of smelling his butt hole with his finger, he was actually quite a good addition to his forces.

When he received the Light Shield of Vitality, he scratched beneath his butt and tilted his head.

"Protect that guy? That guy, he seems a bit off his rockers, but isn't he still the strongest one here?"

"I think he's afflicted with some kind of side-effect from the Werewolf transformation. It will be enough to protect him just until he can transform. I'll give you the signal. You just have to protect him until then."

"I got it. I suppose Pro Kim knows best."

Jungshik Park nodded his head and looked at Ahram with a difficult expression.

Next, Sungchul handed Woojung the Soldier's Crossbow.

"The same to you too. Protect Ahram with this."

Contrary to Jungshik Park, Woojung had a large stature and a threatening aura, but his personality was introverted, and he didn't have the confidence for close-quarter combat. He had almost died of anxiety during the Tam Tam match. However, he happened to have been a Special Forces sniper during his military years and had no problem doing the attack one-sidedly. He would be more than able to pull his weight during the battle.

"Oh hey. This is too much. What will Pro Kim be fighting with?"

Sungchul revealed his beginner blade at Woojung's question.

"Ah…I see…"

Sunghae had already received a weapon from Sungchul. It was the Magic staff, Moonlight. It wouldn't be an exaggeration to say that it was the most effective weapon within the Summoning

Palace. Sungchul decided to not give Sunghae any particular orders because she would never be able to overcome her hatred for Ahram.

"…"

Sungchul, who had finished laying out his orders, looked to the front. The barrier between the Blanche and the Azure Plaza was slowly dissipating.

[The Battle will now begin.]

[Please show us a battle worthy of an event run in the name of the God of Neutrality]

The barrier disappeared, and countless little skirmishes broke out in between the Palace gates of the Plazas. Since the Summoned were inexperienced with large scale battles, they were excessively unorganized and cautious. Both sides moved like the tide with neither side willing to fully commit to the battle. They both instinctively knew that if even a drop of blood were spilled, there would be no turning back from there.

"This is why I don't like Death Match style. I really can't stand to watch this. Fucking pussies."

The influential people within the Observation Towers watching the Rank Match began to grow impatient and spoke harshly. In this world, cowards were considered worse than criminals.

Dolorence wore a glamorously adorned robe that she normally didn't wear and was socializing among the influential crowd like a true social butterfly.

Whenever she met someone's eyes, she would give a refined smile and greeted them with a nod. If they spoke to her, she responded with grace and charm as she willingly became their interlocutor.

One of them complained as they watched the bloodless Plaza.

"Ah! I can't stand to watch this! I heard the Blanche Plaza killed the Tam Tam and had high expectations to see some monsters, but they're all just fucking expendable peasants. At this rate, someone will have to go and ruthlessly cull them down."

Dolorence wore a thin smile and matched the mood with a sensual voice.

"How about we make a bet with the Azure Plaza, then? They're not as good as the Scarlet Plaza, but Azure Plaza is backed by pretty powerful forces. They might have prepared something special after hearing about the news with the Tam Tam."

"Mmm...Azure Plaza, eh...?"

As the man contemplated, Dolorence moved over to the window looking over the entirety of the Plaza and checked her pocket watch

It's almost show time.

A cruel smile formed on Dolorence's lips as something unexpected happened within the Azure Plaza's side.

"Uu...!"

"Kuuu...!"

The people standing at the frontline suddenly collapsed and began to moan as though they were having seizures. Not just one, but six people began to convulse as though it had all been planned beforehand. All eyes from both Plazas, after having nothing better to do, gathered upon this scene.

"What...what's wrong with them?"

All of the Azure Plaza mostly looked confused at the sudden scene, but the Blanche Plaza was different. They had already witnessed something similar. Their terrible premonition suddenly became a nightmarish reality.

"KWAAAAA!"

Their joints became twisted, and fur began growing all over their bodies. Their large eyes were dyed yellow, and their canine teeth filled their gaping maw. Werewolves. The terrible nightmare once again faced the Blanche Plaza and filled them with despair.

"W-WEREWOLVES!"

People began fiercely pushing back towards the Blanche Plaza.

"Grrr..."

The six Werewolves bared their fangs and stepped forward. The Blanche Plaza had already gone as far back as they could and began to completely fracture in response to the pressure. The people in the front continued to push the ones behind them. And as everyone continued pushing one another, the Blanche Plaza completely unraveled before they could even start fighting.

"Hey! Mr. Yuhoon! What do we do now?"

The Preselected who had placed their trust in Yuhoon and stood at the front now looked towards him in despair.

"Let's first calm down and escape to the sides. I'll open us a path!"

Yuhoon gritted his teeth and began using all his strength to push away everyone that was blocking his way.

"What the fuck are you doing! You bitch!"

As someone dared to speak up about his aggressive behavior, he swung his blade without batting an eye. Blood splattered, and a man died. Yuhoon's true, devilish nature revealed itself as people turned to him in surprise.

"Fuck off! I said fuck off! You wanna die? Huh, do you?"

People opened a path for this man whose eyes darted from side to side as he intimidatingly swung about his bloody blade. Unfortunately, cruel fate still headed his way despite his efforts to avoid it.

"I-it's coming this way!"

"It's coming!"

The Werewolves ignored the crowds of people and headed directly towards Yuhoon and his group. Yuhoon weakly sat down as he realized the twelve eyes, filled with bloodlust, only had them in their sights.

"How…"

A single man's face appeared in his mind. The man with a mysterious identity. The man whose thoughts he couldn't decipher. His outer appearance might have been shabby and his looks laughable, but he had been telling the truth. He didn't know whether that man had been lucky or something, but…

I should've listened to that bastard.

Those were his last thoughts as a Werewolf ran him through with its claw and a set of ravenous teeth came from behind to tear apart his flesh.

"Oh. Fuck!"

Sunghae, who was watching the scene from a distance, couldn't help but spit out profanity. It was for the Preselected. Within a moment, the Werewolves had made rags out of the Preselected and moved on to their next target.

[Main Target]

There was something marked within the Werewolves' sights. It was the remaining group of Preselected off in the distance, and it was searching the location of the target that had to be killed first.

"Krrrng...!"

The six Werewolves tore apart people between themselves and split the Blanch Plaza forces in half as they darted off towards the rear. They were headed towards Sungchul.

"Pro Kim! Pro Kim!"

Jungshik Park, holding his shield, repeatedly shouted out with a nervous voice.

"What's wrong, Jungshik?"

"I...My heart feels like it shrank a size, can I run away now?"

"Hold it. You'll calm down once you take a whiff of your butt."

Saying that, Sungchul held his blade and stood to the left as if to protect Jungshik.

"Now, let's hold it a bit longer. Once Ahram wakes up, he'll kill all those low-grade Werewolves for us. We'll just sit to the back and eat some rice cakes."

Jungshik Park felt comforted for some unknown reason. He felt so comfortable that it felt as if he could never be killed if Sungchul was at his side. Even in his wildest dreams, he would never imagine that the person standing next to him was the strongest human...No. The strongest warrior in all of this world.

"Fire!"

Sungchul swung his sword and shouted. Woojung and Sunghae fired off one after the other in coordination towards the Werewolves.

"Krrrr!"

However, Werewolves were still Werewolves. They avoided the projectiles flying at them from the distance with ease and quickly arrived in front of Jungshik Park's shield by dodging all the flying arrows and energy bolts.

"Krrr!"

One of the Werewolves swiped at the shield wall. Jungshik Park felt like he would fly off like a ball, but he narrowly kept his feet on the ground and held back the attack. Sungchul swung his blade and cut the Werewolf's body after successfully blocking its attack. The Werewolf deftly retreated to dodge his blade, then growled with his teeth bared.

"Krrrrr!"

This time, two Werewolves stepped up. The rest of them slowly spread out and surrounded the shield wall. If not for the constant barrage of fire from Woojung and Sunghae, they would have attacked much more readily.

"It's time."

As Jungshik's terror reached its peak, Sungchul grabbed his collar and pulled him back while he tossed something towards the Werewolves with his other hand. The blackened liquid was Ahram's rotten blood.

With the scent of the blood scattered in the air, the Werewolves were once again reminded of Dolorence's objective: Ahram Park. The existence which was behind the shield wall now stood exposed to them with no obstacles in their way.

Ahram continued to swing back and forth up until the Werewolves tore him to shreds. They tore him up so completely that not a single identifiable piece of him remained.

They didn't notice that the fuel for Inextinguishable Fire which was hidden within Ahram's corpse had splashed all over them.

Sanggil, who had been watching from the Observation Tower, was filled with terror, while Dolorence had a smile filled with pride. Sungchul, his expression passive as always, suddenly appeared behind Woojung.

"Stand still."

He quickly tied Woojung's bolt with a cloth and rubbed the Golden Toadstool against the Alchemic Charcoal to set the cloth on fire. It was now a single-use flaming bolt.

Sungchul waved his sword as he quietly said, "Fire."

Woojung pulled the trigger with his finger, and the flaming arrow flew towards the Werewolf that was tearing into Ahram's corpse. The Werewolves agilely dodged the arrow, but when the arrow hit the floor, they couldn't stop the fire from spreading onto their bodies.

"Awoooooo!!"

The Werewolves were burned alive by the Inextinguishable Fire. First, their skin and fur, then even their eyeballs. Black smoke rose into the sky.

"Wow! Look at him!"

Jungshik Chun who had been watching from the rear now led his subordinates as though he had just been waiting for a signal.

"Let's go! Let's go kill everything!"

The landscape of the battlefield had changed. The moment the Werewolves, who had brought so much morale to the Azure Plaza, were burned alive was the moment the Blanche Plaza's victory was more or less assured.

Chapter 9 – Ahmuge

One night, everyone experienced the same dream as God's curse swept through the land. From that moment on, not even a single child's laughter could be heard. The Curse of Extinction. This calamity was interpreted as one of the harbingers of the End. It brought an incurable illness that killed every child born in the cursed land. It didn't discriminate between the rich or poor, strong or weak, noble or otherwise, and killed everyone impartially as all were equal in the face of unrelenting death.

"So, is the kid doing well?"

Captain of the Order of the Iron Blood Knights, Sungtek Jo.

Leader of what used to be the "Strongest Order in the Continent," and currently one of the three most powerful individuals in the Northern Regions. He had lost every single child born in this world to the curse of Extinction. The offspring that had been left behind in the old world was now his final hope.

The reports which made its way to him claimed that the son, who bore his mother's name, was doing quite well. With his natural leadership, he had led by example and displayed remarkable bravery to his people in the Rank Matches. He had even managed to strike down the Tam Tam that was usually known as the nightmare of Rank Matches. When he heard that the son who just arrived in Other World, from whom he never really had hoped much, was doing so well, he couldn't help but devote his attention to him.

"...Your son is doing quite well. The other side managed to prepare six Werewolves for the Rank Match this time, but he managed to overcome them with a clever strategy. Haha, who would have thought of it? To use the Alchemist class for this."

Sanggil reported from the other side of a scrying orb.

"Is that right? For them to release six Werewolves...Who's backing the other side that's using such scummy methods?"

It was difficult for a Summoned to find a way to become a Werewolf within the Summoning Palace. So six showing up at the same time was nothing short of impossible.

Sanggil began speaking again, with a meeker voice.

"That is...it's the Black Division."

"Black Division? You're saying this is Shamal's doing?"

Sungtek's half-white brow shot up. Sanggil felt like he was swimming against sewage.

"T-that is...not verified. We are just speculating at this point."

"Yeah? I mean it's one thing if William did it, but Shamal would never do something like this. I'll go talk to Shamal personally."

"I-it's not verified yet...I don't think there's a reason to bother anyone."

"No, didn't you say that Ahram was a great kid? I might not have raised him, but he's still my blood. If he has this much potential, I can gladly lower my head and ask for favors."

Sungtek waved his arms as he stood up from his chair. The brightly lit scrying orb slowly faded.

"Ah...fuck..."

On the other side of the scrying orb, Grand Knight Sanggil wiped the sweat from his forehead and collapsed onto his chair. A fiery-haired female Mage revealed herself from the shadows from behind him.

"Sir Grand Knight, don't concern yourself so much. It has already gone this far; we're in the same boat now."

Sanggil had almost lost all of his Preselected in the previous match. Even Ahram, who he had to protect no matter what, was not an exception to this. He had been driven into a corner, and Dolorence had slithered in front of him like a viper.

"I gave a false report as you told me to for now. Now...what should we do, Dolorence Winterer?"

Sanggil brushed his hands across his face in his anguish and spoke in a pained voice.

"It's not that there aren't any solutions, Sir Grand Knight. Don't we still have a card left to play?"

"What is it? What is this card you speak of?"

Sanggil desperately raised his head and stared pleadingly into her eyes. She paused for a beat before answering.

"If my guess is correct, the Knight Captain doesn't know his son's face. I haven't seen a Magic Print Maker drop by even once."

"I told him vaguely how the boy looks."

"What did you tell him?"

"That he's good looking and quite handsome…"

Hearing his words, Dolorence broke into a mischievous smile.

"Then that settles it."

"What's settled?"

"Have someone substitute for him. Someone similar. All parents think their children are the most handsome anyways. Don't they say that even ogres think their babies are cute?"

"…Are you for real? Have a stand-in? It'll all be over once the Captain and the replacement meet."

A small portion of Sanggil's suppressed rage peeked out.

"Who says we'll let them meet? Just kill the stand-in, and it'll be ok. Have you forgotten that the next Rank Match is the last one?"

"Kill him…at the Rank Match? The stand-in…?"

With great difficulty, Sanggil's dense mind began to catch up to her vision for the narrative. She smiled a sympathetic smile and continued with her story.

"We'll make him a hero. A hero that fought alone against overwhelming odds and died alone. Understand that it is the Scarlet Plaza that is coming up next."

"Scarlet Plaza…You mean the very Scarlet Plaza that is being handled by the Assassin's Guild?"

"Yes. Luck is on our side."

Sanggil finally understood the entirety of her plan. He swallowed deeply and spoke in a hushed voice.

"War would erupt between the Order of the Iron Blood Knights and the Assassin's Guild after this."

"That could be. But, is a war as important as Sir Grand Knight's life?"

Sanggil suddenly glared at her blunt question, but he couldn't reprimand her. In the eyes of Krill, who was watching from a distance, Sanggil seemed completely constricted by the snake that was Dolorence.

So great, Dolorence Sunbae...I doubted you, but to even manage to toy with the proud Grand Knight...Great...Really great...!!

After she had finished making Sanggil yield, Dolorence approached Krill and spoke to him in a relatively friendly tone.

"Did you see all that? Underclassman? For nameless people like us to spread our name as Mages, we can't stop at anything. We have to use everything at our disposal."

"Amazing. Really...Amazing, Sunbae."

Krill genuinely bowed to Dolorence. He couldn't help but do so. Her opponent was someone who was one of the top ten most influential members, Grand Knight Sanggil Ma. He was someone that Dolorence would usually never dare speak to. Not just anyone could ignore this stark difference and include them into their treacherous scheme through the sheer force of their will.

If I could learn under this person...maybe even my degrading life could...maybe it could open up...!

The ill-will he had for her was already long gone. Krill voluntarily poured Dolorence some alcohol. She smirked and then wet her lips with the strong alcohol before lightly licking it off with her tongue. She looked around the observatory before speaking quietly.

"I need a stand-in. Ideally, try to find me a Preselected or someone that stands out for the job. I would normally have sent the Drill Sergeant, but for some reason, I can't seem to reach her."

Dolorence stared up at Krill.

"Hurry back."

The memory of a person that he had briefly forgotten popped up. The shabby appearance of a wild-looking man that looked ragged.

That person. I wonder who he is.

The man was no longer an essential existence as Sanggil no longer requested bribes. In contrast, this man was now a liability as he knew Krill's weakness, just like Dolorence knew of Sanggil's.

"Ah. One more thing."

Dolorence called out as Krill was about to leave.

"Yes, Sunbae?"

"There's someone that's been getting on my nerves."

"Who's bothering you?"

"There is a woman who picked up the staff I gave to Ahram. It bothers me more that I don't know her name. It bothers me a lot."

Dolorence threw her shot glass towards the ground. Krill could hear her slithering voice as the glass shattered into pieces.

"You want to work for me, right?"

His heart froze at her words. His breath caught in his throat.

"If you want to learn under me, then prove your worth."

"My w-worth? How...?"

"I don't like it. You are trying to act naive when you already know the answer."

Her smile disappeared. It was as she'd said. Krill already knew what she was asking him for.

—

The fierce battle had ended. The survivors digested that the long and tiring Rank Match had ended as they looked at the message that appeared before them. Sungchul stared into the air as he wiped the blood off his blade.

[The Third Rank Match has ended.]

[Blanche Plaza has killed 452 people.]

[Blanche Plaza sustained 242 casualties.]

[You are ranked in First Place among the four Plazas]

His desired goal had been accomplished. He waited for the next message to appear.

[Overall rewards are adjusted by the rankings.]

[You have killed 7 people (Outside your Rank).]

[Your Contribution is 9.2%.]

[You have been rated for S grade rewards.]

Basic Rewards:
1. 12x Palace Token
2. 1x Bottle of Wine
3. 1x Week of Ration
Selective Rewards:
1. Brass Breastplate
2. Knight's Gauntlet
3. 2x Healing Potion
4. Warrior Class Transfer Tome
Please Select Two.

They were adequate rewards. The appearance of Warrior Class Transfer Tome signaled that the final days of the Summoning Palace was drawing close. Sungchul chose the Brass Breastplate and the two healing potions. The Knight's Gauntlet would be more effective than the two items he'd chosen if they were used properly, but he chose to prioritize ease of use. In any case, they were all useless to him.

He'd taken care of seven people during this Rank Match. It was two more than the bare minimum for an A-grade reward. It was incomparable to Jungshik and Ahmuge, who sat at the top with over thirty kills, but he'd managed to reach S-grade with his contributions. Everyone who had participated in killing the Werewolves had received S-grade rankings. Woojung was also acknowledged as having personally killed a Werewolf and got the coveted SS rank. So Sungchul had nothing to complain about.

It was the best results he could have hoped for. He hadn't stood out, yet had done just enough to reach his goal to earn a large amount of Palace Tokens.

I managed to get a hold of thirty-seven Tokens. There isn't much more to go.

The daily common quests would also come to an end. They would get him eight Palace Tokens, which was all that he needed to acquire the Echo Mage class.

"Hello."

Ahmuge approached him after the battle had ended. He felt her properly this time, but she was a woman with a weak presence; it was difficult to notice her without concentrating first.

"Why are you looking at me like that?"

The number of Summoned she had managed to kill was sixty-four. She scored the highest of all of the Summoned. Her innate skill with the sword was a major factor, but the aggressive use of Spirit Wolf staff allowed her to quickly raise her kill score and bypass Jungshik by at least 10 points.

"Why did you come find me?"

She replied softly with a mysterious smile at his question.

"I came to keep our promise from a while back."

"The hidden quest relating to Magic Power?"

"Yes. I'm sure it'll be to your liking."

He could raise his Magic Power to his desired amount with common quests within the Summoning Plaza, but if he considered the future, he also needed to do more than that. He would need a considerably larger amount of Magic Power to contend with the Demon Lord Hesthnius Max.

Sungchul was prepared to use every opportunity he could find.

"Okay. Lead the way."

Ahmuge led him beyond the Palace walls and deep into the forest. It looked as though she had visited the place more than once as the woods were overgrown with no clear signs which made it very easy to get lost in here.

"Do you perhaps have the Alchemist class?"

Ahmuge asked as she brushed past the trees.

"Didn't we agree not to ask about each other?"

"Of course, but it left quite an impression on me. I never imagined that an Alchemist class's ability, the one they call a trap class, could be used to resolve that disaster."

"..."

Sungchul didn't answer. Ahmuge saw his thick face and her eyes curled up in laughter.

"To tell you the truth, I was going to give you a relatively ordinary hidden quest. But when I saw how strong you were, I changed my mind. I have a debt to repay to you, so I prepared a top tier quest."

There was a small pond at the end of the forest; at its center was the statue of a bowing angel. Ahmuge pointed at the statue and said,

"The quest will begin when you touch that statue. You'll earn rewards based on the difficulty you choose. However, be careful. If the difficulty you chose is too high, you'll die no matter how strong you are."

"Is that so?"

Sungchul looked back at Ahmuge and headed towards the statue. She sat at the edge of the pond and spoke brightly.

"I'll give you three hours. If you don't come out by then, I'll assume you're dead. Come back by yourself if you manage to survive past that time."

"..."

Sungchul walked towards the statue without a word.

The moment he put his hands on the statue of the bowing angel, bright letters appeared before him.

[The Forgotten Path of the Seven Heroes – Sajators.]

"Sajators?"

Sungchul's eyes reflected his surprise.

***

After the message had appeared, Sungchul was moved to another space. It was a land without any features like trees, hills, valleys, or buildings. This perfectly flat land extended all the way to the horizon, which was the only means to distinguish the boundary of the land. Another message appeared before him.

[You have arrived at the Forgotten Path of Sajators.]

Sajators. He, along with Vestiare, was one of the two Mages that were a part of the Seven Heroes, but his style was vastly different to hers. Vestiare used echoes to cast her Magic repeatedly, but Sajators was versatile enough with his ability to use several different types of Magic simultaneously. Because of that, he had earned the nickname "Mage of Multicast."

He would simultaneously prepare a multitude of spells, either dodging the enemy attacks or having already sealed off their movement with Magic, before simultaneously unleashing the prepared array of destructive spells to destroy all of his enemies in one go. His Multicast was even able to stack several different high-level spells with enough power to blow away the mountains; even obtaining just a single one of these spells would greatly help Sungchul.

I got lucky. I managed to find the path of Sajators after the path of Vestiare.

He had hoped to also find traces of the other members of the Seven Heroes around the Summoning Palace as they always acted together ever since their conception until their final journey.

"Uuu...I can't breathe...so painful..."

Bertelgia, who was in his front pocket, began to struggle.

"What's wrong, book?"

"I can't breathe...this space...it feels like I am fish out of water. Hurry...into the storage...put me into your storage."

It appeared that this space wasn't suitable for familiars. He put the familiar into his storage. Not long after, a light that was about the size of a firefly appeared.

It was a primitive spirit called Will o' Wisp. The Will o' Wisp which had arrived quietly began to form words.

[Which path of the Seven Heroes do you wish to walk?]

[The difficulty of the trials will vary based on the dream.]

There were five different dreams listed in ascending order of difficulty.

[Gentle Downward Slope]

[Flat Path]

[Gentle Upward Slope]

[Steep Upward and Downward Slopes]

[Unexplored Path]

Sungchul chose the most difficult path, and countless clouds appeared from the horizon. The clouds quickly covered the sky, and dried up and twisted dead grass appeared on the wasteland

He watched the changing environment with cold eyes until he saw something that was familiar to him.

Ah, this place. Isn't this the Path of Lamentation?

There was no doubt. This was the path leading to the entrance of the Demon realm. As if to prove that demons hated and despised all life, grass would not grow where a demon's hooves had trampled on the Path of Lamentation. Only the cold, emotionless rain wet this dead land.

Sungchul watched the flowing clouds before picking a direction. He was heading northwest, walking wordlessly across the desolate landscape until suddenly and without warning, the ground beneath his feet gave out and pulled him into a vortex of earth and sand. It was a Sand Hell, one of the monsters of the Demon realm. Sajators's message popped up before him.

[Due to this monster that swallowed the ground, we lost a large number of support units and beasts of burden that were carrying our rations.]

Sungchul didn't panic and immediately jumped into action, he followed the contour of the sand as he ran towards the center of the vortex where a large pair of jaws awaited him.

"Ahahaha!"

He could hear the soulless laughter of a woman coming from the center. He grabbed the saw-like horns from its gaping maw to withstand the flowing sand.

"Ahahaha!"

The Sand Hell suddenly began struggling more violently and loosened the ground even further. Several tons of sand flew up and then came showering down from the sky. It pushed with an astounding amount of strength. However, Sungchul didn't budge.

He grabbed the Sand Hell's horn and held on solidly until its movements became dull. He twisted off the horn and stuck it deep into the maw of the Sand Hell after it had stopped shaking the earth.

"Ahahaha...Graaaaarkk!"

The Sand Hell spat out violet blood as it convulsed before it flipped over. Sungchul lightly leaped out of the sand pit and hurried on.

A human skeleton blocked his path next. The skeleton wore a brilliant crown and a shining set of armor. As if to prove his former regality, the skeleton warrior had donned equipment that was fit for a king. His body made clacking sounds as he drew his blade. A message appeared before Sungchul.

[A foolish king joined hands with the Demon King in exchange for eternal life. He got his wish, but he didn't retain his past form. We lost many friends due to this foolish king that stood in our way.]

Sungchul finally understood. The scenery before him was composed of Sajators's memories. He was perfectly reliving Sajators's journey through the Demon Realm that was sealed inside this place.

"Mortals...cannot pass...!!"

Several thousand skeleton warriors rose up around the Skeleton King. It was the very definition of a skeleton army. The crowned skeleton swung his blade, and the thousands of skeleton warriors mindlessly rushed towards Sungchul.

Sungchul cut down one or two skeleton warriors with his beginner's blade, but he ended up pulling out Fal Garaz from his storage.

WHAM!

One hammer blow crushed dozens of skeleton warriors and left them sprawled on the floor.

WHAM! WHAM!

Several holes formed within the skeletal army. The army had the ability to replenish their numbers, but the rate of their replenishment couldn't keep up with the rate at which Sungchul destroyed them. Eventually, Sungchul reached the crowned skeleton and finished the battle with a single swing. The crown fell to the floor, and the army cursed with immortality disappeared, sucked into the ground through a mysterious force.

Several more obstacles blocked his path towards the Demon realm, but he overcame them with little difficulty. A Balroq, a high-tier demon, finally appeared before him.

[How much blood had to be spilled beneath the hooves of the Demon General Ugripos, the King of all Balroqs? Our forces numbered 103 when we encountered him, yet the only ones to survive in the end were the Seven Heroes and a nameless youth.]

"…"

Sungchul focused all of his senses on the demon in front of him. It was different than the average Balroq. It was larger and exuded a stronger aura.

"Uwahaha!"

Ugripos let loose a thunderous laughter and swung his massive axe like a windmill. Strong gusts of winds caused the flames of hell to erupt from the ground, dyeing the scene an infernal red. Within the flames and the wind, Sungchul gripped Fal Garaz and stood unshaken against the King of Balroqs.

WHAM!

Sungchul's hammer soon landed a critical hit upon Ugripos, but the moment they made contact, Ugripos evaded the blow by leaving behind an illusion made of flames, just like a cicada shedding its shell.

"Your attacks will never reach me."

The demon spoke, but Sungchul didn't stop. He blindly swung his hammer towards Ugripos again. It wasn't just once, but it was a continuous blow which appeared as though several dozen hammers were attacking simultaneously.

Ugripos tried to use his evasive technique again, but after using the skill for the third time, Sungchul's hammer finally found its mark.

"N-no! Save me! No!!!"

The King of Balroqs, while in the air, clenched his fists as the merciless barrage of blows pounded his body. It was not long until he perished.

" … "

Sungchul loosened his grip on the bloody hammer and calmed his breathing as he stood over the demon's corpse. There was a burning land beyond the dark clouds. Demon Realm; the land of Devils. This was the end of the path of Sajators. The scene of the Demon Realm suddenly vanished. The featureless and barren land surrounded him once more.

"Amazing! I can't believe there was a human capable of brute-forcing his way through the path like this."

He heard a voice from behind. It was a voice full of youth and vigor. Sungchul turned around to respond to the owner of the voice. It was a Mage wearing a pure white robe; he wielded a staff that was taller than himself. Sungchul didn't feel a presence from him, which meant that it was simply an apparition made of Magic. However, Sungchul was still surprised.

So this is Sajators.

He looked younger than Sungchul had anticipated. No, "Childish" would have been more accurate. Unlike the typical elderly Mages who had diligently trained for their entire lives to obtain power, he seemed more like a gifted prodigy who did not have control over his overwhelming strength and was likely to act out on a whim.

"So you're the human that Vestiare was talking about. Your strength is a most thrilling thing to behold and so unwavering to boot. Really, I think you have the greatest potential I have yet to see!"

Sungchul only quietly responded.

"Stop yacking away like a bitch. Hand over the rewards and fuck off."

Sajators grinned so widely that he showed his teeth[5].

"The rewards will come. A promise is a promise! I just want to ask one thing: for what do you fight?"

He coiled his legs in the air and crossed his arms as he looked down upon Sungchul.

"To bash your head in."

Sungchul fidgeted with his hammer while speaking.

"Haha! Truly an interesting friend. Okay. You sound a bit impatient, so I'll reward you first."

Sajators smirked while putting his hands together. Magical letters blossomed like flowers, appearing and disappearing around his hands, and after a while, several items appeared in his palms. Sajators grabbed one of the items and pushed it towards Sungchul.

"How about this? Friend?"

"What's this?"

Sajators formed an evil smile at Sungchul's question and answered.

"Final Elixir."

Sungchul's eyes visibly shook.

He said Final Elixir...? Is this really the Elixir...?!

Final Elixir.

It is the king of all medicine said to even be able to resurrect the deceased, but the true value of the Final Elixir lay elsewhere. The Final Elixir was one of the only two known methods that could undo the Curse of Extinction.

"If you don't like it, I have other items here. Feel free to choose carefully."

Sajators laid down several items that also included legendary artefacts, Magical scrolls filled with mystery, and other items that were difficult to look away from. However, Sungchul's eyes only held the Final Elixir within.

"..."

With his eyes filled with longing, Sungchul reached out for the Elixir. Sajators's cruel smile deepened when his hands finally came in contact with the Final Elixir.

"Dear me. It's a miss."

When Sungchul's fingers touched the Final Elixir, the legendary medicine turned to dust and scattered on the floor. Sajators's heartless words followed after a cold laughter.

"Now I know what you fight for. Fatherly love...Such a painful word for you, isn't it?"

"..."

"Why so quiet? Don't tell me you're angry? Hm?"

At that moment, Sajators's apparition could feel an indescribable pressure bearing down upon him.

"Oh my...?"

A fierce combat aura made from pure wrath billowed out of the poorly dressed young man. The hammer slowly rose.

Sajators's apparition tried to escape, but he discovered that the intangible murderous intent had bound him in place.

"Damn."

The apparition was struck down by the hammer, and it shattered into pieces. However, it never lost its composure, as if still mocking Sungchul until the very end.

"Let's meet again next time, friend. It won't turn out like this that time!"

The cold voice weakly echoed as it broke apart, and bright letters appeared before Sungchul.

[You have completed Sajators' path.]

[You have completed the Objective "Completionist of the Unknown Path (Hidden – Epic)."]

Rewards:
1. Magic Power +25
2. Magic Blade – Infernal Heart (Rare)

***

The first reward on the list was similar to last time. The 25 Magic Power upgrade was a significant boon. There weren't many opportunities to raise a stat by anything more than 20, no matter how low the base stat was. However, he still had one complaint.

They didn't give me any Palace Tokens. Is that because I got the blade?

Sungchul held up the Magic Blade: Infernal Heart.

[Magic Blade - Infernal Heart]

Grade: Rare – Mid grade

Type: Blade – Magical

Effect: Well-tempered edge / +10 Strength / Flame attribute

Note: A blade crafted by a mad blacksmith inside of a molten lake in which a fire spirits resides. He burned to death immediately after the blade was completed.

It was a decent blade. It was meant to be used by beginners, like the Magic Staff Moonlight he had previously received. But unlike the staff, the blade would also be decent enough in mid-level. It might be the best item one could earn within the Summoning Palace.

Within the well-tempered blade, the muted aura of a flame spoke well of the blade's quality. And the balance was good, enough for it to feel weightless.

Sungchul swung the blade as a test, and a streak of flames formed along the path it had been swung in. Using it would cause critical damage by slicing open then searing the exposed flesh.

"Not bad."

However, he also knew that this wasn't everything. It was similar to Vestiare's case. The Seven Heroes rewarded twice.

Sungchul grabbed Fal Garaz and the rewards and waited for the expected message to appear. It did.

[The Seven Heroes – Sajators laughs raucously at your ability to complete the Objective.]

Sungchul's eyes emitted a cold light.

"Laugh it up while you can."

[The Seven Heroes – Sajators has decided to bestow a special reward for completing the Objective.]

Reward:
1. Map made of Goblin hide
2. Blue Ruby Ring

The true reward for completing the Objective had appeared. A single map and a single ring fell to the floor. The rewards didn't make sense, similar to the case with Vestiare.

He first picked up the map made of Goblin hide.

[Map made of Goblin Hide]
Grade: Common
Type: Misc Item
Effect: None
Note: It was made in a hurry due to a commander's order.

The explanation had Sajators's distinct style to it. Other than the preservation, there didn't seem to be any Magical power coming from it; it seemed just like a normal map. The map was made of a Goblin Hide which reeked of savagery, and the quality wasn't much better than that of a drunken pirate Captain's crudely drawn map.

The map pointed to an untamed rainforest set beneath a mountain range called the Screaming Sword's Edge Mountain Range. Screaming Sword's Edge Mountain Range was located at the southernmost tip of the continent and was one of its unexplored territories. There were no sources of income here, and it had nearly no quest rewards in the whole area. There were only frequent status afflictions, stenches, and diseases carried by irritating monsters here; the xenophobic Hermit Kingdom of Lizardmen was all that awaited the visitors at the end. Sungchul, who in this world was second to none in terms of strength, had never even thought of going there because of the pure annoyance the journey would be.

Screaming Sword's Edge Mountain Range…that area's a fucking shithole.

There was some writing scrawled at the bottom of the map.

"Why do you think I gave you the Infernal Heart? If you have a head, try using it."

Beneath that was another set of markings scrawled out with a pen. It was hard to make out as it didn't seem to have been written with ink but had rather been scratched out with just the pen's dry tip.

His laughter escaped through his nose.

"They say a person acts the way he appears…how immature."

Sungchul didn't appreciate the host's need to play pranks rather than simply handing things over. However, they say a thirsty man will dig a well. He grabbed both the map and Infernal heart and began contemplating on how to uncover the trick. He eventually succeeded in finding the secret. When Infernal Heart, with its fiery aura, was placed beneath the map a new message appeared.

It was in an ancient text. It was written in a long-forgotten language that only a rare few could decipher. Fortunately, Sungchul just happened to be one of those few people.

He stumbled through his memories to decipher the message.

Strong...powerful...morning...if...ask...cute...critter...ring...like ...sunlight...shine...earth...release...together...incantation...secret...t hrough

He might be able to translate the text, but his ability to decipher the message was poor. Actually, it was abysmal. At most, he was only able to fit together some of the words that he already knew.

"Mmm..."

However, Sungchul was the master of fitting pieces of puzzles together. He had the ability to pick up the important context from these seemingly unrelated words.

Together, incantation...this...Is this referring to the Multicast? I think this map is a record on how to obtain Multicast.

Sungchul's eyes sparkled with curiosity.

There was also another item; a ring with the Blue Ruby gemstone called Angel's Tear.

[Blue Ruby Ring]

Grade: Rare

Type: Misc Item

Effect: High-Value Item

Note: The Blue Ruby Ring is the greatest reagent, but due to its weak reactivity, it isn't often used. Its beautiful light and pattern makes it favorable for use as decoration.

Similar to the Goblin hide, it was another normal item. No matter how carefully he inspected it, there were no special characteristics to it. The Eye of Truth also gave the same results. There wasn't even a hidden message like there was with the map, but it seemed to be the key to uncovering the clue leading to Sajators's deepest secret: Multicast.

Like Vestiare, Sajators wouldn't leave behind a thoughtless reward.

I guess the actual reward that he left can only be found by crossing over the Screaming Sword's Edge Mountain Range.

Sungchul placed both items into his Soul Storage and watched as the barrier surrounding him broke down. The void space disappeared, and he returned to the scene of the pond that was surrounded by a thick forest.

He heard a familiar voice.

"Already done?"

It was Ahmuge.

As she had been meditating, it seems like she was also diligently performing her common quests. Sungchul looked up to the sky. The sun was already setting to the west.

"How much time has passed?"

"About two hours."

"I see."

Sungchul backed away from the statue and got out of the pond. As soon as he was out, the statue in the center broke and collapsed.

"Hm?"

Ahmuge was taken by surprise, and she rushed towards the statue. She ignored her wet clothes and inspected the rubble with her hands.

Hm? The quest disappeared? How can this be? I heard that the Seven Heroes struck down the people they didn't like, but I've never heard of them destroying a core structure like this...

Her eyes grew wider then turned towards Sungchul.

"How did this happen?"

"Dunno."

Sungchul obviously knew, but he still kept his mouth shut. Nothing good would come from blathering about completing Objectives.

Ahmuge stared at him while getting red in the face, then asked him carefully.

"Perhaps...did you complete its Objective?"

"…"

He didn't make any movement one way or the other. He glared at her and responded calmly.

"Didn't we agree not to ask each other questions?"

It was the single most important promise between them. No matter how excited she'd become, Ahmuge still realized the importance of such a promise.

"Ah…yes…that we did."

She forcibly calmed her breathing and returned to her calm, normal self.

"I apologize for prying."

"Okay."

Sungchul was just moving towards the Plaza when an unexpected noise erupted from his stomach.

GRRRWL.

Going on a rampage for the first time in a while had worked up an appetite.

Ahmuge had clearly heard the noise.

"It sounds like someone's hungry?"

A natural bodily function quickly shifted the atmosphere. An awkward smile formed on her lips, and Sungchul simply nodded with no particular expression. He spoke towards Ahmuge.

"I'm going to prepare a meal. Care to join me?"

"It's okay. I have no interest chewing those bricks they call bread."

Ahmuge politely declined and tried to head back, but Sungchul spoke to her retreating figure again.

"Is that right? I got some meat from the Rank Match. I was prepared to show off some of my skills…"

The hardest challenge Sungchul had faced after he became the Enemy of the World was obtaining a proper meal. He fed himself with poorly cooked meat, fruit, and some grass, but that was only good enough for a couple of days. His desire for a decent meal had kept growing until it could no longer be suppressed.

He ended up choosing Chef as his first sub-class, and since then he had embarked on a difficult worldwide journey to become a true chef. By the time Sungchul qualified for the prestigious title of "Chef De Cuisine," a philosophy had taken root in his heart: when hungry, one should eat delicious food.

He finally developed quite an appetite after a while, so this was the best opportunity for him to eat something delicious. He had decent ingredients with him, and a friendly guest who had taught him about a wonderful quest.

"What do you mean…did you say meat? Are you talking about the mystery meat they gave us after the Rank Match?"

Ahmuge obviously had gotten some meat before. She had earned first place during the Death Match, but it wasn't easy to prepare the meat.

"It smelled strange and wasn't it also too tough to eat? I would have preferred getting a few more apples than that."

She must have already tried eating it, but it sounds like she had prepared it poorly.

A mysterious smile formed on Sungchul's lips.

"The Regal Mountain Chicken is something that can be put on a king's plate."

"Regal…Mountain…Chicken…? Is that the name of the meat?"

"Just trust me. I have complete faith in my cooking ability."

—

Sungchul led Ahmuge towards a cave at the cliff's edge, but a familiar smell emanated from the area around the cave.

"Is this…the smell of human blood?"

Ahmuge's eyes grew cold. Sungchul raised his hand and moved over.

"Wait. It looks like some unwelcome guests may have been here."

Sungchul slowly headed towards the cave. Blood stains and bloody footprints were strewn about the cave entrance. By the shape of the footprints, someone must have gotten punished by the cave's owner and had been chased out.

"Krrrr!"

The cave owner's pair of eyes lit up brightly within the darkness as he revealed himself. It was a massive bear which reached five meters in height. It looked like a bear, but it also had the pattern of a tiger on its pelt. The Tiger Bear, a creature which roamed the vicinity of the Summoning Palace. Despite its fearsome appearance, this monster was an herbivore. It especially enjoyed eating honey. However, this massive beast was still capable of using its fearsome size to injure dozens of amateur Summoned effortlessly.

However, this only applied to a beginner Summoned.

Sungchul stared down the Tiger Bear. It looked defiant, but when its eyes met with Sungchul's, it froze.

"Scram."

His cold utterance hit the bear like a blizzard, and the large beast hastily crawled deeper into the cave. Watching the scene, Ahmuge carefully asked a question.

"Are you... a Druid...?"

"..."

He couldn't say that in the past, he had beaten the bear like a stray dog until the very sight of him would cause the bear to run away in fear. Sungchul entered the cave as he thought to himself,

It was good that I hid this inside the bear's cave. Three weeks after arriving in this world, a few of the Summoned have already grown strong enough to venture this far out.

The meat that had been stored in the cave was certainly safe. He ignored the Tiger Bear that was peeking at him as it trembled in fear, and brought out the portion of meat that had been well-preserved in a cool area of the cave. It was chicken meat that was wrapped in tree leaves.

"Wait, I'll go gather some ingredients."

Sungchul apologized and left his seat to bring out a small box from his Soul Storage. The box contained everything he needed for cooking, from essential condiments to extremely rare and valuable spices worth more than their weight in gold. He only subtly took out some ingredients that wouldn't stand out and wrapped them in a leaf before taking out a different box. This box was filled with dried vegetables and mushrooms and other similarly preserved foods. Sungchul took out a few different types of mushrooms and returned to Ahmuge.

"It might take an hour and a half. Will you wait?"

Ahmuge nodded.

Sungchul packed the ingredients he had gathered into the chicken, wrapped the chicken in a broad leaf, then smeared it in the mud.

"What are you doing?"

Ahmuge, who had been watching Sungchul, asked a question.

"Cooking."

Sungchul, after putting a thick layer of mud onto the chicken, lit a fire and placed the mud-covered chicken on top of it. It looked too primitive to call it "cooking"…at least in Ahmuge's perspective.

An hour and a half passed. Sungchul pulled the crisply cooked mud out of the fire and began to break the muddy exterior with the pommel of his beginner's blade.

THUD.

The mud layer broke apart, and the aroma of meat spread throughout the air. Ahmuge's eyes lit up in excitement as drool filled her mouth.

What…in the world is this? This aroma…?!

Sungchul quietly broke apart the mud, then pushed half of the chicken over to Ahmuge.

"It's not great, but give it a try."

Ahmuge looked at the juicy flesh which was revealing its golden meat then swallowed her drool before ripping off a piece and putting it into her mouth.

"…Ah!!"

As the meat entered her mouth, the Regal Mountain Chicken's life was played out like a panorama before Ahmuge's eyes. His life-or-death battle with the egg shell, his battle for food with his siblings, his teenage years molting out of his cotton feathers into proper ones, and his fateful meeting with a hen on another mountain…then finally, his slaughter.

So delicious. It's my first time eating something so delicious…!!

She could barely contain her tears as she ate her first proper meal in a long time. Reputation or etiquette was meaningless in front of such absolute flavor.

To Sungchul, it tasted rather plain.

58 points. The ingredients and tools weren't on par, so it was difficult to make anything worth over 50 points.

The Chef class had the ability to see the score of any food they tasted. It was quite useless to Sungchul, but it was still a decent meal.

When the meal ended, they both headed towards the Plaza. Ahmuge, who had been silent for a while, caught up to him with soft steps before asking her question.

"How about we make a deal?"

Chapter 10 – Selection Match

"A deal?"

Sungchul's foot stopped. Ahmuge continued to speak to his back.

"You know what the next Rank Match ruleset will be, right?"

Sungchul nodded.

The next ruleset was Representative Match. The rules were simple. Thirty fighters would be chosen from the Selection Matches held in each Plaza to fight the fighters from the other Plazas, and the Plaza with the most victories in the Representative Matches would be declared as the winner. Representative Match was unique in that forfeits and draws were allowed, and there weren't many penalties.

Some complained that it was an unfavorable ruleset since the majority of participants would not be eligible for the benefits. But because forfeits gave the participant a way to guarantee their life, it was also often viewed as the most relaxed of all the Rank Matches. But for the non-participants, this wasn't the case.

The difficulty behind the last Rank Match lay not in the duels itself but in the process of choosing the thirty warriors.

Currently six to seven hundred Summoned were still alive in the Blanche Plaza. Of those, only thirty would be given a chance to fight as the Representative of their Plaza in the arena. The rest were forced to participate in a betting game with their lives on the line.

The "Guess the winner thirty times in a row or die" game.

From the day the Summoning Palace had been established, not a single person had been able to get out of this mini-game alive. In other words, survival depended entirely on making to the top thirty through the hellish qualifier rounds.

"...It is regarding the upcoming Selection Match."

She said after a brief moment of silence.

"I do believe that we have already joined hands, but I just want to confirm whether the feeling was mutual."

No one was trustworthy in Other World. It would be extremely naive for her to take a generous meal as a sign of good faith. This was a world where today's friends could turn out to be tomorrow's enemies. It was better to be even more wary of a formidable ally than of a formidable enemy.

Ahmuge's first impression was that Sungchul was quite average. He looked like a person with no defining characteristics. His swordsmanship was average, and neither his speed nor strength seemed like anything too extraordinary. However, as time passed, she started to feel that there might be strength within him beyond what could be observed with the eye.

Like during the Tam Tam match and during the Werewolf incident. Although it was clumsy, he always found solution to everything. He had even managed to kill the Werewolf Ahram on his own and erased the Path of Sajators by completing the primary objective. The only person who had ever managed to make her feel wary was this "average person."

No one was able to complete the objectives of the Path of the Seven Heroes after the thousands of years that they existed in the Summoning Palace. But this person did it in just two hours.

The objectives of the Path of Seven Heroes were well accepted to be impossible to fulfill, no matter how much training or preparation a person underwent. This was because the Path of the Seven Heroes didn't stop at measuring the participant's capabilities as it also measured their potential.

In the event that someone from the outside relied purely on their high status points to try and brute force their way through, the quest could potentially reject them or even kill them with a trap contained within.

Sajators was also known to be one of the most excessive of the Seven Heroes. For that man to have solved Sajators's Objective within two hours would mean one of two things: his talent was outstanding enough to please Sajators or Sajators himself had taken a liking to him.

I don't know how he managed to complete the Objective, but he's definitely not ordinary. I should avoid making an enemy out of him.

Ahmuge thought as she revealed her most carefully guarded bargaining chip.

"It isn't likely, but if I am about to lose my life, I want you to help me. If I manage to survive the Selection Match safely, I will tell you the location of another Path of the Seven Heroes."

Curiosity lit up in Sungchul's eyes.

"Another Path of the Seven Heroes? Are you saying there are more Seven Heroes quests around here other than Sajators's?"

It was a question that he had already assumed to be the case, but he asked her with an innocent face that managed to fool Ahmuge. She nodded and then began to explain.

"…Before the final battle took place, the Seven Heroes gathered at the Summoning Palace and left behind trials filled with their individual visions. This was so that if they ever failed, they could prepare someone else to carry their burdens for them."

Sungchul fell into contemplation after hearing her explanation. It was a win-win situation for him. He had no plans of fighting her, and it wouldn't be easy for a person like her to fall into danger either. It would be unlikely that he would need to step in to fulfill this bargain. It was also a great opportunity for him. He could memorize the faces of the Seven Heroes through their remnants which would later make killing them a whole lot easier.

After organizing his thoughts, he raised his head.

"In that case…"

He was about to accept when a cold, murderous aura approached from nearby.

"Someone is coming."

It wasn't a monster. It was the aura of a person.

Sungchul quickly hid himself within the forest foliage. Ahmuge felt the presence shortly after and hid next to Sungchul. When she erased her presence, it caused a big surprise for him.

This woman…

Her presence had disappeared completely, to the extent that he couldn't feel her even though she was directly next to him. Rather than an acquired skill, this must be a skill she had naturally been born with.

A small group of people revealed themselves beyond the forest. Using a lantern's light to guide their way was a pathetic group with prosthetic arms and legs and robes made of dog skin. There were seven of them. There were also disfigured Homunculi leashed to dog collars that were crawling along and kicked around by these people.

Sungchul immediately realized who they were.

Slave Hunters.

It was unexpected. The only time Slave Hunters had ever stepped into the Plazas was during the mass Summoning in the first week to mark their slaves, but they normally would never enter the Plaza otherwise. Well, that was unless they had some special instructions from a strange client.

"It is over here, Master! There are footprints leading towards the cliff's face!"

A Homunculus that was missing an arm inspected the floor carefully and began shouting loudly. The Slave Hunters nodded towards each other and moved towards the direction indicated by the Homunculus.

After they left, Sungchul and Ahmuge both came out of hiding.

"What was that about?"

"I'm not sure."

Sungchul walked over to where the Slave Hunters had been and stood on his knee to inspect the floor. There were footprints scattered all about, but he distinctly recognized the footprint that the Homunculus had found.

"…"

It was a familiar footprint. It was Ahmuge's.

So that's it.

As predicted, the Homunculus had pointed out a footprint that matched hers which meant that for some reason, Ahmuge was being targeted.

Has her identity as a Regressor been discovered?

Regressors were not welcome in these troubled times; the world wasn't naive enough to allow those with knowledge of the future to do as they wished. Sungchul was fully aware of how those with powers treated the Regressors. They were seen as bags of meat that could tell them about the uncertain future, nothing more, nothing less.

Most would be captured early on and tortured until they spat out information about the future, despite the irregularity doing this would cause, before eventually dying. It was very likely that Ahmuge would also share this fate.

"…It would be wise to be careful from here on. They are looking for you."

This was the most Sungchul could do. He had no desire to help her out and entangle himself with a Regressor Hunt. The ability to coordinate a Regressor Hunt indicated that the person behind this had quite the background.

"Curious. Why are they following me? It's hard to say with my own mouth, but I'm not all that pretty…Don't worry too much about it. I am confident that I can take care of myself."

Ahmuge responded lightly as though she was unconcerned. Sungchul simply nodded and headed towards the Plaza first.

"Let's split up here. I'll return to the Plaza first."

"Ah…regarding what we talked about before…?"

Ahmuge called out to him before he left. Sungchul didn't stop as he gave his answer.

"Let's just say I agree to the proposal. I'll help you during the Selection Match, but I expect you to follow through on your end of the deal."

Saying that, he hurriedly left the forest.

A small guest was waiting for Sungchul at the entrance of the Plaza. The guest leaped up into the air when he entered then landed on his shoulder.

"Kyu Kyu!"

It was Krill's Sky Squirrel.

Sungchul checked the content of the message in the small pouch around the squirrel's neck.

[I will be waiting at a corner of the outer wall. My little friend will guide you.]

—

The atmosphere surrounding Krill was different at this second meeting. Krill had felt naive and immature before this, filled with the air of a rookie Mage, but the Krill that was waiting beneath the Palace walls now had the air of a relatively experienced Mage.

"It's been a while, Mr. Sungchul Kim."

Rather than a natural leisure coming from the heart, there was an obviously forced leisure surrounding his whole posture.

"...Why did you want to meet?"

Sungchul's attitude was cold, and Krill laughed lightly as he spoke.

"It's just that...there's a small problem. Yes...I need more money. A lot more than usual. The pressure from higher-ups is getting stronger. I have to bear it every day now. I swear they're intending to rob me completely with the way they've been pecking away at me."

Sungchul stared at Krill with passive eyes. Despite Sungchul's silence, Krill began to scratch his head as though he felt some disdain coming from the gaze.

"Help me one last time. It'll be over after this."

"Last, you say?"

"Yes. No matter how much more that person demands, I'll make this be the final one. I promise with my name on it."

Krill thumped his chest lightly with his left fist as to reinforce this promise.

"What value does your name have?"

Sungchul's response was cold, and Krill's lips twitched briefly.

This fucker...

It was for a short moment, but there was no way Sungchul would've missed it.

His head must have grown after all this time.

After a brief silence, Sungchul pulled out three more gems from his possession.

"This is the final one."

Krill accepted the gems with both his hands in a bow.

"Oh, my! Three of these precious things! I'm ever grateful!"

Krill smiled widely as he tossed over a bracelet.

"Actually, the reason for this meeting was to hand over this thing. It's too heavy for the little guy to carry."

It was a worn bracelet made out of brass. Sungchul felt its weight on receiving it; just as Krill had said, it would have been too heavy for the Sky Squirrel to carry.

"What is this?"

Sungchul gripped the bracelet and asked.

"Let's just call it an entry pass to a guaranteed safe passage into the Summoning Palace."

"Speak plainly."

"Yes. Yes. I'll explain again. If you wear this bracelet, you'll be able to obtain a miraculous victory with no effort through the Selection Match and also the final match!"

It looked like a plain bracelet on the outside. As he appraised it, it appeared to be a plain object with no magical effects to it. Krill put away the three gems and flicked his fingers to call over the pet to his own shoulder.

"Just participate during the Selection Match wearing this bracelet, and you'll realize its real value. There is always a chance where something unintended happens, but don't panic. Just go with the flow. There is nothing to gain from acting unexpectedly!"

Krill bowed deeply once more, put on the robe's hood, and disappeared into the darkness.

Sungchul silently fiddled with the bracelet, carefully observing it. It looked like an ordinary bracelet, but Sungchul's Legend rank skill, Eye of Truth, activated to list off all the information hidden within.

[Bracelet of Alias]

Grade: Rare – Midgrade

Type: Equipment

Effect: Hides Midgrade Equipment / Bestows Alias

Alias: Ahram Park

Note: Disguises the user with the desired name. However, cannot disguise stats.

Two tricks were at play here.

One was the veil cast over the equipment. Items with equipment veils would not display their item stats by simply looking at them or using them.

Another was the Alias Bestowal. The one wearing the bracelet would be acknowledged with the alias written into the bracelet.

These two tricks were working together to establish Sungchul as Ahram. Sungchul was disappointed. It was such a pathetic and childish method. However, there might be some heinous and despicable plot waiting at the other side of it. So, despite what he thought of it, Sungchul still put on the bracelet without a moment's hesitation.

"...The only good Mage, is a dead Mage."

Krill would never have dreamed that the person he was trying to trick was a man who held the world record for killing the highest number of Mages.

***

The next day.

The Homunculi met within Blanche Plaza at early morning and gathered in a circle as they began chanting an ominous curse.

"Detderodero…Detderodero…"

One by one, the Summoned were aroused from their sleep to the strange behavior of the Homunculi. The onlookers soon realized that the surface of the Plaza below the hovering Homunculi was rising. A circular arena about the size of a basketball court took shape.

"Now now, humans! It is time to pay attention! This is the debut of the new Drill Sergeant!"

As the ritual of the Homunculi continued, the new Drill Sergeant appeared before the humans. Its size didn't quite match the uniquely large stature of its predecessor, but it was still larger than the average Homunculus, and further stood out by wearing a black hat.

The new Drill Sergeant stepped onto a platform and let out a fake cough before he began his unoriginal speech.

"The Drill Sergeant before you is a Homunculus of ten years that has overseen and led the humans with his bountiful experience, discipline, interest, and curiosity; I have given the lazy humans necessary guidance to adjust to this world…"

It was a Drill Sergeant's acceptance speech.

"It is too cool!"

"I really want to be a Drill Sergeant like that one day!"

Only the Homunculi had looks of envy, while not a single human paid any attention at all.

Once the arena was fully constructed, the Drill Sergeant quickly changed the subject and explained the day's events.

"Now, humans! It's time to perk up your ears and listen! We will be holding the qualification rounds to choose the thirty individuals who will be representing Blanche Plaza in the Representative Matches!"

The Summoned who had been ignoring the acceptance speech quickly changed their attitudes and concentrated on listening to the explanation about the Selection Match. After the explanation ended, they showed a variety of reactions.

"Anyone who didn't qualify to be one of the thirty Representatives will be relegated to a penalty gambling game with their lives on the line...what is this?"

"A Selection Match means we have to fight among ourselves, right? I don't like the sound of that."

"I didn't fight so hard to make it this far only to bid my life in a gamble and die. I'm going to fight to make it in the top thirty no matter what."

The whole Plaza was teeming with whispers.

The new Drill Sergeant watched over the Summoned with a mysterious smile before looking back and waving his hand.

ZIIING~~

A sound which shook the eardrums began ringing from within the arena. A single Homunculus with ear plugs calmly held a drumstick beside a gong several times larger than himself. The massive tremors calmed the chaos within the Plaza. The Drill Sergeant once again had everyone's attention.

"...Now now, the explanation is over! We will now start the Selection Match! As we have explained, the victor will be decided by Duels with Last-Man-Standing rules! Those that want to participate in the competition should now step into the arena!"

People remained hesitant and looked at each other. They weren't familiar with the Last-Man-Standing rules. Like a duel, it was carried out with a series of one on one fights, similar to modern martial arts competition. However, unlike modern matches, the winner would have to face off against new challengers until nobody else stepped forward. It would quickly end if an overwhelmingly powerful challenger stepped forward, but it could also endlessly drag on with mediocre challengers. Many of the Summoned were mediocre and thought it wouldn't benefit them if they hurried into the arena.

After enough time had passed to drink a whole cup of tea, the Drill Sergeant stepped out once again.

"Now, humans! You will regret it if you don't step up for the Selection Match! Come up quickly!"

After hearing those words, one man mustered up his courage and stepped into the circular arena. He was an average man with no distinguishing features. He also wore some tattered casual clothing.

"Now, the first Representative candidate has appeared! Are there no challengers? I'll give you thirty seconds! You must challenge the Representative candidate by that time!"

ZIIING~~

The gong rang out indicating the time, and after a while, the indicated time ended. Surprisingly, no one had stepped up. Everyone was too busy eyeing one another.

I think that even I can win at that level...

Should I just wait to see how things work out for now?

They said that thirty people would be selected. I'm sure it'll be fine if I miss out on the first slot.

Thirty seconds had passed by quickly as various calculations were fiercely being made. The sound of the gong indicating the closing time rang out and the first Representative had been chosen.

"Now now, humans! The first candidate has been chosen! There are twenty-nine slots left! It's time to stop looking around and step up with courage!"

It was such an absurd conclusion. No one had expected the Representative selection method to be this simple. The man who had been the first to muster that small amount of courage simply scratched his head with a disbelieving expression on his face. The faces of those who had hesitated flashed with disappointment. Various thoughts were seeping into their minds.

Ah...should I have stepped out?'

I could have won at that level...

Ah, it's just the first slot. There will be other chances!

216

However, human beings were creatures who tended to think and act the same. A rare scene occurred where dozens of people stepped up at once as the second Representative candidate was being chosen. Several people began crying out in distress; chaos ensued as the arena filled up to the brim with challengers for the second slot.

"One at a time! You will enter one at a time! Trash humans! You will follow order!"

The Drill Sergeant tried to shout, but no one was listening. They were too busy trying to defend their position while shoving and shouting profanities at each other. At that moment, one man stepped up.

"Hey! Hey! Shove off! This fuck…"

A scrawny stature, sparkling eyes, and a distinct, eye-catching tattoo covering his entire body. It was Jungshik Chun. Everything turned upside down as soon as he stepped onto the platform. The humans that didn't budge from the Drill Sergeant's words were frozen like mice staring at a cat when they saw Jungshik.

Jungshik pulled out his Dagger of Swiftness and peered over towards the Drill Sergeant.

"Can I kill them?"

The Drill Sergeant opened his mouth and revealed his saw-like teeth.

"Humans that are quick to understand are always a welcome sight!"

As soon as the permission was given, Jungshik rushed towards the crowd without a second's hesitation. One man pulled out his sword, pitifully trying to defend himself, but he only fell over in a fountain of blood as he lost his head in a single slice.

"Kwaaaak!"

The people on the platform began to jump off as soon as the first person was killed. All the dogs were chased away by the forceful entry of a lion. Jungshik looked down at the people and licked his lips with a disappointed expression. He was chosen for the second Representative slot when the gong sounded the round's end.

The next few selections followed a similar rhythm. Jungshik's subordinates, with their aggression and combat strength, followed him into the proceeding Representative slots. Eight slots were consecutively filled by Jungshik's faction. It looked as though Jungshik's members would take all of the fighter slots.

At the tenth Representative's selection, Sungchul, who had been in a corner, quietly stepped onto the platform. Jungshik's subordinates tried to threaten him with murderous eyes and taunts, but Sungchul seemed totally unconcerned.

"…"

The Bracelet of Alias which was strapped onto his left arm began to respond quietly. The bracelet itself only had the ability to bestow him with an alias, but what effect this would have on the situation was yet to be seen.

"I will step up."

Soon, one man climbed to the platform. It was one of Jungshik's men who had a healthy body and a knife scar across his eye. He was carrying a hefty axe that suited his size.

"A challenger has appeared! Now the Selection Match will begin!"

Sungchul pulled out his beginner sword and prepared to go up. But before he could, someone had already stepped up into the arena. It was a poorly-dressed man wearing a deep fisherman's hat. He was dressed in a red shirt that was closer to a rag and worn jeans which were similarly tattered like Sungchul's. The bright graphic "2002 Be the Red!"[6] was written on the red shirt. A mysterious light flashed across Sungchul's eyes.

This guy…

The new intruder walked past Sungchul and trudged in front of Jungshik's subordinate.

"What? Who are you?"

Jungshik's axe-wielding goon glared at the man threateningly, but the only response he got was the flashing blade of a sword.

CLANG!

The sword edge and the axe edge sparked after clashing. The eyes of Jungshik's goon twitched. The axe was being pushed back without resistance. The axe-wielding man squeezed out every bit of his strength and pushed the man's sword with all his might while letting out a wild shout.

"Hoo Ha!!"

However, the pushed sword smoothly changed its trajectory and flew into his blind spot.

SLICE-

The head of Jungshik's goon who had just let out a roar was sliced off clean, flying into the sky, drawing a parabola as it went.

SPLAT!

The moment his head hit the ground, the headless body shook before it collapsed as well.

"…"

A heavy atmosphere once again enveloped the Plaza. Hosung Ro, another goon from Jungshik's gang, finally broke the silence as he became enraged.

"You bastard!"

"You dare kill Jong Gilly? I'm going to fucking kill you today!"

Jungshik's gang exploded like wildfire. About a dozen men walked into the arena at the same time with their weapons in hand. It looked as though the man in the fisherman's hat was in danger.

Sungchul had been quietly observing the situation. He discovered that the state of the man in the fisherman's hat was quite strange. He wasn't under the effect of some spell or illusion. It felt strange at a more fundamental level. Sungchul finally arrived at the answer.

These fuckers…

Two more people stepped up to the Plaza. They all wore some hiking hat or fisherman's hat to cover their face and wore clothes tattered enough to be rags. Their breathing was synchronized like a machine, and they did not share a single word of communication.

SHING-

Two more swords were drawn. The men in rags slowly walked up towards Jungshik's men.

"Wanna go at it? Huh?"

"Where did these fucks roll up from?"

Scared dogs bark. The goons continued to dig their graves as they relentlessly shouted profanities. About a dozen more men stepped onto the arena. It was now 25 vs. 3. No matter who saw it, Jungshik's men should have the victory. His faction consisted of a group of elites that preferred to operate in smaller groups, and now they also had the upper hand in numbers. However, what unfolded next was completely unexpected.

SLICE! STAB!

The swordsmanship of the ragged men was God-like. Their swords parried and blocked the swords of their enemies before plunging the blade's edge or tip into their enemy's vitals.

It didn't take long for many heads to roll across the ground and cover the floor in blood. In just one minute after losing more than two-thirds of their forces, Jungshik's men ran off in a blind panic.

"..."

The ragged men silently observed below before leaving Sungchul and stepping down themselves. Finally, the Drill Sergeant's joyful voice rang out.

"Remaining time is thirty seconds!"

Sungchul was watching the back of the ragged men as the gong rang out to indicate the end.

As I thought... They were Swordslaves.

Not all slaves captured within the Summoning Plaza were sold off. Depending on the whim of the buyers, some of the slaves were returned before being claimed. However, the Summoned, from the moment they fell into the hands of the Slave Hunters, were left in an awkward position of being neither a Summoned nor a resident of this world. In other words, they were stuck in limbo.

These homeless existences would more than likely be eliminated, but a portion of those that were determined to be talented were utilized for various purposes. There were slaves trained in the way of the sword called "Swordslaves." Their stats weren't outstanding, but they had a high mastery of the sword after being forced to hone their swordsmanship and were even able to cut down enemies stronger than them due to their lack of fear or emotions. Now not only one, but three of these Swordslaves had made their appearance.

They used their heads. Swordslaves are existences akin to tools, so it is easier for the Summoning Palace to overlook them. They can also conveniently be thrown away after.

Under the protection of the Swordslaves, Sungchul gained a Representative match participation slot. Jungshik brought along a small number of his men to approach Sungchul as though he had been waiting for Sungchul to step down.

"Hey, what kind of a fuck are you?"

He looked expressionless, but an inexplicable sense of wrath leaked out of his body. He was glaring at him with a murderous aura that would normally be difficult to even keep eye contact with, yet Sungchul didn't fidget. Instead, he pointed over his shoulder and quietly said,

"Don't bark at me. Directly go talk to the people involved."

Sungchul's finger pointed at the Swordslaves that were standing conspicuously under the arena.

Jungshik peered over towards the Swordslaves, then backed away from Sungchul with his men. The Selection Match continued onwards.

Jungshik's faction's vigor was surely shriveled. The Summoned who were affiliated with Hakchul's faction fought their way onto the arena, and the other Preselected that were observing the situation also began to step into the Selection Matches. An exciting competition unfolded, but the winners were the better-trained Preselected.

Jungshik Park, Woojung, Sunghae, and others that followed Sungchul were able to be selected without problems, as well as two other Preselected who had barely survived the Werewolf attack.

Twenty of the thirty slots were filled within just a moment. Only ten slots remained.

Ahmuge had not appeared yet, but there was a weird atmosphere circling the Plaza. Jungshik had been gathering his men and preparing to strike against the Swordslaves.

The Homunculi were spread throughout the Plaza, but nothing else mattered to Jungshik. His dignity couldn't bear to let these Swordslaves go. As the leader of a group, his faction might end up disbanding if he was branded as a leader that couldn't repay the deaths of his men.

Jungshik pulled out his Dagger of Swiftness and challenged a Swordslave to a fight. It was the man wearing a red devil t-shirt and a fisherman's hat.

"Let's have a go."

"…"

Looking at Jungshik who was pulling out his blade, the Swordslave wordlessly unsheathed his sword in response. Jungshik let out a shout before charging towards the Swordslave.

CLANG!

The swords met in the air and sparks flew. When their swords met, Jungshik felt that his opponent's strength was no greater than his own. He might even be stronger. Jungshik felt encouraged and unleashed a torrent of continuous blows. The Dagger of Swiftness moved blindingly as it targeted several of the Swordslave's vital points. However, he hit a limit as his attacks were pitifully simple and were also completely blocked by the Swordslave's defenses.

Jungshik had been on the offensive until now, but the roles were suddenly reversed. It was at this moment when he realized that there was a difference in skill between them which couldn't be overcome by merely relying on strength. Rusted and gouged in many places, the bloody sword of the Swordslave came stabbing towards his chest. Jungshik had no way of blocking it.

"Hahaha! Shit!"

At that moment, a miracle occurred. The blade that looked to pierce his ribs at any time was blocked by another sword.

It was Ahmuge.

She didn't bother looking back as she coldly spoke.

"Look carefully at their eyes. They aren't human."

"…"

It was then that Jungshik finally saw the Swordslave's eyes under the Fishermen's hat. It was like a ghost's eyes; white with no iris.

W-what the…this bastard…isn't human?!

Jungshik felt a chill, and his body tensed up; the Swordslave left and returned to its original place.

It was almost obvious that Ahmuge would be the next candidate. The other Summoned had clearly seen her skills and didn't even dare to challenge her.

"Are there no challengers? I'll count to thirty, then!"

The new Drill Sergeant's countdown started. Ahmuge looked around expressionlessly. When she found Sungchul looking at her from below, she gave a little wave. Ten seconds before the countdown ended, three men in rags climbed onto the arena; they were the Swordslaves.

***

What a strange feeling.

A wrinkle formed between Sungchul's eyes. He could guess who was behind the Swordslaves the moment they arrived to support him. Krill Regall, when he had given him the Bracelet of Alias, had urged Sungchul not to be surprised if something unexpected happened. He must have been talking about the appearance of the Swordslaves. What didn't add up was why the Swordslaves were aiming at Ahmuge.

To hunt a Regressor in such a public place? Why use a nobody like Krill Regall for that?

The Regressor Hunt was the deepest of secrets, enjoyed by only the most powerful of individuals. The organizers of the Hunt were all famous masters that had the complete trust of those powers. There was no way that such a no-name Mage would be used for such an important task.

Something is wrong. Was I mistaken?

There was no way that Sungchul could have known that a person existed who would issue a kill order over a mere stolen staff. He decided to step back from the situation and continue observing the arena. The Swordslaves simultaneously pulled out their blades.

SHNNNG-

Vicious and chipped blades glistened dangerously in the sunlight. Ahmuge retreated and spoke to the newly appointed Drill Sergeant.

"Isn't the Selection Match a one vs. one battle?"

The Drill Sergeant was loudly and busily chewing on some candy.

"It is time for some snacks. There will be a chance to talk after snack time."

It was deliberate ignorance. Ahmuge smiled bitterly and tried to step down from the arena, but the Drill Sergeant spoke revealing his saw-like teeth, as though he'd been waiting for this exact moment.

"Anyone who steps down after rising to the stage will be disqualified! Thirty consecutive penalty games will be given to all who are disqualified!"

These words felt like a death sentence to Ahmuge.

Is this perhaps…?

Pessimistic speculations were teeming in her mind. It had to be a trap. It wasn't something a newbie Summoned had cooked up either, but something prepared for her by external forces.

STEP. STEP.

The Swordslaves drew closer. She pulled out the Spirit Wolf Staff and summoned the two Spirit Wolves; they protectively drew together in front of her. Holding a staff in one hand and a sword in the other, she watched with cold eyes as the Swordslaves closed in.

One of the Swordslaves dove forward.

"Krrr!"

The Spirit Wolves bared their teeth as they charged towards the Swordslave. He stopped and backed up to where the other Swordslaves were, working together to slay the wolves without much difficulty.

It wasn't an intentional cooperation, but something which occurred coincidentally. The audience cheered, but Ahmuge began chewing her lips while regretting her failed tactic.

I was too impatient. There's still a three-minute cooldown before I can Summon the wolves again...

The Summoned beasts that were supposed to guard the front had been slain all too easily. She only had her sword to attack with, but her opponents were much too tricky for her to rely on that. Swordslaves lacked any form of personality and couldn't be negotiated with or reasoned with. The only way to defeat the Swordslaves was by overpowering them, but Ahmuge lacked the required strength.

SHIK! SHIK!

The Swordslaves lunged at Ahmuge. A sword barely missed, but nicked her on the neck. The sharp assault was just a few inches off from leaving a hole in her neck.

" ... "

Sungchul was within the audience that was overlooking this spectacle. Unlike the others, he wasn't observing the fight itself; he was instead examining the underlying motive to this chain of events.

They don't intend to capture her. They would've aimed at her legs or her arms if that was the case.

At that moment, another sword came rushing at her neck. She dodged the sword once again, but it managed to catch a bit of her hair leaving a few strands fluttering behind. This resolved one of the questions he had. The Swordslaves' aim was not to capture, but to kill her. But why?

Sungchul moved his attention to the audience. There must be someone relaying commands to the Swordslaves. They could be using Magic or some type of primitive signal. A man soon caught his eyes. He was dressed in a worn tracksuit and a white beanie. It was a different style of clothes from usual, but his face was one which Sungchul knew very well.

Krill Regall. So that scum is ordering around the Swordslaves.

He held a small whistle in his hand. It was a whistle used by the Slave Hunters. A fog of suspicion lifted from Sungchul's mind as soon as he saw the whistle.

Krill is holding hands with the Slave Hunters. He must have borrowed the Swordslaves from them, but why is that guy aiming for Ahmuge? I don't know what it could be, but one thing is clear: he's unrelated to the Regressor Hunt.

This meant that there was no reason for him to not go help Ahmuge. However, she was handling herself quite well on the arena. To most people, it would look as if she would soon be killed, but to Sungchul things seemed quite different. She was dodging the attacks by a hair's breadth, but she wasn't facing any real danger.

Should I sit back and watch her skills?

He crossed his arms and leisurely observed the fight.

"Haaa…"

In that same moment, Ahmuge was dodging another blade. She could have parried it, but rather than engaging them she focused on maximizing the distance between them. That was because even though the Swordslaves' blades might be difficult to predict, their feet were still slow. After avoiding a series of attacks, Ahmuge gained some distance and began utilizing more of the arena's available space.

The mode of this battle changed from an encirclement to a chase. The Swordslaves were slowly chasing Ahmuge as she circled farther from the center of the arena. If they had independent thoughts, they might have been able to properly gather their strength and prevent her from escaping, but this proved too difficult for the Swordslaves with their muddled minds. It was thanks to this weakness that Ahmuge was able to utilize clever movements to delay their attacks. This scene was enough to elicit cries of admiration from the crowd, and the cheers for the delicate female underdog only grew louder as time passed.

Three blood curling minutes passed under a roar of cheers. This time, Ahmuge didn't make the mistake of immediately summoning the wolves. She circled the outer limits of the arena while waiting for the Swordslaves' formation to weaken. It didn't take too long. Ahmuge allowed for some distance from the frontmost Swordslave, and he quickly broke formation to stab at her with his blade. She evaded the strike then held out her staff to call out the wolves.

"Awoooo!"

With a sudden flash of light, two Spirit Wolves appeared by her feet.

"Get him!"

Ahmuge rushed over with her wolves at the exposed Swordslave in a three-directional assault. The Swordslave mechanically tried swinging his sword to defend himself, but Ahmuge bravely pushed forward to draw all of its attention to herself. At this moment, the wolves lunged and sunk their teeth into the exposed neck and heel of the defenseless Swordslave.

Belatedly, the other Swordslaves tried to attack the wolves and Ahmuge, but Ahmuge pulled back the wolves and quickly retreated while watching the critically wounded Swordslave.

"U-ugh…"

Color returned to the iris of the Swordslave.

"Mother…"

The Swordslave's shackles were undone on the moment of its death. With his remaining strength, he stretched out his hand before slumping over. Now there were only two Swordslaves remaining.

Her breath was ragged, but her expression had a bit of leisure to it. It didn't last very long, though.

"W-what? What are these guys?"

Another group approached the stage. They were also wearing rags with hats that covered their faces. More Swordslaves. This time, five Swordslaves stepped up to the arena.

Ahmuge's face quickly grew dark.

It's over. There's no chance with this.

As her mind grew dull, her body also lost its strength.

This wasn't why I came back…I still have a mission I need to complete!

The difference in the level of difficulty between facing three versus facing seven opponents was incomparable. They slowly approached, seeking to overwhelm her with their numbers. The Spirit Wolves growled loudly and tried to retaliate, but they were quickly cut to shreds. There was nothing left for her other than slowly backing away and holding up her sword. She quickly approached the end of the stage.

"It is a disqualification if you step off the arena!"

The Drill Sergeant taunted while he continued to chew on his candy. It was a do-or-die moment. Just then, a face that she had briefly forgotten appeared before her.

Ah, that man! What is he doing now?

Help came as if he was waiting for a signal. Ahmuge watched as a man climbed into the arena. Dressed in rags, sporting messy, unkempt hair, he was a man of few words, unpersonable and cold…yet had unbelievable finesse in cooking. Sungchul Kim had arrived.

"Stand behind me."

He curtly said as he drew his sword. Ahmuge simply nodded her head and moved behind him.

The Swordslaves hesitated as Sungchul approached them. Sungchul's eyes flashed.

As I thought…

The Swordslaves wouldn't attack the person wearing the bracelet. It would actually be more accurate to say that they just couldn't. This was because its bearer was someone their controllers absolutely needed to protect, but would a Swordslave who had completely lost their will ever understand such a complex situation?

Sungchul's blade flew towards a Swordslave's heart. It didn't even try dodging or defending itself. The blade easily pierced through its heart.

"U-ugh…"

This was the limit of those that had lost their ability to decide for themselves. Existences that only moved on command could never decide for themselves when one command was contradicting the other. Sungchul used that weakness to drive his blade through the heart of the Swordslave.

"U-ugh…I want to go home…"

The Swordslave, who had been struck in the heart, regained its mind before dying. The Plaza was instantly filled with whispers.

"What…How did that happen?"

"Who…is that person? Is he the leader of those bums?"

Sungchul pulled off the bracelet on his wrist and handed it to Ahmuge as he whispered,

"Wear this, and you won't be attacked."

He stepped off the arena after leaving behind those few words. The Drill Sergeant could not threaten Sungchul with disqualification due to not only having been qualified earlier but also having the bracelet in his possession.

The Drill Sergeant only looked towards Krill Regall with confused eyes, but he didn't receive any answer. The Swordslaves approached Ahmuge in confusion, but when she put on the bracelet, they froze like statues and refused to come any closer. Ahmuge pierced one of them in the heart just as Sungchul had done before.

"Let's go…to victory…!"

The man wearing the red shirt fell with his blood pouring out. There was no resistance nor defiance in him. Ahmuge, who had gotten her second wind, began rapidly "liberating" the Swordslaves. Three Swordslaves fell in just moments, and a very low-pitched whistle rang out.

The frozen Swordslaves fell back and stepped down from the arena. The audience that had been holding their breath while watching Ahmuge's struggle broke out in cheers. Jungshik was not an exception.

"Wow, fuck! That was great!"

Sungchul turned towards a man hidden amongst the crowds within the chaos of cheers. He had hidden his identity with a tracksuit, but the face that was hideously smeared in panic and rage was definitely Krill's.

Sungchul waved his hand at him. Krill grew bright red with rage and disappeared with the Swordslaves.

"Thank you."

Ahmuge approached from behind as Sungchul watched Krill leave. She looked up to him as she returned the worn brass bracelet.

"Really...I'm truly grateful."

A heartfelt gratitude would have a sincerity that could not be expressed through flowery words.

"...I only kept my promise, that's all."

Sungchul turned his back to her and started walking away. There were too many people heading in their direction for them to talk any more personally. And there was also the message delivered by a Sky Squirrel that had drawn his interest.

[There is something we must discuss at length. Come to the Forsaken Church immediately.]

Chapter 11 – Certification

"Son of a bitch…"

By now, Krill was almost entirely consumed by his anger. He couldn't help it. He had failed the important mission that his respected senior Dolorence Winterer had entrusted him with.

The Slave Hunters were following behind him.

"You know how hard it was to raise those Swordslaves? You'll have to pay us back in full."

They were greedy and filthy mongrels, but Krill had no allies more reliable than them. He pulled out two gems and handed them over to the Slave Hunters.

"Thank you for your patience. Come, everyone, let's get this taken care of."

A very jubilant smile formed upon the Slave Hunter's lips. They never expected to receive enough money to live like kings in a brothel for a whole month, even after splitting it evenly. It wasn't often for Slave Hunters, who were the bottom feeders of society, to get an opportunity like this, but not everyone was so pleased.

"This isn't good."

It was the one-armed Slave Hunter that had extended a helping hand to Krill in the past. He refused Krill's request when it was offered, but when Krill began offering it to the others, he caved in and followed. It couldn't be helped.

If he hadn't followed, his companions would have killed the one-armed Slave Hunter and tossed him into the Homunculi's feed.

"Messing with the Summoned is strictly forbidden by Palace rules. Don't act rashly."

He continued to caution Krill. Krill had first let him talk out of gratitude for the past, but even when his goal was so close, the man wouldn't shut up. The anger he had been suppressing burst out.

232

"Hmm? But you do it all the time. I don't think that's something a man whose very job is to turn the Summoned into mindless slaves should be saying to others."

"…"

The one-armed man turned silent.

He knew very well that he had nothing to retort with. But he couldn't simply stay quiet. He gave a final warning with heartfelt sincerity.

"…I am also an Airfruit alumni. I am your senior."

At this, Krill glared icily at the right-armed man.

"I don't remember having a Slave Hunter as my senior."

The right-armed man lowered his head and didn't open his mouth anymore. They soon arrived at the Forsaken Cathedral. Krill couldn't hide his joy at seeing the man he was looking for waiting there as requested.

"Hey, Mr. Sungchul."

Krill stood in front of Sungchul with six other Slave Hunters by his side. Sungchul indifferently looked over at Krill and his group of Slave Hunters.

"Who are these people?"

"Can't you tell, as someone who has come from the outside?"

Krill smirked.

"…"

"Anyways, you seem to think the world is an easy place since you became a bit stronger. Did you think I was such a pushover?"

Krill's voice gradually grew louder. By the time he finished his question, he was practically shouting at the top of his lungs.

"Do I look like a fucking pushover to you? Huh? You smelly Asian son of a bitch!"

Some laughter spilled out of the Slave Hunters standing behind him.

Sungchul slowly opened his mouth.

"Are these the only people you've come with?"

It was the same, firm voice, no different than before.

Krill smirked again and nodded his head.

"Of course. There's only us here."

"Is that so?"

Sungchul replied indifferently, but that only aggravated Krill even further. Getting red in the face and extremely agitated, Krill declared,

"Should I inform you what we're about to do to you? I'm going to capture you with the help of my friends behind me. Then I'm going to torture you until you beg me for death. Finally, I'm going to turn you into a slave. Though I'm going to have to think a bit about just what kind of slave I should be turning you into."

"It is a good plan."

Sungchul was still calm.

Krill moved to one side and gestured towards the Slave Hunters.

"Now. Let's begin."

Each of the Slave Hunters held their own weapon and walked towards Sungchul. They were Slave Hunters now, but they used to be Mages and warriors worth their salt in the past. Their battle experience and skills were on a different level. One man with a blade scar across his face spoke mockingly.

"Someone from the outside with lots of power, coming to a beginner's training center to show off to complete newbies, don't you know shame?"

Sungchul turned his head towards the man and gave a short reply.

"Yeah."

Sungchul's form briefly shook. By the time Krill's eyes registered the visual cues, he heard a dull thud reverberate in the air in front of him.

"Ack!"

Sungchul's fist had dealt a massive blow to the Slave Hunter's chin. Krill could clearly see what had happened to the Slave Hunter's face after being struck so hard. The Slave Hunter's face had splattered into tiny pieces.

GASP

Sungchul didn't stop. After disintegrating one with his fist, he pulled out his sword and slaughtered the others.

They were no match for him.

The Slave Hunters were dead before they even understood how they had died.

The massacre hadn't even lasted ten seconds.

"S-spare me!"

The one-armed Slave Hunter quickly embraced reality and fell to his knees to beg for his life. Seeing that Sungchul was still approaching, he took out a stake with a red cloth attached to it and pierced it into his heart. His eyes shook intensely, but he bit his lips and quickly spoke with a ragged breath.

"I-I swear! This...I, Christian Ashwood, will not speak of what I have seen today with anyone...If this oath is broken...the cost for such a transgression shall be death...So do I swear to the God of Neutrality!"

Once the oath was completed the stake in his heart magically disappeared, and the red cloth burst into flames turning to ash.

"Ho? An oath. Clever man."

Sungchul left him alone and headed towards Krill. Krill's eyes grew wide in fear. Sungchul's rough hands grabbed his face. And only when an unbearable strength transferred from Sungchul's grip into his skull, did Krill come to a realization.

I-I picked the wrong side...the real monster wasn't Dolorence...It was this person...

However, it was too late to regret now. Sungchul gripped harder and spoke in his usual firm voice.

"Now let's hear it. Tell me everything from start to finish."

—

Krill told him everything he knew. From the moment he saw the advertisement that had led him to the Summoning Palace to the moment he met Dolorence. He told Sungchul about how she had wrapped Sanggil around her fingers and ordered Ahmuge's death.

He revealed everything that had occurred within the Observation Tower to Sungchul. After hearing his story, Sungchul quietly stood up from his seat.

Krill trembled as he carefully looked up at Sungchul.

"I-it was all that Dolorence bitch...the red-haired woman's scheme. I just did as I was told."

"Is that so?"

"Of course. If you let me live, I'll pry Dolorence out and present her to you. I swear by my name."

"I don't need help from someone like you. She'll show herself to me on her own in any case."

WHAM!

Sungchul's fist struck the top of his skull. The young Mage's eyes spun in different directions, and all of his seven orifices spat out blood before he finally fell over.

"Kyu Kyu..."

The Sky Squirrel stayed near its dead master, licking its master's feet.

Sungchul gestured towards the Slave Hunter that was watching the scene with fearful eyes.

"Hey."

Sungchul gathered the corpses with the Slave Hunter and set them all on fire. A black smoke rose from the already burnt Forsaken Cathedral. Sungchul peeked over at the Slave Hunter while he burned the corpses. The man didn't move as he sat on the floor. He seemed to have lost all strength after watching such a murderous spectacle. However, Sungchul didn't care to kill him. He was no longer in the position to tell anyone about this scene even if he was allowed to live out the rest of his life. Even if he did try to tell anyone the truth, the oath would immediately activate, and he'd be sent to cross the river Styx. That was the power held by this oath.

However, to be able to perform the oath so brazenly in that kind of situation...A smile formed on Sungchul's lips. More than anything, he wanted to praise this man's decisiveness and quick thinking. As he continued to think to himself, the Slave Hunter approached him and lowered his head.

"Sir Warrior, whose name I do not know."

Sungchul calmly raised his head and looked at the man. He looked to be in his mid-thirties. He also had relatively intelligent eyes.

"What did you want with me?"

"I have no way of knowing who Sir Warrior is or where Sir Warrior came from, but I have seen it. Sir Warrior is definitely not a normal person."

"Speak briefly. I have to go back to the Plaza soon."

"Will you not take me as your underling?"

"You?"

"It looks like you had some kind of deal with Krill Regall…I don't know much else, but I know I can do a lot better than a greenhorn like Krill."

Christian Ashford was genuinely lowering his head. He had seen it. Brock, who had been a Knight of the empire, was split in two with just a single strike and Giron, who held a high-ranking position in the Thief's Guild, had his neck twisted in just one punch. It wasn't enough to simply call this "very strong," it was simply monstrous.

If anything, the man was at minimum at the same level with the Royal Guards of the Empire, and in the context of the Order of the Iron Blood Knights, he would easily deserve a high ranking position. If Christian could tie himself to such a person, it might be enough to pull him out of his current pathetic life.

"P-please use me. I…I'll do anything."

However, Sungchul's reaction was lukewarm.

"I don't really need anyone. What did you do before you became a Slave Hunter?"

"Mage…I was a Mage. I was even an Airfruit alumni. I can't use Magic now, but I know just about everything when it comes to Magic."

"A Mage…"

There might be a couple of uses. A Mage would know the path which lay ahead of him and would also be able to guide him along the way.

Sungchul wrapped his hand around the Sky Squirrel that was pitifully standing near the pile of flame and gave it to Christian.

"Take care of this little guy, and come find me with him during the graduation ceremony."

He then pulled out a gem and tossed it over to the Slave Hunter. This was a symbol of the faith he held towards Christian. Christian tightly held the gem in his hand and watched Sungchul leave with a mixture of fear and anticipation filling his eyes.

—

The Selection Match had ended successfully. All thirty Representatives had been chosen. Sungchul set out to seek the remaining memorials of the Seven Heroes scattered across the Summoning Palace with Ahmuge, but something unexpected occurred.

They set out to find the Path of Daltanius first, but it seemed as if all of the memorials, starting with this one, had disappeared. There was only a fallen pillar in place of the most anticipated memorial which was of the leader of the Seven Heroes, Desfort, and nothing reacted to their presence.

"How could this be…all of them were taken. I'm not sure what happened, but…"

It looked as though Sungchul wasn't overly concerned. Other than Desfort, the remaining Seven Heroes were all warriors. Sungchul, who had reached the peak of warriors, didn't have much to gain from them. He simply wanted to check out their faces.

While blankly looking at the fallen pillar, he gazed over at Ahmuge and spoke.

"Isn't there one last place left?"

"Ah…yes. There's still that Hero left."

The hero that Ahmuge and Sungchul were referring to was called White Shadow. There weren't any records of him other than some reference to him being an assassin, but on the other hand, there were also some alarming legends which had been passed down. It was rumored that the assassin, who didn't like the thought of records being left of him, had killed all the historians and burned their books.

Thankfully, the memorial of White Shadow still remained. Deep in the woods lay a corpse with a slit throat that gave proof that the memorial of White Shadow was still there. However, Ahmuge reacted strangely. She hurriedly stopped Sungchul as he was about to start the quest.

"I'm deeply sorry...but this quest. Could I do it?"

"Tell me the reason."

"I don't know about the others...but I have to complete White Shadow's objective myself. That's the only way I can save the world."

"I don't think I can accept that."

Sungchul continued to show a lukewarm reaction, so Ahmuge briefly fell into thought and responded with a resolute expression on her face.

"I am only telling this to you. Promise me that you won't speak of this anywhere else."

"It's okay. I don't have any friends to tell."

"You don't...have friends?"

Sungchul nodded.

"So...that's the case."

"So keep talking."

Ahmuge settled down again and spoke with a calm voice.

"I don't know if you'll believe me...but I came from the future."

Sungchul's eyes flashed with curiosity. He knew that she was a Regressor, but for her to speak of it herself. It must have taken an immense amount of resolution. This by itself showed just how much she valued White Shadow's objective.

"That means you're a Regressor?"

She nodded.

"My real name is Sujin Lee. I came from ten years in the future. It's up to you whether you believe me or not."

Sujin Lee. It was a pretty name. Sungchul thought idly as he threw out a blunt question.

"Why did you return from the future to this hellish Summoning Palace?"

"I want to save the world from the Calamity of Annihilation."

Sujin spoke without hesitation. There was not a single trace of trickery or falsehood. It was an utterance filled with confidence that could only come from an unwavering conviction. Sungchul was intrigued by her words.

I suppose this means that the world won't be saved by my efforts. Does this mean that I failed?

It was disappointing news, but the future that Regressors spoke of wasn't that reliable, either. Whatever future they had been in could always be changed or overturned. After all, anyone would be curious about what the future holds. Sungchul asked Sujin another question while not really expecting much.

"From what? It isn't the Seven Heroes, is it?"

He, at least, didn't want to hear that the Seven Heroes had won. If the world had fallen to such an opponent, it would invalidate his efforts to obtain strength after turning the world against him.

Sujin carefully looked up and replied after a moment.

"We overcame the second calamity and the third."

Sungchul found himself unintentionally sighing in relief.

So I managed to bash Sajators' head in at least...

But, Sujin hadn't finished speaking.

"But we ultimately faced a great calamity that the Seven Heroes couldn't even compare to..."

Sungchul felt an anxiety that made all the hairs on his body stand on end. He didn't know why, but an unimaginably ominous feeling, which made his body shrivel, was enveloping him like a blaze.

"That…great calamity…what are you talking about?"

As he felt anxious and feeble, Sujin finished speaking.

"…The Enemy of the World, Sungchul Kim."

"…?!"

Sungchul's eyes flared. Seeing his aggressive response, Sujin put on a bitter smile and added a few words of comfort.

"Ah…don't misunderstand. It is a different person. Your face and body are completely different."

However, Sungchul's face didn't look any brighter. The Enemy of the World that she spoke of could only be himself.

I…destroy the world…? How…That can't be true!

"Why are you standing there so blankly?"

Sujin tried to start the conversation again, but Sungchul simply shook his head.

"No, it's nothing."

He muttered to himself under his breath as he closed his eyes. Under the darkness of his eyelids, he recalled the face of the precious existence which he had to protect.

I will not be corrupted.

***

The future a Regressor has come from is never set in stone. There is always a possibility that those living in the present make enough difference in the choices they are given that the future the Regressor foretells never comes to pass. And, despite it all, Ahmuge's words were enough to put Sungchul in a deep state of shock. Haunted by insomnia and filled with doubts, Sungchul spent several days deep inside the forest without moving.

I…will destroy the world…?

It was nonsensical. Who had been the one to rise to the task at a time when those in power had simply prolonged the Calamity and left their burdens onto the next generation? It was Sungchul. How much had he given up for the sake of saving the world since that moment? He had lost his best friend and also all of the reputation he had built. He had turned the world against him in order to gain strength. Wasn't it all for the purpose of saving the world that he was now hiding inside the Summoning Palace and pretending to be a newbie?

Fortunately, the confusion didn't last long. He was a man with conviction stronger than steel. The doubts which had been haunting him like a malicious ghost washed away with the sound of the starting horn for the Rank Match.

"Now now, humans! It is now time for the final trial! Everyone did well for Blanche Plaza so far. Now, go through that door towards the Central Plaza!"

The Summoned headed towards the Central Plaza under the guidance of the Homunculi.

"Where have you been?"

Sujin found Sungchul and began talking.

"It's none of your business."

Sungchul spoke bluntly and made some distance between them. It had to be this way. Sujin was from a future that should have never existed. Her very presence in this world made him feel uncomfortable.

"…"

Sujin didn't continue the conversation but still remained around him.

There were already hundreds of people from the other Plazas crowding within the Central Plaza. There were two circular arenas; the majority of the Homunculi were standing around them and gathered all of the people there.

"Those that were nominated as Representatives, please get up here now."

Thirty people from each Plaza walked up to the arena.

"Unpredictable! Exciting! Humans participating in the penalty game of predicting all thirty consecutive winners step this way!"

Those that weren't included as Representatives were taken to a place where the ground was partitioned into three, where someone had etched an X and an O using a stone in two of the slots and the third was left blank.

Those people without the courage to fight on their own, those who had stood behind others to survive thus far, and those who were too weak all looked around nervously at their surroundings as each one of them stepped onto their designated area. One man stepped forward and shouted out amidst the silence.

"Everyone, let's give it our all. No matter how dangerous the situation, remaining calm will reveal a way out!"

It was Hakchul. He couldn't become a Representative in the end. The latter half of the Selection Match was indescribably competitive despite the fact that it was fought over by the mediocre and the weak. Of the 150 casualties that had occurred over the course of the selection process, about 80% were a result of the fights for the last five available spots. Hakchul had stepped up to the arena but quickly retreated due to how savage the fighting had become. It was a secret known only to Hakchul that he had, in fact, gone up to the stage three times by aiming for the moments the Homunculus in charge was too busy to check his face. However, a man who failed three times was never meant to succeed.

"Everyone! Let's work together and get through this trial! Nothing is impossible if we work with our collective wisdom!"

The gong sounded, marking the beginning of the Rank Matches as Hakchul's words of inspiration began to fade away.

"First Representatives to the front!"

Each of the first Representatives from the Crimson and Blanche Plazas stood facing one another. Blanche Plaza's first Representative was the lucky man who had obtained a slot without contest when no one had the courage to step up. The sound of rumbling feet with hundreds of people rushing around could be heard coming from behind the two fighters.

"Now, the heart-pounding prediction of the winner is taking place! 'O' to predict a Blanche victory, and 'X' for a loss! Stand on the blank sheet if you predict a tie!"

The entire arena became noisy as people began to move about due to the order given by the amused Drill Sergeant. The audience observed the appearance of each Representative standing in the arena. As it was impossible to determine who was stronger at the current moment, people could only make their judgment based on appearance. The Summoned could do nothing but bet their lives on whoever looked like they would be the better fighter. Of course, there were also some that used their wits to make their bets too.

"That guy! It's the one who became the first Representative, right?"

It was Hakchul.

"That guy became a Representative by pure luck, so he'll definitely lose. Let's all go to X! Trust me and follow me!"

Hakchul shouted as he headed to the X area first. Even those who had been ignoring Hakchul felt that what he said was logical. Everyone close by headed towards the X area and stimulated a herd instinct, which caused the majority of the people to stand on the X. Soon, it became so crowded that there was not enough space to accommodate everyone on X anymore.

After a brief moment, the iron gates of the Central Plaza opened, and the Homunculi dragged out a large monster. It was a nine-headed, dinosaur-like creature. By its size alone, it was much larger than a Tam Tam and fearsome beyond compare. The monster was controlled by the Homunculus that was riding on its back and stood behind the humans within the victor-prediction group.

"Grrr…"

Several people fainted at the sight of the drool wetting the floor that was coming from its massive jaw.

"A lot of people have gathered to that side. I guess they think I'm going to win?"

The number one Representative from the Crimson Plaza was a confident-looking youth in his early-twenties. He smirked towards the Blanche Plaza's number one Representative who was frozen stiff with tension.

They might have picked correctly, but unfortunately, they've awoken my sense of mischief.

The man who was talking nonsense to himself turned towards the Homunculus referee and spoke briefly.

"I forfeit."

The Homunculus referee looked over to the Blanche Plaza Representative and spoke.

"Hey, human. Do you agree to the opponent's surrender?"

The Blanche Plaza's lucky guy had no reason to refuse him. He nodded his head, and the Homunculus raised the white flag.

"It is Blanche Plaza's...victory!"

Just like that, the first Representative Match was over. Its name was grand, but the Representative's Match essentially is just a bonus game. What the Summoning Plaza wanted from the Summoned after the fierce combat of the fourth Rank Match was a person that had the courage and ambition to claim their place. The true Rank Matches had been completed before the Representative Match even began.

The nine-headed monster let out a cry as soon as the Homunculus lifted the white flag. After its fearsome cry, the monster began to stomp on and devour everyone on the X area.

"Hey, you fuck! You said that the Crimson Plaza would win!"

Those that were near Hakchul grabbed his collar and shook him, but the water had already been spilled.

"What are you going to do now? Huh?"

Hakchul looked half-insane as he sang a song.

"A B C D E F G, H I J K L M N O P Q R S T, U V W X Y Z...Haha!"

His song was cut short when he was swallowed by the monster. Several hundred survivors were either eaten by the creature or stomped on by its heavy feet meeting their ultimate tragic fate. There was only blood and corpses left on the X spot, looking as though a hurricane had blown through.

"Eh? Did my prank go too far?"

The other matches fell into a similar rhythm, but there were more than a few that fought with their lives on the line. The rewards for these matches were considerably great. It was a big deal to be able to choose your desired class transfer tome from among all of the rewards. Fierce battles and uneventful surrenders passed by until finally, it was Sungchul's turn. He didn't even have a shred of desire to forfeit, and his opponent looked to be the same.

The tall man wielding a large knife began to taunt him.

"Looks like you got the short end of the stick if you've become my opponent."

He released an aggressive aura as he pulled out his blade.

"But what should I do? It's a secret, but I already met the Goddess of Victory before stepping onto here."

Sungchul discovered that there was a magic-induced blessing surrounding the man's body.

He's been plastered with buffs. It must be the red-head who's siding with him.

Sungchul fidgeted with the bracelet before bluntly asking a question to his opponent who was laughing and showing his teeth.

"Does that Goddess have red hair, perhaps?"

Surprise flickered across his opponent's eyes.

"How did you know that?"

In response to the question, he looked up at the Observation Tower that was beyond the Palace walls. The spectators from the Order of the Iron Blood Knights that Dolorence represented were gathered within the Observation Tower linked to the Blanche Plaza. Dolorence, who had been concerned by Krill's sudden radio silence, became relaxed after the man wearing the bracelet appeared.

That stupid son of a bitch. Where did he go? He should have contacted me if he had somewhere else to be. It's fine that everything turned out as planned, but I'm not letting this go after I meet him.

Beside her, Sanggil and other high-rank Knights were socializing while watching the arena.

"Oh. Is that the Knight Captain's offspring?"

"He's not as attractive as the rumors say, but...he looks masculine."

"Yes. Masculine."

Sanggil, who had allied with Dolorence, was sweating profusely as he continued trying to match the mood and sharply turned towards her. She did not flinch as she met his eyes and nodded. Today would progress just as they'd planned.

The gong rang out, marking the start of the match. The high-rank Knights held their breath as they watched the fight before a roar of applause exploded from among the Knights. The Knight Captain's son had skewered his opponent in the heart with just a single strike. Although it was more accurate to say that the opponent couldn't gauge his own strength and had ran into the waiting blade on his own accord.

"How could this be...!! He overcame this opponent who had at least three buffs including Haste, Levitation, and Peerless in such a simple manner..."

"I can't believe it. That calm and calculating nature. Taking action without hesitation. It feels as though I'm watching the Iron Blood Knights' Captain's rookie Summoned days."

The faces of Dolorence and Sanggil grew sour at the cheer that filled the Observation Tower. Sanggil took a moment to approach Dolorence and confronted her in a hushed voice.

"What happened, Mage?"

Sanggil glared at her as though he could kill her on the spot.

Dolorence felt her heart drop but refused to let it show.

"I'll take care of it. Before that man meets anyone else."

"No...do you have any idea what you're saying right now..."

At that moment, two high-rank Knights approached Sanggil. His face was wrinkled in anger, but he was able to straighten out his face and smile when he turned to face his companions.

"Hey, congrats, Sanggil. You are as good as guaranteed a promotion now. With this, we have become the only major faction with a direct descendent of our Order's Founder who is capable of continuing the lineage."

"Ah…well, it was nothing much."

Sanggil wiped his forehead as he replied. Dolorence took that moment to lightly slip out of the Observation Tower.

Sanggil saw Dolorence running off like a stray cat and thought to himself.

It turned out like this because I trusted a Mage's promise. I should have done this by myself from the start.

Sanggil excused himself from the crowd and also slipped out of the Observation Tower. As he stepped out, the Plaza exploded in cheers. It was because another Representative had won a life-risking battle. It was Sujin. She pointed her sword at the kneeling enemy.

"I-I lost." The opponent proclaimed her surrender and Sujin nodded to accept it. Her blade, which had absorbed White Phantom's vision, was a degree sharper than before, and it was also at an incomparable level within the Summoning Palace. Sujin, who had easily earned her victory, headed over towards Sungchul standing below the arena.

"What are you up to?"

She didn't expect an answer. Sungchul peeked over to her before speaking in a low voice.

"It's as you can see."

He was counting his Palace Tokens one-by-one and placing them inside his pocket. There were 53 tokens in total, which meant that he had exceeded his goal.

"That's great. It also looks like your mood has improved somewhat."

Sujin smiled brightly towards Sungchul, but he didn't respond.

"Did I do something wrong?"

She took the opportunity to carefully ask with a bit of emotion mixed in, but he simply shook his head.

"No. It's just that I want to be alone."

Sungchul got up after he placed all of the Tokens in his pocket.

"It is time."

Soon, a bell loud enough to shake the whole arena rang out.

The bell announced the end of all the trials.

***

"Now, everyone go grab your Class Transfer Tomes and move to the altar."

In total, there were 83 Summoned who had completed the trials. The number of graduates was higher than average, but considering the fact that Blanche Plaza alone had 2418 people summoned during the mass summoning ritual, it couldn't be regarded as a large number.

Sungchul looked at the Class Transfer Tome he was holding. It was the Tome of Echo Mage. The moment had arrived for him to absorb the power of one of the Seven Heroes' hidden tomes. He followed the other Summoned up to the altar while holding the Tome of Echo Mage in his hand.

The Summoning Palace's affiliate Mages, wearing thick hoods that covered their faces, surrounded the altar in an orderly line and started chanting an incantation using an incomprehensible language. Runes that were engraved throughout the altar gave off a blue luminescence which shot up into the sky between the Summoned who were standing above them, creating pillars of light. The Summoned watched the spectacle with their jaws wide open, awestruck.

Their surroundings quickly grew dim during this time. It was as though the sun had been swallowed by something unseen; the Summoning Palace was covered in sudden darkness. The

Summoned were, once again, surprised at the change. Sungchul, however, gazed expressionlessly up towards the sky. The eclipse was in progress.

Class distribution had to occur during a full eclipse. This eclipse, which occurred at a regular interval, was the optimal moment for a Mass Class Distribution. The moment the sun was completely obscured by the moon, the chanting of the Mages grew louder, and a message appeared before Sungchul.

[Open the Class Transfer Tome.]

Sungchul opened the Echo Mage's Tome. A pillar of light that was positioned on the altar drew closer to Sungchul and surrounded him in its light. Several tens of thousands of letters written inside the tome separated from its pages and floated within the light before gathering on his body.

[You have been bestowed with the Blessing of the Echo Mage.]

[Congratulations! Legendary Class: Echo Mage has been acquired!]

Reward: Class – Echo Mage acquired

Sungchul immediately opened his class and stats screen.

[Stats]

Strength 999+ Dexterity 853
Stamina 801 Magic Power 32
Intuition 25 Magic Resist 621
Resilience 502 Charisma 18
Luck 18

[Class]
Main Class – Primordial Warrior (Mythic)
Sub Class – Echo Mage (Legendary)
Sub Class – High Class Chef (Rare)
Sub Class – Alchemist (Rare)

He finally managed to get a hold of the Echo Mage class. Even on his status screen, everything that pertained to Magic had increased, even Resilience had increased by a minuscule amount of one. He had managed to fulfill all of his goals in coming here.

Sungchul recalled the Devil of the Demon Realm.

I don't think it will take much longer.

The Summoned looked at their changed status as the ritual came to an end and light returned to the world. The Homunculi, who numbered several hundreds, all took off their hats to show proper respect and etiquette towards these humans.

"Now now, humans! You have done well! We, Homunculi, show proper respect to the humans who managed to survive until this day!"

Within this exciting atmosphere, the Summoned finally experienced the end of this impossibly long and hellish journey. It was during this moment that the massive Palace gates on the south side began to open.

[Congratulations on graduating from the Summoning Palace.]

[You have surpassed all of the trials of the Summoning Palace and have proven your ability to survive this world.]

All the survivors saw the same message appear before their eyes. There were some with tears and others with wide smiles. Each had their own reactions, but one thing was clear: They had gotten through this hell without dying.

The Summoned headed towards the open gates of the Summoning Palace with their expectations and burdens weighing on their hearts.

Beyond the Palace gates lay a wide expanse of grassland, and a shining city shimmering in a golden light was set before them like a beautiful painting.

"Where are you planning to go now?"

Sujin approached Sungchul as she asked.

"…"

He didn't answer her. Sujin's eyes flashed with disappointment, but she briefly said her goodbyes towards his back as he moved away.

"We'll meet again as fate allows it."

After leaving those words, Sujin turned and headed east.

A sigh escaped Sungchul's mouth. He was filled with regret and doubts about whether he should inquire about his future. Whether he should ask her for the reason he had fallen or what kind of events were awaiting him. However, he eventually overcame the sweet temptation.

The future you have seen won't come to pass.

Corruption begins with but a tiny seed of doubt. It was right to cut out the roots, which would slowly consume him and hinder his ability to complete everything that needed to be done because that was just an uncertain future. He trusted himself. There were no doubts in his mind regarding that.

There was also another reason why he needed to separate himself from Sujin. It was because a certain red-headed female Mage was waiting for him behind a fallen stone pillar.

"Hello, Mr. Cute Recruit."

Dolorence spoke with a hint of playfulness in her voice.

"Do you mind talking with me for a bit?"

Sungchul nodded, and Dolorence led him towards the outer edge of a forest.

"Thank you for being so cooperative."

She revealed her true nature once they arrived at a location far enough from prying eyes.

"I'll at least send you off painlessly."

Dolorence conjured an icy storm which roared fiercely from her palms as soon as the words left her mouth. Once she extended her hands, the icy storm grew explosively and consumed Sungchul. After the storm passed, only a pillar of ice in the vague shape of a human remained.

"I do feel bad, but what can I do? This is my job, after all."

Dolorence adjusted her staff and stepped towards the frozen figure of Sungchul. That was so that she could smash it to pieces. When she approached his statue, she felt an unexpected, murderous aura pouring out from behind her.

An enemy?!

As she began to turn, a blunt force struck her. It was powerful enough to cause her mind to go blank.

"Khuk!"

Dolorence briefly caught her breath before coughing up blood on the floor.

"Aaargh!"

She had lowered her guard. She had allowed herself to lose herself in front of such an easy prey and had unexpectedly been ambushed. But...who could it be?

Dolorence fought through the backbreaking pain and slowly turned her head. An unexpected figure stood there towering over her like an Angel of Death.

"Y-you...why?"

The one who had ambushed her was Grand Knight Sanggil Ma. Wielding a hefty Warhammer, he glared at her with murderous intent.

It was at this moment, a passage from a Magic-related reference book from a distant past popped into her mind.

Nothing in this world is fixed.

Everything is in constant flux.

Regardless of how slowly or quickly things change.

"You dare think you can play around with me?"

The beast that had been wrapped around her fingers had broken free and was now baring his teeth towards her. He approached Dolorence, who no longer had enough strength to resist, and lifted his Warhammer.

"S-stop!"

Dolorence, who had realized what he was about to do, could only flail her arms and legs while shouting pitifully, but it was all meaningless. Sanggil crushed her limbs one after the other. She shrieked in pain each time, but the hatred never left her eyes.

"I will curse you…Sanggil Ma‼"

"Do what you want to, Mage."

Sanggil stomped on her head with his military boots after mercilessly crushing her limbs. Her face was then shoved into the ground.

With his foot still on her head, Sanggil pulled out a pipe and began to smoke as he talked to himself and held a smug smile on his face.

"I should have done this from the start. It's just that I'm too soft at times. Isn't that right, Mage?"

He gradually added strength to his foot as he continued speaking. Dolorence tried to scream, but it was buried by the dirt.

Sanggil leisurely puffed some smoke as he looked over at the frozen Sungchul.

"Is this that brat Ahram's stand-in? It looks like he had some luck on his side."

Sanggil casually kicked Dolorence's head before heading towards Sungchul to look over his frozen form.

"Quite a pity, but this is the kind of place Other World is. This kind of helpless situation happens so regularly here."

Sanggil lifted his Warhammer once again, seeking to finish what Dolorence had started, but as he begun his swing, an ironic voice spilled out from the front.

"That's what I think as well."

Sanggil's eyes grew wide. In the next moment, the ice shattered and a rough hand gripped around his neck.

"Ugh…ughp…"

Sanggil's feet were lifted into the air and began flailing about helplessly. His eyes filled with terror on seeing the monstrous person that had broken out of the ice.

W-What is this? This fucker…

It was unimaginable. The Grand Knight, who had reached the qualities of a super human and whose strength surpassed 300, was being oppressed so easily. He tried to break free of the grip on his neck using all of his strength, but it was pointless.

"Kuuh…"

Through his fading vision, Sanggil saw the mysterious man touching his own face. His bones and muscles were making grotesque noises as they were adjusted. It was at this moment that Sanggil came to a terrible realization.

C-could it be?!

When he finally saw the monster's face, he started panicking and let out an incoherent scream.

"E-Enemy of the W-World, K-Kim!!"

CRACK

Sungchul's grip literally pulverized Sanggil's throat. The Grand Knight, who was still in the air, fell limp and a mixture of feces and urine came spilling out from his shining armor.

Sungchul tied a noose around Sanggil's neck then hung him from a tree. He then headed over to the broken-limbed red-headed Mage who lay awaiting death.

"You sure love pranks."

Dolorence spat out the dirt in her mouth and looked at the person that was looking down at her.

Who…?

There was no way a nobody like Dolorence would recognize Sungchul's face. He stood over her and spoke quietly.

"But you were unlucky."

A large hammer materialized in Sungchul's hands. It was the legendary Warhammer forged by tempering the sky into a weapon, Fal Garaz. A forgotten name formed in her mind as soon as she saw this legendary weapon.

Could it be…that this person is…!

WHAM!

255

A refreshing sound wave rang out from the forest. Sungchul left the forest, leaving behind the Bracelet of Alibi in front of the splattered remains of Dolorence's skull.

Sporadic groups of Summoned could be seen walking through the field along a burned-out road that headed towards Golden City.

What should I do now?

He had managed to get hold of a Mage class, but it was just another beginning. He was familiar with how to deal with Mages, but he didn't know as much about Magic itself. One had to enter a School of Magic or a Guild to properly learn about Magic from its foundations, but he had a curse that didn't bode well with that situation.

"Status Screen: Curses"

Sungchul brought up a screen showing the curses that had been cast on him. His eyes were filled with many words.

[Curses]

Final Declaration of Grand Mage Balzark
(Intuition -10)
...
Adelwight, Witch of the Haunted Forest's Common Curse
(-5 Strength / Erectile Dysfunction)
Enemy of the Kingdom
(Faction: Nemesis of Human Kingdom, Blank Check Reward)
...
Enemy of the Allied Mage's Guild
(Faction: Nemesis of Allied Mage's Guild and Sub guilds)

The immediate problem within the screen was the curse which made him the enemy of the Allied Mage's Guild. The Allied Mage's Guild was an alliance formed between every guild, school, and military organizations only excluding wandering or exiled Mages.

This was the kind of organization he had been declared an enemy of.

He might be able to hide his identity with the Deceiver's Veil, but it was another matter to enter a guild or a school with Mages who were naturally suspicious and prone to deception themselves.

"..."

As he briefly contemplated on a plan, a familiar friend lingered around his feet.

"Kyu Kyu!"

It was Krill's orphaned Sky Squirrel. Sungchul held out his hand for the Sky Squirrel to climb onto his shoulder.

"There you are!"

Farther north of the road, a man with a prosthetic limb wearing a dog-hide robe smiled brightly as he walked over. It was the slave hunter, Christian Ashwood.

Sungchul looked over the Slave Hunter without much thought as a serene smile suddenly formed on his lips. He had only now recalled Christian's former profession.

Chapter 12 – Admission

"You wish to learn Magic?"

Christian looked at Sungchul with a surprised expression. Sungchul nodded as he scooped out some red pepper and soy paste from the clay pot he had taken from his Soul Storage. He then mixed a whole ladle worth of sauce into the boiling pot.

"I want to learn Magic. Using the identity of a newbie."

"I-I...see."

Christian was quick to catch on. He knew figures of infamy like Sungchul didn't appreciate being asked questions. He also realized that a unique opportunity had presented itself for him to prove his worth.

"There are a lot of Magic Guilds and academies inside Golden City, but there aren't many places which can compare to Airfruit Magic Academy."

"I've heard of Airfruit Magic Academy."

And killed many of its alumni.

Sungchul added some soybean paste into the boiling water containing some of the river minnows, then tasted the seasoning using a spoon.

"Mmm. It's good."

He had also gathered vegetables from a nearby farm and added them into the pot that was on top of a fire. Next to it was a stone cauldron, which was releasing a crisp aroma while being heated by the fire. Christian was dumbfounded as Sungchul continued cooking.

I wonder what kind of a person he is. Filling his rare Soul Storage with nothing but food...and with such strange and difficult-to-find ingredients.

The Soul Storage was a personal storage which was earned through a Soul Contract; any item could be pulled in and out from it at any time. However, as with most Soul Contracts, obtaining a Soul Storage was a difficult task and required an enormous sum of money. The most common variety, Soul Storage (Common), had ten slots and cost as much as a property located in the inner city. It wasn't necessary to explain how valuable such a storage space was. Yet this mysterious man was using such a precious Soul Storage for storing food. He hadn't seen or heard of someone doing the same. It left Christian speechless.

Sungchul pulled out another consumable from his Soul Storage – an emerald wine bottle and a shot glass. He poured himself a shot and tossed it back whole.

"Kha!"

He put down his shot glass and vigorously mixed the boiling spicy stew with the fluffy rice he had prepared in the stone cauldron before giving it a taste.

"…"

Sungchul closed his eyes, enamored in the taste of his own cooking.

[This Food's Score is…24 points]

It was a "below average" score, but he didn't mind. He didn't know how the Chef Class's scoring system worked, but it would frequently give a low score to traditional Korean cuisines. Especially something like pickled shrimp, which never received a score that was higher than 10 no matter how tastefully he had prepared it.

I don't know on whose tastes the Chef Class's scoring system is based on, but he or she has the preferences of a child.

He cleaned out his bowl of rice, along with the distilled drink in his green bottle, before speaking to Christian who had been spacing out.

"I'd heard that it's tricky to get into Airfruit. Is that true?"

"Yes…It is a bit tricky to get admitted. You have to be young and dressed properly. Also, they weigh the recommendation of the referrer quite heavily."

"And the exam?"

"They do give an exam, but it doesn't mean much."

"Is that right?"

Sungchul wasn't young, and he was dressed quite poorly. He also didn't have someone to give him a recommendation.

"Is there no other place? I want somewhere easy to get into that teaches a lot of Magic and also guarantees fast growth."

When Sungchul asked again, Christian replied confidently with his plan.

"There is no school within the viscinity of Golden City that can comparable to Airfruit. It is easy enough to lie about your age, and your appearance could be sorted out by giving your hair a good combing. The most important part is the recommendation, but I am prepared to find someone for you."

Christian pulled out a gem from his clothes and smiled. The gem was the same one Sungchul had given him as a sign of trust.

"With a gem of this quality, it should be a piece of cake to prepare a recommendation. I am personally acquainted with a Professor who is in charge of admissions. I'll try leveraging him with this gem."

Christian spoke with a confident smile.

After hearing his spiel, Sungchul pulled out another small pouch and offered it to Christian. A pleasant clinking sound could be heard coming from within.

Christian briefly looked into the pouch and swallowed loudly at its contents. It was filled with gold coins with 99.9% purity.

"Use it."

"T-this is too much. A single gem would be enough, but this kind of fortune..."

Sungchul rose from his seat.

"I'll head over to Golden City first. When can I expect results?"

"With this much, I should be able to get it done in no time at all. I will prepare a report by this evening."

"Really? I'll be below the Clock Tower when the sun sets. Give me a progress report then."

"I-I understand."

"Do the dishes too. Make sure to scrub down the pots."

Sungchul left his empty dishes with Christian then headed towards the city that was lit with golden lights.

—

Golden City

It was an independent city, free from any external faction's grip, and was also a gathering point for adventurers, which meant that it was the ideal starting point for all rookie Summoned to begin their journey. A festival was being held within Golden City in honor of the newly graduated rookies from the Summoning Palace that had overcome all of their trials. The scattered few that entered the city were greeted at the entrance by a welcoming crowd.

"For the new bloods of Other World!"

"Over here. To Other World, we welcome you."

Women wearing garlands carrying beautiful smiles on their faces guided the Summoned over towards the plaza. The Summoned, who were completely oblivious to the proceedings, were led by the hands of the city folk to the plaza to receive a surprisingly grand welcome in the middle of an audience.

Food and alcohol were provided to the Summoned while gaudy music and dances were performed in various places within the plaza. People called this the Celebration of Beginnings. It celebrated the memorable moment in which seedlings arrived from the modern world to overcome the trials of the Summoning Palace and take their first steps into Other World. This event was attended by not only the citizens of Golden City but also by people of all classes, including adventurers, clergymen, and even figures who possessed enough power and influence to shake Other World.

An obvious objective was the welcoming of rookie Summoned to congratulate them wholeheartedly, but the real reason was to observe and recruit them. Dimitri Mediov, the favored retainer of the powerful Human Empire located at the center of the continent, came with that purpose in mind. He lazily watched the Summoned who were raucously socializing while eating and drinking heartily.

"How is it? Anyone worthwhile?"

A middle-aged man with a flashy robe took a seat next to Dimitri and struck up a conversation. His name was Armuk Bakr. He was the Lieutenant General of the coalition forces stationed in Storm Battlefront, which was one of the three most powerful forces in the northern regions. Two individuals, each holding enough of a reputation to leave others slack-jawed, had gathered here. Several people had focused their attention on them, and many whispers had started spinning fantasies regarding the purpose of such gargantuan characters in coming here, but the people on whom all of this was revolving around didn't pay them any mind.

"Meh, I don't see anyone useful."

Dimitri swirled his wine glass while furling his brow.

"Didn't you hear? The Summoning Palace stopped spitting out rough gems ever since the 'Preselected' became common practice."

Armuk nodded in agreement at Dimitri's rhetoric, but he pointed at one character. It was Jungshik Chun.

"It turns out Blanche Plaza managed to produce one decent item. He's a rare breed that has the battle sense, ability, and fighting spirit."

"So what? He's already taken by the Ancient Kingdom. They'll probably take him away after the festival ends to eat some dust with them in that worn-down palace."

"Probably right, but did you know...?"

Armuk broke into a knowing smile and tried his luck. Dimitri tipped his glass in indifference, but Armuk's last few words had managed to pique his curiosity.

"They say the Memorials of the Seven Heroes have disappeared. Not just one, but three of them."

"That can't be true. Weren't the remaining memorials determined to be impossible to complete after numerous attempts that were made over several thousands of years?"

Dimitri's body shivered at the memory of Vestiare's Trial.

It was traumatic to gaze into that crazy woman's insanity. No sane person could have gotten through it. Yep, no way.

However, Armuk seemed to be telling the truth.

"That used to be the case."

He was clearly speaking in the past tense.

"..."

Dimitri stared blankly at the empty ground before taking a swig from his wine glass.

"Is that really true?"

"Why would I lie?"

Dimitri's eyes turned back to the rookie Summoned who were now standing there and enjoying the festival.

"So you're saying that among the Summoned gathered here, there are three individuals that managed to obtain the secret tomes of the Seven Heroes? Someone who even managed to watch Vestiare's horrifying nightmare..."

"It could be just one. We can't ignore the possibility of it being a Regressor."

"A Regressor..."

Like the others in power, Dimitri did not think highly of Regressors. It was an infallible rule of reality that those who had failed once, would continue to fail. Armuk observed his expressions and continued to speak.

"And...there's another rumor, saying that one of the rookie Summoned didn't visit Golden City and instead chose to disappear into the Eastern Wastelands. This one had a relatively good result in the Summoning Palace too. Isn't this a typical pattern for Regressors?"

"It can't be a Regressor. The Seven Heroes aren't so generous as to accept those pathetic bastards who have already failed once. Even if it was a Regressor, they couldn't have gone far. The hunters from the religious order wouldn't leave them alone."

Dimitri lightly shook his head and looked over at a woman. She was quite a beautiful Asian woman. He called a servant to confirm her name.

"She says her name is Sunghae Bae. A niece of a High Knight belonging to the Order of the Iron Blood Knights."

His lips curled into a smile after hearing the name of the Order of the Iron Blood Knights.

"The Order of the Iron Blood Knights? I thought they were bygones. I guess they managed to scrounge up some money to grease up the Summoning Palace."

He lost interest and looked over to another person.

What's that? Is he trying to be some kind of a fucking bum?

There was a shabby man wearing drenched military fatigues and a pair of jeans. Dimitri pointed at him and made a joke.

"That guy looks like he rolled around the Summoning Palace by himself for ten years. Look at his clothes."

"Now that I look at it, his clothes look familiar. Just wait a bit."

Armuk suddenly clenched his fist. A blue flame appeared and twirled around his fists before a single book popped out. He turned the pages, patiently skimming through it before letting out a shallow sigh.

"It's some nobody, but his name is quite unsettling."

"What's his name?"

"It is a name I should not speak out loud. He has the same name as the Enemy of the World."

"Ha! That's one hell of a scary name, but his looks don't seem to match. And his physique also doesn't look too impressive."

"It could be someone with the same name. There are plenty of Koreans with Kim as their first name."

"Shall we check out our 'Mr. Enemy of the World's stats?"

Dimitri's eyes lit up.

Several miniature Magic runes appeared in his eyes that spun like a wheel before they relayed the information he wanted in front of him.

Sungchul Kim's Stats & Class

[Stats]

Strength 24 Dexterity 25
Stamina 26 Magic Power 32
Intuition 25 Magic Resist 21
Resilience 18 Charisma 18
Luck 18

[Class]
Main Class – Mage (Common)
Sub Class – Alchemist (Rare)

A mocking laughter spilled out of Dimtri's mouth.

"Only his name is Sungchul Kim. There's no way for *that guy* to come to this place. The entire military force of Other World would be deployed if *he* were to appear anywhere."

The man in the shabby field jacket, who was taking sips of alcohol with a blank expression, did not show any sign of being aware of the powerful men that were watching him.

After the festival was over, he waited for his guest under the massive clock tower which bore the city's time. He didn't need to wait for long.

"Sir Warrior."

Christian Ashwood. The man, who had changed from the dog hide robe to a shimmering black robe, arrived with a face filled with shame.

"The results?"

"I have secured your admission. Even though it cost half of your gold. However…"

His words trailed off, causing Sungchul to burst out sternly.

"Speak."

"There is a bad rumor spreading across the Academy."

"What kind of rumor?"

Christian deeply gulped before replying.

"The Followers of Calamity. People say they are active in the Academy. It made my job easier because of that, but…"

"The Followers of Calamity…"

Sungchul repeated the name as though he was savoring it.

Mages would naturally come to study the source of Magic, which they called "the Truth." If this search for "the Truth" were to stop at a reasonable point, it would be beneficial for both the Mages themselves and to Other World as a whole. But there were some who would sacrifice everything for their research: fortune, flesh, and even their lives. Undead Mages, such as Liches, were prime examples of this. However, there were those that would go even past this point; they were the supporters of the Calamity.

These fanatics believed that the key to the true secrets of Magic was hidden behind Calamities sanctioned by the Gods. All the Mages who Sungchul had casually slaughtered were these very same Followers of Calamity. Christian struggled to continue his story while wearing a pained expression.

"This was my school…but it might not be suitable to go anymore. Death and curses, betrayal, and sinister plots plague any place the Followers of Calamity are found."

It was at this moment when he tried to carefully observe Sungchul's face. Unexpectedly, Sungchul was smiling.

"That would fit me just fine."

***

Airfruit Magic Academy.

A school, which looked more like a castle in size and appearance, occupied the region at the foot of a rocky mountain which ran along the northern region of Golden City.

"…"

266

Sungchul confirmed the admissions form he had received from Christian. As was fitting for a top-rank school, it used neat calligraphy and was well decorated, but the current situation facing the school was not so great. With indifferent eyes, Sungchul looked at the corpses hanging from a nearby oak tree which was standing tall beside the school gates. A ghastly signpost written in deep, red paint stood in front of it.

[Only death awaits the masses who commit heresy.]

[Heresy Inquisitor Magnus Maxima]

"Even an Inquisitor is involved now."

The situation of the school was worse than he had expected. It had allowed him to be admitted by simply greasing a few palms, but Sungchul could see the deep darkness that was looming over the entire Academy.

"I'd heard from Christian."

Head of Admissions, Robert Danton, was a scrawny and tired-looking middle-aged man. He briefly glanced over Sungchul's documents before putting them away; he then pulled a pipe to his mouth and lit it.

"I heard you were a Summoning Palace graduate."

"That's right."

"How did you know of this place? It couldn't have been easy to find, seeing that we're on the fringe of Golden City."

"I was a Preselected. My backer, who I won't name, heard about this school from the Mage that was taking care of me."

Sungchul respond like always with an indifferent tone.

Hearing that he was a Preselected, Robert narrowed his eyes slightly and nodded.

"I see. You did seem different from the average rookie Summoned."

Robert sifted through his folder and pulled out Sungchul's document then stamped a seal on its corner using a hammer-shaped stamp. After stamping it twice, he sucked deeply on his pipe and spoke curtly while releasing a white puff of smoke.

"With this, the admission process has been finished. Anything needed in daily life will be relayed to you by the Residence Assistant that is waiting outside, so just follow whatever he says."

Sungchul got up from his seat and gave him a nod. When Sungchul began to open the door, he spoke again.

"By the way, you have heard the rumors, yes?"

Robert's sharp voice coiled around from behind him, stopping him in his tracks.

Sungchul slightly turned his head and peered over at Robert's face before speaking.

"I've heard the Followers of Calamity or something have appeared on campus."

"You've come here, even after knowing that."

Robert shuffled through his possessions before pulling out a single bright gold coin and smiled.

"Welcome to a dying school."

What he held in his hand was the gold that Sungchul had given to Christian.

A familiar monster awaited him outside the office.

"Hey, disciple. Please come this way."

It was a Homunculus.

Other than the scholarly garb, none of the sickly appearance, annoying voice, and arrogant attitude had changed. Sungchul watched the Homunculus walking closer to him and thought for a moment.

If I recall, these creatures were created from a Mage's flask to mimic fairies.

The Homunculi were counterfeit fairies. They were similar in size and copied a fairy's manner of speech, but compared to the loveable and cute appearance of the fairies, the Homunculi were grotesque and repulsive in looks. Even their Magical abilities were not comparable. In other words, they were the weaker and poorly crafted knockoffs, but they were often used because they had quite the utility when properly trained.

"Disciple! This Residence Assistant is responsible for the general guidance and encouragement of your honor's school life. This teaching assistant only speaks once so clench your butthole and listen carefully!"

The Residence Assistant led him towards the Registrar's Office.

"This Registrar's Office is for choosing what school of Magic you wish to learn! Hurry up and tell the staff what school of Magic you wish for!"

His pace was disturbed by the unexpected intervention of the Homunculus, but Sungchul knew what he needed to do from this point onwards.

So this is the Registrar's Office.

There were folders filled with documents. An elven woman who was seated behind a desk looked over in his direction with wide-open eyes.

Sungchul had asked Christian about the most powerful Magic one could learn in Airfruit, to which he replied without hesitation

"If you're talking about Magical might, the School of Pyromancy is always among the top. If you're talking about the school with the most powerful spells, that would be the school that utilizes the power of the skies: The School of Cosmomancy."

"The School of Cosmomancy? The group that uses Meteor?"

Christian nodded, however, Sungchul's response was lukewarm.

"Cosmomancy. I can definitely attest to their might, but isn't their Magic only useful during large scale war?"

The King of Demons that Sungchul had to get rid of was an experienced warrior as well as a crafty Mage. There was no way he would allow himself to be hit by a Magic like Meteor that had a long casting time and a slow activation rate.

"It is commonly known that Cosmomancy is strong in large scale battles and weak against single foes, but the reality is a bit different."

It was then that Christian put forth a different point of view.

"There are a few experienced Mages of Cosmomancy that can call down the pure light from the Heavens to incinerate most of their foes."

"I have never seen such a Magic."

At least among the ones Sungchul had faced, there were none that had used such a Magic. Christian smiled bitterly before replying.

"It is extremely difficult to learn. The required Intuition and Magic Power is so high that it takes five whole years just to learn the primary spells."

"Five years?"

"Yes. By the standards of an average rookie. It isn't easy to surpass 130 Magic Power and 100 Intuition just through reading and meditations without having any foundation. And as you know, the effectiveness of trying to raise stats using basic tasks gives diminishing returns at higher levels."

Sungchul nodded and said,

"That is correct. It's why people risk their lives for duels and quests; especially missions, if they can manage it."

"However, aren't you a great and powerful warrior? If it is you, Sir Warrior, you would be able to rapidly grow through various quests and events by choosing the School of Cosmomancy as your main school and Magic Swordsmanship as your sub school."

Christian's plan was precise, containing no room for error. He handed Sungchul a booklet with all the quests and the people related to well-known events recorded within. Once Sungchul had read through the booklet, he felt that here was a man that repays his debts. A person like Krill would simply have recommended the School of Pyromancy without a second thought. However, a question formed within Sungchul.

"Why did you recommend the Magic Swordsmanship for the sub school? Couldn't I choose something like Pyromancy or Cryomancy for my sub school?"

Christian shook his head and logically explained his reasons.

Pyromancy, Cryomancy, Metallurgy, Necromancy, Cosmomancy, and the rest which all form the "Schools of Magic" have inherent resonance and flow accompanying them, and using any of them causes a distinct imprint like age-rings on trees to appear on the caster's body. This is what was referred to as a "Magical Fingerprint." A single Mage who held two or more Magical fingerprints would eventually suffer negative side effects from each print working against the other. In minor cases, they might become unable to cast top tier spells, but in some extreme cases, they might die from a volatile reaction. This is the reason for the needed prerequisite that sub schools should not create their own Magical imprints. Schools such as Magic Swordsmanship, Dimensional Magic, Druidism, Divination, Empathomancy, and Alchemy were all included in this category.

"What will you choose for your main school? Both the schools of Cryomancy and Pyromancy of our Academy have a good reputation."

The elven woman handed Sungchul a catalog of all the main schools of Magic. A current list of famous alumni Mages of the school was listed within the five schools of Magic: Pyromancy, Cryomancy, Necromancy, Electromancy, and Cosmomancy.

There are definitely a lot of figures within Cryomancy and Pyromancy. Some with important roles within Magic Guilds and some were even royal Mages...

On the contrary, there was only one name under Cosmomancy: Altugius Xero. Airfruit Magic Academy's Professor. Not even a Headmaster, but just a normal Professor. The weight of his name was incomparably light compared to the weight of the other alumni that were on the list. Regardless, Sungchul didn't hesitate and stepped on the path which had been decided.

"I've decided on Cosmomancy."

"Oh, my. You're going with Cosmomancy? Even if you're a Summoning Palace graduate, that still isn't an easy task."

"..."

His will wasn't so easy to bend.

Looking at his resolute eyes, the elven woman didn't bother saying anything more and wrote something onto a document.

"What will your sub school be?"

Similarly, she presented a complete list of sub schools taught by Airfruit. Magic Swordsmanship, Dimensional Magic, Druidism, Divination, Empathomancy, and Alchemy were listed in the catalog.

Sungchul briefly deliberated between Magic Swordsmanship and Alchemy. It wouldn't be an exaggeration to say there was nothing more for him to learn regarding Magic Swordsmanship, as the Magic Swordsmen he had faced so far were nothing more than swordsmen that happened to know Magic. He had fought with someone that claimed to have reached the pinnacle of the discipline, and so Sungchul had witnessed firsthand its limitations. Thus, he couldn't bring himself to feel even the slightest inclination towards Magic Swordsmanship.

Cheap tricks might work in a close match, but it's meaningless against absolute strength.

He might be able to easily and plentifully gain access to quests and events that existed around the school with the choice of Magic Swordsmanship, but it didn't suit him to walk such an easy path. As long as he had been brought to the hall of learning, it would benefit him to learn at least one single new thing before the final battle.

After a lengthy deliberation, he spoke firmly to the yawning elven woman.

"I'll go with Alchemy."

The elven woman squinted at him and muttered quietly.

"My my, he chose unusual schools for both. Such unique preferences."

"..."

Sungchul didn't mind it and left the office. A red-faced Residence Assistant was waiting for him outside the office.

"This…human! No, Disciple! Did you think you came here to play cards at the senior center? Why did you take so long? Don't you know what a busy Homunculus this Residence Assistant is?"

He couldn't find a reason within himself to reply to such an inferior organism. Instead, he pointed towards the front.

"Next course."

"T-truly an arrogant disciple for a rookie. O-okay. This Residence Assistant has a reputation built up through the years, so I'll hold in my anger this one time. Follow me!"

The Homunculus guided him to a narrow room with a large Mage's hat sitting within. The hat looked unsettling with eyes, nose, and mouth that appeared like a human. Sungchul knew the identity of this hat. It was the Aged Jorgbart.

It was a living hat. When it is placed on a head, the Airfruit Magic Academy's heirloom would instantly understand the student's aptitude and talents and determine the name of the appropriate dorm for them.

"Over there. Hurry and wear the honored hat! Once you wear the honored hat, it will recommend a suitable dorm for the disciple!"

The Residence Assistant began to circle around Sungchul and tried to rush him. Sungchul sat on a chair and quietly looked around as he placed the hat with the human face on his lap.

He said there was a trick to wearing this hat.

According to Christian, the Aged Jorgbart would acknowledge your desire and repeat the desired dorm's name if you were to shout out a dorm's name three times inside your mind. It wasn't clear how such a thing could happen, but he placed the Aged Jorgbart on his head. The next moment, a familiar feeling could be felt on the crown of his head. A smile appeared on his lips.

This…is an incubus.

Sungchul immediately determined the hat's identity. They had placed an incubus within the hat and scammed people into believing that it was a talking hat. He couldn't know what kind of tricks had been used to get an incubus to speak, but he could feel the repulsive sensation of a tentacle peering into his head. At that moment, he stopped all thoughts for a moment and clearly revealed a single, clear objective in his mind.

I'll kill you…!

Next, he thought up the image of an incubus caked in blood.

"Hiiiii!"

The Talking Hat shrieked. It was closer to a beast's cry than a human scream.

"W-what happened! For the Aged Jorgbart to scream! What an unprecedented incident!"

The Residence Assistant that had been watching all of this paled and began running from side to side, while Sungchul redirected his thoughts and loosened his mind before repeating a single word three times.

House of Recollections, House of Recollections, House of Recollections.

When the requirements were met, the screaming incubus stopped his screams and spat out the name Sungchul desired, using a mysterious voice.

"House of Recollections!"

With that, the eventful occurrence finally came to a close. The Incubus were simple and ignorant creatures. As soon as Sungchul took off the Aged Jorgbart and placed it on the chair, the hat simply continued its existence as though nothing had happened, just like an inanimate object. Sungchul approached the traumatized Residence Assistant and opened his mouth.

"He said the House of Recollections?"

"I-I heard it too! But why the House…This feels like a mistake!"

The Homunculus' response was odd.

"The House of Recollections is a dorm that's no longer used…"

"Well, what can we do? The hat has already stated the dorm's name."

All things considered, the Aged Jorgbart would obviously have priority over some Homunculus regarding dorm placement. The Residence Assistant looked skeptical as he led him to the House of Recollections.

A bleak residence under the shadow of castle walls revealed itself. The garden was filled with withered thickets, and the building looked faded as though it no longer saw any use.

"T-this is the House of Recollections! I-I have things to do, so I'm going to leave. Find a room yourself!"

The Residence Assistant left the scene as though he was running away in fear. The terrifying exterior was one thing, but it was also the center of frightful rumors which made one's teeth shiver in the summer[7]. Despite this, there was a reason that Sungchul had chosen to make the House of Recollections his dorm. That was because it was among the oldest of the buildings in Airfruit, and as such, it contained the memorials of noteworthy predecessors. Of course, it was difficult for the average student to deal with, and beings born out of the accumulated malice also existed here, but if he could overcome such difficulties, he would be able to experience the rapid growth that he so desired.

"..."

Without hesitation, he stepped further into the House of Recollections.

***

Once the door was opened, the damp smell of mold assaulted his nose.

Each step he took on the wood panel floor caused it to creak loudly as if someone was screaming.

Sungchul sensed a presence standing up on the floor above him.

The presence quickly ran down the stairs without a sound and hid itself in the darkness that stretched out from the dorms.

Judging from its actions, it probably planned on secretly observing Sungchul.

Sungchul pretended not to notice and walked straight ahead.

After brushing past a few spider webs, he came across a dining room that was illuminated by candlelight.

The dining room consisted of five wooden tables large enough to seat four people, but four of the tables were covered with a white cloth as if they were no longer in use. On the contrary, the last remaining table had a vase on it, together with a freshly preserved flower.

"Who dares to disturb my rest?" It was at this moment that the presence Sungchul had noticed earlier spoke to him.

It was a feminine voice that had an eerie wail as though from a ghost.

It was probably a trick to scare Sungchul away by pretending to be a ghost, but such trivial tricks would never work on him.

Sungchul kept an expressionless face as he continued forward on his way to the stairs, eventually passing by the room where the mysterious woman hid.

"How impudent! Ignoring my warnings!"

Once again, the voice of the woman reverberated from behind.

At the same time, a strange wave passed through the entirety of the dormitory, causing objects to float and shake ominously. At the same time, a thick mist settled in the stairway to block vision, and the objects began to rattle even more violently.

The mysterious spectacle was so unsettling that an unsuspecting passerby would have been scared out of their wits and would long since have been sent running.

But Sungchul remained unfazed as he continued walking up the stairs.

By the time Sungchul had stepped on the last step of the stairway, the floating objects had settled back down, and the mist had vanished.

"You! Do you really want to die?"

The voice of a young girl rang out from behind him.

Sungchul paused to look back.

A blonde girl dressed in white was glaring up at him, full of anger. She had an appearance of a fifteen- or sixteen-year-old.

She had such a beautiful appearance that, given a few years, she would be able to charm a great number of men. But there was one crucial problem.

It was impossible for a child of her age to exist in this world. The so-called "Final Generation" who had narrowly escaped the Curse of Extinction were all in their twenties.

In other words, all children under the age of twenty had been afflicted by the God's curse and suffered from an agonizingly painful, incurable disease, and for the most part, they had all already died. Even if they had somehow survived, they were stuck in a state that was between the living and the dead.

Sungchul believed that the blonde girl before him was an apparition of a child from the latter case. He soon discovered the reason.

This child…she is no longer alive.

He could hear her irregular breath, but not her heartbeat. In other words, her lifespan had already ended; she was now a living corpse.

Soul Engraving – once the Eye of Truth was activated Sungchul spotted a much more severe problem that was plaguing the girl.

From the top of her head to the bottom of her feet, dozens of different types of Preservation Magic were enclosing the girl like a cocoon.

It was a spectacle that showed the Mage's obsession to preserve the girl's original appearance despite all circumstances.

At that moment, Sungchul felt an ache from a corner of his chest and a frown formed on his face.

In the girl, he saw the mad struggle of a man who desperately fought to keep her alive, who would do anything and everything to save the one who was dear to him.

Their methods were different, but what they sought was the same.

"…"

While Sungchul remained silent, the girl took a step closer.

The girl confirmed the frown on his face and gave a mischievous grin.

"Finally, you act surprised."

Sungchul looked at her wordlessly.

"Now, can you get out? This is my house. I'll be troubled if an outsider like yourself comes in brashly."

The girl waved her hands, gesturing for him to leave.

The motion of her hands was enough to wake Sungchul from his heavy-hearted reminiscence.

Ah, I was spacing out.

Sungchul quickly regained his calm while tasting a deep bitterness spreading in his mouth.

He opened his mouth while looking at the girl once again.

"Sorry, but I am not an outsider."

"Hmm? What do you mean?"

The girl crossed her arms while spreading her feet slightly, before donning an attitude of daring him to explain himself.

Sungchul confidently explained the reason why he was here.

"I am a Freshman that was admitted today, and the Aged Jorgbart designated my dorm as the 'House of Recollections'. Do I need any other reason?"

"Really? That ancient Jorgbart?"

There was an effect. The girl appeared surprised.

Sungchul used this momentum, adding in another statement.

"If he didn't, why would I leave aside all those other normal dormitories and choose this eerie place?"

"Mmm…You're not wrong…In any case, if Jorgbart designated this dorm as your own, I have no right to refuse. I can double check with the Homunculus, but that can be put off until later…"

The girl who had been dying to chase Sungchul out became quiet as she fell in deep thought.

Eventually, she let out a sigh and looked defeated.

"Mmm...I guess I can't do anything. I am also a student of Airfruit Academy after all. I will respect the old man Jorgbart's decision. Since that's also part of our tradition."

The unknown girl dropped her shoulder and turned around, but quickly turned back again looking vexed, speaking in a warning tone.

"My name is Sarasa, School of Cryomancy. I don't recommend underestimating me because of how young I look; I am five years your senior."

Finishing her introduction, Sarasa swiftly turned around and ran up the stairs.

"Use any empty room on the first floor. It's a little messy, but the cleaning supplies are in the storage closet next to the dining room, so make use of that. Be sure to put it back after you've used it. The second floor is for female students only, so you are not allowed up to the second floor without getting my permission from the bottom of the stairs first, so don't forget that. I am not very nice."

Once she was done nagging like a mother-in-law, she went up the stairs in a few light movements and disappeared into the darkness.

In the silence that returned to the surroundings, Sungchul stared in the direction Sarasa had disappeared to for a while longer.

An undead who hasn't yet accepted her own death...

Sungchul began walking around on the first floor to pick his room.

Soon, he found an empty room at the end of the hallway that he claimed as his own.

It was a messy room that was filled with dust and cobwebs as Sarasa had warned, but Sungchul didn't mind.

At the very least, it had walls and a roof that would shelter him from the wind and rain and also a bed he could rest on.

"I'll do some cleaning tomorrow."

-

Next day.

Sungchul was led by the Residence Assistant to head to the school building for Cosmomancy.

The building for Cosmomancy was located precariously on the edge of a steep cliff on the northern region, the highest area, within the border of the rocky mountain and castle walls that surrounded Airfruit Academy.

"There used to be a Magically operated lift that would bring us up to the top, but for some reason, it isn't operational anymore!"

Sungchul and the Residence Assistant had to carefully climb a precarious flight of stairs carved into the cliff wall.

There was even a broken segment in the stairway where visitors had to make a potentially life-threatening jump to reach the other side. The Residence Assistant barely made it across, and then shouted proudly

"Now! Disciple's turn! Time to show your courage! Humans who have longer legs and therefore superior jumping power than myself should be able to make it! Being unable to do this would mean you are a poopy human!"

Sungchul leaped over the gap lightly, making the Residence Assistant eat his own words.

The smile on Residence Assistant's face faded as quickly as it came.

"Ah...I guess it is as expected of a Summoning Palace graduate. On a completely different level than your average resident. Well, it's not like there is any resident left to come here anymore, though."

After they climbed the steep set of stairs that felt like a rock wall, they finally arrived at the Cosmomancy school building located at the peak of the mountain.

The building was a stone structure of medium size, and its defining feature was the large telescope attached to its round dome on the top.

"Now, it is time to enter, disciple!"

Sungchul left behind the Residence Assistant and pushed his way through the heavy doors to enter the Cosmomancy school building.

The first thing that caught his gaze was the jade-colored interior.

Another part was that the entire interior of the building consisted of a small number of pillars, with no walls or floors separating the rooms, and an open space with the domed ceiling at its center.

So, any sound made in the building would be amplified, and anyone in the building could see each other at all times.

Within a building which resembled a Cathedral more than an academic building, Sungchul saw two men.

One was an old man whose hair and beard was almost halfway to having turned white.

The wrinkles etched by his age didn't give off the feeling of dignity, but rather the feeling of stubbornness. His tightly shut lips had a "weightiness" that didn't look as though they would open so easily.

The other person was an androgynous youth who looked magnanimous, in stark contrast to the old man.

He was laying in a hammock tied between two pillars and reading a thick book as if it were a magazine.

The first person to respond to Sungchul's appearance was the youth.

"Who is this? It seems that a guest has arrived." He stood up from the hammock and approached Sungchul.

"How did you end up here?"

Sungchul looked towards the old man behind the youth and answered briefly.

"I have come to receive tutelage."

The youth smiled broadly.

"It's been a while since we have had a newcomer."

He put his hand forward and introduced himself to Sungchul.

"I am an inexperienced Mage trying to learn the Cosmomancy Magic of the great Altugius, Leonard Sanctum."

"...Sungchul Kim."

Sungchul revealed his name as he grasped the youth's hand.

"Oh gee, what a terrifying name. Are you a Summoning Palace graduate by any chance?"

Sungchul nodded.

"I see. A Summoning Palace Graduate. I thought it was strange that we would get a newcomer so suddenly, so that's your story. Sorry for dragging things out. I believe the teacher is waiting, so let's step inside."

Leonard politely opened a path.

Sungchul didn't have any opinion on Leonard.

He didn't have anything to evaluate him with aside from his extraordinarily reputable family name.

At the very least, he wasn't so uncouth as to repeatedly stare at any specific feature of Sungchul, nor did he mix any subtle self-praise into his words.

Sungchul approached the old man who sat on top of a stone pile arranged like a tree.

"I have come to receive tutelage."

Sungchul was in no way inferior to that old man, but he decided to lower his head this one time.

This was the proper attitude of someone looking to learn.

The old man stared at Sungchul with stubborn eyes, after which he pointed towards the air and summoned a single book.

He had taken a book out from his Soul Storage.

The old man handed the thick book over to Sungchul and spoke in a clear and piercing voice.

"I am a retired old man with nothing left to teach. Regrettably, you have chosen wrong from many possible choices, and the result was the misfortune of meeting me. All I can give you is this book."

The old man offered the book again.

"I have become old and my arms lack strength. Quickly take it."

Once Sungchul had received the book, the old man turned his back towards Sungchul and lit a pipe.

"After a week, you will be given an opportunity to change your major. You shouldn't fritter your time away, raising your basic stats by reading that book should help you in achieving the path you desire after this."

Those were his final words.

It wasn't a trial, nor an attempt to size him up. He no longer tried to speak with Sungchul.

And it looked as though he would no longer listen to anything he had to say...

Altugius Xero, was it? The old man has already isolated himself from the world.

He had met an unexpected resistance.

Sungchul had heard from Christian that the Cosmomancy Professor Altugius Xero was a cranky and fastidious old man, but he never expected that the man had gone so far as to renounce his duty as a teacher.

"..."

Sungchul, who was still holding the book, stood at a crossroads.

Leonard resumed his spot on the hammock and watched Sungchul with a bemused smile.

Currently, the number of students that had come to seek Cosmomancy was a severe minority already, but when they met Altugius, who rejected even that small minority, they walked away without hesitation.

Using this world's standards, the Summoned standing there would arrive to a similar decision.

How could he hope to learn anything under a teacher who refused to teach?

But something surprising occurred.

Unlike all the other newcomers before him, the black-haired youth who wore a raggedy field jacket and worn-out jeans sat down where he stood and began to read the book given to him by the Professor.

It was assumed that he would quickly grow bored and leave, but Sungchul showed no sign of moving anytime soon.

In this building where even the smallest of sounds were amplified, the sound of each page turning was clearly transmitted into everyone's ears.

Once Sungchul had reached the thirtieth page, the old man finally turned back to take a closer look at the mysterious student who was sitting before him.

Chapter 13 – Altugius

The book's exterior looked plain, but as soon as it was opened, the mystique of Magic that was hidden within became visible. The illustrations drawn in black ink sprang to life and began moving. The lines and shapes it held that were disorderly on the first page began to repeatedly rearrange themselves in a loop. The completed form displayed the shape of a Magical formation. Information regarding it appeared on the bottom of the first page.

["Understanding Magic" is not the ability to vaguely recall the finished product, but the thorough and complete understanding of every component which forms the whole.]

Behind the illustration was a blank page with a question asking whether the illustration was properly understood. The blank page contained a similar Magical power to the illustration that could be filled and erased according to the gestures made by Sungchul's finger or by a strong mental image.

Sungchul was initially intimidated by the book's unusual approach to presenting the material and its questions, but he was curious about the content and began to earnestly solve the questions given. He focused on carefully observing the movements of the ever-changing shapes and in understanding the logic that was behind them. He was soon able to draw out everything he had understood onto the blank page by using his imagination, which resulted in a visual shape.

[Impressive! You have succeeded in solving the first problem in Understanding Magical Formations (Elementary).]

Reward: Intuition +1

Intuition had risen by solving a simple problem. Before moving on to the next page, Sungchul flipped to the final page and confirmed that there were still fifty problems remaining; he returned to the front and resumed solving from where he had left off. By the time Sungchul had reached the thirteenth problem, he saw through the many windows of the Hall that it was already dark outside.

Leonard Sanctum, who had been lying on the hammock leisurely, must have left the Hall in the meantime.

It seems like a lot of time has passed.

He had managed to raise his Intuition by five just through solving some problems over the course of the day. Whenever the problem felt slightly difficult, he was assured to gain additional Intuition. He wanted to solve the problems for a while longer, but he had promised that he would go to meet with Christian tonight. He slipped a bookmark into the page that he was currently on and returned it to Altugius.

"I have prior engagements, so I'll take my leave. I'll return the book for now and come back tomorrow."

"…"

Altugius looked at Sungchul with a scowl before receiving the book with an emaciated arm. Sungchul nodded and headed towards the exit. The old Mage opened the book and took a peek at where the bookmark had been left. Suspicion rose in Altugius's eyes.

"You, over there."

He called out to Sungchul who was reaching for the door. When Sungchul turned around, Altugius spoke with his steely voice laced thick with disdain.

"Did you really solve it up to this part?"

He opened the book to the page marked by Sungchul and pointed at it with his finger. Sungchul lightly nodded his head.

"Is there a problem?"

"No. No problem at all."

Altugius closed the book and returned to his seat. When the old man turned silent once more, Sungchul opened the door and headed outside towards the setting sun. When the door finally closed, the old man, who had shown nothing but disdain from the start, stared at the book in utter bewilderment and disbelief as he looked at the page marked by Sungchul.

A Freshman who could solve up to the thirteenth problem within a quarter of a day? Unbelievable! Isn't this a talent that has not been seen in the past hundred years?

Rather than talent, it would have been more accurate to attribute it to his experience. Sungchul had been fighting fallen Mages with his life on the line even before he had managed to obtain his overwhelming strength. The tense moments of life and death that repeated continuously led Sungchul to acquire the instincts to cope with Magic as he experienced it first-hand with his body. After a certain point, he had grasped how to predict what kind of Magic his opponent would be using by the brief flicker that appeared as the Mage chanted; in other words, by looking at the shape of the Magical formation. He had struggled at first and had almost lost his life a few times by predicting it incorrectly, but his experiences gradually helped in perfecting this skill.

Even during the battle with the Grand Mage Balzark, the head of the infamous Followers of Calamity and the devourer of souls, Sungchul overcame his opponent of higher renown than his own by predicting the Mage's Magic and acting first. For someone who was able to accurately predict spells based on Magic formations that didn't last over a tenth of a second, Altugius's book was nothing more than a low difficulty rite of passage.

"Mmm..."

Altugius logged into the Magic network which was available across the entire Academy. He was looking for information on this unknown student who had left quite an impression on him.

He was alarmed at the name, and then once again when he read the name of the dorm the student was assigned to

"What...? He was assigned to the House of Recollections? How can that be...that can't be...?!"

Between these two shocking events, it was the latter that caused him to tremble so intensely. The old man's eyes fluttered vigorously. He immediately pulled a staff from the air and tapped it on the ground. The Magical lift that had been inoperable until now spewed mystical lights as it reactivated. The old Mage then rode the lift down the cliff and headed towards the House of Recollections.

"Sarasa. Sarasa!"

The old Mage called out a girl's name with a hurried voice as soon as the tightly shut doors of the eerie dorm flew open. The blond girl revealed herself beyond the hallway like an apparition. The old man approached the girl and held her hand tightly in both of his and asked her cautiously.

"Sarasa. Did anything strange...happen?"

The blond girl looked at the hurried old man as though he was crazy before pulling her hand away and spoke with a shocked expression.

"Eh? What is this crazy talk? There's no reason anything strange would happen."

The girl who had been looking at the old man with an exasperated expression suddenly recalled something and said, "Ah, some weird guy came here. He said something about the Aged Jorgbart assigning him to this dorm. I tried to scare him away, but maybe because he's a Summoned, it didn't work."

"I see. Sarasa, I was worried. I thought something might have happened to my sweet Sarasa because of that guy..."

Altugius looked at the girl with a worried gaze once more and expressed concern. Sarasa only looked annoyed and shot back with a sharp tongue.

"What do you mean something could happen? I'm the strongest student on leave. It might not seem like it, but I'm still a Lich, you know?"

At that moment, her eyes lit up with a frightening blue glow and froze the surrounding air instantly.

"I...know."

Regret flashed across the old man's eyes. He worried that his excessive concern had reopened a past wound for the girl.

Sarasa looked directly at the conflicted old man before placing both of her hands onto his that held his staff.

"Don't worry, Grandpa. Shouldn't we be more worried about you than about me?"

The little girl's hands were as cold as the breath which came from her lips.

—

"It still isn't too late. It might be wiser to transfer from Airfruit to Logotete."

When they met, Christian's appearance had improved once more. Especially his crude wooden claw, which had been in place of his left hand, had been replaced with a prosthetic that somewhat resembled a human limb. Sungchul watched Christian manipulate his new prosthetic to hold his drink with a passing gaze before speaking.

"Is the state of Airfruit that bad?"

"Yes. There was a full-time Headmaster before, but after Magnus' questionable death, the Headmaster's position has been empty for three years now. There have been several motions to appoint a new Headmaster from the faculty, but the fierce conflict from the main schools, the School of Pyromancy and the School of Cryomancy, has continuously delayed it, which caused the Academy to fall into its current desolate state. To make matters worse, the Followers of Calamity have also appeared...It could be said that Airfruit's fate is sealed."

Christian hung his head and deeply apologized to Sungchul for his poor decision. However, Sungchul didn't show much of a reaction. He was only interested in one thing.

"Is there more to gain from Airfruit, or is there more to gain from Logotete?"

Christian answered readily as though he had been waiting for this question.

"Logotete is a rising name. It can't be compared to Airfruit that has stood for thousands of years, but it has proven to be very stable without much internal conflict in comparison. It also has the greatest Professors of the Necromancy School of Magic."

"Necromancy School…"

This school of Magic was useless to Sungchul. What he needed was a single powerful blow, rather than an army of corpses.

"It is difficult for me, who had recommended it, to say this, but Airfruit has lost its ability as an educational institute. If I had known of this ahead of time…"

If Christian went as far as to say this much, it had to be the truth. At the very least, he wasn't someone who would bluff or exaggerate the truth. With just this much, Sungchul's heart already settled on transferring from Airfruit to Logotete, but there was something he wanted to confirm before making up his mind.

"Do you know of the old man named Altugius Xero?"

"Yes. I have heard of him. He never managed to leave much of a name behind, but there is a rumor that he is the greatest Cosmomancer that Airfruit Academy has ever made."

"Hooh?"

Curiosity flashed in Sungchul's eyes. The old man looked like someone that had been forgotten in the flow of time, but to have such a history…Sungchul recalled the old man's back when he was sitting alone in the empty hall before he asked his next question.

"Then why couldn't he leave his mark on anything?"

If one had the skill, his name would naturally be left behind in history. Whether that was through fame or infamy.

"I'm not sure. That's something I can't confirm, but according to rumors, I heard he caused a huge incident during his formative years."

"An incident?"

"Yes. It even led to him killing the Vice-Captain of the Assassin's Guild in a duel."

"That's hard for me to believe."

Suspicion rose in Sungchul's mind. The Assassin class was known to be the bane of the Mage class. In a duel between two equally skilled opponents, it was certain for the Mage to be killed by the Assassin. Assassins had many techniques that could be used for negating a Mage's attack and could force a critical blow to a Mage in just an instant. And if this Assassin was the Vice-Captain, the second best of the Assassin's Guild? In a one on one combat? This was a scenario any average Mage would have no hope of winning.

"Is that the truth?"

"Could be. I can't say that I know the truth behind it. I've only heard of it as a rumor that was floating around, after all."

"But if it is the truth, the Assassin's Guild wouldn't have left Altugius alone, would they?"

If Christian's story was true, there was no way that Professor Altugius could still be breathing. The Assassins lived by the ironclad rule that ten brothers had to take revenge for the death of a brother. If someone with the rank of Vice Captain were to die, then the head of the Guild himself would call for a kill command. He recalled a certain dark-skinned man's face in his hazy memories.

Shamal Rajput. If that guy handled it personally, not only Altugius, but the entire Airfruit Academy would have been eliminated overnight.

Sungchul looked at Christian with a bored expression while having these thoughts. Christian, who felt that he was being interrogated, spoke nervously.

"I can't guarantee this, but as far I know, the Assassin's Guild that lost their Vice Captain and Airfruit Academy entered into some kind of an agreement, and Professor Altugius disappeared from the public eye."

Sungchul stroked his chin and nodded. That made more sense. The news of the number two of the Assassin's Guild, the guild that was known to be the gathering of the greatest of Assassins in the world, losing a duel against an unknown Mage would have plummetted the Guild's reputation into the dirt. It would have been a more profitable trade for the Guild to simply hide the truth by locking up Altugius within the school.

"What will you do, then? If you wish to go to Logotete, I'll get you set on the procedure. After all, there is still some gold and jewels remaining."

Sungchul stood at crossroads once again. Airfruit Academy had lost its function as a school, and the rumors regarding Altugius weren't reassuring. Thus, if he remained within Airfruit, it would mean he would be taking on a very heavy risk. However, Sungchul still favored Airfruit in his mind.

He couldn't say for sure, but this moment felt extremely similar to when he had first stepped onto Eckheart's trials. Whether it would be a boon or not was something that could only be determined after he took off the lid. But Sungchul was an unreasonable glutton when it came to growth. He would take the path with the greatest danger if it also had the greatest rewards.

"I'll remain in Airfruit. If I can learn Magic from the man who defeated a Vice Captain of the Assassin's Guild, there would be nothing better than that."

The next day, the newcomer made his way to the Cosmomancy building. Rather than a student, the man's clothes resembled that of a homeless person. The man climbed up the cliff to report to the Observatory every morning. He borrowed the book from an old and stubborn Professor and read the book until late into the night. After a week had passed, he had completed the book he had received from the old man and spoke when he returned it this time.

"Are there no other books?"

"..."

The old man didn't speak as he pulled out another book from his Soul Storage.

One book, two books, three books…The books he pulled out from the storage continued to increase in number. When Altugiushe had pulled out the eighteenth book, he curtly spoke to this mysterious man he had yet to accept as his disciple.

"I'll lend you these books, but I'm only going to lend you books, nothing else."

Sungchul steadily looked at the books that were piled up to his height, grabbed one, and went to a corner to pour over it.

What an odd fellow.

It wasn't an act or a trick. Sungchul was genuinely holding the Magic tome and reading its contents as he turned the power written within the tome into his own. That genuine passion was enough to awaken some forgotten emotion that lay buried deep within Altugius. The way he looked at Sungchul began to change, but he couldn't find it in himself to express any such emotions, which was all because of the wolfish bastard lying lazily on the hammock who was watching him carefully. When their eyes met, Leonard Sanctum gave a strange smile while muttering aloud.

"Ah! When will I get to learn some Cosmomancy? Doesn't anyone feel bad for the disciple that only has his dear old teacher in his heart."

This former disciple of his was currently a Follower of Calamity.

***

"You, over there."

It was unprecedented for Altugius to be the first to speak to Sungchul.

"…"

But Sungchul didn't respond to this. He was instead devoting all of his attention to reading his books.

"You there. Summoned."

On the second beckoning, Sungchul raised his head and looked at the old Mage. Leonard Sanctum, who had been lying on his hammock, heard the voice and began to raise his body to look over as well. Altugius started to speak.

"It looks to me that you've spent all your time here since you've been admitted. Do you have a Guidance Counselor?"

"No, I do not."

Sungchul couldn't recall ever hearing of such things. A soft muttering spilled out of Altugius' lips.

Even if the school is in its current state, to not share such basic information…

Leonard seemed to share this opinion.

"Oh, my! A week has passed, and you still haven't chosen a Guidance Counselor?"

The lighthearted voice echoed in the empty hall. After a brief moment, Sungchul asked his question.

"What is a Guidance Counselor?"

Altugius' silver brows trembled lightly upon hearing his words. To not know such basic information that all Freshmen ought to know. It was a damning proof that showed that the academy had begun to crumble at its very foundations. This would have been unthinkable back when Altugius, or even Leonard, were Freshmen at Airfruit.

The Observatory rang out in Leonard's laughter.

"Oh my goodness! A Freshman that doesn't even know what a Guidance Counselor is. These truly are some dark times."

He fell back onto the hammock and closed his eyes, a smirk on his face. As the silence returned, Altugius looked directly at Sungchul and spoke quietly.

"I apologize, but as I have said before, I have no intention of teaching anyone, and therefore I cannot be anyone's Guidance Counselor. Seek someone else."

"I understand."

Sungchul spoke indifferently and returned to reading his book with intense focus as usual. Unrelentingly. There wasn't a more joyous sight for an educator than to see such a studious attitude from a brilliant student, but it only made Altugius burn with anxiety.

This fellow...Maybe he isn't aware of the consequences of not selecting a Guidance Counselor?

All Freshmen must choose a Guidance Counselor within ten days, and those who didn't find an educator within ten days would lose the right of being a student. This was initially a rule set in place to allow Professors to work together to cast out undeserving students who entered the school using underhanded methods, but the circumstances had changed. If the academy had been operating normally, the Freshmen orientation would have been organized, and through the orientation, the students would have been informed of all of the academy's expectations of them.

However, in the current state with the stunted flow of students they had, the welcoming ceremonies had all long since been done away with, and there was no one left for them to teach. If he had chosen the popular schools of Pyromancy or Cryomancy, the assistants would have given him the proper procedures, but there was no such service within the School of Cosmomancy.

Sungchul continued to wrestle with the books for another day in the Observatory, clueless about what was about to happen to him. Altugius' concerns only grew deeper.

That fellow. At this rate, he'll be expelled in three days from now.

The problem was that Leonard Sanctum, who had promptly left the Observatory during the evenings, was almost spitefully holding his ground. He would only get up from his hammock and leave the Observatory after Sungchul left. His intentions were clear. He wanted to rid himself of the annoying presence that had appeared at the Observatory. And he could do so without having to get his hands dirty.

A similar situation occurred the next day. The shabby man, who didn't even have a uniform, immersed himself in the pile of books which towered as high as he was. He didn't speak and instead devoted himself to the books, except when he went to leave for lunch.

Altugius waited for this opportunity to warn Sungchul about the impending danger, but Leonard rose from his hammock each time so as to remind Altugius of his presence. He smiled brightly on the outside, but Altugius knew of his heinous personality hidden within. If Altugius expressed any concern for Sungchul, Leonard would use that as an excuse to try and force Altugius to teach the Secret of Cosmomancy that was held by Altugius. That would be absolutely unacceptable.

If the Secret of Airfruit, which has been guarded for generations, were to fall into the hands of the Followers of Calamity, the destruction of the world would only accelerate.

It is ok with just me getting my hands dirty.

Altugius remained silent in the end and didn't rise.

Two afternoons passed like this. There was only a single day remaining on the clock. But Sungchul remained fixated in his studies. Altugius wasn't observing Sungchul because of his brilliant mind, but for his incredible tenacity. A question rose in his mind. Why would a Summoned from the other world be so attached to a niche school of Magic? And so, he ended up asking directly.

"That book, do you understand what you're reading?"

The question had a hidden meaning behind it, one which revealed the old man's intent. Leonard, who knew about it, smiled widely again as he said,

"Teacher is getting quite mischievous."

He knew about the book that Sungchul was reading, and the books within the pile that were towering over Sungchul as well. The ball was now in Sungchul's court.

Sungchul, who was face-down reading his book, raised his head, not too quickly nor too slowly and looked at Altugius. There was a brief moment of silence after which Sungchul shook his head.

"I have been digging into it for a week now, but honestly, I don't understand it one bit."

A breath of sigh escaped from Altugius' lips. It wasn't to rebuke Sungchul's ignorance, but rather rebuke his inability. The books that he had given to Sungchul were not meant to be understood from the very beginning. They required foreknowledge and a certain amount of Intuition before their contents could be understood. As long as the prerequisites had not been met, the reader could do nothing but become lost in the maze of words. The answer Sungchul had given was the expected one.

This fellow...

The time that seemed to be crawling along now sped up as Altugius opened his mouth once again.

"Why have you not asked me a question if you didn't understand?"

At this question, Sungchul closed the book and spoke in a matter-of-fact manner.

"Isn't that because you are not yet my teacher?"

A feeling of shame and anger churned within Altugius as he met Sungchul's firm gaze. He didn't express it, but his guts were violently twisting, and his legs felt quite weak. Altugius wordlessly returned to his own seat. He could feel Leonard's gaze searing into his back, but he ignored it and thought of Sungchul. He thought of a convenient, yet undesirable truth that he had been forgetting.

That's right. He was in the House of Recollections!

That evening, Altugius Xero sought out his granddaughter who was residing within the House of Recollections and began a conversation with a voice full of affection amidst countless eavesdropping ears.

"How is the new student? Does he look to be doing well? He has been very busy since the last time I saw him, and he doesn't even have his own uniform, either. No matter if he's a Summoned, what kind of Airfruit student doesn't keep such basic decorum!"

Sarasa's face, who had been listening to her grandfather's story, grew sour.

That night, Sungchul encountered an unexpected guest in his room. Sarasa had pulled up a chair and had been waiting for him in his room.

"It is time for some special 'ethical education', Freshman."

The Lich girl's eyes had an azure glow…

—

Sungchul felt that the girl's sudden visit was quite odd, but he remained silent and waited for her to continue. Sarasa held something out towards Sungchul.

"You. Have you gotten this? You haven't, have you?"

It was an official student handbook, made from lambskin. There was the name of its owner written on the first page of this well-used notebook clearly looking worn with all of its frayed edges.

[Sarasa Xero]

Ho?

Curiosity sparked in Sungchul's eyes, but he didn't express any of it and simply nodded in response.

"I haven't received such a thing."

Sarasa sighed and spoke again.

"I'll lend you this one, but read over the 'Freshman's Attitude' that's written on the second page carefully."

He couldn't quite understand the reasoning behind her actions, but there didn't seem to be any hostility. Also after having read so many phrases of undecipherable text, he felt drawn to read something legible for once. Sungchul obediently did as Sarasa had asked.

<Freshman's Attitude>

[1. As an Airfruit student, I will maintain its dignity.]

[2. I will not become involved in unnecessary conflict.]

[3. I will not overeat.]

[4. I will return the library's books before their due date.]

[5. I will always keep a respectful attitude towards my teachers. I will not look down on them regardless of their majors.]

…

Sungchul took his eyes away after this point and looked towards Sarasa.

"I don't feel there is a need to read this so carefully."

"What if there's something more important written at the bottom?"

Sarasa crossed her arms and spoke in a smug voice. He moved his gaze towards the notebook once again. There was another passage below the 'Freshman's Attitude', written as finely as grains of sand.

<Important! Things Freshmen need to do>

[1. Receive a uniform from Bington's Clothier]

[2. Receive a dorm designation from Aged Jorgbart]

[3. Complete the basic course in etiquette from Professor Robert Danton]

[4. Attend Senior Student's Orientation]

[5. Select a Major with the Registrar's Office]

[6. Select a Professor from a major / perform introductions]

[7. Attend Freshman Welcoming Ceremony]

[8. Select responsible Guidance Counselor]

...

Sungchul's gaze stopped at the entry regarding the Guidance Counselor. There were five stars next to the entry with the words 'Expulsion!' written beside it.

"Do you now know what you've done wrong?"

Sarasa's eyes flared as she suddenly rose from her seat.

"Are you referring to choosing a Guidance Counselor?"

When Sungchul asked, Sarasa forcefully shook her head and pointed at the first entry in the notebook.

"No. Not wearing a uniform!"

"..."

"Even if the school is falling apart, how can a student of the renowned Airfruit Academy be dressed like that? Clothes are the minimal civility towards others which reveals one's own nature. No wonder Gramps was nagging at me."

"Who is your Grandfather?"

"Who do you think? It's Professor Altugius Xero. Haven't you heard of the legendary figure that took care of the mad dog of a Vice-Captain from the Assassin's Guild that was causing a ruckus on our campus?"

"Ah, is that right?"

Sarasa began nodding to Sungchul's reply and continued to nag. She continued to prattle on, but her words could actually be condensed into a single sentence: "Wear a uniform." However, Sungchul was more interested in another part.

"What should I do if no Professor of my major will agree to become my Guidance Counselor?"

"That's how it ends up if you don't wear a uniform. Well, you should then request a minor Professor. Of course, only after you have received the uniform from Bington's Clothier!"

The next day, Sungchul visited the Office of Admissions. The Residence Assistant was waiting within.

"Where is Bington's Clothier?"

Sungchul didn't plan on completely ignoring Sarasa's advice. There weren't many people on campus, but the laborer's fashion that he was currently wearing was undeniably conspicuous. However, the Residence Assistant gave him an unexpected reply.

"Student! Are you referring to Bington? Why are you looking for some human that was fired ages ago?"

"Then what about uniforms? I don't have to wear one?"

"Uniforms have to be bought with personal funds from an external clothier based on your personal preference!"

He had already failed the first objective that a Freshman must achieve. Sungchul moved on to the next objective recorded in Sarasa's notebook. He discovered that many things Sarasa had experienced had either been removed or were missing.

"What orientation is this when there are no students? Other than Palace graduates who barely got in, the rest are all inferior stock, or from the Final Generation!"

Helplessly, Sungchul moved on to the next destination that he had set for himself. School of Alchemy, House of Malleability.

Contrary to the School of Cosmomancy, the name was apt, though the building itself wasn't a structure, but rather a collapsing tent.

"…"

He opened the tent and entered. Several students who couldn't be seen anywhere else had gathered here. Many of them looked to be in their early twenties. They were from the Final Generation.

"What brings you here?"

A student approached the unfamiliar guest and asked cautiously. Sungchul didn't hesitate to state his purpose.

"I came looking for a Guidance Counselor."

A man with sunken eyes came out from deeper within the tent while scratching his head.

"A Freshman? Hm? It's a Summoned."

He looked directly at Sungchul, then smiled, revealing his yellowed teeth.

"You. You wouldn't have received Eckheart's quest within the Summoning Palace and become an Alchemist, have you?"

When Sungchul nodded, he slapped his knees with laughter while holding his belly for quite some time.

"Oh…my stomach. There hasn't been anything really to laugh about recently, but I've finally found something worth laughing on. Anyways, you're looking for a Guidance Counselor? Okay then. I am Basil Philrus. I will gladly be your Guidance Counselor."

He asked for Sungchul's personal details before opening his school-wide Magic Network and perusing Sungchul's records.

"Oh my, you're carrying such a terrifying name. Anyways, you've cut it very close. One more day and you would have had to pack up your things and leave!"

Hearing all of the information, Sungchul recalled Altugius within the Cosmomancy Observatory, and then the face of Leonard.

The Professor is one thing, but I wonder why that guy didn't tell me any of this.

That question was resolved, more or less, on the next day.

"Hey. Mr. Freshman. You can't come in here."

Leonard blocked the entrance with a bright smile. When Sungchul asked for the reason, Leonard put on a sorrowful face as to sympathize with Sungchul's misfortunes while speaking.

"It is because you have been expelled. You'll get the news soon...but to explain, you have yet to find a teacher to accept you within ten days of your admittance, in other words, you haven't found a Guidance Counselor."

"If it is only the Guidance Counselor, then I've already found one."

Sungchul spoke firmly. It was for a brief moment, but Leonard's lips twisted in a strange fashion.

"You've...found one?"

Leonard looked back.

"Not him."

Sungchul said.

"The Alchemy Professor, Basil Philrus."

"Ah...is that right?"

The displeasure on Leonard's handsome face was clearly visible, but Sungchul didn't pay it any mind. He passed by Leonard, who was holding his head down, and sat at his usual spot to begin reading through the pile of books. Altugius let out a stifled sigh of relief as he closed his eyes and listened to the amplified sound of the turning pages in the Observatory.

Chapter 14 – School of Alchemy

"I believe it might be because Sir Warrior lacks the requirements to view the contents of the book."

Christian solved the conundrum that had been plaguing Sungchul in one breath.

"Some Magical tomes require being acquainted with a separate tome. Having extremely high Intuition makes it possible to circumvent some of the peculiar requirements, but in most cases, the problem Sir Warrior is facing will occur."

Sungchul nodded while watching the Sky Squirrel eat some nuts at the corner of the table.

"So that was the case."

Other than the explosive growth at the beginning, he didn't manage to advance his Intuition at all during this past week. It was a heartbreaking waste of time for Sungchul, who liked to optimize every second of his growth.

I should have met with this fellow a bit earlier to consult with him.

However, Sungchul was the type of person who tried his hand at overcoming obstacles on his own before asking for help, but now that he knew that Altugius had given him indecipherable texts, an alternative method would be required. Christian declared that he would find out the solution for him.

"...I'll use my network of people and investigate regarding the book. Once we know the prerequisites, such as which books you'll need to read and the level of Intuition required, it should become possible to decipher that book."

The problem now was time. It wasn't Sungchul's intention to waste his time while he was waiting. He looked directly at Christian and asked him a question.

"What do you suppose I should do in the meantime?"

"Since you have chosen Alchemy as your minor, how about you use this time to receive some teachings regarding it while I try to decipher this book?"

"Alchemy?"

Sungchul's mind recalled the image of the humble tent with the lifeless students that were all chattering away.

"That's right. Although they can be regarded as the delinquents of the school, they won't chase away any student. In that way, you can also receive Magic Power and Intuition. As Magic Power and Intuition are the lifeblood of Mages, it could only be of benefit for you to raise it."

"That's a good idea."

He also recalled the talking book that he had forgotten inside his Soul Storage. Despite everything, the book would be helpful in regards to Alchemy.

Sungchul briefly opened the status window to check his stats.

[Stats]			
Strength	999+	Dexterity	853
Vitality	801	Magic Power	32
Intuition	35	Magic Resist	621
Resilience	502	Charisma	18
	Luck	18	

I have to drag my Magic Power and Intuition over 100 as soon as I'm able.

The basic spell for Cosmomancy required 130 Magic Power and 100 Intuition. Currently, he couldn't learn the spell even if Altugius had wanted to teach it to him. This meant that he would need to change his plans if he wanted to meet his goals. He organized all the things that needed to be done in his mind.

I'll go to the Alchemy building first to raise my Intuition, and I'll then perform the quests inside the House of Recollections. Finally, when my Magic Power and Intuition exceed 100, I'll come and find the Cosmomancy building again.

It had been a winding journey, but now that he had set out on a direction, he could see the end in sight. He pulled out a jewel to reward Christian.

"It is always a pleasure."

Christian bent down to receive the jewel with a wide grin on his face.

Having accomplished everything he had wanted to, he turned to leave when a certain someone's face appeared in his mind.

"Do you know of Leonard Sanctum?"

He hadn't thought about it much before, as he hadn't been very inconvenienced by Leonard, nor had he ever run into the man. However, Leonard had revealed his true nature today. He had an unexpected amount of interest in Sungchul and wanted him expelled. It wasn't clear whether Leonard was an enemy with a purpose or simply a delinquent who enjoyed the suffering of others, but what was certain was that Sungchul didn't like either possibility. There was nothing wrong with having information ahead of time.

"Leonard...Leonard   Sanctum...I've   heard   that   name somewhere..."

Christian spent quite a while struggling to recall when his head shot up along with his finger.

"Did that person have brown or blonde hair? His nose slightly crooked like a hawk's beak?"

"Perhaps."

Christian pulled out a pen and paper, grabbed it with his prosthetic, then quickly sketched out a person's face. The drawing overall was nothing more than a chicken scratch, but the identifying features were well emphasized. Sungchul looked at the portrait briefly and nodded.

"This is accurate. It is this man. When did you have such a talent for art?"

"It is because my minor was in Dimensional Magic. Surprisingly, they taught us music and art there as well. Anyways...I don't know him directly, but he's quite a famous figure. Why are you looking for him?"

"He was in the Cosmomancy building."

Hearing this information, Christian tilted his head.

"Is he still in school? That's strange. I only know him because his face was on a poster back when I was attending."

"For what reason?"

"He got expelled. He was found guilty of intentionally causing the death of five students during an in-school competition known as the 'Gauntlet.' Whoever is expelled can never return to the school for any reason."

"Well, he was inside the Cosmomancy building."

Sungchul took some time to digest the information from Christian.

"It looks as though someone is backing him."

"Could you look into it for me?"

Sungchul placed another jewel on the table as he rose from his seat.

"Excuse me, Sir Warrior. I have a question I have wanted to ask for a while now."

Christian carefully inquired from behind while scratching his head.

"Ask."

"Isn't it a waste? Even if you give me this much money...Well, it's not something someone on the receiving end should be saying, but...I feel that the compensation is excessive."

"That is not something you have to concern yourself with."

Christian would never have dreamt that the man who eight years ago had emptied the pride of the Allied Merchant's Guild, "The Infinity Safe," was standing right before him.

Sungchul moved to his next destination, leaving behind the two bright jewels.

—

"Yes, I am the former tailor of the Airfruit Academy, Bington."

Originally, Sungchul hadn't intended to wear the uniform, but he gained a bit of interest after Sarasa's fervent emphasis on it. He pulled out a single gold coin and spoke to the tailor.

"I'd like to get fitted for one uniform."

"Oh my, you're a Freshman. That's fine. Please wait for a bit."

The skinny tailor wore a monocle and was intensely staring at him through it.

Sungchul's Soul Contract – The Eye of Truth detected that the man was looking at him through Magical means.

"Okay. Your measurements are complete. Do you prefer clothing to be a bit loose or snug?"

"I'd like an appropriate fit."

"Ah, the most difficult of requests. Well, I'll have to show off a bit of my skills then."

Bington began making the uniform using scissors and needles that moved independently, one after the other, with unbelievable proficiency deserving of his former title of as a tailor of Airfruit Academy. Sungchul watched with an interest which he hadn't felt in a long time, the rare performance of Bingon's work.

Regardless of anything else, this man has reached the pinnacle of his field. He truly deserves to be called a master.

It didn't take even thirty minutes for him to complete a full uniform.

"This is the famous Airfruit Academy Uniform, made from the best material by the masterful hands of the very best tailor. Would you like to try it on?"

It was called a uniform, but it had the form of a robe. Sungchul removed his outerwear and put on the school robe, before looking at himself in the mirror.

"Oh, my. Sir customer! You look quite striking. An extraordinary aura seems to flow out of you, and it wouldn't be an exaggeration to say that you could become a Grand Mage by tomorrow!"

Bington rubbed his hands together as he obviously buttered him up, but Sungchul's response was quite passive.

What's this...

It was too tight to be called a robe. It was something like a skinny shirt which hugged his body's muscle lines as though his body had been perfectly measured. It reminded him of something the thugs would wear back on Earth. His sleeves had been lopped off and were patternless as well. The worn, yellowing shirt he wore underneath being visible below the sleeveless and shapeless robe was nothing short of a crime against fashion. Bington was weakly smiling while rubbing his hands together and lingering at Sungchul's side, as though that part was also bothering him.

"Your shirt from the old world is quite worn out! We also sell sleeveless shirts in our store that are just as good as the other world's clothes."

However, his words didn't reach Sungchul's ears. He spoke plainly while looking in the mirror.

"Isn't this too small? Why are there no sleeves?"

"It is the latest trend!"

Bington chatted away proudly.

"The latest trend?"

"The days when Mages stay cooped up in the laboratory studying books are long past. Aren't you the Magic Swordsman that lacks for nothing? Sir customer seems to have a marvelous male physique as I see it, which is why I made it so that it accentuates Sir customer's appeal to the maximum."

"..."

Sungchul pulled off the robe and wore his military fatigues once again. The familiar looseness made his body feel relaxed.

This feels much better.

A pine caterpillar has to eat pine needles.

Sungchul thought of this idiom as he left the shop, leaving the trendy uniform behind.

—

The next day, Sungchul headed towards the Alchemy tent rather than the Cosmomancy Observatory. He was different from the usual, as his front pocket was quite full.

"How could you! Sticking a lady in such a place for days and not even checking once! Isn't that just too much?"

Bertelgia was thoroughly peeved. She had been stuck inside the Soul Storage since the Path of Sajators. Sungchul had completely forgotten about her existence until now when he had pulled her out.

"Really! You're the worst. The WORST! Starting from passing the trial with such an inappropriate method, how can you not have a single thing that is good about you? Are all Summoned like this?"

Bertelgia continued to nag and hop about in his pocket, but Sungchul didn't show the slightest response. He spoke the moment they began to approach the Alchemy tent.

"I'll stick you back into the Soul Storage if you don't quiet down now."

"..."

Bertelgia was silenced with a single sentence; even her squirming within his pocket diminished. After calming Bertelgia, Sungchul entered through a straw mat door flap into a tent that was called "The House of Malleability." When he entered, however, he smelled something unpleasant. The place reeked of marijuana.

Sungchul observed that several students were sitting on some placemats within the tent while smoking some marijuana. They were peeking over at him while whispering amongst themselves and snickering.

Sungchul ignored them and sought out the Alchemy Professor, Basil Philrus.

"Ahem. Who's this? Isn't it the Freshman?"

A man with a burly physique suddenly blocked his path. His clothes appeared to be that of a student's, but his eyes looked befuddled as he occasionally snickered from being inebriated by the marijuana.

For them to be so happily smoking marijuana this early in the morning.

That wasn't all. The rest of the students were also rolling around the ground with empty alcohol bottles. The people and the bottles littered the ground alike as if they were the same thing.

Sungchul glared at the student blocking his path and spoke quietly.

"Where is Professor Basil Philrus?"

"Basil Hyung? Basil Hyung is inside sleeping with a barmaid."

The burly student snickered again and pointed into the tent.

Sungchul discovered two bodies, one male and one female, sleeping together, wrapped around one another inside a closed-off section separated by a portiere.

It's a complete circus. Even beyond what I'd expected.

He regretted coming so early in the morning.

***

However, he couldn't just waste time after getting this far. Grasping at straws, Sungchul asked the man in front of him.

"I wish to learn Alchemy. Where do I start?"

"There are textbooks scattered on the floor, with the ingredients and the cauldrons all outside the hut."

The man clucked in laughter before returning to where his friends were waiting for him while speaking loudly for everyone to hear.

"That guy is so earnest! You know what he said to me? He said he wanted to learn Alchemy!"

He exploded with laughter as though it was the greatest joke he had ever heard.

"Why would someone like that come HERE!"

The rest of the students snickered along as they continued to puff on marijuana cigarettes with smoke pouring out of their nose and mouth. In some sense, it had a similar atmosphere to that of the School of Cosmomancy.

Sungchul didn't bother with their taunts and began to look through the floor that was littered with beer bottles and trash in search of the lost textbooks.

"There. That book."

Bertelgia whispered from his pocket. Sungchul discovered a thin book that was "stored" under a pile of bottles and grabbed it with his hand.

<Beginner's Alchemy that even Ogres can Follow>

The students who were watching Sungchul with interest burst into laughter at the sight.

"Look at that. Mr. Serious Summoned managed to find a book!"

"Worthy of being Eckheart's successor!"

With such an eye-catching title, the book appeared to be intended for children. Upon opening the book, it revealed the illustrations of a goofy-looking Ogre stirring a cauldron. They were laughing because they knew about this.

As usual, Sungchul was not fazed by the mockery of such insignificant people. He left the torrent of mockery behind him as he exited the tent.

He could see several cauldrons and a storage made out of wooden planks stuck together. The cauldrons were filled with dust and spider webs, and the storage cabinet was left neglected.

"Whew. Who were those bastards? Really? They dare call themselves Alchemists! What a disgrace!"

Bertelgia squirmed once again.

"Alchemists are treated like dogs even now! They are all pathetic people who can't see how great Alchemy really is."

Sungchul listened to her complaints and took a seat on a tree stump near an alchemic cauldron before opening the book. A distinct feeling came into mind as he turned the first page. Easy. It looked stupidly easy. He read through the entire "Beginner's Alchemy that even Ogres can Follow" in one breath. There was quite a bit of content, but that wasn't a problem for Sungchul. It was a moment when having being lost in the maze of indecipherable text for the past week had finally paid off.

"A warrior like you should know that combat raises associated status points; Alchemy and Magic also increase related status points the more you use them."

Bertelgia piped up when Sungchul closed the book as though she had been waiting to speak. He pulled her out of his pocket and nodded.

She tottered along Sungchul's palm like a human and spoke like an educator.

"Another thing. There seems to be some connection between that cauldron next to you and the book. In other words, successfully 'synthesizing alchemical solutions within the boundaries of the Academy using the cauldron and textbooks provided' is considered as the completion of a quest, and a suitable reward is given. This is a common teaching mechanism in Magic Academies."

"Is that so?"

"Yep. Academies are, in essence, culminations of massive quests created by their predecessors. Even the oft-ridiculed Alchemy operates under the same principle."

While listening to her insight, Sungchul made a note in his mind.

Bertelgia. She can prove surprisingly useful at times.

If what she had said was correct, then it was time for some hands-on experience. Sungchul stood up from the stump, found a suitable branch, and brutishly snapped it off. It was about as thick as a grown man's arm, but it broke off like styrofoam in his grip. He stripped off all of the straggling branches using nothing but the strength of his hand before pulling out his beginner blade from his Soul Storage.

The sword had been used extensively during his time in the Summoning Palace, but now it was a piece of junk which was simply taking up space inside his Soul Storage.

Sungchul held the sword over the flame that was burning underneath the cauldron until it had heated into a red color, then punched the blade with his fist to flatten it.

"Dear Lord..."

Bertelgia was speechless.

He looped the flattened metal around the branch a few times, using it to tightly secure smaller branches to it, creating a sturdy book holder. He embedded the book holder against the cauldron and placed "Beginner's Alchemy that even Ogres can Follow" on top.

"...Clap. Clap. Clap."

Bertelgia couldn't help but applaud as she looked over this spectacle.

Sungchul took a step back to observe his handiwork before he headed to the storage made of planks. The storage was locked shut with rusted chains, but it came apart as easily as cobwebs when tugged by Sungchul.

"You look as though you've done this often?"

Bertelgia teased carefully. Sungchul nodded at this and responded.

"It's one of my few hobbies."

"..."

There were countless ingredients placed on display. Bertelgia looked like a fish in water as she flew about taking a look around the storage. Sungchul couldn't figure out how a book that had no nose, eyes, or mouth could observe the ingredients. On completing her examination of the materials, she returned to his shoulder.

"The ingredients aren't preserved well, probably due to neglect. But it should still be possible to synthesize the lowest-grade alchemical solution with them. Take this, this, and that for now. Yes. And that too."

Sungchul picked out everything Bertelgia recommended and smelled them.

[Blindman's Grass]

Level: 1

Grade: F

Attribute: Wood

Effect: None

Note: It is commonly seen along the roadside, but due to its stabilizing nature, it acts as a neutralizing agent to otherwise reactive ingredients.

This is something I used before.

There was a noticeable difference between being clueless and having a dabbling knowledge, especially in regards to generating interest in a subject; the latter carried a significant advantage over the former. His interest reignited with such vigor that Sungchul gathered some other ingredients to check their alchemic properties.

"It's a good habit to smell as many ingredients as possible. Like a lion spares no effort when hunting a rabbit, a great Alchemist would never overlook even the most common of ingredients!"

He managed to gather all the necessary ingredients during Bertelgia's stream of encouragements and laid his jacket next to the cauldron, placing the ingredients on top

Then, shall we begin?

It was a rare moment of gentleness. Sungchul opened the textbook on his handcrafted book holder and chose an ingredient among those laid out before him.

"It is effective to remove the roots of the Blindman's Grass before synthesis. There are some impurities contained within the roots that hinder the neutralizing effects of the plant."

Bertelgia continued to advise him by his side. Sungchul followed her instructions and carefully removed the roots of the dried Blindman's Grass, and proceeded with a similar preparation for the other ingredients. For example, a dried ingredient called "Flower of Happiness" needed to have its stamen and pistil removed, and only the dark caps of Shadow Mushrooms were considered as useful alchemical ingredients.

"You're quite good at preparing ingredients! I thought you were only good at smashing things."

Bertelgia, who had been observing Sungchul while floating by his side, threw out a rare compliment. While preparing the ingredients, Sungchul realized how preparation for cooking and Alchemy seemed extremely similar. Good ingredients were needed for good results, and dedication to cooking began from the preparation of ingredients.

Considerable time was devoted to preparing the ingredients before they were tossed into the cauldron. Sungchul then vigorously stirred the contents with a scoop. Mana continuously leaked out with each stir, and the alchemic cauldron filled with a vibrant light.

[Synthesis Success!]

A green liquid filled the alchemic cauldron. Sungchul filled an empty bottle with the green content and proceeded to examine it.

[Healing Salve]

Level: 1

Grade: E

Attribute: Wood

Type: Recovery Item

Note: It is effective when rubbed onto wounds.

A message popped up when Sungchul finished observing it.

[Congratulations! You have succeeded in your first synthesis as an Airfruit Alchemist student.]

Reward: Magic Power +1, Intuition +1

Sungchul's eyes flashed when he saw this message.

"It raises Magic Power too? Not just Intuition?"

"Of course. It takes Magic Power during synthesis. It isn't as simple as just reading a book and understanding the theory."

+1 Magic Power and +1 Intuition. It was an insignificant amount, but to Sungchul who had been thirsting for growth, it felt like finding an oasis in the middle of the desert.

He immediately opened the next page and attempted the alchemical process within, and with Bertelgia's assistance, he managed to complete it in no time. By the time the sun had reached its zenith, he had completed the volume and all of its assignments. It had only raised his Magic Power by five and his Intuition by three, but Sungchul wasn't discouraged. There was a mountain of resources to be found within the tent.

Sungchul again entered the tent and found another book before turning to leave. The students, who were finally preparing to start their lessons of the day, saw this unfamiliar man wearing military fatigues and couldn't help but tilt their heads.

"Who is that guy?"

Since all the students that had been smoking marijuana had left, there was no one there to answer them. There was also no one to give it a second thought. While being ignored by the students and the Professor of the School of Alchemy, Sungchul steadily plowed through the textbooks at a breakneck speed under the instruction and guidance of Bertelgia.

By the time the pothead students saw Sungchul again, they were shocked to see the book he held in his hands.

"W-what? He's already looking at Advanced Alchemy?"

Their disbelief was to be expected. The shabbily dressed man had been looking at the introductory textbooks for children just a week ago. And they couldn't help but be surprised that this same man was now referring to Advanced Alchemy after merely a week's time that even they wouldn't dare attempt to read.

"He's probably just pretending," a student said, looking unimpressed as he breathed out a puff of white smoke. With his reassuring words, the other students all laughed along in agreement.

"That must be it. How could that guy be looking at books that even we can't understand? Elementary Alchemy is decently easy, but even Intermediate Alchemy makes me shit blood when I try to read it."

"Agreed. And beginning with the introductory level Alchemy, knowledge of how to correctly use alchemical tools becomes necessary. How can anyone self-learn the proper use of the tools without an instructor?"

Their Professor, Basil Philrus, was wasted on alcohol and lying naked in his tent today as well. More mindful students might have pitied Sungchul and taught him some basics, but no such students were left within the School of Alchemy. They could only conclude that this man was holding on to the Advanced Alchemy book for show. However, they had no way of knowing that the alchemic tools that had been gathered into a corner of the tent had disappeared and that Sungchul had a much better teacher than some random Alchemist.

"Good. Good. Pour it like that before squeezing out the rest. Though not too roughly!"

"..."

Sungchul carefully turned the centrifuge's handle under Bertelgia's guidance. As he could snap off the handle by being careless, he adjusted his strength as he cranked it to the highest possible speed and then noticed the liquid separating into two layers inside of the centrifuge.

"Good! Now use a mesh to filter out the upper layer!"

Under her guidance, Sungchul managed to fill a bottle with a clear, white liquid. One of the benefits of being an Alchemist was being able to know the rate of success beforehand.

[Synthesis Success!]

He broke into a faint smile before taking a break. Contrary to what the students believed, Sungchul had already comprehended Intermediate Alchemy and had taken a step into Advanced Alchemy.

His Intuition and Magic Power each had risen over 50 within the week, and his only obstacle now was his lack of mana. He was synthesizing so frequently that he was running out of mana, which resulted in failed synthesis. However, this problem was easily solved by using the power of money. He began drinking expensive Mana Drinks to restore his depleted Magical Power and continued with developing his Alchemy.

Sungchul managed to grow beyond anyone's expectation, but it still wasn't enough to satisfy him. No, this was simply the beginning. Sungchul, whose Magic Power and Intuition had exceeded 50, set his sights on the House of Recollections.

Chapter 15 – House of Recollections

Like the passage of time forming wrinkles on the human skin, old buildings would also gain bone-chilling ghost stories; these were like badges of honor for the structure that has stood for several centuries. It might have been inevitable that the House of Recollections, a building that had been erected over a thousand years ago, would be as much the focus of numerous unexplained wonders as the countless students who had passed through these doors. Not many students remained within the Academy, and the vital flow of new admissions looked to have run dry, but seven ghastly rumors circled within the House of Recollections.

The first wonder was regarding the immovable door at the end of the basement hallway. According to rumor, it was a room used as a prison before the House of Recollections had been renovated into a dormitory, and the room in question had been used as a sinister torture chamber similar to other prisons. It is said that many of those who were tortured to death became poltergeists, and had wandered within the chamber ever since. Sungchul now stood in front of the focus of the first of these stories: The Immovable Door at the Basement.

[On the night of the waxing crescent and upon the stroke of midnight, rust water will flow like blood through the cracks of the immovable door, and a quest will begin.]

There was a note from Christian inside Sungchul's hand. He read over the note once again and waited for the rust water to flow from this infamous door.

After some time had passed, a dreary feeling crept into the air, and a slithering voice could be heard.

"Uh…oo…oooo…"

It was a frightful wail, enough to make any weaker man make a beeline to the door.

"Can't we...just turn back?"

Bertelgia, who appeared to be plenty scared, dug deep into his pocket. On the other hand, Sungchul wasn't bothered at all as he continued to observe the edges of this door. Bright red rust water soon began flowing from the door's edges like blood.

Sungchul placed his hand upon the doorknob as though he had been waiting. There was a surprising chill that was surrounding it. He could see bright words appear from the doorknob soon after.

[What, pray tell, has compelled you to take hold of this doorknob?]

A list of choices followed.

[1. Curiosity]

[2. Courage]

[3. Foolhardiness]

Sungchul wanted to select the third option, but he chose the ideal answer as given to him by Christian, which was the first choice.

[Curiosity? Curiosity can be the flame of knowledge to brilliant Mages, but be wary. Curiosity will often lead to death.]

Sungchul read through the words as he picked his ears.

After a moment, the rusty water, which had flowed out from the door, began to float up on its own and wrote out bright red words and symbols over the door as though it were written in blood.

[Answer me this: What is this Magical formation trying to convey?]

There was only one purpose to the shape-shifting rust water: the examination of the challenger's capabilities. It especially examined the Intuition. Sungchul would not have been able to understand the shapes of the rusty water a week ago, but he wasn't the same as before. He grasped the underlying pattern and meaning behind the dizzying motion of the rust water and answered calmly.

"Fortune."

As his voice rang out, the rusty water that had been dancing in the air burned away into nothingness, and another message appeared before him.

[You have the qualifications to enter the door.]

The door slowly began to open. What laid beyond this immovable door, feared by students as a torture chamber, now revealed itself to Sungchul. He felt slightly disappointed. There was a single Devil tied down by metallic chains beyond the doors. It had a ram's head and a bat's wings, a human's body, and a goat's hooves. It was a Baal.

A Baal was known to be a grade higher than Balroq, but they had both met a similar fate without much difference to Sungchul's hammer.

"Kekeke…a long awaited guest. You've come right in time. I was just about to grow bored of this and escape."

The chained Devil spoke. Upon closer observation, one of the Devil's eyes was blind, and his Magic strength felt weak. He looked to have been captured after losing his strength due to a loss from a human or a Devil.

Sungchul looked over the Devil with uncaring eyes and bluntly spoke, "…Let's begin."

A twisted smile formed on the Devil's lips and he laughed loudly. Dozens of chains that shackled his body shook with his every movement.

"A human with some spunk! Good. Let the Devil's Game begin!"

A Magical formation bloomed on the Devil's fingertips, and a single table appeared between them. A single die and three cups had been placed on top of the table. The Devil turned the cup over and placed a die within before he began to mix the cups with practiced movements. Intrigue sparked in Sungchul's eyes.

It's a Shell Game.

It had been written on Christian's note that it would be a dice game, but Sungchul knew that it was a Shell Game.

"Now. The rules are simple. I'll mix the cups, and you guess the location of the die. If you get the location correct, I'll reward you."

The Devil looked down upon Sungchul, arrogance in his eyes as he put forth his challenge.

"Do you accept?"

Sungchul nodded. As soon as he accepted, the Devil's hand that held the cups moved fluidly and tried to confuse the eyes. The die soon stopped, and the Devil asked his question.

"Now. Which cup is holding the Die of Fate?"

It wasn't a difficult question. Sungchul pointed towards the center cup. When the Devil lifted the cup, it held the die.

"Pretty good. For a human, anyways. To be able to see through the great Crustes's deception!"

The Devil shook his fists as though he was frustrated. His chains shook violently and made a loud racket.

"However, a promise is a promise, so I'll reward you."

When the racket from the chains died down, the Devil pointed his finger with a sharp nail shooting out towards Sungchul.

[What a great challenger! You have won the gamble against the Devil Crustes!]

Reward: +1 Magic Power

As a Devil, a race with a high affinity for Magic, the reward wasn't Intuition but Magic Power. It was quite insufficient for a gamble against a Devil, but there was more to come. Crustes smiled and spoke amiably.

"Truthfully, I made a mistake this time around. It's been so long that my fingers got all twisted up. Why don't you try again? This time, I'll bet 2 of my Magic Power. Of course, you, a human, don't have to bet anything."

A tempting offer. There was no reason to refuse. Sungchul nodded once again, and the second game soon began. The results was another victory for Sungchul.

As expected, it's just as Christian said.

The Devil imprisoned within the basement of the House of Recollections was one that had fallen to the human realm after being defeated during an internal fight amongst the Devils within their realm. This Devil, Crustes, was granted a secret space within the dormitory among students in exchange for helping Mages and led a pitiful life tricking students.

The Devil's methods weren't that different from the traditional tricks that swindlers would use. He would lose a couple of games to the students to raise their greed and lower their guard before he devoured their souls through a single massive gamble.

[After the fourth game, please quickly escape from the room. The Devil will get extremely upset if you don't!]

Christian warned him to only go as far as the fourth bet that didn't require any risks for the student. It was because the Devil would require the students to bet some of the earnings after the fifth game.

"How could such a human thing happen! For Crustes to lose four times consecutively!!!"

The metallic chains shook loudly without reservation, and the Devil's body trembled in anger.

"10 Magic Power. Let's put 10 Magic Power on the line for the next gamble! I can't let you leave like this!"

Sungchul had won exactly 10 Magic Power through the four matches. Even with the consideration that the stat was easy to raise due to its initially low number, it wouldn't be an exaggeration to call it a top tier reward for a common quest.

Rather than calling it a common quest, it looks as though this is just simple gambling like the Devil had said.

Most quests are classified common quests.

Quests are a collection of trials and rewards created by blessed beings with the permission of those who control the world; Gods and Lesser Gods. Those who created quests were referred to as the quest hosts, and the difficulty of the quest trials and the size of the rewards were relative to the strength of the quest host. Legendary existences, like that of the Seven Heroes, could create high-tier quests, like objectives, but the lesser existences could only create quests that are suited to their level. However, this Devil's gamble had an excessive reward to be considered as a low-tier quest. This meant that this quest was not set up like other quests, and was created in a way that could harm the quest host depending on its results.

"Now, human! Do you dare gamble for 10 Magic Power? If so, come and try your luck."

If Sungchul managed to win, he could earn another 10 Magic Power. It was an opportunity to gain 20 Magic Power overnight with no particular effort involved on his part. However, the Devil would never deal in such a losing bargain.

"However, not even I can give away this much for free. I have bet thus far, and now you must bet something as well."

"What do you want me to bet?"

When Sungchul asked, the Devil spoke with a sinister smile.

"What else do you have to bet, other than your soul?"

It was easy enough up until now for anyone could choose the correct cup by paying a bit of attention to the Devil's sleight of hand. It was simple and straightforward. An ignorant person might have been drunk on his winnings and stepped into this formidable challenge not knowing that this temptation would be his destruction.

"I'll do it."

However, Sungchul entered the game with an entirely different mindset than the others who had all been sacrificed to the Devil. He crossed his arms and activated his Soul Contract- Eye of Truth as he observed the Devil.

"You agreed?"

SLAM!

The immovable door slammed shut. The room became dyed in a bloody hue. The Devil smiled and laughed loud enough to blow off the roof.

"Shall we begin? Human? The final gamble, my 10 Magic Power, or your soul?"

The Devil's hand that held the cups began to move. It was fast. It was a speed that was levels beyond the previous games as the die shot between the cups like a bullet, intending to confuse the eyes.

"Kehahaha!"

The Devil broke into a lighthearted laughter, and he put in more speed. By the end, his hands and the cups began to move faster and faster until only the afterimage of it could be seen with the naked eye, and the wooden table began to burn from the sheer friction of his movements.

The hands stopped after some time while a portion of the table continued to burn. The Devil looked down on Sungchul with his last remaining eye and oppressively asked him.

"Now, human. It is the time of destiny. Choose."

The Devil was laughing. It was impossible to choose correctly. It was because this was a gamble that couldn't be won even if the Goddess of Fortune was smiling upon the human. The die was not in the cups, but rather it was hidden inside the Devil's grasp.

I'll get to dine on a human soul after such a long time.

The Devil was licking his lips in anticipation as he hurriedly waited for the decision.

"Now, human! Why hesitate? I don't have much patience, you know?"

At that moment, something the Devil hadn't anticipated occurred. Sungchul grabbed the Devil's wrist.

"Cease all movements."

The last remaining eye of the Devil shrank in terror.

H-how?!

He couldn't move his hand. It was something that had never happened before. Despite his status as a fallen Devil who had lost his former strength, he was still an existence whose strength couldn't be compared to that of an average human, but now it had been overcome so easily.

"Kuwaaaa!"

The Devil felt like his hand was being crushed, and so he released his grip as he screamed in pain.

Roll...

The die that had been hidden in his grip rolled onto the burning table.

W-what the...this bastard...

The Devil had finally realized it. The one who had been tricked in this gamble wasn't the human, but rather himself. Sungchul stared at him with eyes that were more Devilish than a Devil's and spoke firmly, using a heavy killing intent.

"Keep your promise, Devil."

"H-how could I refuse!"

Crustes gave up what little remaining Magic Power he had left to Sungchul. The message alerting of the quest's success came up.

[ ]

Reward: +10 Magic Power

Seeing that the message was blank, the Devil himself must not have expected to lose the fifth gamble. Sungchul quietly spoke to the Devil who was staring at him wide-eyed.

"The next time I come to find you, it will be your funeral day."

The chains that held the Devil shook weakly. Sungchul could feel the Devil's terror through the meek noises from the chains as he stood at the door. The immovable door swung open, and Sungchul checked his stats as he left through the door.

[Stats]			
Strength	999+	Dexterity	853
Vitality	801	Magic Power	71
Intuition	58	Magic Resist	621
Resilience	502	Charisma	18
	Luck	18	

There are six remaining quests within the House of Recollections. I'll tackle the Alchemy class books at the School of Alchemy during the day, and continue the quests inside the House of Recollections during the night. My time limit is a week. I have to hit my goals within a week.

It wasn't a coincidence that Sungchul had managed to achieve such divine physical strength. He knew what he had to do to continue growing.

***

Outside the Airfruit Academy campus, there was a store for Magical tools with a carbuncle symbol. This store, which had been steeped deeply in history and had already been passed down for eight generations, was now at risk of closing down due to the impending calamity and the degeneracy of the Airfruit Academy. The current owner, however, was currently standing slack-jawed.

"You…wish to buy all of this?"

He always believed that the infamous "windfall" was a stroke of fortune which only happened to others.

"Everything. How much will it be?"

The black-haired Summoned arrived without warning and brought with him enough profits to put him back in the black after suffering many years of losses.

"The total comes to 31 gold coins…but since Sir Customer is a regular, we'll call it an even 30 gold coins."

The man had bought 31 low-tier Magic Essence, which was more commonly known as Mana Drink. It was infamous for having a ridiculous price despite its actual effectiveness at recovering Magic Power, but this man had just purchased 31 of them. There were only 2 within the store's inventory, but it was possible to get the other 29 through other stores and Alchemists.

The man had previously purchased 11 of these Mana Drinks and just like then, no haggling had taken place; The man simply bought at the named price even when the transaction amount surpassed dozens of gold coins. This instance had been no different. The wholesale value of the 31 mana drinks that had been sold to the man was only valued at 12 gold coins. The owner was prepared to lower it to 20 gold coins if he started haggling, but the man hadn't even bothered with questions or complaint as he unhesitatingly handed over 30 gold coins. It goes without saying that the owner couldn't help but smile.

The man's gold coins were much purer than the average gold coins, so their value would be much higher than regular gold coins. Even if they were all gold coins, their prices could vary depending on the date of manufacture, weight, and purity.

"Then, if you'll excuse me."

After the man left, the owner carefully examined one of the gold coins. It was unmistakable. It was a perfect gold coin with 99.9% purity. The owner's mouth couldn't help but split into a wide smile.

"Dang. What does that man do for a living?"

He examined the other side of the coin to confirm its mint. That was because common coins have the mint site recorded, but the coin he now held in his hand had no such marks on it; an unmarked coin. He had no way of knowing its origins, as someone who only traded minor tools with average students, but there was only one faction who had the authority to produce unmarked coinage in the Other World: The Allied Merchant's Guild. They weren't openly dominating, but their near bottomless economic might and their information network of merchants allowed the Guild to become one of the hidden masters that ruled Other World. The circulation of unmarked coinage was a topic they had a great interest in for a while now.

"The unmarked coin is being checked."

It was late in the evening when the head of the Allied Merchant's Guild, Viceroy Horneko, received the report regarding the unmarked coin. There was black bread and a block of butter on the table. It was a humble meal which didn't quite fit in with the image of the head of the Allied Merchant's Guild, who held the power to move mountains of gold at will. Viceroy Horneko chewed on the stubborn bread as he lazily looked to his aide.

"…Is that right?"

He continued his meal even after he heard the report. After placing the butter on the black bread, he held some warm water in his mouth as he thoroughly chewed the buttered bread before downing it with the water. After completing his meal in this way, which was reminiscent of a cow's mastication, Horneko finally opened his mouth.

"Where was the unmarked coin in question found?"

"It was Golden City."

"Golden City?"

One of Horneko's brow shot up.

"Yes. Not only that, but we also confirmed the information that several jewels we are familiar with have been identified within that district."

"Unmarked coins, followed by the gems…"

The gems could be considered as a coincidence, but the unmarked coins, which had been securely locked away inside the Infinity Safe, being circulated could only mean one thing: The man who had emptied the Infinity Safe eight years ago was active again within the human territories. They had lost him by a hair's breadth last time, but they couldn't afford to miss this opportunity again.

"Contact the Assassin's Guild. Tell them to gather their best possible force. No questions will be asked, regardless of the price."

—

The reason for purchasing the Mana Drink in bulk was simple. The second hidden quest within the House of Recollections required a large amount of Magic Power.

On the desk of the currently empty House Head's room was a precious orb, which reflected a dark, unpleasant light.

Bertelgia recognized the orb's identity in a single glance and spoke,

"This is the Stone of Soul Absorption."

"I see."

Sungchul also knew this. There were some Anti-Mage specialists who had these stones embedded into their weapons. The Soul Absorption Stone inside the House Head's room was significantly larger than the ones he had seen, and its surface also looked polished as if to prove that it had been passed through the hands of countless students.

"Hm. Whether it is in the past or now, a place called 'school' will always be the same."

Bertelgia popped out of Sungchul's pocket as she spoke. When she noticed Sungchul's lack of response, she spun around in the vicinity of the stone while continuing with her words.

"Even the school that I attended had a Soul Absorption Stone at every dormitory. You know, because a Freshman with extraordinary Magic Power would come by from time to time. And to pick out those talented kids, they left the stone there. The real deal would end up breaking the stone with just their mana."

"That's what I'm also trying to do."

Sungchul pulled out a bag from his Soul Storage. It contained the thirty Mana Drink within.

"This doesn't seem right…"

Bertelgia drooped her body.

"This is a scam. A total scam!"

"…"

Sungchul didn't pay heed to her words and instead placed his hand on the Stone of Soul Absorption. Accompanying the sensation of his Magic Power draining away was a bright message that appeared before his eyes.

[Welcome to Airfruit Magic Academy's Magic Power Measurement.]

[You are currently touching a stone that drains Magic Power, called "the Stone of Soul Absorption." If you experience a chill, dizziness, weakness in your legs, or fatigue, please remove your hand from the Stone of Soul Absorption immediately.]

"…"

His vision became blurred. Sungchul immediately poured a Mana Drink into his mouth. It was only as large as a baby chick's tear, but he could feel his Magic Power reinvigorate immediately after it entered his body.

[Good! You possess great Magical power. In that case, the measurement of Magic Power will now begin.]

[The Magic Power Measurement will continue for the duration of five minutes. The moment your hand is removed, or your Magic Power is completely drained, the test will end.]

[The test will begin in 5...4...3...2...1...]

[Start!]

When the countdown ended, the stone began to drain Sungchul's Magic Power intensely. One of his hands remained on the stone while the other was busy emptying Mana Drinks into his mouth. His Magic Power was simultaneously replenished as it drained away. A white light began to fill the Stone of Soul Absorption as Magic Power came flooding in.

"This shouldn't be. This...shouldn't...be..."

Bertelgia stared wordlessly at Sungchul's method of solving the quest. The test came to an end when half of the 31 Mana Drinks he had prepared were used up.

[Impressive! Your high Magic Power can only be found in 1 among 500 people!]

[The 12th House Head of the Airfruit Academy, Mardiastes extends a gift with respect towards the possessor of the most important talent: great Magic Power.]

Reward: Magic Power +5, Intuition +5

It was a generous reward. But this still wasn't the end. Sungchul did not remove his hand from the Stone of Soul Absorption. The exterior of the Stone of Soul Absorption filled with milky light and began to grow turbulent.

[Is this still not enough?]

Sungchul held the Mana Drink in his other hand then nodded.

[That is fine. The actual trial shall now begin. However, the test from this point can be extremely dangerous, so please proceed under the supervision of the Residence Assistant of the dormitory.]

There was no Residence Assistant. Instead, there was only Bertelgia flapping beside him. When Sungchul looked over at her, she shouted with a relenting look.

"Begin!"

The test began at that moment. The stone began to absorb Sungchul's Magic Power at a rate incomparable to before.

"Eh? Isn't this dangerous?"

Bertelgia spoke out in concern, but Sungchul didn't take heed. He still had about 15 Mana Drink left. He consumed the essence when his mana was drained and continued on like a machine in this fashion.

SLAM! SLAM! SLAM! SLAM! SLAM!

In an instant, the clear sound of 10 empty bottles rang out over the top of the desk. Bertelgia, who was watching the scene froze in shock.

"Is…this something a person should do?"

With only 4 mana drink remaining the surface of the Stone of Soul Absorption finally began to crack. Sungchul's drinking of mana essence also stopped.

[Impressive. You are the possessor of astounding Magic Power that only appears once every 10 years.]

[I congratulate the birth of a great Mage who will carry the future of Airfruit, and pray for endless glory in the years to come.]

Reward: Magic Power +5, Intuition +5

He had managed to get his hands on additional rewards.

For a time, the Stone of Soul Absorption and its related quest would not be available, as it would take a considerable amount of time to restore a shattered Stone of Soul Absorption. However, Sungchul discovered a more urgent problem. He felt a familiar presence coming from beyond the door.

The Lich girl. She must have caught onto my plans and come by.

They were fated to meet again at some point. After all, the girl had been carefully observing everything that was happening within the dorm.

Sungchul shoved Bertelgia, who had been flying beside him, into his pocket and whispered to her.

"Keep quiet for a moment."

"…"

She fidgeted once as to show her acknowledgement.

The figure outside the door was the person he had been expecting.

"Whatcha' doing there?"

Her crystal blue eyes shot forth a piercing gaze, taking a peek at the scene behind Sungchul.

"I was performing a quest related to the Stone of Soul Absorption."

There was no reason to make up a lie for something that was so obvious, so he spoke the truth. Hearing his explanation, Sarasa moved past him to look at the precious orb on top of the House Head's desk.

"Ara?"

The surface of the Stone of Soul Absorption appeared cracked, like a field dried out by drought. Sarasa looked surprised as she turned towards Sungchul.

"This…was this your doing?"

Sungchul nodded, and Sarasa's form wavered like a reed.

"How can this be?"

Sarasa placed a hand on the cracked orb and recited a spell in her mind.

Vision.

A visible projection appeared between them with information on display.

<Those that have Shattered the Shell>

Mardiastes

Great Lagrange

334

Vitto

Armin Cruz

...

A familiar name appeared within the words that were scrolling away like the credit reel of a movie.

142. Altugius Xero

...

148. Leonard Sanctum

149. Sarasa Xero

And finally, Sungchul's name appeared.

151. Sungchul Kim

Sarasa stared piercingly at the name before turning towards Sungchul once again. A small Magical formation appeared in her eyes which flickered with a cold and blue light.

Sungchul's stats			
	[Stats]		
Strength	24	Dexterity	25
Vitality	26	Magic Power	81
Intuition	68	Magic Resist	21
Resilience	18	Charisma	18
	Luck	18	

"You've shattered the Stone of Soul Absorption, and your Magic Power doesn't even reach 100?"

This was impossible, in her mind at least. Sungchul obliged her by tossing a small bottle in her direction. Sarasa instantly recognized the liquid within the bottle.

"This is...Mana Drink?!"

Sungchul nodded, and Sarasa finally looked at the rest of the room. There was a massive amount of empty Mana Drink bottles which had been piled high on the House Head's desk.

My god... how much is this.

Sarasa's eyes grew wide, and a cold breath poured out from deep within her lungs.

"This is a sham."

Sarasa shook as she spoke.

"You're right. This is a sham."

Sungchul spoke while looking back at her with indifferent eyes.

"But, it couldn't be helped. My teacher won't teach me any Magic, so I could only conclude that I had to raise my stats regardless of the method."

"T-that is…!"

Sarasa opened her mouth to speak but quickly shut it again. She was well aware of the situation Altugius Xero had fallen into.

Sungchul continued to watch her with passive eyes and spoke quietly.

"I'll briefly go to visit the second floor. There is a quest there that I want to complete. I have no ill intentions, so you're welcome to come observe from the side."

"…"

Sarasa made no reply. Silence implies consent. Sungchul used the momentum of the situation to move past her and stepped onto the second floor's stairs.

Once on the second floor, Sungchul felt that the chill which permeated the entire dorm was one step stronger.

The area in front of Sarasa's room had the most intense concentration of Magic.

She coated the place with Cryomancy.

Sungchul moved past her room and headed towards the next quest's location. The quests within the House of Recollections were infamous for their high difficulty and degree of risk, but to Sungchul, who was already familiar with both the strategies on overcoming them and the various contingency plans he could follow in case of mistakes, the obstacles didn't amount to much.

Going to the School of Alchemy in the morning and the House of Recollections during the night, Sungchul continued to grind through this ebb and flow for a whole week. He looked at his status page as he celebrated his accomplishments with some of his personal cooking.

[Stats]			
Strength	999+	Dexterity	853
Vitality	801	Magic Power	130
Intuition	101	Magic Resist	621
Resilience	502	Charisma	18
	Luck	18	

Sungchul drained a shot glass in one go.

"Kaaa!"

The alcohol was sweet, especially after raising Magic Power which had been particularly difficult. When the beginner's threshold of 100 was met, growth would naturally come to a halt. This was why he had to rely on Alchemy so heavily, despite completing all of the hidden quests within the House of Recollections. After full days of synthesizing he had barely managed to raise his Magic Power by 1 or 2 until he finally met the goals he had set.

Should I slowly begin to move towards that place?

He hadn't received any positive news from Christian, but he had set his mind on returning to the Observatory of Cosmomancy after so long.

—

"Look who it is? Didn't you decide on Alchemy? You must have come by because you were lonely without any friends. How sad…there don't seem to be any friends here either."

Leonard passionately greeted Sungchul when he returned to the Observatory, but he ignored Leonard completely as he entered. Altugius, who was obstinately sitting under a pillar with his back turned, took a quick peek before putting his head down to feign ignorance.

"…"

Once again, Sungchul took a seat next to the tower of books that had been haunting him and grabbed one. It was the thickest of the pile and was the one that had hurt his brain the most. Leonard began to taunt him while lying on his hammock.

"I'll say this from the kindness of my heart. That book is not something a beginner like you can understand through brute force."

The warning would have been better served much earlier, but things were different now. Sungchul was watching the words, which couldn't be understood before, slowly form into something coherent.

"…"

The Magic tome slowly lifted itself and opened before him. Leonard's eyes grew wide in shock.

W-what…that bastard!

Nothing could be hidden within the Observatory, which was a place that amplified even the smallest of sounds. The book that was now levitating in the air began to turn its pages at a rapid pace. When the information within it had finished transferring over to Sungchul, Altugius turned his head, and his aged face became full of astonishment.

No…that man…?!

During that moment of shock, a small change appeared within Sungchul. The change was then manifested into physical form.

[You have broken through the basic tome of Cosmomancy: Light that Shines through Stormy Clouds.]

[The Knowledge of the Skies and the Universe is now hidden within you.]

Reward: Magic-Glare

Chapter 16 – Difficult Assignment

Sungchul felt the new skill imbued to his body and took a moment to familiarize himself with it.

"Status window. Magic."

[Magic]
1. Glare

Sungchul stared at the spell "Glare" intensely. Eventually, a more detailed screen regarding the skill appeared.

[Glare]
Rank: 3
Type: Offensive Magic
Attribute: Null Attribute
Effect: Single Target Attack
Note: Calls down a Heavenly Light to burn your foes.

Even the most basic Magic was categorized as a third rank. Was it more accurate to say that it was to be expected?

Sungchul was gripped by a compulsion to test out his new Magic, but there was a problem that needed to be solved before he could do so: the people within the School of Cosmomancy.

"No...you. How did you do it? How...could you read that book?"

It was the first time that Altugius made such an expression of surprise. He even dropped the pipe in his mouth onto the floor from the shock, but there was another person who was even more surprised; that person was Leonard Sanctum.

"This is impossible. That man's Intuition was definitely at the level of some chimp…"

Immediately after he spoke, a Magic formation unraveled within his pupils and Sungchul's stats appeared before him. The new numbers only confirmed Leonard's suspicions.

This is IMPOSSIBLE! His Intuition is 101?! How did he manage to raise it so high? What kind of person is he?

Altugius was also looking at Sungchul's stats using a similar Magic. Only praise escaped from his lips since this was a truly monstrous growth rate.

"W-what kind of sorcery is this?"

Altugius asked, and Sungchul replied with honesty.

"I synthesized at the School of Alchemy during the day, and performed quests within the House of Recollections during the night."

It was an inadequate explanation, but the only truth that mattered was that he had managed to achieve such rapid growth, regardless of what method was actually used.

To this answer, Altugius spoke genuinely;

"Truly impressive. I've seen countless students but never someone who progressed so quickly."

No matter how much help one were to receive, growth was the merit of the individual.

Even with the best and the most thorough of assistance, without effort and diligence improvement is impossible.

"Amazing."

It was rare praise from Altugius, who was someone who usually kept silent on such matters. Leonard became enraged. He pulled himself from the hammock and briskly stepped towards Altugius.

"Are you going to give your teachings to that bastard?"

His sharp voice echoed throughout the Observatory. Altugius turned to face Leonard but ultimately decided to avoid his gaze.

"I haven't said a single word on such matters."

"Then why did you hand over the basic tome to him? Out of so many books, why that one? Is there some conspiracy that I'm not aware of?"

Leonard's voice grew increasingly aggressive with every step he took towards Altugius. Sungchul, who was watching the scene, further solidified his impression that Leonard was not simply Altugius's disciple. He was acting more like a loan shark than a disciple.

According to Christian, Airfruit had already processed his expulsion once before. Though not only has this person set foot in the school again, he's also harassing his Professor. There must be a variety of forces at play here.

A building with a rotten foundation will eventually collapse, but there was no reason for Sungchul to step in nor was there a need for him to. He continued to observe the situation.

Leonard continued to press his so-called teacher while aggressively baring his fangs.

"This puts me in a difficult position, Professor! Don't you already know that patience isn't my strong suit?"

Altugius didn't speak a word with his head facing the floor. When his teacher didn't appear to be responsive to him, Leonard let out a sigh and turned around. His bloodshot eyes locked onto Sungchul's figure.

"Hey, Freshman."

Leonard pointed a finger towards Sungchul, and when Sungchul acknowledged him, Leonard spoke cheerfully with a sinister smile.

"I...I don't like you. Do you mind just leaving?"

The words were brightly spoken, but they came interlaced with hidden threats.

"..."

Sungchul stared at Leonard with his mouth shut. Leonard thought it foolish at first and laughed bitterly at the gesture, but the laughter didn't last long.

W-who is this piece of shit?

He saw an insignificant man, frozen in place and unable to say a single word, but he could also feel an intangible chill come crawling up his spine.

Leonard vehemently denied this feeling, but he couldn't rid himself of his uneasiness. His insides began to boil in anger.

This is why I never liked those fucking Summoned graduates.

Unlike those that were born into this world, the Summoned crawled through hell upon their arrival. Not just any random people could survive within that hell. This was why they would be more militant than the average Other Worlder.

Leonard never liked the attitude of those Summoned. He had to thoroughly step on them with oppressive strength to make sure they were never allowed to crawl up to him again. He smiled as he began to recall the faces of those arrogant fucks that had been killed by his hands.

"Haven't you heard of me? What I, Leonard Sanctum, has done within the Airfruit Academy? Perhaps it's because you had no friends who could tell you?"

"I've heard that you've killed students in combat."

The silent Sungchul finally opened his mouth, but his voice and expression were still quite indifferent.

Leonard chuckled as he nodded.

"You know of it? Then why are you looking at me with such a stiff back? Feelin' cocky? Or maybe feelin' brave? Or maybe you just don't know how to act at all?"

"..."

"Well, either way, it doesn't matter. I'll give you a chance. If you disappear from my sight right this instant and I never catch you again, I'll forgive you."

Sungchul didn't even bat an eye at the blatant threat. He simply pointed his finger towards the exit. It was a gesture of challenge.

Leonard exploded in laughter. He roared in laughter for quite a while like a madman. As the Observatory filled with Leonard's laughter, Altugius who had been silent during this whole time let out a thick sigh.

"Leonard Sanctum."

Altugius' voice rang out within the Observatory. Leonard continued laughing, but his eyes peeked over in Altugius's direction. Altugius spoke again.

"I don't believe you've received a full pardon yet."

Leonard's laughter was cut short. Instead, his bloodshot eyes that were bulging out glared at his own teacher with murderous intent.

"I've received a full pardon, from my second Professor, the Head of the School of Pyromancy."

"I believe the Head of Cryomancy has opposed your pardon."

"That school does not represent our Academy," Leonard replied, becoming agitated. In contrast, Altugius remained calm and collected as he answered.

"Isn't it also true, that the School of Pyromancy does not represent our Academy?"

Leonard, who heard the rebuttal, let out a short outburst.

"Are you taking that fucker's side?"

He pointed towards Sungchul. Altugius held his expression as he replied with a soothing voice.

"I'm just concerned about you."

That single phrase slightly defused Leonard's explosive anger. Altugius continued to speak.

"You've finally managed to return to school, and you're going to throw it away over this small incident? Aren't you a prodigal existence within the Airfruit Academy blessed with the ability to wield two markings and have broken the shell[8]?"

Leonard's fierce eyes softened at the rare praise from his teacher, but he sharply threw out a question as he took a step back.

"Then why won't you show me the Secret of the School of Cosmomancy?"

"It is simply not time yet."

Altugius had led the conversation with such skill until that point. His final answer felt vague and insincere.

Leonard, who had been hesitating, felt like cold water had been thrown over him once again.

What a fucking lip service.

However, his fire had also died down. He no longer had the desire to make things any worse than they were.

"Well, I understand what you mean. It looks as though I was too fired up. I apologize."

Leonard approached Sungchul after a half-assed apology and held up his hand with a big smile as if nothing had happened.

"Ah, I'm truly sorry about this, Mr. Freshman. I just have a fiery temper at times. Let's just let bygones be bygones with a shake."

"..."

Sungchul only stared at Leonard's hand. Leonard showed a surprised expression with a playful whistle before retracting his hand; he then continued to loiter around his hammock.

"You didn't look so petty."

It was meant to provoke, but Sungchul couldn't be ignited by such an insignificant person. He only had a single desire at this moment, to try out his newly learned Magic.

Sungchul lowered his head towards Altugius, who had returned sitting with his back turned, and left the Cosmomancy building.

As soon as the door shut, Leonard spoke towards Altugius.

"Now that I think about it, I really need to chase that guy out."

Altugius simply shook his head.

"Duel...especially Gauntlet isn't allowed. If you start a Gauntlet with the fellow, Cryomancy will attack you and your second Professor. Isn't that against what your true Professor wishes for?"

Leonard gave a sinister smile at Altugius's words as he lightly swung his body on the hammock.

"My true Professor is only Professor Altugius. Professor Fregius of the School of Pyromancy is a good man, and I am indebted to him, but isn't he a bit lacking to guide me along the true path of Magic?"

Altugius didn't reply. Leonard continued to speak through the silence.

"I have no intention of starting a Gauntlet. I thought of a better method. A peaceful and a legal method."

"What are you planning?"

Altugius caved in to curiosity and asked Leonard, who put on a satisfied expression and replied, "I'll get rid of his place here."

Leonard's gaze fell somewhere far away.

—

The first Magic of the School of Cosmomancy: Glare. It was an offensive type spell that Summoned a Heavenly light that burned away all enemies in sight. Sungchul dressed a scarecrow with an old abandoned suit of armor from the dorm so that he could test out his newly learned Magic in the backyard of the eerie House of Recollections, which was visited by none.

The method to use Magic lay instinctively within his mind. First, he thought of the spell he wanted to cast. He then thought of its complex formations which he had seen within the Magic tome, made of symbols he understood but could not explain. The symbols turned in his mind like the gears of a clock whose rotation and motion brought out the power of Magic. After the preparations were completed and the spell's name and chant were shouted out, vocally or mentally, could the spell finally be activated.

This entire process was called the Aria. The time it took to complete an Aria differed from spell to spell, and the wording of the Aria varied greatly as well. The Aria of Sungchul's first Magic, Glare, was short enough to be called instantaneous.

Should I give it a try?

The Magic formation passed through his mind as though he had hit fast-forward, and his Intuition alerted him when the spell was ready. Sungchul looked at the suit of armor he had placed 25 meters away and recited the name of the spell in his mind.

Glare.

In that instant, a beam of light burst from his fingertip. The pillar of light accurately landed on the chest region, causing black smoke to rise.

"..."

Sungchul could see a coin sized hole had appeared at the "heart" of the armor. It was a monumental first experience with Magic, but Sungchul didn't rate it so highly.

"Shit!"

It was weak. Significantly so. It would be difficult to even imagine killing the King of Demons, Hesthnius Max, by using Magic of this caliber. His opponent was a Mage who could freely wield 6th rank spells, and also had a considerable Magical Resistance. Glare might barely be enough to singe his skin.

Sungchul wouldn't be satisfied with this first bite. He quickly changed his attitude. It was more than greedy to expect his first Magic to split the mountains and the seas. Looking at it objectively, his Magic Power and Intuition had only just surpassed beginner levels, and Glare was a low tier Magic that didn't exceed the third circle of spells. It might look weak in the eyes of Sungchul, who was called the Enemy of the World, but it would be plenty useful in the eyes of the average person.

It had the powerful advantage of having a short Aria, allowing it to shoot a burst of light instantly, which would make it difficult to dodge. With good accuracy, it could be used to give consistent damage to an enemy, or even suppress them under a barrage of fire. Mages had the unique characteristic of being able to grow their Magic's efficacy, relative to their Magic Power stat. If he could raise his Magic Power, he would also be able to pour out a much more destructive beam of light.

In other words, it looked weak now, but it had the potential to be his main form of attack when his Magic Power grew. Sungchul finally concluded something along these lines.

It is a spell that is bound to become more useful as I raise my Magic Power.

He tried a dual casting of Glare as well. It was to test the main ability of his class: Echo Mage. However, for whatever reason, the echo had not rung out. He recalled Vestiare's voice and conjured the echo with more strength, but it ended after a single cast. However, the reason for his inability to utilize echo appeared before him as in response to his conjuration.

[A voice without a soul cannot hold an echo.]

Sungchul could vaguely understand the explanation after looking at the message.

Could it be that I'm still lacking in Magic Power?

A small voice cannot produce an echo. Only a thundering voice from the top of a mountain could make an echo that would stir the entire mountain range. Sungchul's current Magic Power could be compared to a whisper in terms of volume. His current state was like taking his first steps compared to Vestiare of the Seven Heroes. The true strength of an Echo Mage would only reveal itself through further training and growth.

This is but the start. Let's not rush it.

Sungchul calmed his briefly excited heart. A clutter of problems returned to his mind when he regained his calm. One thing that he needed to do also came to mind.

Sungchul cleaned up his surroundings and left Airfruit campus towards Golden City's downtown. He planned to go meet Christian who he hadn't seen in a while.

***

As shadow accompanies light, dark alleys also lay within the shimmering Golden City. Slave Street was one such back alley. A crowd of slavers were putting their slaves up for auction just as Sungchul stepped into the dirty plaza. He passed by the auctions and watched the faces of the slaves out of the corner of his eyes.

A familiar head of black hair. They were a part of the most recent mass summoning which had brought them to Other World. Their eyes, lacking intellect, looked at their potential owners with dull gazes. Sungchul left the auction house looking bored.

When Sungchul left the auction house, a street filled with thugs, beggars, and prostitutes opened up before him. He sought out a particular store and headed towards it. It was a glamorous inn with a sign that read, "Palace of Pleasures." Christian was spending a joyous time surrounded by several beauties in a room inside the Palace of Pleasures.

"Oh, my! Look who it is? It is Sir Warrior!"

Christian, who was thoroughly drunk, greeted Sungchul with a loose smile on his face.

"You've come at the right time. Please sit over here. There are beauties for everyone!"

He began to scold the women with fake anger in his voice.

"What are you doing? Take care of Sir Warrior!"

"Send them all away."

Sungchul spoke briefly, but with force. Christian tactfully judged that Sungchul was not in a good mood. He hurriedly sent out the girls, then stammered with a different attitude while fidgeting with his prosthetic hand.

"Uh...regarding Professor Altugius's book...I am looking into it, through someone knowledgeable at Logotete's side. They are working hard at it, so I assume that the results will be in soon."

"I'm done with that."

Sungchul raised and smelled a glass of the alcohol on the table, then frowned.

"Is it not to your tastes?"

"I can't even tell the number of different spits mixed in here anymore. It looks like this establishment mixes leftover alcohol, so unless you've got guts of steel, stay away from the drinks."

"I-I'll keep that in mind."

"And I came by to learn about another topic."

Sungchul wanted to hear detailed information about the person called Leonard Sanctum. When he first heard about Leonard, the man had been a secondary problem, but it had quickly become his primary concern. Christian, who had been depressed, revitalized as though he was confident about the topic.

"Ah, Leonard Sanctum. I know plenty about that son of a bitch."

Christian said frankly.

"That bastard is suspected of being a Follower of Calamity."

"Follower of Calamity?"

Sungchul's eyes lit up.

"That's right. He has Professor Fregius of the School of Pyromancy supporting him, and Fregius is already publicly known as a Follower of Calamity."

"I want to hear more."

It had been quite a while since Sungchul had an enemy within Airfruit Academy. It was about time that he dug into the situation behind the school. Christian explained the current situation within Airfruit Academy with his own knowledge as well as the information he collected.

According to Christian, the rapid decline of Airfruit Academy ultimately began with the death of Headmaster Magnus three years ago. When the Headmaster in charge of the school disappeared, Fregius and Robert Danton, both respective heads of the schools of Pyromancy and Cryomancy, and also the most powerful forces within the school, began fighting to fill the vacancy.

If one side had been able to oppress the other completely, it would have ended with a few small incidents, but it was as if a tiger had been pit against a dragon[9]; they were both equally matched. Time continued to slip away as their feud grew deeper in the endless rivalry, and during this time, the school's ability to function had fallen to the wayside. Rumors that the school was teeming with the Followers of Calamity also sprung up around the same time. And another rumor, one that said the Followers of Calamity had killed the Headmaster, also began to circulate, with the actual killer never being found.

"...Leonard Sanctum is THAT Fregius' main disciple. He was originally under Altugius, but after he was expelled under dubious circumstances, he began to follow Fregius. As Fregius is the ringleader of the cult residing within the Academy, it could only mean that Leonard must also be a Follower of Calamity."

"I see."

He understood the gist of it. Of how the atmosphere of Airfruit Academy truly was. He suppressed an urge to vomit from the sheer repulsion he was feeling.

"Ah. There's one more interesting tidbit."

Christian carefully gauged Sungchul's reaction.

"Spit it out."

"It's not confirmed, but they say that Professor Altugius has a huge debt to Professor Fregius."

"Debt?"

"That's right. I don't know the reason, but the rumor is that it is quite an astronomical debt. They say it is because of this, that Professor Altugius cannot oppose Professor Fregius. Well, it is still just a rumor in the end."

"I see."

He had everything he wanted. Sungchul finally rose from his seat.

On the table, there was a large pile of gold coins that Sungchul had put out earlier. He grabbed one and examined it. Coinage without a mint–unmarked currency. He looked at the coin with disinterest before he left the room.

"Excuse me, Sir Warrior. Are there no other orders?"

"Make a list of everyone within the Airfruit campus suspected of being a Follower of Calamity."

"Followers of Calamity...It's a difficult ask, but this Christian will devote his all to this task, Sir Warrior."

Sungchul held out a gem for gratuity, and Christian received it happily with both hands.

"Send the Sky Squirrel if anything happens."

"I understand!"

As he left the room, he was plunged into dizzying decadent red lights. But what truly befuddled him were not the lights, but the situation ahead. He couldn't see an easy path to obtain the knowledge behind Cosmomancy. In order to unravel such a difficult problem, he would need to resolve the issue with the Followers of Calamity quickly. Especially Leonard and his cabal. However, he could meet an undesirable result if he were to approach this situation rashly. The Followers of the Cult were a vile group, akin to a reptile with many heads. If he wanted to strike, he needed to cut off all the heads at once. Otherwise, there was a chance he might be bitten by the poisonous fangs of a remaining head.

The known Followers of Calamity members are Leonard and Fregius, but there are bound to be more of them hidden within the school. An influential person must be leading the cult.

Sungchul was the reaper of the Followers of Calamity. He thoroughly understood the enemy's methods. The first ironclad rule for dealing with the Followers of Calamity was to suspect everyone. Altugius himself might be a Follower. Even if that was true, Sungchul was prepared to use any means necessary.

—

At the same time, several Mages had gathered within the House of Recollections to perform a ritual. The person at the center of the Magical formation was Sarasa Xero. Her body wasn't covered with the usual thick robe, but only a thin, light nightgown. She was allowing the spells the Mages chanted to seep into her body slowly.

"..."

Altuguius looked upon his Granddaughter with a worried gaze. Sarasa, who lay there with her eyes closed, felt her Grandfather's gaze and briefly winked at him. As the spell that came pouring into her grew even stronger, she couldn't resist furrowing her delicate brows and clenching her eyes. Altugius deeply furrowed his own brows. A man standing near him spoke in a soft voice.

"You do not need to concern yourself. There will be a brief moment of pain, but your Granddaughter's loveliness will be preserved for eternity."

There was the clear image of a skull drawn on his robe. He was a Necromancer and knew of methods to stop the decomposition of the dead. He offered his services in exchange for a small fortune or gifts. Sarasa's appearance had been maintained by their Mage craft.

"Mm...it appears that the payment is a bit light?"

Like a ghost[10], the Necromancer knew that the payment was lacking by the weight of the coin pouch. Altugius felt a cold sweat trailing down his spine.

"Let's see here...You're lacking three entire coins. May I ask the reason for this?"

"T-that is...I'll give you the rest the next time we meet."

The Necromancer's response was apathetic. He looked at Altugius callously as if he was looking at a corpse, and spoke perfunctorily.

"If I recall, this happened once before. I trusted in the Professor's reputation and overlooked the matter, but if the problem continues to present itself, I suggest you look into other Necromancers."

Unfortunately, the other Necromancers would not help Altugius. That was because the Necromancers were all affiliated with the rising star, Logotete Magic Academy. He would be falling out with the Logotete-affiliated...no...all of the Necromancers within the entire Golden City if things turned awry with this man.

"I will try to prepare the missing amount as quickly as possible."

Despite his own pride, Altugius lowered his head to a Necromancer from a rival school. The Necromancer looked upon the bowed Altugius with disinterest then nodded with an unsatisfied expression.

"This is the last time. Any more of this, and you leave us in a difficult position."

The ritual continued as expected. The Preservation Magic upon Sarasa's body regained its original vigor, and her appearance would retain its original form for a short duration. However, this would be the final time. Altugius needed money. Lots of money. There was only one way he could earn a lump sum within a short amount of time. He sought out a man that he never wanted to meet again. The figure wore a crow mask and was dressed in immaculate, white judge's robes.

The man, looking out a window at the sun with his hands held behind his back, felt Altugius approaching him and turned to speak in a gentle voice.

"Did you finally resolve to save the school?"

The man's identity was the Heresy Inquisitor Magnus Maxima. He was the man who had been sent to investigate the rumors of heresy surrounding Airfruit Academy and was known to resort to any method when it came to eradicating heresy.

—

"Are you going to the School of Alchemy?"

Bertelgia popped up from his breast pocket and spoke. Sungchul nodded as he said,

"I'll spend some time within the School of Alchemy for now."

Leonard Sanctum was bound to be waiting at the School of Cosmomancy to pick a fight with him. Sungchul wouldn't avoid such a fight, but there was also no reason for him to create any more problems through conflict. It wouldn't be too late for him to act after the information regarding the Followers of Calamity had been gathered.

"Great choice!"

Bertelgia trembled slightly within his pocket as she brightly continued,

"Yesterday, I noticed that your spells looked wimpy as hell due to you lacking in Magic Power, and I thought that there was a need to train up your Magic Power by spending a lot of time at the School of Alchemy."

"I doubt it'll go up by that much."

He had managed to raise his low Magic Power past 130 through the manual labor known as synthesis, but his growth rate had plummeted after breaking through 100. Ineffective growth was the opposite of what he sought.

"Growth by synthesizing is too slow compared to the amount of effort required."

"That's what an ignorant person would say."

Bertelgia retorted immediately.

"There are innate levels for all alchemic items, you know? Your growth rate is garbage because you keep making low-level alchemic items, but you'll get faster growth with higher-level items!"

"Is that right?"

"Yes! The downside is that ingredients are hard to come by...and also expensive...but..."

Sungchul couldn't obtain ingredients that were hard to find, but cost was not a problem. He decided to try his hand at synthesizing the high-level alchemical concoctions which Bertelgia had mentioned when he got back to the School of Alchemy. However, he witnessed something completely unexpected when he arrived at the site of the school.

"..."

The tent for the School of Alchemy had vanished.

***

Sungchul discovered familiar faces gathered behind the worn-down ingredient storage house. It was the Professor of Alchemy, Basil Philrus, and his students. Around this time, they would usually be sleeping or smoking pot, but they were gathered in the empty plot with lost faces as though they had lost their homes. Sungchul approached them.

"What happened here?"

No one answered. They only sighed with their heads down towards the floor. Sungchul asked once again, directing his question towards Basil this time, hoping to get an actual answer.

"What in the world happened here?"

The man who would be sleeping in the nude wore proper attire this time around. He looked up at Sungchul with a dejected expression on his face and spoke bitterly.

"Our school received a notice to disband."

"Disband?"

The complete story was this: The School of Alchemy, at some point in time, turned into a form of garbage dump of students that had been rejected by the other schools within Airfruit. The quality of students and the quality of the educator reflected this fact. Sungchul was fully aware of this. As the academy continued to fall into ruin, there was a movement to remove the useless schools. The School of Alchemy rapidly declined and couldn't show any results as the final person with any form of renown, Philrus's predecessor, had died. In the end, the School of Alchemy was forced out into the tents and had simply been waiting for the day they would be kicked out and be forced to disband. Sungchul had arrived just before that fated moment.

"Professor, we aren't truly disbanded yet."

A female student with thick dark bags under her eyes looked at her teacher and spoke with a sad voice.

"That's true. It isn't final yet, but that will only remain true for the week!"

Basil began pulling at his hair dejectedly while hanging his head down.

"What will happen if the decision for disbandment finalizes?" Sungchul asked.

"I'll be kicked out, for one, and my students that can't find another Guidance Counselor will meet the same fate."

"We'll get kicked out too. Only kids that have been rejected are gathered here."

The female student with bags under her eyes spoke frankly, and Basil scratched his head in agreement.

"As long as something short of a miracle doesn't occur."

Sungchul's eyes lit up at those words.

"So, there is a way."

He could resolve their financial problems if nothing else, but the "solution" that Basil spoke of was unexpected.

"It's in regards to what the Emergency Management Committee talked about...They said they would disregard the disbandment if our School of Alchemy manages to produce some satisfactory final result."

"Something satisfactory?"

It didn't look easy.

Reluctantly, Basil continued speaking.

"That's right. They require an alchemic item that is of the fifth-level, minimum. Embarrassingly...there isn't anyone among us who is capable of such a feat."

It was at that exact moment when Sungchul's breast pocket began to thrash about violently. Bertelgia vigorously vibrated her body like a cell phone on vibrate. She wanted to speak.

Sungchul excused himself before moving to a quiet location when Bertelgia shot out of his pocket, as though she had been waiting for this moment, and blurted out words that had been held back for so long.

"What? They can't make a measly fifth-level item? Phew, what kind of idiots are they?"

Bertelgia was fuming.

—

Alchemic items synthesized through an Alchemic Cauldron had a different level system from other items. The Alchemic items were given levels categorized from one through nine with one being the lowest and nine being the highest. However, the highest grade

Alchemic item ever synthesized by humans was known to be of level seven, but no Alchemist existed today who could produce that. Along that line of thinking, it might appear as though level five was a mid-grade alchemic item, but in reality, its relative difficulty was quite high. The Emergency Management Committee didn't commission the School of Alchemy to produce a fifth-level item for just any reason.

"Sigh…Pathetic. Truly pathetic. How could a big-name school like this not have an Alchemy Professor that could synthesize a fifth-level item? This is ridiculous."

Bertelgia appeared to be upset for some reason. Sungchul only looked upon the situation with amusement.

"So, do you have some method to solve this?"

"Of course. I am a codex of alchemic knowledge. I would obviously have level five items recorded in me!"

Bertelgia flipped through some pages with various alchemic items' recipes as if to prove her statement, but he couldn't understand any of it. As he had grown more adept with Magic tomes he understood that he lacked the necessary Intuition to understand, so he shook his head.

"Unfortunately, I can't understand any of your pages."

"Ah. How high is your Intuition? Just over 100, right?"

He nodded.

"Mmm…It'll be hard to decipher for you, then. In that case, I'll tell you the recipe directly. Although…I'm not supposed to, as the guide of the Creationist!"

"Ah. There was such a thing as a Creationist, wasn't there?"

He had put it out of his mind after completing Eckheart's quest.

"What? Have…have you forgotten about it? Forgotten that you're walking on the path of the Creationist?!"

Bertelgia dropped out of the sky, seemingly from trauma, then popped back up before she hit the ground. She rose to Sungchul's eye level and flapped her pages.

"Isn't it enough that I remembered now?"

"Really...how can anyone be so rude! Whatever! Doesn't matter! Whether you walk the path of the Creationist or not, I have no obligation to force you as a guide."

Bertelgia looked peeved, but she did her job as expected of her.

"Anyways, I'll list some fifth-level items that I know of which seems possible for you to make. Pick one that seems right for you."

Bertelgia listed names of some alchemic items. Candlestick of Twilight. Rainbow Ingot. Buoyant Crystal. Alchemic Bomb (Dark), Medicine of Elfir. There was a total of five Alchemic items. Even the almighty Sungchul had only heard of the Buoyant Crystal.

"What's the easiest among these?"

"Well, they're all pretty tough, honestly. You're going to have to prepare yourself for a lot of failures. I only recommended these because their ingredients are easily accessible."

As Bertelgia had said, fifth-level alchemic items weren't so readily synthesized. The gathering of ingredients could be overcome through the power of money, but each item also required a distinct high-level Alchemic technique. For example, the characteristic of the Candlestick of Twilight required a unique crafting method from the Alchemist, the Rainbow Ingot required a deep knowledge of heat, and Alchemic Bomb (Dark) required dexterous handwork, along with proficient experience with weight scales. The rest of the items had similar problems. Each required a unique skill.

"Which will you make?"

Sungchul thought on it for a while before choosing the Alchemic Bomb (Dark) in reply. He thought it would be easier to "appeal" to the upper echelon through force.

"All right! Then let's go tell those fools! We will make the item, but the idiots will have to request the procedures for an assessment!"

He listened to Bertelgia this time. Basil Philrus was still shocked and was making a pathetic face along with his pupils.

Sungchul revealed his plans with a firm voice to those waiting in front of the tent.

"I seek to make a fifth-level alchemic item. It'll take about a week. I only ask that you put in the request for judgement to the Emergency Management Committee."

"What? You are going to make a fifth-level alchemic item?"

Basil, who seemed to lack the will to hold himself together, suddenly perked up at the news.

"That's right. I want to give it a go."

"It hasn't even been a month since you entered the School of Alchemy. Third-level...no...have you tried making second level items yet? At the very least, I don't remember telling you about such an item."

"A knowledgeable person I know is quite the Alchemist. I am receiving personal tutelage from that person."

"Mmm..."

Basil looked as though he thoroughly disapproved of the plan, but still nodded reluctantly.

"I understand. Leave the request to me, but remember this, the judges that will be sent from the Emergency Committee will be the Professors of Pyromancy and Cryomancy. Playing a prank with those people will be very dangerous."

Basil made it clear that he would make the request, but the name on the request would be of Sungchul's. It meant he would take no responsibility for this incident.

Sungchul simply nodded.

"It doesn't matter."

He then headed on the path towards the city center of Golden City with Bertelgia and sought a store for Alchemic ingredients.

"Give me everything."

Sungchul not only took the ingredients for the Alchemic Bomb (Dark) but the ingredients for the remaining four items as well. It was just in case the production of Alchemic Bomb did not turn out as expected. He had to expend a small fortune, but he had plenty left.

He bought out all other viable ingredients at the store before heading back to the school. The Alchemy students lounging beside the storage were already popping off their wine bottles during midday. There was also a thick musk of marijuana present in the air. Basil, who should have been leading these students, was laughing and enjoying himself among them.

Sungchul overheard their conversations despite his lack of interest; they were mostly lowbrow humor regarding sex. He went to the farthest possible location with the cauldron from them. Then, he pulled out a table that had been stored, laid a tablecloth on top, then arranged the various, purchased Alchemic ingredients and the required tools.

"Shall we begin, then?"

Bertelgia spoke confidently from his breast pocket.

"Right. What do I have to do first?"

"You should prune the Porous seeds from the Firecracker Tree first."

Sungchul picked up the seed covered with thick hair among the ingredients on the table. It was about the size of a peach seed, and it felt rough. He held the seed to his nose and smelled it. It generally had the distinct vegetative aroma, but there was also a smoky smell of gunpowder underneath.

[Porous seed of Firecracker Tree]

Level: 4

Rank: C

Attribute: Tree

Effect: Explosion upon impact or contact with flame

Note: Seed of the Firecracker Tree originating from the Great Meadow of East. Once the seed ripens, it grows more explosive until it self-detonates. This spreads the spores over long distances.

A single one of these seeds required twenty silver coins. The price was small potatoes to Sungchul, but it was enough to match a month's wage for an Airfruit Academy staff.

"Delicately grab the seed's shell and mark the exterior with the knife, then we need to extract the explosive extract contained inside."

Sungchul quickly began his work.

"Careful. It could explode. This guy is dangerous enough to take a finger with a single slip."

Bertelgia warned him to be careful, but the knife work of the master chef, Sungchul, was relentless. He smoothly handled the seed despite his inexperience with this foreign ingredient and extracted the thick red grains contained within.

He's good. This guy.

Bertelgia was slightly touched. She had felt it before, but the way Sungchul handled the ingredients was not normal. The porous seed of the Firecracker Tree was difficult even for properly educated Alchemists to handle.

"What's next?"

"Uh...we just use the mortar to turn it into powder, but it's easier if you prepare five seeds worth of extracts at a time before powderizing it."

Sungchul immediately moved onto the next step. He handled the seeds with extreme precision and placed five seeds worth of extract within the mortar.

"Should I powderize it now?"

"No! You can't JUST powderize it. You need to make and add a counteragent beforehand."

"A counteragent...you mean the thing we made with the Blindman's Grass?"

Bertelgia shook once forcefully within his breast pocket, and he immediately reached for the Blindman's Grass. Bertelgia stared carefully at his fingertips at this moment.

I definitely told him to prepare the ingredients before adding them. Should I watch and see if he does it properly this time?

Sungchul was lighting a fire under the Alchemic cauldron and pouring the distilled water. It was common sense up to this point. What was important lay after.

"..."

He once again grabbed the Blindman's Grass that he had picked out and looked at it carefully until he eventually began the process of pruning the roots and the dried ends of the grass.

Gasp! He's actually doing it right! This person!

It was all beyond her expectations.

***

It was a peculiar thing. Seeing a man who looked worlds apart from the words "diligence and perfection" preparing each ingredient so naturally. Sungchul carefully placed the pruned Blindman's Grass and the other prepared ingredients into the Alchemic cauldron and diligently stirred it with a wooden spoon. Soon, a neutralizing agent with a green tint began to form.

"Do I have to pour this into the mortar?"

"Y-Yes! Use about three Alchemic spoons worth."

"..."

Sungchul added the neutralizing agent into the mortar, and he began to carefully crush the Firecracker Tree seed extracts softened by the neutralizing agent with a pestle. After five minutes had passed since the process began, the moisture from the neutralizing agent evaporated away leaving only the red-colored powder within the mortar.

"Is this enough?"

Bertelgia shook once in reply to Sungchul's question.

"Yep. It's enough. Next, we'll be using the scales."

"The scales."

Sungchul looked at the scales with a blank expression. It wasn't a tool he was familiar with.

"Alchemic bombs are a type of tool that requires very specific amounts of materials. That's why it won't do without a very precise scale capable of detailed measurements, you know?"

Bertelgia had a few more thoughts that she kept to herself.

He couldn't possibly do something crazy like succeeding in one go, right? I don't know about the other tools, but the scale isn't a tool that's easily handled with beginner's luck!

The process of measuring with the scale began. Sungchul gently poured the red powder onto one arm of the scale, then judged the weight by hanging the counterweight on the other arm. It went slowly as it was his first time, but he approached it with focus and precision.

"What next?"

Bertelgia stared intensely at the swaying scale. It was a perfect measurement with no real flaws. She didn't want to admit it, but she could see that Sungchul had the dedication to detail that was the core virtue of all Alchemists.

However, the final step of synthesizing the Alchemic Bomb (Dark) resulted in failure despite his innate talent.

BOOM!

While he was stirring the mixture, Sungchul detected large quantities of his mana draining away and drank Mana Drink to replenish it, but his focus wavered during the most critical moment, causing the entire process to fail.

[Synthesis Failure!]

A groan escaped from Sungchul's lips. He had not blinked at most situations, but it took an unexpectedly heavy toll to expend so much mana and concentration to synthesize a high-level Alchemic item.

For someone on my level to struggle this much...Alchemy isn't something to take lightly.

The students that were enjoying their booze besides the storage began to look over his direction. They pointed at the Alchemic cauldron with black smoke trailing out and started laughing out loud.

"Whew…those idiots. Why do they choose to live that way?"

Bertelgia muttered angrily, but Sungchul was different.

I don't know why, but it feels as though my Intuition has increased. This fatigue reminds me of a sense of fulfillment after a drawn-out battle.

He immediately pulled up his status screen to check his stats.

[Stats]			
Strength 999+	Dexterity	853
Vitality 801	Magic Power	132
Intuition 103	Magic Resist	621
Resilience 502	Charisma	18
Luck	18		

It was a negligible amount, but his Magic Power and Intuition had increased. He had failed the synthesis, but it wasn't a complete failure. He felt a second wind reinvigorating him once again. Sungchul chugged down a few bottles of Mana Drink, then went to butt heads with synthesizing the Alchemic Bomb (Dark) again. When he began setting up for his next attempt, Bertelgia spoke against it.

"It might be better to take a breather. It's too much to repeatedly try making a fifth-level item at your level."

"You think so?"

"People often think Alchemy and Magic are separate things, but at its core, it is an undeniable branch of Magic that transforms something through techniques and sheer force of will. Also, the Magical fingerprint sitting on your body could be ruined by excessively overusing your Magic Power. You should at least know that you can't use Magic anymore if the Magical fingerprint gets destroyed, right?"

Bertelgia's warnings were not something to ignore. Sungchul immediately understood her sentiments and quietly asked a question.

"How many attempts a day would be safe?"

He asked regarding the maximum amount he could handle. Bertelgia took a moment, then answered in a soft voice.

"Three times. Anything more than that would be trouble."

"Okay. I'll keep that in mind."

Sungchul tried synthesizing two more times and failed at them. He became depleted of mana at the last moment each time and failed pitifully at the last second as his concentration wavered. However, Sungchul was not downtrodden. He was only getting a feel for the process, and his stats increased marginally with each failed attempt at creating a high-level product.

Okay. With the way things are going, I should be able to succeed in at least three days' time.

The Alchemy students, who were not able to understand Sungchul's condition, used the freak newcomer that was consecutively creating explosions in the distance to fuel their alcohol binge.

"Ah! That idiot. He made such a ruckus about creating a fifth-level Alchemic item, and what's he doing now? Is he planning on blowing up the entire school?"

"That's what I'm sayin'. He's all show. Look at the way he's using that scale."

At that moment, a single figure walked in their direction. The students who had been drinking or smoking weed froze at the sight of him.

"Whew. The stench of trash. Truly repulsive, isn't it?"

The identity of the man wearing a robe dyed in the crimson color of the School of Pyromancy was Leonard Sanctum. He looked at the Alchemy students like insects as he stepped over to them then smiled brightly as he saw Sungchul standing beside his Alchemic cauldron emitting black smoke.

"Ah ha!"

His figure vanished instantly along with the Magic circle he created and soon appeared before Sungchul.

"Hey, Mr. Unwelcomed-Guest-of-the-School-of-Cosmomancy. How are you doing?"

He pulled his face closer to the Alchemic cauldron then formed an expression of shock as he looked at the failed synthesis product.

"Oh, my. Are you perhaps in charge of presenting a product for the School of Alchemy?"

"It's as you can see."

"It looks as if you've failed, though."

"..."

When Sungchul shut his mouth, Leonard let out a sharp laugh through his nose then walked past him.

"There isn't much time left, so try your best. You'll be processed for expulsion otherwise."

Sungchul surmised that Leonard was behind the sudden decision to disband the School of Alchemy.

Mages have always been like this. They like their cloaks and daggers.

However, it didn't make much difference to Sungchul regardless of what Leonard chose to do. Sungchul was confident that he could synthesize a fifth-level Alchemic item at this juncture. That result came to him a day later than he had expected, on the 4th day. What Sungchul had tried wasn't the Alchemic Bomb (Dark) nor Buoyant Crystal, but Elfir's Medicine.

The process of making Elfir's Medicine was similar enough to the method of a favorite recipe of his that it was almost indistinguishable. He had to decoct precious medicinal ingredients to milk their juices, then mix it with even more precious medicinal ingredients to create a medicinal soup. He had to use a ladle to carefully mix several Alchemic ingredients containing Magic Power with the medicinal soup, which is where it differed from his cooking recipe. Thankfully the experience he accumulated during his previous attempts to create Alchemical items was proving to be beneficial.

He replenished his missing mana with Mana Drink and learned to cope with the draining mental focus thanks to his practices. And it finally happened on his second attempt at synthesis; he was able to witness the spectacle of blinding brilliance flooding out of his Alchemic cauldron.

[Synthesis Success!]

"Wow!"

Bertelgia passionately shook her body. It must have become a habit. Sungchul didn't appreciate her making a ruckus but happily accepted her gesture just this one time. He could feel the long-forgotten feeling of accomplishment whet his thirsty heart as he filled the fifth-level alchemic item of his creation into a glass bottle. He headed towards Basil Philrus afterward.

"This is the promised fifth-level alchemic item."

—

The judging proceeded efficiently. Professor Robert Danton, from the School of Cryomancy, and Fregius, from the School of Pyromancy, were expected to attend the judging, but Fregius could not be reached, so his second-in-line Professor Maloouf attended in his stead.

There was a face Sungchul recognized sitting beside Armin Maloouf, Leonard Sanctum. He made a gesture to pretend to show friendliness as Sungchul entered the meeting room of the Emergency Management Committee with Basil Philrus.

"We'll begin the judgment."

The Professors in charge of judging each utilized a different method to examine the item created by Sungchul. The examination methods were used to determine the Alchemic item's type and properties, along with the authenticity of the item. The proceeding didn't take long.

"This is a fifth-level Alchemic item."

Robert Danton made his acknowledgement first, followed by Armin with the same opinion. Leonard's face began to become twisted as it took an ugly shape.

"This can't be. How could this be...?!"

Sungchul lightly tossed the remainder of Elfir's Medicine towards him and firmly made a suggestion with his characteristic tone of voice.

"Why don't you see it for yourself, then."

Leonard did as Sungchul asked. There could only be one result. Sungchul had created the real thing.

"This...can't be!"

As his superiors finished making their judgements and were prepared to announce the result, Leonard shouted with sheer arrogance in the face of the situation at hand.

Robert Danton looked at Leonard who had lost his composure with cold eyes and mumbled, "Fucking cocky bastard. If it weren't for Fregius, I would've already dealt with such a fucker."

Armin's attitude wasn't much different, but he didn't express it as such. The result was announced in the midst of Leonard's disruptive muttering.

"The decision of disbandment is null as we accept that the assigned task has been completed satisfactorily by the School of Alchemy. However, the duration of the annulment is a year; the School of Alchemy will have to provide another reason to continue their existence within the Academy within a year from now."

It was a triumphant moment. Basil and his students, who had been holding their breaths with their hands clenched while eavesdropping on every movement within the meeting room, let out a cheer together. Sungchul returned as roaring cheers slowly filled the hallway. At that moment, Leonard suddenly jumped up from his seat.

"You!"

Leonard was losing his sense of reasoning.

"You piece of shit! Sungchul! Come over here! I can't just let you go."

Sungchul quietly turned and looked directly at Leonard.

"?!"

Leonard felt a suffocating terror engulf him in that instant, but brushed it off as a moment of insanity and continued to shout.

"It's a duel! Let's settle this with a Gauntlet! You can't refuse if you're a man, right?"

Robert stood from his seat with an unpleasant expression on his face as Armin also rose from his seat. In that same moment, the shut door of the Emergency Management Committee's meeting room flew open, and the desperate face of a student wearing the robe of the School of Pyromancy appeared.

"I-it's a disaster!"

Robert paused and looked over at the student.

"What is it?"

The Pyromancy student replied tearfully at the question.

"P-Professor Fregius...has been murdered!"

That single sentence was enough to drive everyone listening into a shock. The most traumatized by the news was the quick-tempered Leonard Sanctum. Fregius was the one whose protection allowed him to return to the school and the one with authority to fight back against the head of the School of Cryomancy.

He had lost both his protector and his backer in a single moment.

Robert's chilling gaze fell onto Leonard.

"You, get out of my face. You fucking garbage."

Leonard's face burned bright enough to be visibly seen, but he couldn't say anything in return as he left the meeting room with his head down as though he was escaping. The landscape of power within Airfruit had suddenly changed. Sungchul, who had been in the center of the whole spectacle, looked out the window with his closed mouth.

I can feel a storm brewing.

The premonition was predictably accurate. When Sungchul returned to the House of Recollections, a familiar rodent leaped in his direction.

"Kyu Kyu!"

It was the Sky Squirrel, but its condition was strange. The creature, with no letter or message attached to it, had its front paw stained red with blood. Sungchul could smell it. It wasn't from the Sky Squirrel. It was the scent of human blood.

Chapter 17 – Gathering Storms

It was within a musty darkness. A young man in his early twenties was vacantly staring at an incapacitated corpse with its hands tied around the chair. He was looking down at the remains which were in a state where it was more accurate to call it a pile of meat marinated in blood rather than a human corpse. The youth continued looking at the corpse with curious eyes before he grabbed one of the torture devices and pushed it deep into the body of the corpse. The dead don't move. The youth looked behind him and asked with an innocent voice.

"Mom, why did he die?"

The youth's question rang out in the darkness as two silhouettes appeared from the shadows. One male and one female. They both wore black robes with feline masks.

"This person's heart contains a Covenant."

The female's voice echoed in the dark.

"A Covenant?"

When the youth asked, the woman approached the corpse tethered to the chair and pulled the prosthetic arm attached to his left side, then pointed its finger toward the heart that was currently exposed.

"The moment an oath taken under the Divine Mediator's name is broken, your life is forfeited. He must have broken his oath the moment he decided to reveal the name you sought. That was why the heart exploded."

Listening to the woman's explanation, the youth looked deflated and dropped the small knife in his hand.

"Ah, so unlucky. It was my first interrogation! To meet such an idiot."

A man appeared behind him. He was a tall youth wearing the same black robe and feline mask as the rest. He slapped the discouraged youth on his back and spoke with malice.

"You are a disgrace to the family! Why does everything you do turn out like this? You can't even do one interrogation right. I'd have made this guy spit out the name of the fucker we wanted in a minute!"

"Brother, don't be too harsh. This is our Pict's humble beginnings."

Black fog smoldered behind the teen. The fog transformed into a young woman with a sensual body shape. Black hair and blood red eyes. She wore a playful smile under the feline mask.

"All hear me."

The man who appeared at the beginning spoke with a solemn voice. He accepted the gaze of the four before him and extended his left arm in a disciplined gesture. There was a tattoo of lightning piercing a skull etched onto the back of his hand. It might appear to be normal, or even tacky, but those that knew its meaning would never underestimate it. It was because the tattoo represented one of the four families that controlled the Assassin's Guild, Almeria Family. It wasn't the most powerful among the four families, but it was known to be the most sinister. They always moved as a single unit on missions.

"This time, we face off against the Enemy of the World. He is a monster among monsters whose strength exceeds the 600 mark. One mistake could cost us our lives. Don't lower your guard. Always step carefully. As a father, I don't wish to lose any of my family."

The current patriarch of the Almeria family, D'vici Almeria, finished his brief speech then disappeared with his wife into the darkness on the far side. The oldest son and daughter, Kaz Almeria and Myra Almeria, quietly followed after their parents.

The only one remaining was their youngest, Pict Almeria. His face was still twisted as though his anger from the previous incident hadn't been resolved. He picked up the prosthetic arm that had been left on the ground, opened the dead man's jaw, then tried to shove the entire prosthetic inside. The corpse, tied to the chair, thrashed about wildly.

"Shit...! All because of this fucker!"

The teen left the scene, leaving a mangled corpse behind. A man sought out the blood-soaked room after a considerable amount of time had passed.

"..."

Sungchul steadily looked at the pitifully disfigured corpse.

Christian.

His face could not be recognized due to the grotesque methods used in the interrogation, but the prosthetic embedded into his jaw revealed his identity.

"Ew...What the...I can't look at this..."

Bertelgia dug deeper into the breast pocket. Sungchul looked around at his surroundings. They didn't leave behind a single clue besides the horrendous torture tools and blood. This wasn't done by just anybody, Sungchul felt that in his guts.

But why?

He fell into deep contemplation briefly beside Christian's corpse. In the end, he discovered something shiny next to the blood-soaked torture devices. A gold coin reflecting a golden light. The unmarked coin.

Did they use this to track him...?

He wasn't fully aware of the ongoings of the world of merchants, but he had heard stories. There was a rumor which he found hard to believe that a skilled merchant could use a single coin to uncover everything it had experienced. He had brushed it off with a laugh before, but this was the only clue he had at this point.

Is this an act by someone who's targeting me?

There was no other way to interpret this. It was difficult to imagine that anyone would pour so many resources to chase down a single worthless Slave Hunter. Sungchul was also still in the superior position. His unknown enemies must not have been able to uncover anything about him.

This was the power of the Covenant.

Sungchul pulled out the prosthetic from Christian's mouth, attached it to his missing limb, and then looked at his figure for a bit. He hadn't been a bad friend. There were stories Sungchul had wanted to hear from him. How he became a Slave Hunter. How he had spent his school life. There was never a time to ask him about his life, and now Sungchul would never know.

BUZZ! BUZZ!

Flies began to gather at the scent of rotting flesh. Sungchul poured oil over the corpse and lit it on fire. Turning his back on the roaring fire, Sungchul blended into the dizzying lights of the Slave Street once again. He could hear a panicked scream regarding a fire.

"…"

His mouth was firmly shut, but his eyes radiated a wrathful glare that was sharp enough to cut through the moonlight in the night.

—

When Sungchul returned to the House of Recollections, he could see Sarasa standing at the entrance. However, her facial expression looked different in some way. The usual haughty expression that she had on her face while she nitpicked each and every issue was nowhere to be seen. Instead, she looked more like a problem child who was caught stirring trouble. The reason was soon revealed to him.

"Kyuuiiing…"

It was because he could hear a familiar cry behind Sarasa's back.

"Ah…it was out and about."

Sarasa avoided Sungchul's gaze and handed him the Sky Squirrel. When her cold grip released the Sky Squirrel, it broke free and hopped up onto Sungchul's shoulder.

"Kyu Kyu!"

The Sky Squirrel enjoyed the touch of people, but it didn't seem to like Sarasa's cold hands. She looked at it with a bitter expression and spoke harshly.

"Our dorm bans pets and livestock."

"...It's just for a little while."

Sungchul spoke simply before brushing past her and headed to his room. Sarasa stared at his back and followed him closely with short, small steps.

"I said it was forbidden. I'm the dorm's owner."

"I can't help it as the owner of the Squirrel had died. I just need a single day."

Sarasa was always quite forceful, but hearing that the owner had died, she backed down a notch.

"I-is that right?"

Sungchul nodded. He left Sarasa behind and headed towards his own room once again. The messy interior, as it was when he had first arrived, greeted him. He placed the Sky Squirrel on top of the bed before sitting down himself to organize his thoughts.

If it is an Assassin that's targeting me, I don't have much time.

It could have been a coincidence, but this person had arrived within Golden City at least. The existence of the gold coin at the scene bothered him the most.

Sungchul had visited the tool shop in front of the school before he had returned to the dorm. The store owner seemed to live away from the store. There was no sign of life within, and no sign of forced entry. It was also quite late, so no one was around to ask for any explanation. To know the complete story, he would have to wait until the sun was up.

With Christian dead, there really isn't anywhere I can reliably get information from.

On the other hand, Sarasa had been waiting for him in front of the door for a while now. She looked as though something was on her mind.

He stood up from the bed and opened the door.

"What's up?"

Sungchul asked with no inflection in his voice. Sarasa avoided his gaze and hesitated, but then her expression changed and she looked straight back into his eyes.

"About that incident before, I don't have any ill will towards it. I think it was immature of me to lash out."

"It's not something to apologize for."

Sunghul closed the door. Or at least he tried to before Sarasa's pale hand forced itself through.

"W-wait!"

He opened the door again.

"..."

Sungchul's frosty gaze landed on Sarasa's face.

"You don't have to look at me like that. I just wanted to say...you've been here for a while now, so as students sharing the dorm, we should be conversing every now and then. Anyways!"

Her eyes looked past Sungchul and at the Sky Squirrel curled up on his bed. For whatever reason, it seemed that she took a liking to it. Sungchul noticed the gaze and recalled a long-buried image of the past.

That kid also particularly liked animals.

The forgotten reverie was cut short by Sarasa's voice.

"Anyways, you. It looks like you were chasing down the quests within the House of Recollections. You're welcome to ask me anything you don't know about. It looks like I made a mistake today, so I'll be especially nice."

"What can you teach me?"

"A strategy against the Devil of the Immovable Door."

Sarasa looked quite confident. However, Sungchul reaction was cold.

"Are you talking about the Devil with the shell game? I already beat him."

"Oh yeah? How about the Underground Well's Skull Soldier quest?"

"Beat that one too."

"Oh yeah...?!"

She listed several more quests, but the results were the same.

"How could this be...you're lying, right?"

She looked incredulously at Sungchul. Sungchul, who saw her hesitation, thought up one question.

"Do you know about the Magic tool shop outside of the campus?"

"Ah, Carbuncle? Yeah. Of course, I know."

"About the owner too?"

Sarasa opened her eyes wide and nodded.

"You're talking about that plump man with a booming voice, right? Yeah, I know him. I've known him since I was an undergraduate."

A strange light flashed across Sungchul's eyes. He continued to ask her more questions.

"Do you know where he lives?"

"I know, but why are you asking?"

"I have some items to deliver to him. It'd be nice if you could tell me his location if you know it."

As he said that, Sungchul let out a whistle to call the Sky Squirrel.

"Kyu Kyu!"

Sarasa's eyes became fixed on the Sky Squirrel. It trembled as though it feared Sarasa's interest, but due to Sungchul's grip, it ended up in Sarasa's grasp.

"I'll leave him to you since I have something to deliver to him."

"Ah...ok."

She gathered her hands to hold the Sky Squirrel. It shrieked, but as Sungchul handed it a peanut, it calmed down. Sungchul handed her a small paper pouch of peanuts and said

"The fastest way to get close to an animal is through its belly."

"I-I see!"

She handed over the information regarding the Magic tool shop owner with no resistance.

Sungchul headed out into the darkness towards the shop owner's house. The interior of the home was pitch black. He hid his presence as his Eye of Truth surveyed the surroundings for potential dangers while he entered the house.

"..."

It wasn't too late. The murderer's reach hadn't extended here just yet. The owner had simply fallen asleep.

Sungchul shook the man awake. The shop owner who had been muttering in his sleep rubbed his eyes away and met the unwelcome guest.

"W-What is wrong, sir?"

Sungchul pushed the bloody gold coin towards the frightened shop owner.

"Do you remember this?"

The owner finally realized the unwelcome guest's identity; it was the man who was the source of his recent windfall. Various thoughts crawled around his head, but he couldn't imagine something as shocking as what was revealed by the customer.

"I am Sungchul, 'the Destroyer.' People seemed to have taken to calling me the Enemy of the World."

He pulled out Fal Garaz, the weapon fabled to have been bestowed upon the Dwarves by their god, as if to prove his identity. Once the shop owner saw the weapon surrounded by brilliant light, he was overwhelmed with shock as his breath got caught in his throat.

"Kuh…uh…uh…"

Sungchul glared at him and spoke with a soft, but forceful voice.

"Take your belongings and leave Golden City. Head to the province of the Human Empire and seek an Imperial Audience with the Emperor."

"Uh…Uhh…"

Sungchul pulled out a sword made of ivory from his Soul Storage and handed it to the shop owner who was still having trouble forming a single sentence.

"Show this to the Imperial Court, and the Emperor will grant you an audience. However, never forget that if you reveal this truth to anyone else..."

Sungchul reached behind the shop owner towards the display cupboard. The decoration made of copper crumpled in his grip and parts of it squeezed out of between his fingers like butter.

"Hiii!!!"

"If you mistakenly think that you can hide from me, you're welcome to try it. You're welcome to gamble your life on that bet."

Sungchul placed the bloody gold coin in front of the man and turned around.

"Leave immediately."

"Y-Yes, sir!"

The man stumbled out of his bed and pulled on some clothes in a hurry to begin packing. Soon, a carriage quickly braved the cold night air as it went off towards a distant location.

"..."

Sungchul watched the horse-drawn cart disappear before turning around.

"Quite unexpected of you?"

Bertelgia spoke from his pocket.

"What is?"

When Sungchul asked, Bertelgia popped out of his pocket and landed on his shoulder like the Sky Squirrel had.

"I thought you'd kill the man. It is you we're talking about."

"I don't arbitrarily kill innocent men."

"That's what I didn't expect. I thought you were someone ruthless. Like the Seven Heroes."

"...I am different from them."

Sungchul spoke as though he was making a promise to himself, then looked off towards the sky. The light had already begun to peek out from the Eastern horizon.

I bought myself a bit of time, but there still isn't much left. It's time to change my plans and rush getting the Secret of Cosmomancy, then leave this place.

His gaze fell on the domed structure sitting high on top of the mountain range.

***

The death of Fregius, the head of the School of Pyromancy, came as a great shock to Airfruit Magic Academy. Early in the morning, Sungchul could see a truly rare sight. Hundreds of students were gathered on the campus. It was something that hadn't occurred often since the vital flow of new students had been cut from the school. They were looking at the large poster on the plaza message board. The news of the head of the School of Pyromancy's passing was written within.

"My God…for Professor Fregius to have died."

"One of the pillars that supported this school has collapsed."

"Where is Airfruit headed for now?"

Sungchul met a familiar face as he walked while listening to the conversations among the crowd.

"Ey! Genius Alchemist!"

It was Basil Philrus who looked closer to "that older kid" you knew around the neighborhood rather than a Professor. He acted like he was his longtime childhood friend and offered his hand for a shake. Sungchul simply stared at the outstretched hand indifferently. Basil, looking a bit embarrassed, began to scratch his head.

"Ah, well. Isn't my face feelin' quite heated?"

"What's wrong?"

Sungchul had seen Basil Philrus hit rock bottom so he could not find a reason to treat Basil with respect.

"Greetings. More importantly, have you seen the poster?"

Basil, as though he acknowledged his own incompetence, didn't mention Sungchul's attitude towards him. Sungchul looked at Basil's smirking face and asked a question.

"Are you referring to Professor Fregius's death?"

"Yes! Of course. However, that's not all. There's a critical behind-the-scenes story!"

"Another story?"

This time, Sungchul showed an interest. Christian's death had been such a major issue for him that he had been preoccupied, but information about the death of the one labeled as the leader of the Followers of Calamity was certainly very interesting indeed. When Sungchul's frosty exterior seemed to have melted slightly, Philrus became excited and kept on blabbering.

"Ah yes. You'll be surprised when I tell you. Come this way."

He brought Sungchul to an isolated spot, then looked around once before speaking with a soft voice.

"I overheard this from the meeting between Professors. They say that Professor Fregius was murdered in the same method as our former principal, Professor The Grand Magnus[11], three years ago. Presumably, it was the same person."

"What was the method?"

Philrus took a moment to gather his thoughts before making his reply.

"One-half of the corpse was torn asunder as though it was struck by a great force. They say it's a horrid scene that they couldn't sit through and it was as though someone had taken a Meteor directly to the face."

"Meteor?"

Meteor was the best known spell within the School of Cosmomancy. It was a powerful spell that summoned a comet from the sky to make a massive strike against an enemy on the ground.

"That's what they say, but as you know, Meteor isn't something that can be used indoors. If they had used it indoors, they would have blown away not only the Professor but also the building with it."

"He died indoors? Professor Fregius, I mean?"

Basil nodded. Sungchul had more real combat experience than anyone else, but he had never encountered such a spell.

I can't discount that it could be some derivation of a summoning spell.

A Magic Academy with a wide variety of Magic couldn't make head or tail of this Magic, so anything was possible.

"Anyways, who could the criminal be? To kill The Grand Magnus and now the Headmaster candidate Fregius, he can't be a run-of-the-mill Mage."

"The criminal is a Mage?"

"That's right. We found remnants of Magic. That's why they're so frantic. What kind of Mage could have done such a thing? It had to have been a powerful Mage that could overcome those powerful Mages. People are suspecting that the head of the School of Cryomancy, Robert Danton, is the murderer, but as I see it, this kind of deed isn't something Cryomancy can do."

At that moment, soldiers wearing shining silver armor were marching onto the campus. Countless students took the hint and began scattering away; the area naturally fell under the soldier's jurisdiction. Basil frowned at the sudden commotion.

"Phew, they're back. Those dogs from the Order of Purity."

Sungchul's gaze turned towards the soldiers as well. He also glimpsed at the man that was being escorted by the soldiers. With his white judge's garb and a crow mask, he looked closer to a divine entity than a man.

Is that the Inquisitor of Heresy?

The Inquisitor of Heresy was an incredibly religious crusader of faith that worked as a clergyman within one of the two orders that followed the God of Neutrality; the God of Neutrality being one of the five main gods of the Other World. However, it wasn't uncommon that the blind faith of these people gave off a bad vibe. Sungchul had witnessed a certain innocent northernmost frontier village located close to the Demon Realm disappear.

He had also killed three of these Inquisitors. They weren't particularly powerful foes. He only felt that they had the resilience of a cockroach.

I want to avoid confrontation, if possible.

Basil piped up as Sungchul was organizing his thoughts.

"That Inquisitor. There are rumors that he is the half-brother of our former principal, The Grand Magnus."

"Half-brother?"

"That's right. The Magnus name is a Mage family known for their deep history, but the Inquisitor, who was the child of the legal wife, was sent to the Order due to his lack of talent. The Grand Magnus, on the other hand, as the son of a mistress, was so talented that he managed to earn the Grand title to his name. As you can imagine, they were very antagonistic towards each other. Well, according to rumors that is."

Basil continued to tell more stories, but they were all irrelevant gossip. Sungchul ended the conversation appropriately, then turned to head towards the School of Cosmomancy. It was at this moment that a crowd of Mages headed towards his direction. It was a group of students wearing uniforms dyed in blue, accompanied by a middle-aged Mage. He was acquainted with the middle-aged Mage.

Stocky jaw with a sharp nose. A face with indifferent blue eyes. It was the head of the School of Cryomancy, Robert Danton. Sungchul recalled the scene of him tossing Leonard Sanctum out in the most humiliating manner immediately after hearing the news of the head of the School of Pyromancy's death. That Robert Danton was looking at Sungchul right in the eye. Without notice, he stopped before Sungchul.

"Can we speak briefly?"

"If it's only very brief."

Robert didn't react to Sungchul's brash reply, but the students behind him were livid.

"No manners. Who do you think this person is that you can speak to him without lowering your head?"

"A mere Alchemist. Know your place!"

Robert held up his hand to command his underlings to cease the racket, then looked at Sungchul to speak again.

"Just a moment is fine, so come by my room."

"I can't spare a lot of time."

The ends of Robert's lips twitched. He turned and headed to his room first, then Sungchul followed behind while receiving nasty looks from his students.

"Oh, my. Why did he come already? I...I couldn't make my request yet!"

Basil had wanted to ask Sungchul to help him keep his spot as the Professor of the School of Alchemy.

—

"I heard the rumors. They say you're a Preselected among the Summoned."

Robert began speaking as soon as he took his seat. Sungchul simply nodded.

"I am also from a Preselected group. It has been fifteen years since I arrived here."

He spoke as though it was a distant past, but to Sungchul, he was still green. Sungchul had been summoned approximately twenty-five years back. Though his appearance and age looked years apart.

"So, let's cut to the chase as you've said that you haven't got much time. I'll speak plainly."

Robert rose from his seat, closed all of the room's curtains, then took a brief glance around before slowly walking round towards Sungchul's back as he began talking.

"If I may ask, who is your backer? It doesn't matter if you can't say, but it'll help me understand you better to overcome any misunderstandings, so think carefully and speak."

He directly asked for Sungchul's background. Sungchul could only think that he was an honest person before considering several candidates to name as a backer. He filtered the names based on their strength and the difficulty for Robert to get in contact with. Soon, a faction appeared in his mind, and he spoke its name firmly.

"The Ancient Kingdom."

"The Ancient Kingdom...?!"

Robert wet his lips.

"Isn't the Ancient Kingdom a place that forbids Magic? Why would a group that stands against Magic send you here?"

"You should be well aware that they use plenty of it behind the scenes, right?"

Robert broke into laughter after hearing this and didn't ask any further, but it wasn't clear whether or not he believed in Sungchul's words. Tension flowed between the two of them as Robert opened his mouth once again.

"I saw your skill first-hand, although strictly speaking, it is the strength of the backers behind you. On that line of thought, why not lend your strength to me?"

"What do you mean?"

Sungchul threw out his question while still standing.

"Join my side. After Fregius' death, there is no one but me to lead the school. It is but a shell of an institution, but we can try to lead it into a better direction. I need a lot of support for that purpose."

Sungchul circled the room as Robert returned to his seat and spoke again.

"Is that your actual name?"

Sungchul nodded.

"I had thought it was an alias. I was so sure of it when you created that fifth-level Alchemic item. I thought, 'Ah, this friend wants to attract the school's attention with such a name.'"

He misinterpreted the situation to match his own expectations. Sungchul continued to listen to Robert's fantasies and managed to determine a single line of thought within his dull story. Robert didn't believe that Sungchul produced Elfir's Medicine despite the truth of the matter. It could have been that the man wasn't familiar with Alchemy, or that there was no one to advise him otherwise. Whichever case it was, it was to Sungchul's benefit. It was due to this misunderstanding that Robert was about to begin negotiations with the most dangerous man that had no friends or allies.

"Anyways, I don't know who your friends are that stand behind you, but I can tell that they are willing to devote their heart and soul for you. I know this because I was also a Preselected. I guess one could call it the difference in temperament felt between Preselecteds. I know this better than most."

Robert continued to speak vaguely until finally, he said what was on his mind.

"I need gold coins. A significant amount of gold coins. It is almost assured that I will be the principal, but there are many areas that will require large funds to expedite the process."

"What can you do for me?"

Sungchul asked sharply.

"If you become my strength, I'll give you an important position within Airfruit. Naturally, a position that your backer will be pleased with. People might say that Airfruit is finished, but its name still holds value, so it isn't a bad trade."

Regarding this, Sungchul stared unflinchingly at Robert as he spoke.

"I want to hear more details."

"I will give you a position as a Professor if you want. As you know, the current Professor in charge of the School of Alchemy,

Basil Philrus, is quite incompetent. He's someone that has to be kicked out."

"Isn't it too early? I'm a foreigner that hasn't even been here for a year."

"I didn't mean to give it to you immediately. Several preparations need to be made first, but once I am the Headmaster, I can prepare you to be on Airfruit Academy's greatest elite course to set you on the path to valedictorian. How about it?"

"…"

Sungchul didn't reply. Robert wasn't pleased with Sungchul's response, but exerting more self-control, he spoke softly.

"Is it not enough?"

"I only want the Secret of Cosmomancy. If you can notify Altugius to allow him to hand over the Secret of Cosmomancy, I'll ask my backers."

"Altugius…"

Robert began to frown. It looked as though something was on his mind. After significant time had passed, a thin smile formed on his lips, and he nodded.

"I'll give it a go, but it won't be easy."

"What does that mean?"

"Altugius is quite stubborn. I'll put in a word, but he isn't someone who is liable to listen to others. He wouldn't listen to that vicious Fregius, so what are the chances he'll listen to me?"

"Then it complicates things."

"But, he also has a weakness. It is time. Once that girl he treasures so much begins to rot, I'm sure his ears will open. Will you wait for me until then?"

Sungchul nodded for now. He knew nothing would change whether he agreed or not at this point.

Robert, who was now much happier, looked at Sungchul attentively. The man who had been observing Sungchul's face with narrowed eyes like a viper suddenly opened his mouth.

"Now that I think about it, you must be trying to gather some strength if you desire the Secret of Cosmomancy."

"Isn't strength everything in Other World?"

Robert rolled his eyes and spoke as though he had been waiting for that exact reply.

"I can't attest to the quality of the Secret as I've never seen it myself, but I feel as though it's greatly exaggerated. It also seems as though there might have been exaggerations mixed in with the rumor that Altugius managed to kill the Vice-Captain of the Assassin's Guild. Mayhaps, the Vice-Captain wasn't in peak form."

Robert continued to speak empty words until he slipped in his true intentions.

"Why not put aside Cosmomancy for the Secrets of Cryomancy?"

Sungchul sharply shook his head, and Robert's face twisted ever so slightly. Sungchul, seeing this reaction, had an immediate thought.

Should I test him?

During the time he had fought against the Followers of Calamity, he had learned more than just combat techniques. He experienced commonalities in mental states and habits of Mages and learned how to agitate, anger, or calm them.

"I was ordered to learn the Secret of Cosmomancy or something equivalent."

The trap was set.

"Is it not possible for Cryomancy to be that substitute?"

"Cryomancy or Pyromancy aren't suitable as substitutes."

"Why do you believe so?"

"It is too common."

These words were to agitate Robert's pride. Mages tended to be crafty but were also known to be extremely prideful. As expected, Robert's eyes changed. It fell into the same patterns Sungchul had experienced countless times before.

Robert took a deep breath before fixing his eyes onto Sungchul, then spoke.

"If you seek a path that leads to true enlightenment, I can help guide you a bit. Not too deep, but just a little. Just enough for you and your backers to be satisfied with."

"What are you speaking of?"

When Sungchul asked, Robert made a wicked smile.

"To witness extinction very briefly. Just a bit of it."

Bad vibes always proved to be accurate. Sungchul looked at Robert in a different light.

Is this bastard also a Follower of Calamity?

The entire school was rotten. He briefly thought of the possibility that most of the core members of the school were Followers of Calamity, but his expression remained unchanged. Instead, he made a leisurely smile instead and held a hand out towards Robert.

"That is exactly the purpose I came to Airfruit for."

As he spoke, he opened his Soul Storage and pulled out a crate.

Oh…to already have a Soul Storage. This guy is an unexpectedly powerful figure.

Robert's heart skipped a beat as he waited for the crate to open. Sungchul opened the crate with crude movements. Blinding golden light flooded out of the crate and obstructed Robert's vision. Sungchul felt a wide smile form on Robert's lips as he grabbed one of the golden coins.

The golden coin without a mark.

The unmarked golden coins.

Sungchul handed Robert one of these golden coins and spoke to him in a firm voice.

"Never mention that you got these coins from me. Unless you wish the entirety of the Ancient Kingdom as your enemy."

"I swear upon my name."

Robert replied with a smile from ear to ear.

The fish had bit down on the bait.

***

When he returned to the Cosmomancy building, the atmosphere within the Observatory had changed for many reasons.

"You've finally come."

Altugius walked over and called out in his gruff voice as Sungchul entered the building. Sungchul nodded then looked over to the side. Leonard's hammock had been folded away. Instead, he sat on the floor upright looking studious with a book in his hand. He paused in his studies, moving the book slightly to give Sungchul a heinous glare. Sungchul ignored his gaze and continued to move towards Altugius.

"Were you expecting me?"

Altugius nodded. Sungchul felt that the man looked ten years older than he was in that moment. It wasn't due to his physical health, but rather he looked extremely exhausted.

"I have put you at a distance due to personal reasons, but I have decided to teach you in earnest from this point on."

Altugius handed Sungchul a single necklace. It was a medallion depicting the form of a planet in the sun's orbit with a ray of light striking its center.

"This is the insignia of the School of Cosmomancy. Wear it on your neck."

Sungchul did as he was told.

"It is actually quite an impressive medallion, but it doesn't seem to fit with your attire."

It looked as though Sungchul's fashion resembling a laborer didn't quite suit Altugius.

"First, I feel as though you should get a fitted uniform. It has been bothering me for quite a while, to be honest."

There was no way for Sungchul to know, but Altugius was referred to as the Tiger Professor, as he strictly enforced student morality. Leonard, who had been listening in on their conversation, let out a laugh. Altugius turned his head and shot him a look.

"Anyways, we have an unwelcome guest."

Altugius pointed a finger towards Leonard's face.

"What is this strange creature that I have never taken in as a disciple doing here?"

The chilling sarcasm echoed loudly throughout the Observatory. Leonard's expression immediately changed. He had believed that Altugius had accepted him, as Altugius had never commented about his presence here, but it now appeared that the Professor had been patiently enduring him for the opportunity to chase him out when Sungchul arrived.

I should have killed that fucker...

His insides were boiling with anger, but it was already too late. He got on his knees and put on a strained expression in hopes of inverting his situation.

"I'm sorry, master! I...I couldn't be more sorry. It was all due to Fregius' schemes..."

"I don't need anything from you. Leave immediately."

Altugius was ruthless. As he held out his hand, a brilliant staff with five different gems embedded within it appeared from his Soul Storage.

"Or are you prepared to have a Gauntlet with me?"

Regardless of Leonard's renown within the school as an individual with great strength, he would not be able to contend against Altugius, who had left behind a legend. He paled, then turned around to escape while uttering unintelligible babble, screaming as he retreated from the building. Altugius let out a refreshing laugh after watching this scene.

"Don't come back! You're expelled!"

This old man. Was this his original personality?

It was unexpected. The old man who always had his back turned towards him had such a magnanimous personality.

"That kid is a Follower of Calamity. You should also know who they are, right?"

Sungchul nodded.

"Damnable fools. True degenerates. I wanted to kill him, but seeing that he was one of our school's pupils, it would have left a bad taste in my mouth."

Altugius put a pipe in his mouth before inhaling deeply as he looked towards the ceiling of the Observatory. There was nothing of interest to see on the domed ceiling that was plastered in white.

"How was the Summoning Palace?"

Altugius pulled out his pipe and suddenly asked his question.

"It's not a place for leisure," replied Sungchul.

"That seems right. It is a hellish place. However, it is a necessary evil. People from your world think too differently from ours. When too many people with different ideas arrive, the world will inevitably change."

It was an interesting perspective. Sungchul had always believed that the Summoning Palace was a special rite of passage designed to filter out the greatest from the rest, to find individuals who could become the saviors of the Other World. Those who were the Summoned would generally receive better treatment anywhere they went.

Altugius breathed out a smoke-infused sigh as he took his eyes off the ceiling.

"However, this place has also turned into hell. It doesn't matter what the others think."

"Are you referring to the Followers of Calamity?"

"Maybe. Maybe not. They aren't the important part, but the Calamity that they worship is. The Calamity is eating away at us bit by bit until we all become insane. It is enough to bewitch even the most noble of us."

Altugius tightly shut both his eyes and fell into deep thought. Soon after, he pulled out volume two from his Soul Storage.

"Take this for now."

Sungchul opened the book as he received it, but it wasn't something he could understand as of now.

"It's the book relating to Meteor, the popular spell that is the core of the School of Cosmomancy. You'll need to exceed 210 Intuition to learn it."

"Isn't this progress too fast?"

"Might be, but this is a dangerous world. We never know what is going to happen next. First with the Principal, and now Fregius, I might also disappear at any time."

Altugius' voice trembled slightly. Sungchul saw concern and anxiety within his expression.

"It has been a while since I've seen a student as diligent as you. A very rare thing to see, even if we take into consideration details like your motivations or your backer."

Altugius, like Robert Danton, suspected Sungchul of being out of the ordinary with someone supporting him from the shadows. It simply exceeded common sense to witness such a rapid growth otherwise.

"That is why I'm gifting you with this. I don't know when you'll be able to make Meteor your own, but it also isn't any of my business."

Altugius finished speaking and returned to his old spot, then turned his back once again. He shot out an unexpected final sentence at Sungchul who was staring at his back.

"Now, get going since I gave you what you wanted."

"What do you mean?"

"This is everything I can teach you. I'll give you that book, so take it and go."

It was an unexpected development. Sungchul felt slightly annoyed at the shameless old man's change of heart.

This old man...

He calmed his heart and spoke again.

"I can't leave with just this."

"Then?"

"What I want is the Secret. I don't have any intention of leaving here before I receive the Secret of Cosmomancy."

Sungchul could sense Magic emitting from Altugius at that moment. A beam of light shot towards Sungchul in that exact moment. A blinding flash. It was Glare. Glare's light was aimed slightly off from Sungchul's face. It was the same Magic, but due to the difference in Sungchul's Magic Power, it vastly outstripped his own Glare's brilliance and firepower. The beam of light pierced through a bookcase around the outer edge of the Observatory and left a hole in the wall.

"…"

However, Sungchul did not even flinch. Altugius let out a fake cough and stood up from his seat.

"What a greedy friend. Can you not be satisfied with just the medallion and Meteor? I didn't say it before, but with the medallion, other competitive Schools of Cosmomancy will accept you as a student."

"It can't be anything other than the Secret."

Sungchul didn't budge at all. Altugius let out a groan. His eyes contained a deep sadness.

"Excessive greed can be your downfall. Like those of the Followers of Calamity."

"It isn't excessive. There is a reason that I must receive your Secret."

"And that reason is?"

Altugius asked. Sungchul replied firmly without any hesitation in his voice.

"To stop the Calamity."

Altugius' eyes were dyed with surprise as he heard these words, but it lasted only briefly before he let out a chuckle.

"That's impossible. Nothing can stop the Calamity."

"The Seven Heroes have done it. Nothing is impossible."

Sungchul spoke with finality. Altugius looked upon Sungchul with mixed emotions until he finally turned away.

"Leave. Before I become truly angry."

"It isn't my business whether you grow angry or not."

Sungchul did not retreat a step. Instead, he stepped forward. Altugius sighed once more.

I don't want to rough him up, but I suppose I have to suppress him with minimal damage.

Sungchul immediately stopped moving and suddenly looked behind him. Altugius was confused by his abrupt action, but the cause soon revealed itself.

A presence?!

A presence that couldn't be underestimated was felt beyond the door. Altugius felt a chill crawling through his body. The presence he felt was not much different from the figure that had made him famous in battle.

"Oh my, I was caught. Such good Intuition."

The door that had been firmly shut flew open. Beyond the open door, an uninvited guest wearing a black robe with a feline mask stood in wait. He looked at Sungchul and Altugius in turn before speaking in a bright voice.

"I would like to ask you: is this the School of Cosmomancy?"

Saying this, the man took off his mask. A striking face with a long scar across his left eye was revealed. Sungchul could smell the scent of death from the young man.

Is he an Assassin?

Murderous intent openly dripped from his presence. This was a luxury that only a few with absolute confidence in their strength could enjoy. Generally, an Assassin's strength lies in their ambush, as usually it was their weakness to be exposed in direct battles.

The mysterious youth continued to look alternatingly at Sungchul and Altugius.

"Hm. The one I seek doesn't seem to be here. I'll be taking a gander at both of your strengths, if I may."

He pulled out a scroll and tore it before Altugius could put in a word otherwise. At that moment, his eyes filled with a Magical formation and the stats of both men before him appeared.

"Young man: Average. Old man: Extraordinary."

An anecdote came to the youth's mind. A humiliating anecdote whispered in hushed tones within the Assassin's Guild.

"Ah, are you Altugius?"

"Ill-mannered child. How dare you come here and speak such ridiculous things?"

Altugius straightened his white beard and scolded in a thunderous voice. The youth showed a surprised expression, but that was it.

"Pffft, don't torment the young so much. I just wanted to speak briefly."

Altugius suddenly shot Glare towards him. The brilliant beam of light shot in that instant had been aimed just beside his temple. But like Sungchul, the young man also did not move. However, their reactions were different. The young man snarled in anger.

"Ey! You trying to start something here?"

He brushed his robes open revealing dozens of hidden weapons underneath. Altugius let out a laugh.

"Are you the Assassin's Guild's lackey? It is uncanny how you and that retard with red-hair act alike. If only you had seen how that idiot died, you wouldn't dare show yourself here."

"I'm stronger than him, old man."

The youth didn't back down at all. The situation was quickly reaching its climax.

Not bad. I might be able to witness Altugius' skill at this rate.

Sungchul took a step back to witness this scene, but the fight Sungchul desired didn't come to fruition. A female voice from beyond the open door calmed the young man.

"Orabeoni Kaz[12]. What are you hoping to achieve by fooling around in a place like this?"

Another figure with a black robe and feline mask entered the Observatory.

"It looks like he isn't here anyways. Let's just go."

"Why are you being like this, Myra? I just wanted to play around a bit before I left."

The youth made a fuss, but his temper had been calmed. He looked at Altugius from the corner of his eye and turned around to leave.

"Sorry, old man. We'll settle the score another time."

Altugius crossed his arms and laughed once again. The two figures that left the Observatory descended the gentle mountain slope at a slow pace.

"Ah, I'm pissed."

Kaz, the eldest son of the Almeira family, looked towards the sky as he muttered to himself. He knew it was a difficult assignment, but the trail was more than a bit bare. He had expected to get his hands on the legendary villain when he first discovered the Slave Hunter that had been using up the gold coins like they were water, but the Covenant enchanted on the Slave Hunter's body had ruined all of that. The man who couldn't bear the torture uttered a single word: School of Cosmomancy. The man's heart proceeded to combust into flames and was sacrificed to the God of Neutrality as soon as he uttered the word.

"But why the School of Cosmomancy?"

Kaz looked back upon the domed building. The Enemy of the World and the School of Cosmomancy. There was no common ground to be found. He had ended up visiting the school in the end, but other than the famed old man, there was no one that could possibly fit the description.

"Anyways, Myra. How is it on our parents' end? Did they find the other one using the unmarked gold coins?"

Myra shook her head at his question.

"Gone. Without saying a word to anyone."

"...Mmm. Could he have caught onto our scent?"

"Maybe. It could also be a coincidence. Either way, there is no reason to rush."

Amidst the conversation, a lone figure caught Kaz's eyes. It was a handsome man wearing a robe dyed in red. He had been sitting in the forest far from the School of Cosmomancy by himself, screaming for some reason.

"What the hell? Who is that guy?"

"Who knows. Seems insane to me?"

Myra brushed it off as though she wasn't interested, but Kaz was different.

"I'm going to check him out for a bit."

Kaz approached the screaming man like a child who had discovered a new interesting toy.

"BITCH! FUCK!!!"

The identity of the man sitting in the forest screaming was none other than Leonard Sanctum.

Chapter 18 – Stinkbug

He had killed countless of those weaker than him. He had been openly caught five times, but he had too many sins to name that were committed secretly. Leonard, who had lived such a life, finally met his match.

"Kuu..."

He was hung by his feet and exposed to unrelenting violence. Whips and clubs struck every inch of his body, and when he lost consciousness, a blast of cold water shook him awake. His opponent was a complete stranger.

Leonard, who was beaten down to a pulp, asked himself why he was in such a position. He couldn't think of an answer, despite his best efforts to squeeze out an explanation. Other than a stroke of misfortune, that is.

"Now, shall we begin our story time?"

Kaz opened his mouth with a wicked smile. There were shiny torture tools in his hand in place of the whip, and Leonard who saw that began to thrash about wildly from his incapacitated position.

"When I first saw you, you had quite a handsome face. It pissed me off. So, choose one: eyes, nose, mouth, or ear. To give up."

A single blade lingered in front of Leonard's eyes. He began to scream something unintelligible and thrashed about once again. Kaz, who saw this ridiculous scene, started laughing while holding his belly. He gripped Leonard's right ear, then sliced it off.

"Uwaaaaak!"

A pitiful scream rang out, but there was no one around to help Leonard. A sound barrier cast around the trees prevented his scream from leaking out any further. He was now facing the same final moments that he had forced on those weaker than him in the midst of this complete isolation. However, Kaz pulled out a medicine and put some on Leonard's bleeding injuries as though he had something in mind.

"Want to live?"

Leonard endured the pain and forced his head to nod.

"If you tell me what I want to hear, I'll let you live."

Kaz made a gesture towards Myra, who was sitting underneath the tree watching the scene silently.

"Myra, lend me that thing."

Myra extended her hand without a word. When she did, a colorful insect about the size of a plum crawled out of her sleeve. It was a stinkbug shaped like a trapezoid.

Kaz grabbed the bug carefully and tore away Leonard's shirt revealing his back full of bruises and cuts from the constant beating and whipping. Kaz placed the tail of the bug on his back. The bug's six legs flailed about as its sharp tail end began to bore itself into Leonard's back.

"Kwaaaaaak!"

Leonard thrashed about violently. The stinkbug was tearing through his flesh and laying its eggs. One. Two. Three. Kaz smiled with satisfaction as he saw ten eggs, then returned the bug to Myra.

"Thanks, Myra."

Myra returned the bug to her sleeve and spoke with a frosty voice.

"Father won't be pleased if he hears of this. You have to take responsibility."

"I'll bear it. Don't worry. Anyways, don't you think Father's methods are too old-fashioned? Efficacy drops when we can only lay our hands on those involved."

Kaz looked over at Leonard, who was shaking like a twig, and made a cruel smile.

"In this era of Calamity where we're all destined to die anyways; we should use every tool available."

—

Sungchul continued to confront Altugius. It was Altugius who broke first.

"Do what you want. I won't take responsibility for whatever misfortune you meet by staying here!"

He let out a loud harrumph before sitting at his designated spot and sucking on his pipe. However, Sungchul was second to none when it came to stubbornness. He didn't budge an inch as he demanded what he wanted.

"You don't have to worry about me. Just let me know the Secret."

Altugius continued to puff his pipe with a displeased expression when he suddenly pulled something out from his Soul Storage. It was a small box marked with the insignia of a comet. Orbs composed of gold, silver, bronze and all other kinds of alloys were revealed when Altugius opened the box with his wrinkled hands.

"Activate."

When Altugius softly touched an orb, they floated around him on their own as if they were alive.

"These are the training tools used by Cosmomancers to learn their craft. People of the past called them the Stars of the Cosmos, but people of late have taken to calling them as pinballs. Anyways, they are used to gauge the proficiency of that Glare spell you've learned."

Altugius pulled out another item from his Soul Storage. It was a Magic scroll. He lightly tossed over the container with the orbs charged with power along with the scroll towards Sungchul.

"Perseverance is a type of talent. I have accepted that you have quite the talent in it. However, there are many different types of talent. The tool I have given you contains the quest refined by countless ancient masters. The quest will test you on another talent required by Cosmomancers. You want to learn the Secret of Cosmomancy? We'll talk after you've overcome this quest."

Sungchul held the orbs and Magic scroll separately. The orb contained Magical energies, and the scroll was for a Magic barrier.

"Also, make sure to use the scroll before attempting the quest. I don't want this sacred structure of Cosmomancy harmed by your crude Magic."

Altugius spoke these words and puffed on his pipe while looking at Sungchul with a relatively relaxed expression on his face.

They had called me a rare genius that hadn't been seen in hundreds of years, and it still took me fourteen months to complete that pinball quest. Even that Leonard who was praised as a "once in a decade Genius" couldn't even think it was possible for himself to complete it. No matter how gifted and perseverant this man is, there is a limit to how far one can go with pure talent. This is not something he could solve easily.

For those that couldn't be forced away, one must confuse them with an overwhelming assignment. It was a saying handed down from ancient times within Airfruit's School of Cosmomancy, which held a particularly powerful Secret.

"…"

Sungchul looked over the orb first.

"Activate."

When he uttered their activation command, the six orbs composed of gold, silver, bronze, steel, tin, and white gold flew into the sky and slowly revolved around Sungchul's vicinity. A brightly lettered message appeared before him.

[The Stars of Cosmomancy]

[The Stars of Cosmomancy will orbit around your vicinity.]

[As the sovereign of these astral bodies, you must shoot down those that defy you with the Authority of Light.]

[The Stars that are in defiance will be dyed with darkness, so observe carefully with both of your eyes.]

[Please care to observe your surroundings before starting the trial so as to not create casualties.]

It was a ubiquitous type of quest among those he had experienced within Airfruit. It also used vague language that was typical of Airfruit's quests.

What does the light's authority refer to? Is it talking about Glare?

Altugius, who had been watching Sungchul, shouted with a loud voice.

"It's a trial for shooting down the dark orbs with Glare. The Magic barrier was a one-time gift, so buy one at your expense before you reattempt the quest!"

The price of Magic barrier seals was significant. They reached 50 silver coins in price, and their supply was low, so it was hard to get a hold of one. This was well within Altugius' intentions.

This quest takes up more than just a lot of effort. It also digs into the pocketbook of the one being tested. Now, let's see how this friend's talent fares in Cosmomancy Magic.

Altugius reclined to a more comfortable position as he looked over in Sungchul's direction. Sungchul activated the scroll and deployed the barrier, then turned his attentions to the orbs circling him.

[Shout the phrase "Begin" once you are ready.]

Sungchul calmed the Magical energy in his body and took a shot towards the barrier as a test.

Glare.

A beam of light fired out from his fingertip and struck one part of the barrier before it disappeared. Altugius smiled with his eyes.

His Magic Power is still weak. It looks to be around 140, I think.

Sungchul, who had tested out his Magic, now turned to the orbs circling him and spoke quietly.

"Begin."

[Level 1]

The path of the orbs circling him began to change. The golden orb suddenly became dyed in darkness and flew past his face. Sungchul didn't hesitate in using Glare. A beam of light shot out from his finger to strike and peel away its darkness. One of Altugius' brows shot up.

Is it luck...?!

After striking one orb, Sungchul turned his focus onto the copper orb rushing at him. The orb that had appeared from his blindspot flew past him and approached another blindspot when it began to dye itself in darkness. Sungchul's eyes had caught it, but his inexperience with Magic caused his aim to waver and strike feebly onto the barrier.

As expected, beginner's luck. It couldn't have been anything else. For sure.

Altugius inhaled from his pipe and let out a sigh of relief.

Soon, the first level had finished.

[Your score]

[3/10 (Number of Heavenly Bodies struck / Number of Heavenly Bodies that defied you)]

[Judgement...Failure!]

"..."

It was a shameful result for Sungchul. He could hear Altugius' laughter.

"Ha ha! It looks as though you're a bit lacking to be demanding the Secret of Cosmomancy!"

The orbs that had been orbiting Sungchul fell into their container. Sungchul pulled out a Mana Drink from his Soul Storage.

Altugius, who had been laughing, looked on with shock.

What? This guy also has a Soul Storage?

Sungchul drank two bottles of Mana Drink at once, dropped them onto the floor, then rubbed the orb once again.

"Activate."

It wasn't just a grudge. The first attempt at the test was nothing more than an attempt to adjust his sights. His perception honed to its limits and decades of combat experience during his time as an absolute warrior wasn't just for show. During the first test, after missing his second shot, he focused on improving his control over the output of the spell, rather than its accuracy. And by the final shot, he had already commanded complete control over the spell as he scored a hit.

"Begin."

There was nothing to stop him once he managed to get a feel for it. He looked on at the orbs spinning dizzyingly around him. Altugius felt an unusual aura surrounding him, but he ignored it and continued smoking his pipe.

The first orb soon became dyed in darkness and flew past Sungchul's face.

Glare.

The beam of light shot out from his finger and accurately struck the center of the orb, peeling away the darkness. The second one with the tricky flight path flew past him from his blindspot to another blindspot as before. Sungchul didn't flinch as he took a step back and smoothly shot the orb to banish the darkness.

Altugius' eyes flew open.

No...that one?!

In the first level, the second orb was known to be the most difficult target. It was the quest host's intention to throw off the tester's balance with a high difficulty curve ball that would affect his future attempts within the level. However, this mysterious man overcame that second shot with ease. He continued striking every other orb in their tricky flight paths with little difficulty. Altugius ended up dropping his pipe after a short time passed.

[Your score]

[10/10 (Number of Heavenly Bodies struck / Number of Heavenly bodies that defied you)]

[Judgement...Pass!]

Sungchul looked at the score that appeared before him with disinterest and drank another Mana Drink.

[Astounding! You have completed the first level with a perfect score.]

Reward: +3 Magic Power, +3 Intuition, +3 Dexterity

It even raised Dexterity, unlike a typical Mage quest, but the quest wouldn't be able to raise Sungchul's Dexterity.

[Error! Your Dexterity is higher than the Dexterity of the quest host, and thus you will not be able to receive the boost in Dexterity.]

Quests gave an opportunity for unspecified people to receive boosts in stats, but unless it was like the Devil in the basement who gave out his own stats, it wouldn't raise the recipient's stats beyond that of the quest's host. There weren't many who could exceed Sungchul in his physical stats. This was also the reason why Sungchul didn't bother much with the quests of the remaining Seven Heroes other than the Mage Heroes. He was sure that there was no one among the Seven Heroes who could come close to his physical stats.

[Would you like to begin Level Two?]

Sungchul's eyes were now focused on the next level. And Altugius couldn't take his eyes off from the figure of the indescribably amazing man.

***

Mages generally preferred and were trained to fight one-sided battles that could be handled elegantly with no risk of injury. Combat vision, quick judgement, psychological warfare, flexibility to respond to developing situations, quick reflexes. These sweaty, crude, broad categories of combat were largely ignored. However, within the School of Cosmomancy, or at least the Observatory run by Altugius, there was a different atmosphere.

The Stars of Cosmomancy, or pinball as they were more commonly called, was more of a physical training that emphasized quick reflexes and the ability to deal with extraneous circumstances, rather than being actual Magic training. Sungchul grew surer of his assumption as he drew closer to the third level of the Star of Cosmomancy. The dark stars no longer lingered around his vicinity. They either rushed in recklessly or attacked him discreetly, and they ceaselessly and ferociously drove him to a corner.

The Stars of Cosmomancy tested more than just reflex and quick response; a particular star was designed to be too quick and irregular to hit.

Sungchul was initially stumped, but he discovered that this star, too, had a complex pattern designed to disguise its repetitive nature. Using suppressive fire, Sungchul was able to push its movements to its limits and was able to obtain a point without much trouble.

"I can't believe this even as I watch it."

Every time Sungchul achieved victory, Altugius' breath grew increasingly rough. His eyes didn't see an amateur recently spat out by the Summoning Palace, but rather a master's expertise honed by dozens of years of swordplay.

Is he a genius...or is he a well-trained swordsman?

Sungchul's stats were barely adequate for an apprentice Mage, and his strange movements could be better associated with experience rather than sheer stats. When calm finally settled in the Observatory, Altugius instinctively knew that the man of unknown origins would be the very first figure to break through the Stars of Cosmomancy in a single day since the conception of the Airfruit branch of the School of Cosmomancy.

Sungchul lazily looked over the rewards that appeared before him as he opened his status window.

[Stats]			
Strength	999+	Dexterity	853
Vitality	801	Magic Power	151
Intuition	131	Magic Resist	621
Resilience	502	Charisma	18
	Luck	18	

It was still an unsatisfactory amount, but to other people, his growth could be considered nothing short of miraculous. Altugius thought along the same lines.

Is this man...a monster?

The "monster" approached Altugius and pushed the box containing the orbs back into his possession.

"Now that I have passed the trials as you've requested, will you pass me the Secret?"

"Y-You have yet to complete all the trials!"

To be exact, he wasn't quite prepared yet. His heart wasn't prepared to accept this astounding result. Altugius pardoned himself with nonsensical excuses like a pouting child and turned him away for the moment.

"Return for now. I have some thinking to do!"

Sungchul looked at Altugius passively and nodded.

"I understand. I'll return tomorrow."

He had passed the trial in one go, but it was a trial that consumed significant amounts of mana. Sungchul felt that he was quickly approaching the threshold of using Magic Power that Bertelgia had talked about. This was why he obediently followed Altugius' request.

But when I return tomorrow, your heart better be ready for what needs to happen.

After Sungchul left the Observatory, Altugius felt heavy fatigue wearing down on his aged shoulders. Too many things had happened at the same time. Time alone was the medicine to calm the turbulence of the mind, but reality wouldn't give him the opportunity.

KNOCK! KNOCK! KNOCK!

Someone knocked upon the Observatory door.

"Who is it?"

When Altugius asked, a cold, emotionless voice responded from beyond the door.

"I have brought the item sent by the Inquisitor of Heresy."

"Leave it at the front."

When the footsteps faded away, Altugius dragged his old, yet spry body towards the door; a large sack full of gold coins had been left there. Altugius let out a sigh and placed it into his own Soul

Storage. He looked down at the panoramic view of the school beneath the cliff of the mountain as he put the sack away. The view that opened up beneath his feet wasn't much different than the view he had seen when he first stepped foot into the Observatory as the Professor of Cosmomancy, but he knew better than anyone that the school had begun heading down the path of no return.

The face of a certain somebody appeared clearly on his mind as he looked on at the faded scenery. The man, with an impressive beard that had gone partially gray, had a mild temper, but had led the teaching staff with his powerful voice and strong personality. The world would remember him as The Grand Magnus, the final Headmaster of Airfruit. Altugius recalled the final conversations he had had with the man who had been a friend for most of his life. The man had said to him:

"The world is a sea, and we are but rafts floating on top of it. The rafts can navigate the sea, but it cannot affect the sea in any way. We can only acknowledge the flow of the world. That is all."

It wasn't widely known, but The Grand Magnus was a Follower of Calamity. He had sought to leave behind achievements as a Follower of Calamity, but he had died by Altugius' hands. Altugius believed his decision to be correct at the time, but after these three years, his resolution was wavering.

"If only I had died instead by that bastard's hands at that time…"

—

Sungchul was en route to the House of Recollections.

GROWL…

Maybe it was due to the amount of concentration spent on the trials; he felt quite ravenous. It was his policy to always eat something delicious when he was hungry. He would expend some of his own effort to prepare food when he was in the middle of nowhere, but a must for foodies is the exploration of hidden restaurants. He began scrolling through his memory to seek out the hidden gems within Golden City, but the food joint of his memories had become some Guild's office that he had never heard of.

"Hey, Mr. Summoned! What are you doing here? Are you perhaps here to apply to our Guild?"

The man standing guard in front of the Guild with an overbite called out to Sungchul.

"…I have no business here."

Sungchul ignored him and moved on to the next location, but when he walked along the main street, a familiar face appeared. It was Philrus, the Professor of Alchemy, and his disciples.

"Shit! Trash discovered!"

Bertelgia peeked out from his pocket and lightly shook her body. Basil soon discovered Sungchul. He suddenly looked quite amiable and began talking to Sungchul.

"Hey. Look who it is? If it isn't my best pupil!"

Sungchul looked on with an indifferent expression. It was because he couldn't recall ever becoming that man's disciple.

Basil laughed awkwardly, scratching his head, and opened his mouth once again.

"Ahaha! Man, isn't it a bit hot around here?"

"If you'll excuse me."

Sungchul squeezed past Basil and his students. Their view of Sungchul had changed compared to the day they had first met him at the run-down tents. Their eyes were now filled with envy, greed, jealousy, and the like. Sungchul did not lock eyes with any of them and walked past quickly. It was at this moment when Basil followed along at a quick pace and struck up another conversation with great affection.

"Where are you headed?"

"To eat."

"If that's the case, why not join us? You are a part of the School of Alchemy, after all."

"…"

When Sungchul grew silent, Basil carefully looked at him and asked, "What's wrong? Perhaps...you don't want to eat with us..."

"I am quite picky with food. I don't want to go somewhere that's not up to par."

When he heard this, Basil broke into a satisfied smile and pulled Sungchul close.

"Then that's great. We are planning on going somewhere with a great chef!"

"Is that so?"

Sungchul's frozen heart melted slightly. Regardless of everything, Basil was someone that had resided within Golden City for quite a while. It might be faster for him to rely on the man for good food. Sungchul pleasantly agreed with such thoughts.

"Okay. I'll trust you this time."

"You'll be glad you listened to me."

Basil's eyes were filled with confidence as they always were. After a while...

[This food's score is...18!]

As someone of the chef class, Sungchul could see the score of dishes he tasted.

"Mmm..."

He had expected the score to be a bit low as Basil's wallet was tight and he had ordered the cheapest food with the largest quantity, but that wasn't the only reason. No matter how cheap the food was, there was a standard that must be maintained. He took another bite.

[This food's score is...17!]

"..."

A flicker of anger leaked onto Sungchul's face. It was a bit of rage that was kept in check even during Leonard's flurry of insults.

This isn't meant for human consumption.

What was laid in front of Sungchul was a soup made mainly from pig intestine and potatoes that had been flavored with enough spices to numb the tongue.

Its preparation was half-assed. They didn't even bother to remove the undesirable smells from the intestine. The chef only bothered to suppress the disgusting scent with strong spices, and he completely failed at even that.

The other dishes were the same. They were decorated to look decent, but the flavor entirely depended on strong spices.

There are no narcotics used here, but there are some addictive substances to flavor it that are quite similar.

Sungchul managed to unravel all of the secrets behind the restaurant in just two bites. This wasn't something he would dare call food. It lacked any sort of dedication or consideration for those eating it. It was just a dish made to be sold in large quantities for profit. Despite all this, the restaurant was packed. Whether this was due to the people of Golden City having crude tastes or the provocative dish serving its purpose, it was clear that the restaurant was thriving.

"Is the food not to your tastes? The dish of the greatest restaurant of Golden City?"

Basil asked after devouring his food gluttonously when he noticed that Sungchul had left his plate largely untouched. Sungchul nodded, excused himself quietly, then rose from his seat.

"Where are you going?"

"To get a bit of air."

Sungchul followed the street around the restaurant to peek into the kitchen. He witnessed a traumatic scene within. Sungchul's eyes grew wide in shock.

"Now now! We must quickly make the fodder for humans!"

"Just scoop out a bit of the poop inside the pig intestines and wash it once or twice! The tastes of the people of this city have already adjusted to the taste of pig shit!"

It was the Homunculi that were handling the food. They were pretending to be chefs, going as far as donning chef hats, and were carrying out the directions of another Homunculus who was giving orders and preparing the meal. The actual chef of the restaurant was handed the food prepared by these Homunculi and created the dishes by caking it entirely with enough spices to paralyze the tastebuds before putting it up for the customers.

"They are finding flavor in food soaked in pig shit water! Filthy humans!"

One of the Homunculi shouted as he soaked vegetables in the water used to wash off the intestines. The other Homunculus bothered to wipe down the containers piled up to the side, but Sungchul's angry expression didn't relax.

"Mmmm…"

He had only wasted his appetite.

I should have just made the food myself to eat.

Sungchul firmly decided to bid Basil farewell and returned to the restaurant, but a group of Mages wearing familiar clothing stood in front of the restaurant's entrance. Their uniforms were dyed in blue. They were the Mages of the School of Cryomancy.

"Iya. It's been so long since we ate here."

"My guts are going wild. Let's enjoy a proper meal."

The Cryomancers were looking quite excited. They were licking their lips as they entered the restaurant and smiled as the scent of spices within the restaurant entered their nose. The one who looked the oldest among them spoke with the manager.

Sungchul took a step back and watched them converse.

"We are ten here. Do you have room?"

The manager paled at the question.

"U…um. As you can see, it is a full house."

The Cryomancer looked displeased as he glared at the manager, and looked about the restaurant. The man finally smirked and looked back towards the manager.

"Look, there is room over there."

His finger pointed towards a corner of the restaurant where a group of students was eating the cheapest meal with gluttonous vigor. It was the School of Alchemy.

"But, dear customer, those customers have not finished their meals yet…"

"I'll talk to them myself, so just prepare the food. Bring out the most expensive meal with the most expensive booze. The money is here."

The man smirked as he handed a shiny gold coin to the manager. Sungchul's eyes flashed with a strange light as he saw the gold coin.

It is the unmarked gold coin.

It looked as though Robert had begun circulating the gold coins he had received from Sungchul to his subordinates already. This meant that the battle between the ones that killed Christian and the Followers of Calamity was going to begin in earnest. Sungchul had planned on taking a step back and quietly watching the two fight, and when the opportune moment arrived...

As Sungchul was drawing out plans for the future in his mind, a crowd of students looking quite upset headed towards his direction. It was the Professor of Alchemy and his students that had been eating excitedly just before they lost their spot.

"Those sons of bitches...Not even dogs are bothered during a meal."

"I want to get out of the School of Alchemy."

Sungchul looked over at Basil and his students, who had to leave their spot with slumped shoulders at the cost of chump change, and opened his mouth as though he was waiting for them.

"Thank you for the meal."

The food was atrocious, but more than that, he had managed to get meaningful information. He could always eat some more food at the dorms, but information wasn't so easy to come by.

Sungchul returned to the dorms with a light heart, when he felt an unusual aura seeping from the dormitory.

A sound seal?!

The seal often used by Assassins had been cast over the entirety of the dormitory.

-

At the same time, a dark shadow was drawing over Altugius as well.

The vigilance seal over the House of Recollections has been severed?! Is Sarasa in danger?

Altugius hurriedly dragged his aged body from his seat and pulled out the staff from his Soul Storage. When he swung his staff, the Magic formation of the lift carved on the exterior of the Observatory lit up as it activated. He rushed to enter the lift.

But before he had managed to even take a few steps, a chilling light flashed before his eyes. Altugius reflexively deflected the light with Glare.

CLUNK.

A sword that had been partially burned away rolled on the floor. Altugius' expression changed. He was suddenly staring at the dark-robed assailant that stood in his path.

"Where are you rushing off to, Altugius?"

He had heard the man's voice behind the feline mask before. Kaz Almeira. The bastard had sought out this place once again.

***

"Get out of my way. I don't have time to deal with you."

Altugius felt his stomach burning a hole in itself from impatience, but Kaz walked leisurely with a chilling aura about him as though he knew of the exact situation.

"I had always been curious about this…How did some pathetic Mage manage to kill the Assassin's Guild's Vice-Captain?"

Altugius tried to move past him in hopes to salvage even a second of time, but the Assassin named Kaz stood in his path once again as to purposefully obstruct him.

"Disappear from my sight if you don't want to die."

"It looks like that Mage was telling the truth. Seeing how you're so impatient with your weakness exposed."

Kaz made a sinister smile as he approached Altugius.

"That Mage? Who are you talking about?"

Altugius' face grew ugly. He already knew the answer.

Leonard. That bastard. Did he actually...?!

The Assassin pulled out two blades and released his chilling aura instead of a proper answer.

SHIIING.

The cold blade flashed in front of Altugius' eyes.

—

It was the moment when he broke through the sound sealing barrier.

CRASH!

A corner of the second floor came crashing down. Sungchul saw wooden planks flying about and realized that a battle was taking place within the House of Recollections.

Who's fighting whom?

Through the newly created hole on the floor, he witnessed a blonde girl in robes escaping while deploying Magic formations. It was Sarasa.

The man chasing her from behind was wearing a red uniform.

Isn't that Leonard?

He was laughing maniacally as he shot Glare towards Sarasa without restraint.

"Eeehehehe! Die! Die!!"

They disappeared to the far side of the hole, and another blast of sound struck the ear drums.

"..."

Sungchul broke through the second floor and saw them. Sarasa and Leonard were both staring hatefully at each other as they continued their fight. The decorum of battle had yet to break down, and also, it wouldn't be too late to intervene later. Sungchul erased his presence and disappeared into the darkness.

"Why are you attacking me?"

Sarasa spat out a breath of cold air as she asked her question. Leonard answered with a smiling face.

"I don't have any personal feelings towards you one way or the other. What could I want from a corpse like yourself?"

Sungchul thought on that reply. There had to be a reason for Leonard's sudden action. He always looked to be mentally on edge, but he was no fool. At the very least, he should have been aware that a vigilance seal was protecting Sarasa's residence, and that disturbing her would cause the terrifying Altugius to charge over right away. There had to be a reason for which he still initiated this situation.

Sungchul discovered the reason from Leonard's appearance. His face had a bluish tint like that of a zombie. Also, his clothes had been torn away at the shoulder, revealing bumpy holes along his backside. Sungchul knew what this meant.

Someone planted some venomous bugs inside his body. It looks like the handiwork of the Grimada Family of the Four Families of the Assassin's Guild, but why is he also missing an ear?

The insect eggs embedded into the body. The torn-off ear. Sungchul immediately came to a simple conclusion that combined both of these facts.

The Assassin's Guild has involved itself.

There was no way to determine the reason for their involvement, nor should one ever try to find out. They were a group that would do anything for proper compensation, and they would kill anyone for any number of reasons.

"I'm not the bad guy here. It's your gramps that's the villain. If that old bag had just taught me the Secret of Cosmomancy, it wouldn't have had to come to this."

Leonard Sanctum was letting out flames from his staff for intimidation. On the other hand, Sarasa stood as still as ice, as cold as the freezing air that she surrounded herself with, while glaring back at him with a chilling stare. But she was unable to bring the full extent of her might to bear.

It was due to a small scratch left on her face. Leonard had aimed for her face during his ambush and disrupted a portion of the Preservation Magic put on her body.

Such a small wound would appear harmless, but it was actually a fatal strike against Sarasa since utilizing a large amount of mana while the Preservation Magic was in disarray would lead to an extremely rapid decay of her face. It was a cheap and cowardly trick fitting of Leonard.

"…"

Sarasa, who didn't want to lose her face, could only remain defensive.

If I can drag this one, it'll be my victory.

"Kyuing…"

The Sky Squirrel in Sarasa's pocket was suffering from the frosty air surrounding her. She whispered in a small voice.

"Please hold on a bit longer…"

She glared at Leonard who was mocking her and suddenly gathered her Magic Power.

"Ice Wall!"

A wall of ice unfolded between Leonard and Sarasa. Sarasa attempted to quickly retreat at that moment, but Leonard shattered it with a blast of Magic Power as soon as the wall was erected as though he had been anticipating it.

"Where are you off to?! Let's play some more! Meat puppet!"

Sarasa still wasn't exerting all of her strength, but she expertly fended off Leonard's attacks. However, her skin was losing its vigor and began wrinkling as the battle went on. A small bit of respite came after a lengthy exchange of blows and neither were seriously hurt, but Sarasa was clearly exhausted.

"Whew…"

However, Sarasa did not lose her fighting spirit. She had someone to trust.

If I hold on a bit longer, Grampa will come.

It was at that moment Leonard opened his mouth.

"Are you perhaps thinking it'll be okay if you buy some time?"

He struck the heart of the matter.

"…"

Sarasa's eyes that contained a glowing blue light glared at Leonard. He smirked before spilling his spiel.

"Stupid. No matter how long you wait, Altugius isn't coming."

Her eyes shook violently upon hearing this.

"What are you talking about?"

"Someone real scary is planning on getting in his way. There is also a sound-sealing barrier cast outside. No one will come to help you nor save you."

Leonard, who could wield two Magic markings, held a ball of light in one hand and a ball of fire in the other. He was now prepared to finish her off.

"Why do you think I assaulted you? Wouldn't I have come at you before otherwise? Now that things have gotten this far, I don't plan on showing you any mercy."

"Try me."

Sarasa's eyes radiated a chilling light. Leonard let out a laugh.

"I'll tell you what I'm going to do to you. Listen carefully. I'm going to take you down and make a piece of art while you still hold breath."

"A piece of art?"

"Yep. An awe-inspiring masterpiece that will be enough to sweep that old man off his feet."

Leonard's eyes became dyed in lunacy.

"You're insane."

Sarasa spat back coldly, but it had shaken her. The lunacy in Leonard's eyes held no doubt.

"I'll say this again, but you have no fault in this. If you want to blame anyone, blame your Gramps. The same Gramps that turned me into this!"

Sarasa gathered all the Magic Power available to block the combination of light and fire, but she felt strained. Something unexpected also occurred.

"Kyuing..."

The Sky Squirrel couldn't endure the chill any longer and fainted. Sarasa, who could feel this, lost her concentration and was thrown against the wall. The fight had ended.

"Ehehehe!"

Leonard walked toward Sarasa.

"Should I call this the silver lining? I really thought the world was ending when that fucker beat me, put eggs in my body, and cut off my ear. Who could have thought that it was a shortcut to such sweet revenge?"

Leonard had a greater hatred for Altugius' relative than for the Assassin who had cut off his ear. It was due to the grudge from what he believed to be Altugius' betrayal, added by the rationale that none of this would have occurred if Altugius hadn't cast him out.

"Don't fret. Once I kill the lot of you, I'll soon follow."

"What?"

Sarasa asked with a pained expression.

"There is no way that guy will let me off once he figures out that you guys have nothing to do with the Enemy of the World. Well, maybe it's better this way. I can haunt you guys after death."

Leonard pulled out a single blade in his possession.

"Now, what kind of masterpiece shall I make!"

As Leonard's blade flashed, a man revealed himself from the shadows.

"…"

Leonard felt the sudden presence and turned around. His eyes, which were overflowing with lunacy, shook violently. It was Sungchul.

"Who is this?"

Leonard abandoned Sarasa and headed to Sungchul like a predator who had found a tastier prey.

"I was meaning to find you for some fun."

"Just answer my question." Sungchul suddenly spoke.

"What?"

"You said that the Assassin was looking for the Enemy of the World. Is this correct?"

Leonard laughed instead of replying.

"What does it matter to a fucker like..."

As Leonard was about to finish his sentence, Sungchul's crude hand wrapped around his face and plummeted him towards the ground. The floor shattered and Leonard's head was embedded halfway into the floor.

Fear flashed across Leonard's face, but it was already too late for regrets. Sungchul grabbed his head and smashed it onto the floor again.

SMASH! SMASH! SMASH!

It continued repeatedly and soon an indecipherable whimper spilt out of Leonard's mouth.

"S-save me! S...v...! Me!"

Sungchul relaxed the grip on his head. Instead, he grabbed Leonard's body and stomped on the places that the venomous bugs had planted their eggs in with his military boots.

POP! POP!

The insects embedded into Leonard's body writhed violently as they were squashed by Sungchul's boots. Every time they thrashed, it translated directly into Leonard as pain.

"KWAAAAAAAAAK!"

Leonard twisted his body wildly like a beast struck by lightning. Sarasa held the Sky Squirrel with both hands and watched the scene with concern and surprise.

After a series of torture had ended, Sungchul once again asked his question to Leonard.

"Answer me, Mage. If you don't remember my question, I'll gladly remind you."

Leonard choked on some air before spitting out his answer as soon as Sungchul's words finished.

"T-That's right! That guy…he was looking for the Enemy of the World! He asked…where the Enemy of the World was…and that I need to find him…that's why…"

He was already halfway gone. Sungchul held Leonard's right arm and pulled it off.

"KWAAAAA!"

The presence of Magic is known to be varied among people, but it is commonly gathered in the right hand. So those without the ability to use their right hands were also unable to use Magic.

Sungchul tossed Leonard, who had become an invalid, to the side and approached Sarasa.

"Are you injured?"

"No injuries, but…who are you?"

Sarasa's eyes sparkled.

"…I am a passing Freshman."

At that moment, he could hear a familiar shout.

"Sarasa! Sarasa! Are you here?"

It was Altugius's voice. It was ragged and out of breath, but the vigor behind it was unchanged. Sungchul noticed a dark fog following behind him.

Is that the Assassin?

Sungchul extended a hand toward Sarasa.

"Go and tell your Grandfather of your state."

Sarasa nodded and grabbed his hand. It was rough and battered but felt dependable. Holding Sungchul's hand, she righted herself before approaching the dormitory window and waved to her Grandfather.

"Grampa! Here! Over here! I'm fine!"

Altugius, who had been wandering the yard, heard her voice and raised his head. After confirming her safety, a small tear formed in his eyes. However, it was only a brief moment before he poured out a fearsome aura as he turned around.

"Now, shall we start this for real?"

The dark fog following Altugius dissipated as soon as the assailant heard those words.

"Mmm. That useless bastard. Looks like he failed."

Kaz who had been bothering Altugius as a fog returned to his human form and retreated a step. He looked as though he had lost interest and looked towards Sarasa.

Mm?

He noticed a certain man. Kaz combed through his memories to recall that the man had been at the School of Cosmomancy building. He was the most worthless of the three, but he could detect something strange about the man that he couldn't quite put his finger on. The feeling didn't last long as a powerful Glare was fired by Altugius, aiming to take his life.

Kaz returned to his fog form before leisurely leaving the scene. Once Altugius confirmed that his enemy had left, he ran over to Sarasa's side. An emotional reunion soon followed.

Sungchul took a step back and watched their reunion with indifferent eyes.

"Leonard Sanctum. How dare you do such a thing?"

Altugius, who heard the whole story, looked over at Leonard who was half dead with eyes full of pity.

"When I first saw you, I thought of you as a rough gemstone. You had outstanding talent and potential, and I figured you were someone who was good enough to take up my mantle within Airfruit."

Realizing that his former student's death was not far, Altugius unhesitatingly poured out his heart. Leonard, who had been slumped over letting out an incoherent whimper, trembled weakly.

"But, you couldn't hold yourself back and committed too many sins. God has given you talent, but he has also given you a container unworthy of such talent. Leonard Sanctum. This is all I have to say to you."

Could he have truly understood the meaning behind Altugius' words?

Leonard was hunched over like a shrimp and let out an indecipherable scream. Something was crawling out of his back. It was a stinkbug with a pattern sparkling like a jewel. Sungchul didn't hesitate in walking over Leonard's corpse and stomped on the stinkbug.

"Did you...save my Granddaughter?"

Altugius spoke to Sungchul with a shaking voice. Sungchul nodded.

"But...how could you...he should have been an opponent that you couldn't win against."

"That's not important. What I want is one thing only: the Secret of Cosmomancy."

Altugius could see it once again. The eyes of Sungchul were firm and determined, unclouded by doubt.

Just who could this man be?

It was something he could never know even if dozens of years passed. The only thing he was sure of was that the man was destined for greatness in the field of Magic. Altugius decided to not refuse that fate any longer and nodded.

"Fine. In return for saving my Granddaughter, who is to say anything about handing over a Secret of a dying school? I'm not sure if it'll be enough to repay you."

The Secret of Cosmomancy was finally in his grasp, but at that moment, Sungchul could hear the noise of countless military boots entering the sound-sealing barrier.

"Kyu Kyu!"

The Sky Squirrel cried out nervously from Sarasa's grasp. Soon, Sungchul's companions could confirm the identity of the unwelcome guest.

"Altugius Xero!"

It was the minions of the Inquisitor of Heresy. Among them a man had unfurled a long scroll and began to shout loudly.

"You have been charged with heresy and/or abetting heresy, along with the crime of murder of a devout follower and thirteen other criminal charges, and thus we have come to apprehend you."

Chapter 19 – The Hunt

Altugius looked towards the Inquisitor of Heresy with disbelief. "No…How did you…"

The Inquisitor of Heresy shoved past the surrounding people and approached Altugius. He spoke to him in a quiet voice that only Altugius could hear.

"This is an act. All for the effort of restoring your school."

The entire situation was like a bolt from the blue, but since the Inquisitor said it, then it must be true. Altugius' eyes shook restlessly, but his shoulders finally gave way and accepted the situation. The Inquisitor's minions bound Altugius and gagged his mouth.

"Grandpa!"

Sarasa ran towards the minions with a sad look on her face, but Altugius only shook his head. His words couldn't be understood at the moment due to the gag around his mouth, but he sent out a warm gaze instead. Finally, he looked towards Sungchul. He tried to signal Sungchul with his eyes, but Sungchul was also trying to convey something. He had a rigid expression as he shook his head, then glared coldly at the Inquisitor.

Does he mean not to trust the Inquisitor of Heresy?

There wasn't much time for thought. The Inquisitor of Heresy, Magnus Maxima, left the building, and his minions roughly dragged Altugius along with them. When the crowd of people departed, the pale girl and the silent man were left behind with the cold corpse.

"W-what should we do? What should we do now?"

Too many things had happened at once. Sarasa could feel all of her strength leaving her body as she collapsed where she stood.

"W-what should I do now?"

She suddenly became alone. There was no one left to look after her. To make matters worse, the Preservation Magic contained in her left cheek had been shattered, causing her skin to start withering slowly. She would soon lose her beauty until she would look no different than any other Liches with their mummified face. Despite all this, the thing that shook her most deeply was the frustration of the unforeseeable future unfolding in front of her.

When sorrow replaced despair, she felt enough pain to make her chest ache, but her eyes could not shed a single tear. The dead cannot cry.

It was at that moment,

"Get up."

The man of mystery spoke firmly, yet with force.

"Stand up and face reality."

It was a simple command, but his words contained some strange persuasiveness. Sarasa found herself righting herself as he had told her to. The preservation in her right arm had been partially destroyed during the battle, causing her right arm to also shrivel up like a corpse.

"How should I face this reality?"

Sungchul pointed towards the House of Recollections at the words of Sarasa, who had turned into a half-corpse at this point.

"When there is nothing you can do, you will have to rely on someone you trust and just wait."

Sungchul let those words linger and walked forward.

"Wait here. Without fear. Time will give you an answer."

Sarasa tightly made a fist and nodded. Sungchul stood before the sound-sealing barrier which was on the verge of collapse and spoke once more.

"Don't forget to feed the Sky Squirrel."

He then stepped past the barrier.

That Assassin. He was looking for me.

He had no intention of returning empty-handed today.

-

Kaz Almeira was a genius among geniuses that the family managed to produce for the first time in decades. He had narrowly escaped the threshold of the Curse of Extinction and had all the qualities of an Assassin, such as brutality, precision, and patience in spades, along with his innate talent, allowing him to master a variety of assassination techniques from the maternal family along with the paternal family.

He also carried the inevitable characteristic of arrogance that all geniuses had, but for him, it was closer to a form of confidence from knowing the exact measure of his abilities than true arrogance. He put himself in extreme situations and enjoyed pulling himself out of any obstacle, and he managed to gain great benefits from this dangerous method. The Almeira family gave warnings regarding his methods while ultimately being unable to stop him.

"Thanks to the commotion you've created in Airfruit, our existence has been made aware to the Inquisitor of Heresy. If I didn't make negotiations, we would have had the Order of Purity, the Enemy of the World, and the Followers of Calamity besetting us on all three sides."

D'Vici sternly scolded his son, but he knew that his words were falling on deaf ears.

"Ah. I don't know, Father. I only heard that the Mage held hands with the Enemy of the World and decided to take a stab at it."

"So, was Altugius someone you could handle?"

"He was plenty powerful. Honestly, I might lose by myself with my current abilities. That guy is a Mage, but moved with the Dexterity of an archer and suppressed me with Magic that was difficult to dodge while sneaking in some powerful spells."

Kaz spoke without any particular joy in his expression or voice. Pict, who had been watching beside them, rose from his seat to leave. He didn't want to look at his more powerful and successful brother. Kaz peeked over at his brother's backside as he spoke again.

"But, Father, I have learned it. I learned what Altugius' secret is."

"Is that so?"

"That person is hiding a weapon called Dimension Magic. It was remarkable. If I hadn't retreated halfway through the fight, I would have been flattened like the Vice-Captain."

"It won't be too late to explain all of this later. For now, go to your dwelling and confine yourself."

"Yes, I understand."

Kaz, who was returning from his scolding, met his youngest brother Pict again. Pict looked as though he was waiting for Kaz. He laughed as soon as he saw Kaz.

"I'm going to go hunt the Followers of Calamity right now."

"Ah? Is that right? With your strength?"

When Kaz mocked him, Pict gave him a frosty glare and left.

"Let's see how long you can mock me for. Ten years. I'll catch up to you in ten years, you bastard."

"Calling your brother a bastard. You bitch. Did I let you have it too easy for too long?"

"You only got the respect you wrought. Anyways, just watch. I'll bring the head of the Enemy of the World."

Pict stuck out his tongue and disappeared into the darkness in a hurry. Kaz looked at such a brother with a smile and shook his head.

"Catch up to me? You'll have to train for at least a thousand years."

He said this, but he knew that his brother was a possessor of great talent. That kid had handled his first torture brilliantly. He unmistakably had the Assassin's characteristic of brutality and apathy towards his victims.

Brat. Once you're a bit older, I'll guide you myself.

Pict was too lacking for Kaz to teach personally, but he planned on going on assassinations together with Pict after his brother accumulated more experience and intuition. Without knowing his brother had such intentions, Pict could only feel bitter towards Kaz.

"A genius, my ass! I'll teach you that true geniuses need time to cultivate."

Pict's mission of the day was to hunt down the Followers of Calamity picked out by the Inquisitor of Heresy. D'vici had told him it was enough to hunt down a single one, but Pict had decided for himself to find three of them and interrogate them all at once. He had failed his first interrogation due to a Covenant that bound the man, but he knew he could succeed this time. He could still vividly feel his blade cutting through his victim's flesh.

"Let's see."

There were Mages wearing robes dyed in blue on the other side of the road. They were insignificant in Pict's eyes. They were weak folks that could be killed with a single slice, but his objective was live capture. He began to stalk the Mages while waiting for his opportunity. His deft movements allowed him to roam from alley to alley while pursuing the Mages diligently and watched with bated breath as the Mages retreated to their individual quarters.

Like beasts who lower their guards within their nests, humans were also the most relaxed within their beds. Christian, the Slave Hunter, had also been captured in his bed. Pict relived the sensation of that day and revealed himself slowly from the darkness. It was at that moment when he discovered a vague figure reflecting in the moonlight standing on the ground beside him.

"...?!"

There was no time to react before a hand gripped his throat. It contained a tremendous amount of strength. When the grip held his throat, he felt a terrifying pain as if his eyes would pop out and his brain would burst.

"Ugh!"

Rather than the cry of a person, it sounded like something from an ugly fowl. The man who held his throat soon spoke.

"Are you guys the ones responsible for killing a Slave Hunter named Christian?"

That person's identity was Sungchul. He relaxed his grip on the young Assassin's throat ever so slightly with indifferent eyes.

"Answer the question."

Instantly, Pict tried to squeeze all the strength in his body to let out a scream to call upon his family that had surrounded the area, but Sungchul's reaction on his throat was faster than the time it took for the voice to spill out from his throat.

"Kwek!"

Pict could feel the voice being squelched within his throat and his vision being dyed with a yellow tint.

Assassins are a tenacious bunch as expected.

Assassins of the Assassin's Guild were taught to tolerate pain from an early age. The result was that half-assed interrogations had no effect at all. Not only that, the greatest virtue of Assassins was to put their mission ahead of their lives. They were actively developing and practicing countless methods of suicide in case any secrets could be leaked. Pict was also thinking up methods of taking his life.

This...looks to be my limit.

He firmly decided to take his life, regardless of the method, at the first opportunity. However, Sunghul would not relinquish such an easy death to the Assassin. He discovered torture tools and some effective medicine on Pict's body. Sungchul tore Pict's clothes and shoved it down his throat before striking his right arm. Pict's arm twisted in a strange direction before being torn away in a mess. The youth thrashed about wildly, but he couldn't let out a scream.

"I have no intention of interrogating you, Assassin."

Sungchul applied Pict's medicine to the open wound before hanging the feline mask to the wall with Pict's arm placed below it; then he wrote a message with the blood flowing from Pict's arm that was cut off.

[If you wish to save the kid, come inside. You must come alone.]

Sungchul forcefully turned Pict's head to have him witness the message.

"You lot sure like to think your level of brutality is something spectacular."

Sungchul dragged Pict in a way so that his stump of an arm, which bled despite the medicine, painted the floor red, and then threw him into a storage room. The bloodstain marked the route from the feline mask to the storage room like a red carpet.

"Today, I'll teach you a little about brutality."

Sungchul leaped onto the roof of a building where he had a clear view of both the mask and the storage room. A different Assassin soon followed in. It was Myra, who dealt in venomous insects. She flinched at the scene of Pict's mask and amputated right arm. They were Assassins trained to tolerate great amounts of physical pain, but in the end, they were still human. They were apathetic towards their victims but warm towards one of their own. She hesitated again at the message written in Pict's blood, but she stepped forward as though she had already prepared her heart.

No! Sister! Don't come in!

Pict flailed about with all his might, but it was all pointless. Myra mentally prepared herself for battle and slowly moved step by step into the storage room. It didn't take long before a dark shadow appeared behind her.

The man had appeared like a ghost. Before she had time to blink, he grabbed the back of her head and lifted her straight up only to smash it down into the ground and grind her face against the rough floor. The feline mask shattered and Myra's bloodied face revealed itself.

"Uwaaaa!"

Sungchul, who had shredded her face across the floor, tied a rope around her neck and lifted her above him. The person's body spun around like some toy. At that moment, all the venomous insects hidden on her body rained down onto the floor. Myra gripped the rope tied around her neck with both her hands and all of her strength, but ultimately succumbed to exhaustion and fell unconscious.

Sungchul had no intention of allowing her a comfortable death either. He slugged her bloodied face to wake her up before hanging her upside down in front of Pict. Sungchul glared at Pict before speaking in a steady voice.

"Are you guys the ones who killed a Slave Hunter named Christian?"

Pict did not answer. Sungchul searched the floor while stomping on the venomous insects until he found the most suitable one. It was the stinkbug that lays eggs in human flesh.

Sungchul grabbed the stinkbug and held it over Myra's body until it laid its eggs. Myra's body resisted weakly, but Sungchul kept his eyes on Pict. Pict realized that the man had no intentions of showing mercy.

At that moment, a miracle occurred. Myra, who looked as though she had lost consciousness, suddenly opened her eyes.

"Pict! I'll be going first."

Myra's bloodied eyes shook violently before they rolled over, revealing only the whites of her eyes. Sungchul confirmed her death indifferently. Pict found renewed confidence at his sister's exemplary death and glared at Sungchul with hate-filled eyes once again.

Try whatever interrogation you want. I'll take it all with the name of the Almeira family at stake!

However, Sungchul gave it no importance. He let Myra's corpse fall to the floor and squatted down to start some kind of procedure. The stench of blood began to flood the room. Sungchul then held the corpse and walked out of the storage room. His two hands held Myra's corpse that hadn't even cooled yet and pressed on it tightly. Soon, something unbelievable occurred.

"Aaaaa."

The corpse began to cry out. It was something unintelligible, but it had Myra's distinct vocals. Sungchul held the corpse and looked puzzled before muttering to himself.

"It's not working so well since I haven't done it in so long."

He lifted the corpse and began to manipulate it to his whim.

"Aaaaah!!!"

Myra's jaw flew open and let out a terrifying shriek. Much more strongly. Pict, who was watching the scene, knew the monster's intentions.

That bastard...he's calling them. He's calling my family...!

It would be problematic for more victims to come out of this incident.

Pict began to thrash about wildly to draw Sungchul's attention to himself, and when his eyes finally met Sungchul's, he nodded vigorously.

"That's right. I killed that Slave Hunter. We done now? You happy?"

Sungchul only continued to look at him indifferently and shook his head.

"I'm just getting started."

***

On a tall throne there sat a man wearing a golden suit of armor. He looked to be in his early thirties by appearance with his thick blonde hair and faded blue eyes, exuding a powerful spirit. William Quintin Marlboro. People of this world referred to him as the Emperor of the Human Empire.

He received a report that a seemingly insignificant man sought an audience with him who was the leader of the most powerful nation in Other World. Typically, he would've been stopped at the gate, but the man said that he must show some object to the Emperor. The Emperor wasn't pleased with it, but he did feel curious. He commanded the man be brought to his throne.

A middle-aged man with a naive look about him was brought 100 paces before the throne and made to kneel. The Royal guards received some item from the man and presented it cordially to the Emperor. William flicked his fingers and manipulated the wrapped object into the air from the soldiers who had brought the item and had it float to him. The item was wrapped in a silk cloth.

When he unraveled the cloth, he found that it contained a single sword made of ivory.

"Mmm."

A low rumble escaped from the Emperor's mouth. The scene twenty-five years ago, when he had completed the Summoning Palace and entered Golden City, appeared before his eyes.

"Allow him within 50 paces."

The middle-aged man hurriedly stepped forward and bowed down before the line marked bright red. The Emperor finally asked his question.

"Who gave you the sword?"

The middle-aged man readily answered his question.

"The E-Enemy of the World, your Majesty the Emperor."

The middle-aged man spoke his account of the events without reservation. A faint smile formed on William's lips.

You've finally shown yourself, Sungchul.

He rose from his throne and looked at his surroundings.

"Which of our military units are closest to Golden City?"

An armored man answered from a distance with a bow.

"It is the 2nd Armada lead by our retainer, Dimitri Medioff."

"Mmm, the 2nd Armada."

The Emperor stroked his beard as he fell into thought, then gestured grandly with his arm before making his command.

"Send the 2nd Armada to Golden City. Their objective is the Destroyer, Sungchul Kim. Eliminate him at all costs."

When the Emperor's words were spoken, the military commanders quickly began to move. Mages wearing white uniforms used the stone of telepathy to make communications, and a Platoon of Dragon Knights rode their Wyverns into formation towards the north. As the entire Empire stirred awake, the Emperor gazed towards the distant north with his cloudy blue eyes in deep thought.

It's been eight years already.

Eight years ago. The most influential existences within the continent were gathered to halt the upcoming Calamity. They were named the Thirteen Champions of the Continent. Currently, the title exists only as a type of formality, but in the past, the title was used to represent the group of people who were the only hope the denizens of Other World had of salvation from Calamities. Unexpectedly, they betrayed that grand expectation in a spectacular way. Only a single voice among them shouted in rebellion, but no one was listening. That man soon took on the moniker of the Enemy of the World.

"Sungchul...why have you returned?"

A question rose in the Emperor's eyes.

—

Within a dark basement, Altugius was tied in the center like a piece of meat ready to be butchered.

THWAK!

A whip with sharp hooks tore away the flesh of his back.

"Uggggh!"

Altugius felt his sight turn yellow as he let out a painful scream, but the torturer had no such mercy. They proceeded to flog him every ten seconds without rest. Altugius' back looked pitifully ragged, caked with dried blood, and torn. His consciousness was hanging by a thread. The Inquisitor of Heresy, Maxima, appeared as he was drawing his final few breaths.

"Bestow the grace of the God of Neutrality upon this man."

The servants wearing crow masks used restoration Magic on Altugius' body. The wounds on his split back became sealed, the pain receded, and the light behind his eyes returned. As some of his consciousness came back to him, he recognized the man standing before him and let out a shout.

"How...How could you do this to me...?!"

The Inquisitor of Heresy held up a hand, and the torturer struck Altugius' abdomen with the hard shaft of the whip. It felt as though it would pierce his gut.

"Kwuk!"

Altugius spat out a glob of dark blood. The aggravating noise of clanging metal chains echoed in the small room. When some semblance of silence returned, the Inquisitor of Heresy spoke softly.

"Xero Altugius. You have bravely fought for the revival of Airfruit until now."

"T-then why do this to me...?!"

Altugius gathered a series of shallow breaths to speak. The Inquisitor raised his hand in response, making the people within the torture room rush out like the tide. When they were left alone in the eerie torture chamber, the Inquisitor put his hands behind his back and began to circle Altugius slowly.

"The situation has become much worse, Altugius. Did you know that the Enemy of the World has been spotted here?"

"The E-Enemy of the W-World...?!"

"Whenever the Enemy of the World appears, the most powerful within the continent will be advised to send their forces. It means that the Crusaders of the New World will be formed. I have an obligation to finish things here before those people arrive. In other words, there is now a need to pick up the pace."

"What does that have to do with me? Why do I have to be in this state?"

Altugius shook his chained arms. On the other end, the Inquisitor didn't show even the smallest of movements; like an object in a painting. A small voice muttering beneath his mask rang out.

"It is quite unfortunate, but I have decided to put you up for execution. I have concluded that it is the only way to clean up the various problems plaguing Airfruit."

"How is that the only solution?"

Maxima replied Altugius' question with an odd laughter.

"Kekekek..."

It was a laughter that sounded like the final gasping breath of a patient dying from a virulent disease. Altugius opened his eyes wide and looked towards the Inquisitor. Finally, he spoke.

"Soon the teaching staff under Robert Danton shall all be killed by hands of the Assassin's Guild. That will leave you as the final pillar upholding Airfruit. What will happen then when I pluck out that final pillar?"

It was then when Altugius finally grasped the true intentions of the Inquisitor.

"You mean to get rid of Airfruit?"

The Inquisitor nodded.

"Twenty years ago, I was found to be mediocre by Airfruit and left the school of my own volition. I spent many sleepless nights forced to watch a bastard son of a mistress take my rightful place and wield the powers of my birthright."

"For such a petty reason…?!"

The Inquisitor's body squirmed in an odd way at Altugius' rebuke. He turned away from Altugius with strange movements akin to a wind-up doll, then slowly took off his crow mask. Altugius let out a brief scream at the sight. Beneath the mask, there was a mummified face of a corpse.

He was not dead. Hot blood flowed within his veins, pumped by a still-beating heart. It was intense tenacity through a nightmarish hell that had turned his face into what it was. The Inquisitor put on his mask again after revealing his true face, then spoke poetically.

"My motivation may seem petty to you, but to me, it might be something important enough to stake my destiny on. Conversely, your haughty motivation might look as petty to me."

The Inquisitor clapped, signaling the torturers and guards to enter the torture room once again. He moved past them and spoke in a low voice.

"The execution will proceed tomorrow at noon."

Altugius did not speak again. He thought of Sarasa, who would be waiting for him alone.

No...I can't die like this!

However, the chains that bound him were all too solid. The torturers held their whips.

—

A flashing blade cut through the throat of a Mage in the cover of darkness. The Mage took a mortal wound before he could even open his eyes and scream. D'vici put a pillow on the face of the wounded Mage to confirm his kill. The Mage gripped the hand that held down the pillow and thrashed about wildly before it lost its strength and slid away.

This was the fifth one. D'vici had managed to wipe out the teaching staff of the School of Pyromancy in a single day. A similar series of events would be happening over in the next room. His wife from the Grimada family, Illia Almeria, released venomous scorpions to kill the head disciples of the School of Pyromancy. Dozens of people died in their sleep, completely clueless to the cause.

The couple, who had now finished their silent slaughter, met up at the entrance to the School of Pyromancy. Two headless corpses were growing cold at the entrance. D'vici looked toward the dark sky and spoke.

"All done?"

"Yes. All done. Not a single one left."

Illia pushed back a scorpion trying to escape her sleeve and made a sinister smile. D'vici wiped off a bloodied sword and began to think.

Just the School of Cryomancy is left. Pict and Myra. I hope they're doing well.

D'vici thought this as he looked over to his wife and spoke softly.

"Anyways, I'm not sure if Myra's side is going well."

"Should I go and find out?"

At Illia's question, D'vici nodded. He was a traditional Assassin with a serious and cautious personality. At the very least, he liked to avoid any risks and succeeded his tasks without any losses, but due to this they were unexpectedly rated abysmally by his peers, and so his family was ranked the lowest among the four great Assassin families. Despite this, he never regretted his decisions about his methods. His family was far more important than some ranking. Illia, who knew this about her husband, pulled out a small bottle and opened it. There was a blue-winged Moth inside that crawled out and wiggled its antennas in the night sky, before flying off somewhere.

The Moth was called the Lovebird Moth, and it was one of the few bugs that Illia had with no venomous or dangerous properties. However, it had a very unique and useful ability. The male of the Lovebird Moth is known to seek out its consort across any distance. The Lovebird Moth released by Illia expectedly flew off rapidly in search of a companion. Finally, it found its mate inside a dark warehouse. However, its mate was unfortunately squashed into an unrecognizable shape. The Moth raised itself and began to fly back out into the night sky.

"..."

A figure in the darkness watched the direction in which the Moth flew off to. It was Sungchul. Behind him were two corpses hanging side by side. These were the corpses of Myra and Pict.

Sungchul, who looked to be frozen for a moment, left behind the two corpses and made a beeline towards the direction of the Moth. The Lovebird Moth split the night sky as it made its way to its owner, then landed on her hand. Illia's face froze.

"Honey. There is a problem."

D'vici was not shaken.

"You're sure?"

"Yes. It lost its mate."

D'vici let out a shallow sigh and disappeared into the darkness.

"Let's fall back."

His body slowly turned into fog and melted into the night. Illia melded into that fog to hide herself. However, Illia soon discovered hostility in the air lurking nearby. She had discovered hostile rumblings in her webs cast about in the surroundings and spoke quietly.

"Honey. It's an enemy."

"Is it him?"

"Most likely."

D'vici instantly calculated the amount of power he possessed, along with any other advantages that he might have.

Enemy of the World. His strength is estimated at 600. Dexterity and Vitality are known to be about 500. His combat strategy is just one: oppressively crush with sheer stats. It is the most simple, but effective strategy.

After a quick deliberation, he knew that he currently had no chance of winning. He might be able to delay and escape if his strongest son, Kaz, was here, but at this rate, he would die a pointless death.

"Honey."

D'vici hid his expression. Illia caught onto his intent and nodded before looking at her husband with tearful eyes.

"I'll buy us some time. I should be able to delay him for at least three minutes."

" … "

"At the very least, you must escape to find Kaz and leave this place. Tell the client that the bastard is here."

"I understand."

Illia kissed his cheeks a final time before disappearing into the night. This was the last farewell between the Assassin lovers.

D'vici, who was now alone, regained his original expression and waited for his oppressive enemy to arrive. Soon, a man in worn-out clothing waded out of the darkness.

He looks different. I had heard he was a giant over two meters tall.

The man who appeared in the darkness spoke.

"Are you the head of the Assassins?"

"That's right. I am D'vici Almeira, the 32nd Head of the Almeira family."

D'vici replied honorably, reaffirming his plans once again.

'Three minutes. I have to hold firm with the belief that this is my final stand.'

However, before even three seconds had passed, D'vici knew that he was outmatched by a monster much stronger than he had ever realized. He died instantly as his skull shattered with a single blow to the head.

Sungchul watched the figure of the woman fleeing in the distance after his kill, but he didn't pursue right away. He patiently stalked his prey until it guided him to its nest, but the prey appeared to have caught onto his plans. She led him to an odd location then turned around.

"Kill me too, Enemy of the World."

Illia's eyes swirling with tears and vengeance glared at him as she let loose all of her venomous insects in her possession. There were so many that it looked as though a black smoke was spewing from her body.

Sungchul pulled out his beloved Fal Garaz. Illia's expression froze.

"You might be able to kill us tonight, but our family will live on!"

Sungchul swung Fal Garaz. Illia's form was swept away with her venomous insects. Sungchul watched the mixture of human and insect viscera dripping around his feet with indifference then stared off into the night sky.

Was she talking about that guy from before?

He already knew the face of the last surviving member of their clan, as well as the client who had hired them. That was enough. That day, the entirety of the Almeira family that had spread fear through the continent had been killed, except the eldest son.

In that same moment, those wearing crow masks were raising a pyre at the entrance of Airfruit Academy.

Chapter 20 – Primordial Light

At the break of dawn, Airfruit became a place of horrors. The teaching staff of Pyromancy that had been leading the corrupted school had been slaughtered, and their promising students had all met their deaths. Those who were still around gathered in disparate groups and wandered the campus, seeking the assassins with tensed nerves and torches in hand, while the rest lined up the corpses and mourned the dead. Sungchul arrived here at this time.

A group of students holding torches stood in his path. It was because of his unusual appearance.

"Who are you? Identify yourself!"

A man shouted bravely. Five staves were trained in Sungchul's direction. Sungchul glared at them and spoke curtly.

"I am a student here."

At this point, one of the students recognized him.

"Wait, this man. I've seen him before. Put away the staves."

It was a student wearing a robe dyed in blue. He asked for discretion from his fellow students, then approached Sungchul to speak to him discreetly.

"You are the fellow from the School of Alchemy, right? I greet you. I am a junior at the School of Cryomancy named Sidone. It is truly a blessing for you to have survived this fearful night."

It was apparent that the man wished to become an acquaintance of Sungchul. When Sungchul remained silent, he offered to lead the way to Professor Danton.

"Did he also survive?"

Sungchul didn't know of all the casualties yet. He knew that the Almeira family had been behind the attack on the school, but he had no way to know where their blades had been directed. Sidone briefly spoke of the known casualties so far.

"For now, it isn't an exaggeration to say that the School of Pyromancy has been completely obliterated. The teaching staff has been wiped out. There are plenty of rumours, but I think that the Assassin's guild might be behind this attack."

The School of Cryomancy had suffered almost no casualties according to the man's report. It would most likely be like this because Sungchul intervened before the Almeira family could fully commit themselves to the assault on the school. He decided to wait until later to consider this a blessing or a curse. Meanwhile, he took up Sidone's offer to be guided toward the School of Cryomancy, which was believed to be the most secure building on campus.

"You were quite fortunate to be able to survive this horrid night unscathed."

Robert greeted Sungchul warmly, and he nodded in response. Sungchul then spoke of everything he had seen at the entrance.

"It looks as though the Order of Purity will burn Professor Altugius on the pyre."

But for some reason, Robert looked unfazed at the fate of his fellow professor.

"Whether that stubborn old fool dies or not is none of our concern. The most important news is that the Assassin's Guild has attacked us. In other words, the Inquisitor of Heresy has drawn his blade."

He didn't hide his anger. His eyes burned with vigor and a twisted smile formed on his lips.

"If the Inquisitor wants to play like that, we also have our ways."

"Our ways?"

Robert let out a carefree laughter and nodded his head.

"Our way to retaliate, that is."

All Robert had was a handful of Mages beneath him. Furthermore, the majority of the fighting force other than Robert and the teaching staff were students. Sungchul judged them to at most being able to clean up the mob soldiers of the Order of Purity.

"Follow me, my friend protected by the Ancient Kingdom. I will reveal to you our secret weapon."

Robert brought Sungchul and a small number of guards down to a basement. He swung his staff at a wall of the basement where musty air flowed, and then the aged bricks began shifting to reveal a secret passageway. Sungchul recognized that the passageway looked relatively new compared to the rest of the architecture.

"Only a few know the truth that our former Headmaster the Grand Magnus was a Follower of Calamity."

Robert watched a few gutter rats become spooked and scurry away before he spoke again.

"However, most people with a similar status to me should have suspected it. It was challenging to find any Mage who dissented against the Great Mage Balzark when he was recruiting for the Followers of Calamity."

"Is that so?"

"It was even worse among the higher-ranked Mages since they had already hit a plateau. They needed some way to break through their limitations, something to stimulate their growth. Like..."

At that point, they had reached the end of the tunnel where an enormous golem stood in their path. As Danton shook his staff, the golem moved to the side and the end of the tunnel revealed itself to Sungchul.

Unlike the passage covered in darkness, they approached an area filled with light. They could see nothing but the vague mass of light in the distance, and as soon as Sungchul stepped into this area, he could see his surroundings right away. They were inside a massive cave with a spherical structure that stood in the center.

"Like this!"

Robert said with pride in his voice, and Sungchul's eyes lit up.

It's a Dimensional Door.

Large forces such as the Human Empire and the Ancient Kingdom had set up massive Dimensional Doors in several places to move their large military forces. It wasn't immediately clear why a

Dimensional Door was needed at a Magic academy, but Robert quickly provided an explanation.

"This Dimensional Door is connected to the Demon Realm."

"Ho?"

"The former Headmaster had completed most of it, but it lacked a few critical components. With the funds that you provided, I was finally able to complete the Dimensional Door."

Robert spoke in an excited voice. Sungchul looked back toward the Dimensional Door and then at Robert with a cold gaze.

"What's the grand plan?"

Robert let out another carefree laugh and pointed towards the Dimensional Door.

"At high noon today, Altugius will be executed according to the notice put out by the Inquisitor of Heresy. Much of the Inquisitor's force will be gathered there as well. That is when I will utilize the Dimensional Gate."

Robert flicked his finger which caused a flower of ice to form in the air and then shatter.

"After that, they'll become like this. All due to the unexpected visit from the forces of the Devil in Golden City."

Robert's heroic laughter echoed within the large cave while Sungchul only gazed at the spectacle quietly.

"This Dimensional Gate. How do you activate it?"

—

The underground prison of the Inquisitor of Heresy was not a place just anyone could enter. They had to satisfy one of two requirements: they had to be sentenced by the Inquisitor of Heresy, or they had to provide enough bribes to satisfy the wardens. Sungchul entered the dimly-lit underground prison through the latter method.

"Be quick. You have until the Inquisitor finishes his midnight prayer."

The warden with the crow mask tactfully retreated. Sungchul flung open the unlocked door and stepped into the torture chamber. Within the center of the chamber, there was an unconscious man whose body showed apparent signs of torture while being held in chains.

"..."

Sungchul approached him. Altugius regained a bit of consciousness and put in some effort to open his swollen eyes. His eyes, peering through the thin gap his eyelids created, were filled with fear. His stubborn spirit had been drained out of him during the span of the torture. Sungchul, who had seen his powerful personality when the man had fought against Kaz, and when he had chased away Leonard, felt a bit of pity towards his current transformation.

"It is your disciple."

Sungchul revealed his identity before Altugius could get a good look at him. Altugius' body shook ever so slightly.

"S-Sungchul Kim? Are you actually here?"

When Sungchul nodded, Altugius desperately rushed to speak.

"W-water. I need some water..."

Sungchul looked around his surroundings. There was some water in a few barrels, but it was tainted with blood and filth. Sungchul opened his Soul Storage to pull out a transparent bottle that blended with the surroundings and brought it to Altugius' lips.

When a single drop of liquid from the container touched his tongue, Altugius' eyes flew open. A miraculously refreshing sensation traveled from the tip of his tongue to the rest of his body. Sungchul drained the contents of the bottle completely into his mouth.

"What a remarkable flavor of water. T-Thank you! I feel as though my vigor is returning!"

Altugius would never know the truth even in his dreams. What Sungchul had given him was the sap of the World Tree grown in the land of the Fairies.

"Okay then. Why have you come here?"

After regaining his senses Altugius looked towards Sungchul and asked in a low voice, so Sungchul let known his intentions.

"I came here to learn the Secret of Cosmomancy."

A sigh escaped Altugius' mouth.

"What a waste. I don't have it with me at the moment."

"Then?"

"The Secret lies in the place that I've spent my life guarding. The Observatory of the School of Cosmomancy."

"The Observatory of the School of Cosmomancy?"

"If I weren't a prisoner, I would follow your side to deliver you the Secret…but as of now, it is not so easy."

"I shall break you out then."

Altugius simply shook his head weakly.

"I would keep my life if I escaped, but I will not be able to deliver you the Secret of Cosmomancy. It takes a considerable amount of time to inherit the Secret of Cosmomancy, and Maxima Magnus will not stand by once he hears of my escape."

"You are quite honest."

Other Mages would have begged and pleaded for freedom, regardless of their actual intentions to keep any promises made. It was the modus operandi of Mages which Sungchul had ceaselessly dealt with. Following what Sungchul said, Altugius obtusely asked as he looked wide-eyed.

"Why bother lying about something soon to be discovered anyway?"

A faint smile formed on Sungchul's lips.

"I only said so because there never seems to be an end of people willing to make those short-lived lies."

Altugius, too, broke into a smile, but it was soon replaced with an expression of deep concern.

"Can I ask a single favor from you?"

"Is it about your Granddaughter?"

"That's correct. Please take care of Sarasa for me. I don't mean forever, but her father lives along the frontier borders of the Demon Realm. Far north."

"Sarasa's father?"

"He should be active as a mercenary Mage at the 'Storm Battlefront' under the alias 'Deckard.' He's a man-child, constantly busying himself in the harsh Demon Realm trying to save the world. Please lead Sarasa to that man. It won't be the Secret of Cosmomancy, but he shall provide an adequate reward in return."

"..."

Sungchul lowered his head as though in thought.

"Time's up. It is about time for the midnight prayer to end."

The annoyed voice of the warden rang out in the distance. Sungchul raised his head once again, then looked towards Altugius. It was a gaze that was like the calm sky of a starry night.

"I am sorry, but I will have to learn the Secret of Cosmomancy."

Altugius' face was filled with horror.

"But at this moment...!"

"I will be back. At a more appropriate time."

Leaving behind these ambiguous words, Sungchul left the dimly lit torture chamber. Altugius looked towards Sungchul's back with a complicated gaze mixed with terror and anticipation.

Just...who is that man?

He could already figure out that the man was not ordinary, but his limited knowledge could not even guess at what his identity might be. The individual named Sungchul Kim was such a man.

—

Sarasa was looking at her face in the mirror. One-half retained the beauty of her life, while the other had the grotesque form of a mummified corpse. However, Sarasa did not despair or falter. She calmly asked the man who was facing away from her.

"You want me to begin packing?"

Sungchul nodded.

"By noon today, you and your grandfather will be escaping this place together."

"Will that be possible with your strength? I will do all I can to help," replied Sarasa.

The eye on the decayed half revealed a sharp gaze. However, Sungchul shook his head.

"You would only be a burden."

"Do you really think of me as being so weak?"

Sarasa let out a laugh.

At this point, he quietly took out his beloved weapon. Fal Garaz, the most powerful hammer said to be forged by the Dwarven gods caused the very air surrounding it to destabilize and tremble in its sheer presence.

Sarasa who saw the weapon was filled with terror.

"Is that...Fal...Garaz?"

There was a single incident that had shaken Other World before her death. It was the earth-shattering news that a devilish man known as the Enemy of the World had destroyed the temple of the Dwarves and had stolen their holy weapon. She had only heard of the name then and learned of its origins and appearance by researching it within the library. The holy weapon that she had seen only through books had graced her with its appearance. The awe and danger she felt now were incomparable to what could be felt through illustrations.

The man holding the weapon finally opened his mouth to speak.

"I am Sungchul Kim."

It was neither an alias, nor just a man with the same name. He was literally the former "10th Champion of the Continent." The man who is now better known as the "Enemy of the World."

"I...I can't believe it...Why would...that Sungchul come to us...?"

"I have sworn by my name to rescue you and your grandfather."

Sarasa gripped her fists tight. What was there to say if none other than the most dangerous man in the world had promised to protect you?

"Kyu Kyu!"

As though it understood Sarasa's torrent of emotions, the Sky Squirrel within her grasp began to bother her for kibbles. Sarasa stole a peek at her sleeves out of the corner of her eyes and petted the Sky Squirrel's head.

***

Kaz looked over the corpses of his family members in disbelief. Everything had happened in a single night. His brother, sister, and parents had all met their untimely demise without discretion.

"Are these the corpses of your family members?"

A man wearing a shiny golden helmet asked matter-of-factly. The ones that gathered the bodies were the Dragon Knights of the Human Empire that had been dispatched to Golden City last night. They swiftly dispersed within the entirety of Golden City to seek out any traces of the most dangerous man, which led them to find the unsightly form of the four corpses.

"They are my family's remains."

Kaz gritted his teeth as he spoke, then looked around his surroundings before shouting.

"Where is this Enemy of the World? Where did that bastard go?"

"The forward team is tracking the Enemy of the World. You don't have to concern yourself with that. The air fleet led by Retainer Medioff will arrive here soon. When the military might of the air fleet is on full display, there will be nowhere for even the Enemy of the World to escape to."

"…"

Kaz nibbled on his nails as he held his silence. He felt as though his anger would explode out of his chest, but the cold calculations of an assassin led him to believe in the Dragon Knight's words.

"On a subject besides the Enemy of the World, the Inquisitor of Heresy from the Order of Purity sent notice that a Purification will occur today at the Airfruit Magic Academy. If there is any indication that the Enemy of the World has joined hands with the Heretics of Airfruit, it may be that he'll show his face at that location."

The Knight fixed his helmet then hopped onto the large Wyvern waiting for him.

"Kweeeeh!!"

The Wyvern rose up into the sky with an ear-splitting cry as it flapped its massive wings. The air current formed by its wings caused Kaz's hair and clothes to thrash about wildly.

"..."

Kaz, who stood alone now, gave a silent prayer to his family's remains, then left the scene.

Sungchul Kim. You will die by my hands.

His eyes flashed with killing intent denser than ever before.

—

When the sun reached its peak, those that wore shining armour gathered in front of Airfruit Academy. A pyre with wood stacked high sat beside an aged tree decorated with dangling corpses with rotting flesh. The Inquisitor of Heresy, who was still wearing his crow mask, arrived in a Palanquin with a solemn atmosphere about him. A bloodied old man with his hands tied behind him rode on a donkey which followed the carriage.

The executioner pulled the man off the donkey and tied him onto the pyre while cuffs that interfered with Magic activation were strapped on the old man's wrists. A priest in a crow mask appeared in front of the restrained old man on the pyre holding a long scroll, then listed his sins one by one.

"Sinner Altugius Xero, despite his responsibilities as a professor of a Magic Academy and a guardian of knowledge, could not overcome the temptations of corruptive knowledge and had fallen to become a member of the Followers of Calamity. For the countless crimes that he has committed and the greatest crime of murdering his friend and superior, the Grand Magnus..."

Altugius shut his eyes and did not refute a single charge. Trying to reason now was an effort in futility, and shouting and begging would only serve to further humiliate himself. He wanted an honourable death as a student and educator of the hallowed Airfruit Academy. Even though the servant in the crow mask continued listing false crimes while smearing his image, he no longer cared for it. Still, he had but a single regret.

He sought out through the crowd of countless people in the Plaza for a single face through cracked eyes.

Sarasa.

He couldn't find his precious granddaughter, who was the apple of his eye. It could have been that she alone hadn't heard the news from the House of Recollections or the man named Sungchul had taken her away from here.

"...for this, Altugius Xero has been charged for judgment by the Purifying Fire."

The announcement of his execution, which he had ignored for a brief moment, rang out clearly in his ears. Altugius let out a dull sigh before gazing out towards the people staring at him.

They were students wearing robes of various colors, professors of unpopular schools, and faces that he had met once or twice without knowing their names. He discovered anew that their faces were drained of energy with shadows of depressive dread looming over them. It might have been due to the endless years of deterioration wearing down on him or out of the literal fear of imminent doom, but he didn't like it. The school he had protected his whole life was far more honorable, worthy, and proud than any other.

Altugius' mouth, which had been tightly shut during this whole time, opened shortly after his execution had been announced.

"Why are you looking at me with rotten eyes like some dead fish?!"

Altugius suddenly shouted. It was a booming voice that couldn't have come from a dying old man.

"Even if I die, or the scraps of the Followers of Calamity die, Airfruit will remain. Are you all not the proud educators and pupils of the proud school of Airfruit? Even if we are unable to practice Magic some day, Airfruit will live on as long as even a single person etches the name Airfruit into his heart. It will live on!"

Altugius agitated the shame within the survivors. Their ashamed faces looked towards the floor and let out a sigh. Altugius turned his head and then glared at the Inquisitor of Heresy who was sitting arrogantly in the corner of the Plaza.

The Inquisitor didn't react, as usual, but Altugius smiled towards such a man and soundlessly mouthed a message.

"Talentless Bastard."

No sound could be heard, but the message was deciphered clearly by the Inquisitor. His hand rose.

Suddenly, a massive Magic formation appeared at that moment.

"Look at that! It is the Air fleet!"

"It's the flag of the Human Empire! The Air Fleet of the Human Empire has arrived!"

Following a ship resembling a massive plate, a total of six ships appeared above Golden City airspace from the Dimensional Door. It was the appearance of the oppressive Airship Fleet that represented the might of the Human Empire.

Dimitri Medioff, a powerhouse within the Human Empire, was looking at the distant ground below with a scornful gaze within the flagship, Bengard.

"The Enemy of the World appeared here? He's got balls. Why couldn't he just continue to linger around the Demon Realm? How dare he show his face this deep into the continent!"

He swung his baton as he barked his orders.

"Disperse the ground forces to seal this city!"

At the same moment, a particular man was looking over the scene from Robert Danton's study with aloof eyes. The man was

Sungchul. He quickly ran to the secret passageway, and then stopped to gaze up at the Dimensional Gate which stood at the center of a large cavern hidden underneath the academy.

Several corpses were lying about with eyes wide open around the Dimensional Door's activation device. Sungchul approached Robert's corpse at the center of the many corpses and tore away the necklace around his neck.

It was the key to the activation of the Dimensional Door.

The slabs of stones surrounding the Dimensional Door rotated slowly as soon as the amethyst key was entered. The rotation of the stones grew increasingly rapid until it caused a crack in the space at the centre of the Dimensional Door.

"Uuu…are you really going through with it?"

Bertelgia asked from his pocket. Sungchul nodded as he looked over at the Dimensional Door.

"It's to reduce casualties as much as possible. The Demons are easier to fight against than me."

Sungchul saw a familiar earthen flame beyond the crack.

"Krrrrrrr!"

At the same time, he could also hear the cries of beasts in the distance.

"…"

Sungchul left the cave while leaving the Dimensional Door activated.

The execution was about to proceed. The man wearing the crow mask was pouring oil over the wood, and the executor with a torch was waiting for his moment. The Inquisitor of Heresy rose from his seat and held up his hand as all the preparations were finished, and the moment he lowered his hands, the pyre below Altugius would light ablaze.

The Inquisitor's hand soon fell.

The torch fell onto the wood below, and it began to burn with dark smoke pouring into the air. Altugius shut both his eyes and prepared himself for death, but at that moment, a powerful gust of wind blew onto the execution ground with enough force to blow away Altugius' beard, if not even his skin. The fire that had been growing with vigor disappeared without a trace, and the execution ground fell silent. One of the students gathered the courage to look over in the direction of the wind.

"T-that man is?!"

One of the Alchemy students pointed a finger at the man in question. The man who wore a tattered field jacket with shabby jeans was a famous figure within the School of Alchemy. However, he was holding an item that hadn't been seen on him before. It was a beautiful and extraordinary hammer with a lengthy shaft.

"Who is it?!"

The Inquisitor of Heresy roared in anger.

Sungchul suddenly moved. His movements weren't fast or slow, but they exuded heavy pressure that didn't allow just anyone to stand in its way. The soldiers of the Inquisitor wearing glamorous armour hesitated, making the sergeants and the commissioned officers bark their orders at them.

"What are you waiting for? Stop that man!"

With the command, the soldiers pulled out their short swords and stood before Sungchul.

SLAM!

A dull sound filled the execution ground. The people could see dozens of soldiers flying into the air. These dozens were blown away by a single blow of the hammer. Sungchul pushed past the soldiers as if it was as easy as sweeping a dusty floor. One of the spectators recalled something and shouted at the top of his lungs.

"T-That is the Enemy of the World!"

Terror filled everyone by that single phrase. Soldiers no longer moved, despite the commands from their superiors, the spectators began stepping back, and the state workers started to struggle to leap from the platform. Only a single man, the Inquisitor of Heresy, stood before Sungchul.

"Who dares disrupt the holy procession of the God of Neutrality!"

Sungchul's only reply was a single blow from his hammer.

WHAM!

The Inquisitor's upper body was crushed and embedded into the ground, but the Inquisitor of Heresy was a man blessed by the God of Neutrality. He was the embodiment of holy strength. His broken form was reborn to its original shape under a blinding light. The soldiers of the Order of Purity watched the holy scene with tears in their eyes.

"Oh! Look and see! The Inquisitor of Heresy, Maxima Magnus, has received the blessing of God!"

However, resurrection did not resolve the root of the problem. Sungchul fixed the issue of Maxima's resurrection with a very simple method.

SLAM! SLAM! SLAM!

It was to whack away at him until he died. The final thing that Maxima witnessed was an irrational hammering and a similarly irrational strength behind it. Maxima continued to resurrect until the seventh time, upon which he died, flat as a pancake.

Inquisitors of Heresy are definitely cockroaches.

Sungchul, who had killed the Inquisitor, headed towards Altugius who had been restrained to the execution grounds. No one dared to stand in his way.

Altugius looked at Sungchul with shock in his eyes.

"A-are you the Enemy of the World?"

Sungchul nodded, then spoke bluntly.

"But why does that matter?"

It was a simple sentence. Altugius was taken aback by the excessively haughty phrase, yet simply smiled. However, the danger had not yet passed.

The ground troops of the Human Empire swarmed to the execution grounds by teleportation and on foot.

"There! The Enemy of the World!"

"Engage with all forces to stop him!"

Elite fighters and mages numbering in the hundreds gathered with Sungchul in their sights. Altugius looked at them, coughed, and then spoke.

"Shit. Leave me and go. You should at least be able to save my Granddaughter, right? Isn't that so?"

Sungchul freed Altugius from his restraints, then spoke in a firm voice.

"No one can stop me from doing what I intend to do."

As soon as the final word escaped his lips, a blood-curdling scream pierced high into the sky and a black mass rose into the air like a cloud of locusts. They were the invasion forces of the Demon Realm, summoned through the Dimensional Door.

The soldiers of the Air Fleet that had surrounded Sungchul with glee fell back into a defensive position and began to shout.

"It is the Demons! The Demons are here! Raise the alarm!"

A hurried sound of bells rang into the air causing Airfruit to descend into chaos. Sungchul took that opportunity to grab Altugius and disappeared in the madness.

"The Enemy of the World! You shall not escape!"

There was one who followed after them. It was the orphaned Kaz. He had taken on his mist form, a technique passed down within his family, to transform into a fog and stalk Sungchul. However, transforming into fog did not make him immune to Sungchul's attacks. Sungchul lightly swung Fal Garaz, splitting the fog, and it did not reform again. The fog soon took a human shape and fell onto the floor.

Sungchul, who had rid himself of all the pests, now fled towards the Observatory of the School of Cosmomancy with Altugius. It was time for Altugius to keep his promise.

"I will not judge you for who you are. I would have helped you even if you were the Devil himself as the only one that extended a hand of salvation was you alone."

Altugius spoke the words in a simple manner before removing the Magic-suppressing cuffs. As he felt the power of Magic flowing back into him, he pointed towards the roof of the Observatory.

"Glare."

The beam of light shot from his extended finger easily tore away the plaster on the roof. Dust fell onto the floor, and in the midst of the rain of dust, Sungchul could see the glittering constellations beneath the plaster. After Altugius revealed all the constellations, he spoke in a solemn voice.

"That is the Secret passed down within the School of Cosmomancy."

Altugius displayed his Glare once again. The beam of light which was fired from his hands accurately hit a gem arranged into a constellation, covering the entire constellation in a bright light. Once it received enough light, it fired a beam of light into another gem in another constellation.

From the scorpion, to the unicorn, to the oyster; once all twelve of the constellations were lit, Sungchul was gripped by a strange feeling, as if a secret he could never come to comprehend was revealing itself to him.

[Primordial Light]

The true Secret of Cosmomancy was now in his grasp.

***

"Don't put your guard down now. The real challenge has yet to begin." Altugius gave a warning.

Sungchul would soon know the meaning behind his words. A tidal wave of overwhelmingly massive knowledge descended onto his consciousness. Within his mind, he experienced being different existences.

First, he was a comet existing within the infinite void of space. He felt fearful of the unending journey, trapped in frozen isolation that was colder than ice, and when the scenery changed, he was but a rock within the unnamed comet. Time went by very quickly for the rock. The sun and the moon spun past like the hands of a clock, and he saw the unceasing rotation of light and darkness.

Everything changed once the scenery suddenly collapsed around him, but the flow of time didn't change. Various experiences of a similar nature continued. The one thing that he would never forget within all of the countless, yet equally memorable worlds of wondrous fantasy, was the existence of the giant sun.

Abruptly, he stood facing the exploding sun. It looked like the sun, but at a second glance, it felt like it was simply a different star that only resembled the sun. It looked ablaze in a golden flame, but once the bias that clouded his judgment faded away, he saw that the fiery light now appeared blue and sometimes seemed to cover the surface in pure white, like snow.

Regardless of what color it actually was, the most important thing was the unending light pouring from the burning star. Just by looking upon the light composed of primordial might, Sungchul was able to sense the source of an unforgettable power. Even after this experience, the various knowledge continued to invoke different hallucinations to project different experiences, but Sungchul only remembered that infinite light. That primordial light.

"…"

Sungchul let out a shallow sigh as his eyes flew open. He came back to reality as the torrent of various knowledge that had flooded his mind faded away.

"Have you seen the light?"

Altugius looked at him softly as he guarded Sungchul's side. Sungchul nodded in response.

"What light was it?"

"A very bright light."

"What did you experience there?"

"Oppressive strength that could burn everything away."

Altugius smiled faintly at Sungchul's responses.

"They say that the light changes based on the observer's perception. The light I saw was wisdom itself, but that is not what matters to you."

Altugius pointed a finger to the air, creating several floating Magic formations and starting to mumble a spell. The twelve Constellations in the Observatory dimmed and within the light came out a single tome. Altugius slowly guided the tome down with his staff and handed it to Sungchul after grabbing it.

"Take it."

"This is…?"

"Primordial Light. It is the Secret of Airfruit's School of Cosmomancy that you have sorely sought."

"Thank you."

Sungchul graciously received the tome. A message in bright letters appeared before him.

[Primordial Light]

Rank: Legend

Type: Magic Book

Effect: Acquisition of Primordial Light (Cosmomancy)

Note: The light that you saw contains everything you imagined and more.

Restriction: 500 Intuition

Requirement: Stand before the Light

The Secret of Cosmomancy was not at a level he could simply access.

"To gain a glimpse into the book, it requires two things. One is the ever-present requirement for Intuition: 500 Intuition in total."

It was a fearsome number. A stat requirement worthy of the Secret of Cosmomancy.

"Is it a Seventh-Circle Magic?"

Sungchul's eyes lit up brightly as he asked.

Altugius nodded his head.

"You know well. As expected of the Enemy of the World."

"What's the other requirement?"

"You've already met it. Haven't you seen the light?"

Altugius spoke as such as he turned his concern beyond the window. There was the sound of war in the distance. The sound of demonic drums. The Magical bombardment of the Air Fleet. The battle cry of humans and the roar of Demons. Sungchul also noticed that the light peering in from the window was turning a red tint. The sun was beginning to set.

What appeared to be a brief experience consumed quite a bit of time as Altugius had warned.

"My part in this is complete. All that is left is up to you."

"Thank you."

"Don't mention it. Anyways, where is Sarasa? I had only heard that she is in a safe location."

"She is already in the outskirts of the city. I'll lead you there personally."

Sungchul pulled out his beloved Fal Garaz and led the way. Altugius followed behind and broke out into laughter.

"I guessed it might be possible, but for you to actually be the Enemy of the World. I thought you were a rare sort, but I would never have imagined you were someone so great."

"I am nothing special."

Sungchul said as he flung open the doors of the School of Cosmomancy.

When the doors flung open, the chaos that was the campus of Airfruit unfolded before their eyes. The Demons covered the sky and the fleet of the Human Empire that opposed them were in the midst of fighting the final battle to decide their fate.

"Kyiiii!!"

Sharp talons of a monstrous flock swooped down towards Sungchul and Altugius.

WHAM!

The monsters turned into a bloody paste and dropped to the ground in a fine mist when Sungchul swung his hammer. A single one survived to fly off into the sky once again. However, the monster did not realize that there were two unwelcome riders on his back: Altugius and Sungchul.

"Hold on tight."

Sungchul tightened his grip on the monster's neck and turned to the side.

"Kyyiiii!"

The creature let out a pained cry as he turned toward the direction directed by Sungchul. He continued to freely control the creature with his grip tightly on its neck. Altugius watched the scene with wide eyes and asked.

"Just when did you learn this?"

"If you hang around the Demon realm long enough, you just pick up a few things."

At that moment, a squad of Dragon Knights flew past the monster from the other side. The man with a golden helmet turned to the side to see Sungchul and Altugius and his eyes were dyed in shock, but they could not chase after the monster. One of the Demons had broken into a warship of the Air Fleet and was engaging in close-quarter combat. Capturing the Enemy of the World was their mission, but the military had a standing order which preceded any other order: ensuring the survival of the fleet.

"Shit! There is no end to them. What is the scale of the Dimensional Door to allow so many Demons to pass through?!"

It was enough to have the Fleet Commander of the Second Armada of the Human Empire, Dimitri Medioff, foaming at the mouth. The Enemy of the World that he had been hunting for had appeared, yet he had to deal with the Demons that had gathered like flies. It would be simple enough to deal with ordinary Demons, but it looked as though their opponents were a seasoned force that had been prepared for a while.

The sheer quality and quantity of the enemy forces were difficult for the common soldier to deal with. They were only managing to fight to a standstill because they were the powerful Air Fleet of the Human Empire.

"Kekekekek! Are you the leader?!"

A Balroq with a bulky frame stood on the deck of the warship. Dimitri Medioff pulled out his Rapier and stood against the Demon while grinding his teeth.

"Shit! Quickly send out the ground forces and demolish the Dimensional Gate! Do it before they bring in more of their kin!"

The Balroq's axe flew toward him. Dimitri parried the massive axe blade and let loose a powerful battle roar.

As the battle continued to devolve into greater chaos, the monster carrying Sungchul and Altugius landed on the outskirts of the city. Or more accurately, Sungchul had broken its neck to force it to crash land.

Sungchul and Altugius put the corpse of the monster with twitching wings behind them as they approached an aged shrine. A girl with a face that was partially decayed waited for them.

"Grandpa."

It was Sarasa. Altugius lovingly looked at the girl's grotesque face and hugged her deeply.

"You went through so much trouble."

Tears hung on the rim of Altugius' eyes.

"What trouble? Grandpa went through all of it."

Sarasa firmly gripped on to her grandfather's back.

"There isn't much time."

Sungchul interrupted. He had pulled out a sack filled with gold coins and gems from his Soul Storage and pushed it towards Altugius.

"All this?"

"It is my tuition."

"That and this…"

"Don't worry about it. It isn't even my money."

"Even so…"

"When you sell these coins, I suggest you erase the coin's mint from its surface. If you're unlucky, the assassins from the Allied Merchant's Guild will track you."

Sungchul moved to leave with these words. Altugius called out to him once again.

"Can I ask one thing?"

Sungchul stopped without looking back. Altugius looked at his back as he asked his question.

"Why would someone so powerful like you learn Magic underneath someone like me?"

"I need Magic in order to kill the Demon King, Max Hesthnius. That is all."

"Just for that reason…Is that all the reason why you admitted yourself into Airfruit and acted like a freshman…?!"

Sungchul nodded.

It was ludicrous, but it was persuasive because it was coming from Sungchul. Altugius thought as such before wondering if there was anything more he could do. Soon, something came into mind.

"Does your Magic Power and Intuition match with what I saw?"

Sungchul nodded.

"Those two numbers match exactly with my current stats. Although, I will need to train further to bring down Max."

"If that's the case, seek out my son on the Demon Realm battlefront."

"Your son?"

"The kid thinks he's saving the world like you and left for the battlefront to seek out ways to improve his Magic Power. If it's you, you might find your own method to grow, but it might grow a little faster with a bit of his knowledge to help you."

"Deckard…"

Sungchul turned slightly. He never overlooked any method when it came to his growth.

Altugius tossed out a single book and a ring from his finger.

"It is embarrassing, but the book is my own composition. It is something I created in order to hand down in case I found a talented disciple. Also, show Deckard the ring, and he'll at least give you a listen."

Sungchul held the ring and Altugius' book and gave a deep bow. Sarasa stepped forward as though she had something to say.

"I apologize if I did anything to offend you, and I'll return this child to you."

There was a Sky Squirrel in her grasp.

"Kyu Kyu."

It looked as though he had adapted to her touch enough to not reject it. Sarasa looked glum as though she hated the idea of parting from the little beast.

Sungchul looked at her, then spoke calmly.

"Take good care of the squirrel."

"Huh? You're not taking it?" Sarasa asked in surprise.

Sungchul nodded.

"Now, if you'll excuse me."

He then took a deep breath and rushed forward, leaving behind a gust of wind. The powerful whirlwind left in his wake roughly passed through Altugius and Sarasa.

"Grandpa. I don't think the rumours are true."

Sarasa spoke quietly.

"What do you mean?"

"I heard that the Enemy of the World resents humans the most, but why was he so nice to us?"

"I'm not sure."

Altugius' meeting with him had been brief, but he had had a small insight into the man named Sungchul Kim.

"It might be that the world had just pegged him wrong."

The man called the Enemy of the World was charging toward the center of the bloody battle between the Demons and Dragon Knights. Thousands upon thousands of soldiers were blocking the road towards his destination, but he freely charged through the heart of the military forces then entered the opened Dimensional Door.

"The Enemy of the World entered the Dimensional Door!"

The soldiers of the Human Empire shouted hurriedly, but no one existed who could stop him. If there was a single change, it was that no Demons appeared after the moment Sungchul had entered the Dimensional Portal

"...come."

Sungchul stood before the thousands of Demons that had set up a formation around the Dimensional Door and blocked their path. No Demon dared move towards him. Soon after, Airfruit's Dimensional Door lost its strength.

—

The incident in Golden City made waves throughout the entirety of Other World. The movement of the Demons and the reappearance of the Enemy of the World. It was a headache for the powerful within Other World. One of these powerful figures, Shamal Rajput, the head of the Assassin's Guild, looked upon the disfigured body of a young assassin with cold eyes.

"Kaz Almeira. You were soundly defeated."

Kaz had lost his entire arm from the shoulder down, leaving him in quite a pitiful state. If the blow had been any deeper, he would have been split from his neck.

"..."

He prostrated himself before the leader with his head bowing towards the floor. Tentacles that resembled the limbs of an octopus were attached to his stump.

"You have to continue training. You are the one who will lead the guild the moment I am defeated."

"...I will keep it in mind."

"Also, I will post someone to your side."

Shamal snapped his fingers. Suddenly, the silhouette of a woman appeared in the darkness. Kaz glared at the woman in surprise.

Who is it? This bitch. There was no one like this among the inheritors of the four families.

Shamal's next words cleared up his confusion.

"She is a Regressor."

"A Regressor…?!"

"That's right. She is a Regressor from a future that is most likely to occur. She is still quite lacking, but with enough effort, she will be someone who will do great work for us."

Shamal gestured with his hand for her to stand before Kaz. She stood before Kaz with a hooded face then spoke with an elegant voice ill-fitting for an assassin.

"I am called Ahmuge."

Afterword

Road Warrior (Author)

Thank you for reading. This is the second book I have released in the Western market. I wrote this story with the desire to create an epic adventure with a large overarching plot as opposed to my previous works which were more limited and confined in scope. The fact that the Main Character is overpowered was often a double-edged sword since the story would quickly become boring if the protagonist could overcome any situation without difficulty. So, I had focused the story around the idea that there were many reasonable and believable restrictions placed on the Main Character. And I especially placed a high priority on the restrictions so that they were closely tied to the overarching background story. It wasn't all planned-out from the start, but it was a personally satisfying experience, and I believe the story flowed well until the very end.

Oppatranslations

It was quite a task for us to translate Enemy of the World and release the book especially because Korean novels generally lack in certain elements which are widely seen in English Literature like dialogue tags and they also have their own quirks like the use of "..." in many areas. Also, grammar is fundamentally structured differently making it overly ambiguous in meaning compared to English. It is not an exaggeration to say that this was the single largest accomplishment of not only the many contributors who spent thousands of hours into this project but also for our young Company. We have worked hard to ensure quality of work, and I can happily say that this is only the first of many to come.

I would like to make a shoutout to our many fans and friends who supported us and helped us along.

And for those of you who are curious about how the story continues, it is actually available to read on our website! Visit the link below-

https://www.oppatranslations.com/and-the-story-continues/

[1] Hyung is used by korean males to address another male older than them who they are close to.

[2] This is actually a Japanese word meaning tsun - cold and dere - lovey dovey. A person who acts cold but is actually a loving and caring person. There are varying degrees of Tsun and Dere.

[3] Ahram is talking to the woman standing beside Jungshik.

[4] Korean word for senior/upperclassmen.

[5] Showing teeth is considered rude in Korea.

[6] The shirt slogan "2002 Be the Red!" refers to the 2002 World Cup when Koreans called themselves the Red Devils.

[7] Korean idiom- Koreans say they like to watch the horror genre in the summer because it gives them the "chills" to chase the heat away.

[8] Shell here is the Stone of Soul Absorption. If you remember his name had popped at 148 last chapter in the list of those who had broken the Stone of Soul Absorption.

[9] "Dragon versus Tiger" means rivalry between two opponents who are evenly matched and are unable to overcome each other.

[10] Korean idiom meaning the person is able to see through and know things they should not be able to see or know (uncanny).

[11] Grand in this world is a title of nobility. Hence, "The" being added before it

[12] Orabeoni- It is the most elevated (formal respectful) version of Oppa (a woman's older brother). It is also used in place of "Young Master."

Made in the USA
San Bernardino, CA
15 June 2018